PRAISE FOR
AND I DARKEN

"A dark and twisty fantasy. . . . Think *Game of Thrones* . . . but with teens." —*Seventeen*

"Sinister, suspenseful, and unapologetically feminist."
—*Buzzfeed*

"Will completely spin you into another time and place."
—*Bustle*

"Takes no prisoners, offering up brutal, emotional historical fiction." —NPR.org

"Gleams with fierce, cunning characters—absolutely riveting." —#1 *New York Times* bestselling author
ALEXANDRA BRACKEN

"As richly complex and glittering as the Ottoman Empire itself." —ROBIN LAFEVERS

PRAISE FOR
NOW I RISE

"Kiersten White is a genius." —JUSTINE LARBALESTIER,
author of *My Sister Rosa* and *Liar*

★ "Gorgeous, rich, and rewarding." —*Booklist*, Starred

"This complex historical fiction offers a gender-switched take on the story of Vlad the Impaler, and Lada is as cold and bloodthirsty as her real-life male counterpart. . . . Readers will find her and (perhaps even more so) Radu relatable and human, flawed and engaging." —*VOYA*

"Lush and ominous . . . teens will be entranced." —*SLJ*

BOOKS BY KIERSTEN WHITE

NOW
I
RISE

KIERSTEN WHITE

EMBER

Text copyright © 2017 by Kiersten Brazier
Cover art copyright © 2017 by Sam Weber
Map art copyright © 2017 by Isaac Stewart

All rights reserved. Published in the United States by Ember, an imprint of Random House Children's Books, a division of Penguin Random House LLC, New York. Originally published in hardcover in the United States by Delacorte Press, an imprint of Random House Children's Books, New York, in 2017.

Ember and the E colophon are registered trademarks of Penguin Random House LLC.

GetUnderlined.com

Educators and librarians, for a variety of teaching tools, visit us at RHTeachersLibrarians.com

The Library of Congress has cataloged the hardcover edition of this work as follows:
Names: White, Kiersten, author.
Title: Now I rise / Kiersten White.
Description: First edition. | New York : Delacorte Press, [2017]
Identifiers: LCCN 2016038757 | ISBN 978-0-553-52235-8 (hardback) |
ISBN 978-0-553-52236-5 (glb) | ISBN 978-0-553-52237-2 (ebook)
Subjects: | CYAC: Princesses—Fiction. | Good and evil—Fiction. |
Transylvania (Romania)—History—15th century—Fiction. | Istanbul
(Turkey)—History—15th century—Fiction. | Turkey—History—Mehmed II,
1451–1481—Fiction.
Classification: LCC PZ7.W583764 Now 2017 | DDC [Fic]—dc23

ISBN 978-0-553-52238-9 (trade paperback)

Printed in the United States of America
10 9 8 7 6 5 4 3 2 1
First Ember Edition 2018

Random House Children's Books supports the First Amendment and celebrates the right to read.

For Christina, who will never have time to
read this book, but who gave me
the gift of time to write it

———•———

For Christine, who will be answering to

and who I could not write a line or

the sake of take to matter

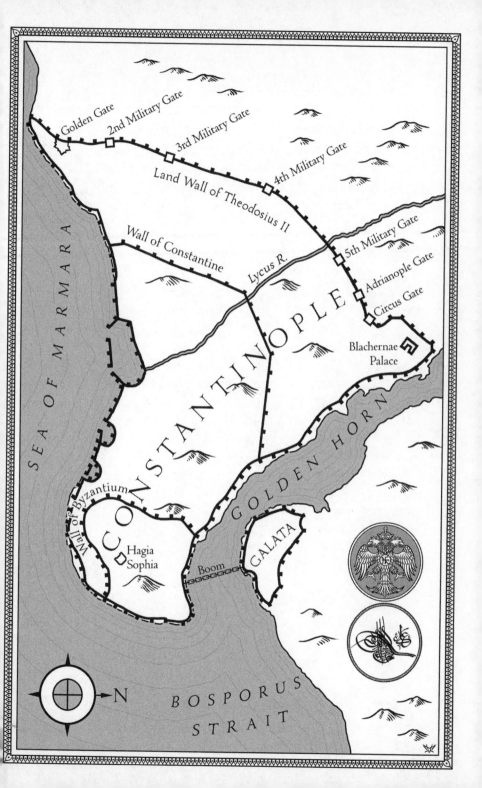

NOW I RISE

1

January 1453

HELL WAS A PARTY.

At least, Radu was fairly certain that whatever hell there was would certainly resemble this party.

Music drifted like perfume on the air, enough to sweeten but not overwhelm. Groups of musicians were scattered across the island; they could be glimpsed among the hardy green that had survived the winter months. Though the main meal would come later, blue-clad servants floated through the crowds with food-laden trays shaped like lily pads. On either side of the island, the Tunca River flowed leisurely by.

Whatever else he had been, Murad—Mehmed's dead father and Radu's onetime benefactor—had not been one to skimp on luxury. The harem complex he built on the island had been out of use since his death, but it had not faded in glory. The tiles gleamed. The carved stones of the walls promised luxury and peace. The fountains tinkled in cheery companionship with the surrounding river.

Radu wandered between buildings painted like geometric

gardens, pulled along as surely as the course of the river. He knew it was useless, knew that it would not make him feel better. But still he looked.

And there—next to the bathhouse. Radu was drawn to him like a leaf spun on the river current. Mehmed wore his now-constant deep-purple robes and a swirling golden turban. A jeweled chain fastened a cloak around his broad shoulders. Radu tried to remember Mehmed's full lips parting in a smile, his eyebrows rising in mirth rather than mockery. The two young men, both having finally finished growing, were the same tall, lean height. But lately Radu felt small when Mehmed looked at him.

He would have taken even that today. But Mehmed did not look in his direction, immune to the connection Radu could not escape.

"Truly glorious," Halil Vizier said to Mehmed, his hands on his hips as he looked up at the new bathhouse complex. Three connected buildings, with domed roofs echoing those of mosques, had been added in the past few months. They were the first new construction anticipating Mehmed's grand palace complex. It would rival anything his father had ever built—anything *anyone* had ever built. To celebrate this investment in the capital of the Ottoman Empire, Mehmed had invited everyone who mattered.

Ambassadors from various European countries mingled freely with the Ottoman elite. Mehmed stood apart, but was free with his smiles and sweeping promises of future parties at his palace. Along with his usual attendants, he was joined by Ishak Pasha, one of his most powerful spahi; Kumal Pasha, Radu's brother-in-law; and, as always, like a bitter taste that could not be swallowed, Halil Vizier.

Radu hated thinking of his old enemy Halil Pasha as Halil Vizier. He hated even more that it had been his own plan to put Halil in a place of trust and power to keep a closer eye on him. Maybe Lada had been right. Maybe they should have killed him. Things would be easier, or at least they would be more pleasant. That should be Radu's place at Mehmed's side.

As though sensing Radu's poisonous envy, Halil Vizier looked at him. His mouth curled in a sneering smile. "Radu the Handsome," he said. Radu frowned. He had not heard that title since the end of fighting in Albania, when Skanderberg, their foe, had coined it. Mehmed glanced over, then away as soon as their eyes met. Like a butterfly alighting on a flower and finding it lacking.

"Tell me," Halil said, that nasty smile still on his bearded face. "Is your pretty wife aware this is not a functioning harem yet? I fear she has false hopes about entering it."

The men around Halil snickered. Kumal frowned, then opened his mouth. Radu shook his head, a minute movement. Kumal looked sadly away. Mehmed did not acknowledge the insult—the implication that Radu's wife would enter Mehmed's harem to divorce Radu—but he did nothing to refute it, either.

"My wife is not—"

A gentle hand came down on Radu's arm. He turned to find Nazira. Nazira, who was not supposed to be here. "His wife is not pleased with anyone else monopolizing his attention." Beneath her translucent veil, her smile was far brighter than the winter sun. She wore the colors of springtime. Still, Radu felt cold looking at her. What was she doing?

Nazira turned Radu away from the men and led him down a path draped in more silk than most people would ever see in their lives. It was extravagant, excessive, absurd, like everything about this party. A reflection of a sultan too young and foolish to think of anything beyond appearances and his own pleasure.

"What are you doing here?" Radu whispered urgently.

"Come on a boat ride with me."

"I cannot! I have to—"

"Endure mockery from Halil Vizier? Try to regain the favor of Mehmed? Radu, what has happened?" Nazira pulled him into the shadows of one of the buildings. To onlookers it would appear as though he were stealing a moment with his beautiful wife.

He gritted his teeth, looking at the wall above her head. "I have business."

"Your business is my business. You do not write us, you never visit. I had to learn from Kumal that you have fallen out with Mehmed. What happened? Did you ... does he know?" Her dark eyes were heavy with meaning, the weight of it too much for Radu.

"No! Of course not. I— It is much more complicated than that." He turned away, but she grabbed his wrist.

"Fortunately for you, I am very clever and can understand even the most complicated things. Tell me."

Radu ran the fingers of his free hand along the edges of his turban, tugging at it. Nazira reached up, taking his fingers in her own. Her sharp eyes softened. "I worry about you."

"You do not need to worry about me."

"I do not worry because I need to. I worry because I care about you. I want to see you happy. And I do not think *Edirne* holds any happiness for you." She emphasized *Edirne*, making it clear that it was not the capital she spoke of, but what—or rather, whom—that capital held.

"Nazira," Radu hissed, "I cannot talk about this right now."

He almost wished he could. He was desperate to talk to someone, anyone. But no one could help him with that problem. Radu wondered, sometimes, what Lazar could have told him if they had ever talked openly about what it meant for one man to love another. Lazar had been anything but discreet about his openness to something ... more ... with Radu. And Radu had rewarded Lazar's loyalty and friendship with a knife. Now he had no one to talk to, to ask these desperate questions. It was wrong, was it not? For him to love this way?

But when Radu looked at Nazira and Fatima, he did not feel anything other than happiness that they had found each other. Their love was as pure and true as any he had ever observed. Thoughts like this made his mind turn around in circles upon itself, until not even prayer could calm it.

Radu looked down at Nazira's hands on his. "The palace may not hold my happiness. But I cannot look anywhere else."

Nazira released him with a sigh. "Will you come back with me? Spend some time at home? Fatima misses you. It might do you good to be away."

"There is too much to do."

"Too much dancing? Too many parties?" Her voice teased, but her eyes lacked an accompanying sparkle of sincerity. Her words stung him.

"You know I am more than that."

"I do. I simply worry you might forget. You do not have to do this to yourself."

"I am not doing it to myself, or for myself. I— Damn. Damn, damn, damn." Radu watched as a man in naval uniform—a sturdy cape, a tighter, smaller turban than the ones worn by ordinary soldiers, and a sash of Mehmed's colors— walked past. He was accompanied by one of Halil Vizier's trusted friends.

"What?" Nazira followed Radu's gaze.

"I need to talk to that man. Without anyone else being able to hear. It is the only reason I am here."

She was suddenly excited. "You do? Is he—" She raised her eyebrows suggestively.

"No! No. I just need to speak with him. In secret."

Nazira's smile turned into a thoughtful frown. "Can you be seen together?"

"Yes, but it cannot look like we met on purpose or are discussing anything of importance. I was hoping to find some quiet moment, but there are so many people here. He has not been alone since he came to the capital. Halil Vizier has seen to it."

"Your party attendance is more complicated than I thought, then."

Radu gritted his teeth. "Much."

"Well, you are very fortunate you married so well." Nazira put a hand on his arm and steered him onto the walkway. "Tell me about him."

"His name is Suleiman, and he is the newly promoted admiral of the navy."

Nazira laughed. "This will be easy."

She danced effortlessly from group to group with a coy smile and a word of greeting for all. Radu was on the fringes of these parties lately, a contrast to when he had been a shining focal point. But with Nazira on his arm, more people were willing to stop for a moment of conversation. He craned his neck for a view of Suleiman. Nazira pinched his arm, hard.

"Patience," she whispered.

After several more stops to chat with the uncle of her deceased father's best friend, the cousin of Kumal's deceased wife, and any number of other people Nazira treated with delight and deference regardless of their place in the Ottoman social hierarchy, they plowed directly into Suleiman. Somehow Nazira had managed to turn and walk so that Radu knocked the man over.

"Oh!" Nazira squeaked, putting her hands over her veiled mouth. "I am so sorry!"

Radu held out a hand to help the man up. They had never met before, but Suleiman's eyes lingered on the boat-shaped gold pin on Radu's cloak. "Please forgive me."

"Of course." Suleiman bowed. "I am Suleiman Baltoghlu."

Radu bowed as well. "Radu."

"Radu . . . ?" Suleiman paused expectantly.

"Simply Radu." Radu's smile was tight. Lada had left him behind under the mantle of the Draculesti family. But Radu had rejected his father's name. He would not take it up again, ever. "This is my wife, Nazira."

Suleiman took her hand, bowing even deeper. "They make wives prettier in Edirne than they do in Bursa."

Nazira beamed. "That is because the wind blows too hard in harbor cities. The poor women there have to expend all their energy merely staying upright. There is no time left for being pretty."

Suleiman laughed, a loud burst of sound that drew attention. But the attention was focused on him and Nazira, not on him and Radu.

"Tell me, what do you do in Bursa?" she asked.

"I am an admiral."

"Boats! Oh, I adore boats. Look, did you see?" Nazira pointed to the collection of delicate boats bobbing in the river. They were carved in fanciful shapes. One had a prow like the head of a frog, and its oars had webbed feet carved into their ends. Another looked like a war galley, tiny decorative oars sticking out both its sides. "Radu is afraid if we take a boat out, he will not make it back to shore. But surely if we had an admiral with us . . ." Nazira looked up at Suleiman through her thick eyelashes.

"I am at your service." Suleiman followed them to the dock, helping Nazira into a boat carved like a heron. A head on a slender neck pointed their way forward, and silk wings extended on either side. The tail was a canopy arching overhead to protect passengers from the sun, though it was not quite warm enough to be necessary.

"This is lovely!" Nazira sighed happily, leaning over to trail one hand in the water. Radu was not quite so pleased—he hated boats—but he shared a secret smile with Nazira. She had done his job for him.

Suleiman took the oars. Radu sat gingerly in the back of the small boat.

"I am going to chatter very brightly, waving my hands a lot," Nazira said as they pulled away from the shore, and away from any prying ears. "In fact, I am going to talk the whole time, and you two will be unable to get a word in edgewise."

She continued her one-sided conversation—a silent one. Her head bobbed up and down, she laughed, and her hands punctuated imaginary sentences. Any onlookers would see her entertaining Suleiman while Radu tried his best to keep his stomach.

"How soon can you build the new galleys?" Radu muttered, clutching the sides of the boat.

Suleiman shrugged like he was trying to loosen up his shoulders for rowing. "We can build ships as fast as he can fund them."

"No one can know how many ships we really have."

"We will build a few galleys in Bursa for show, so it looks like I am doing something. The rest will be built in secret, in a private shipyard along the Dardanelles. But I still need men. We can have all the ships in the world, but without trained sailors, they will be as much use as the boat we are in now."

"How can we train that many men in secret?" Someone would notice if they conscripted men for a navy. A few new boats could be attributed to a foolish whim of an immature sultan. An armada, complete with the men to sail it, was another thing entirely.

"Give me the funds to hire Greek sailors, and I will give him the finest navy in the world," Suleiman said.

"It will be done." Radu leaned over the side, barely avoiding heaving.

Suleiman laughed at some new pantomime of Nazira's. "Whatever you do, keep this one around. She is truly a treasure."

This time Nazira's laugh was real. "I am."

Radu did not have to feign relief when Suleiman finished their loop around the island and pulled them back to the dock.

He stumbled onto it, grateful for the solid wood beneath his feet.

"Your husband has a weak stomach," Suleiman said as he helped Nazira out of the boat.

"Yes. It is a good thing he is so handsome." Nazira patted Radu's cheek, then waved prettily at Suleiman. "Our navy is in most capable hands!"

Suleiman laughed wryly. "My little bird boats will be the terror of the seas!" He bowed theatrically, then strode away.

"Thank you," Radu said, letting Nazira take him back through the party, then into a secluded corner. They sat on a bench with their backs to the bathhouse wall. "That was brilliant."

"Yes, I am. Now tell me what is really going on."

"I am— We are— This is very secret."

Nazira rolled her eyes, exasperated.

"I am helping Mehmed with his plans to take Constantinople. We have to work in secret so that Halil Pasha—" Radu paused, grimacing. Halil's new title always tasted foul on his tongue. *Why* had he insisted Halil be elevated from a pasha to a vizier? "So that he does not discover our plans with enough time to sabotage them. We know he is still in league with Emperor Constantine. My elimination from Mehmed's inner circle was deliberate. I need to appear unimportant; that way, I can organize things Mehmed cannot be seen to care about, like the navy. Everything we do in public is to divert attention from his true goals. Even this party is a farce, to show that Mehmed is frivolous and cares only about Edirne. Why would he invest so much money in a palace if he intends to make his capital elsewhere?"

"But if everything you are doing is in secret, could you not do all that and still be one of his advisors?"

"My actions would draw too much attention if I were constantly at Mehmed's side."

"Not if it were widely known that you were merely his friend. Sultans can have close friends who are not necessarily important, but are merely beloved." Nazira looked down, her expression pained but determined. "Do you never wonder if, perhaps . . . Mehmed understands more than you think he does? And this separation is not so much a strategy as a kindness?"

Radu stood so quickly he nearly lost his balance. "No."

"He is not a fool. If I saw in one evening how you felt, surely he has seen the same over the years you have spent together."

Radu put a hand up, wishing he could make Nazira swallow the words so they had never been spoken. If Mehmed truly understood how he felt, then . . . It was too much to think about. There were too many questions that had no answers Radu wanted.

"Maybe your sister was wise to leave. She realized a sultan could never give her what she needed."

Mehmed's plan made sense. It was the only path. That was why Mehmed had chosen it. "I am staying because my life is here," Radu said. "Lada left because she wanted the throne, and she got it."

Sometimes he wondered what would have happened if he had not pushed Lada to abandon them last year. Because he had chosen that, too. Chosen to say exactly what she needed to hear to decide to leave Mehmed—and Radu. It had been a dark, desperate move. A move he thought would bring him closer to Mehmed. Radu held back a bitter laugh.

He had pushed Lada away, and she had ridden to Wallachia and glory. To everything she had ever wanted, without a second glance for the man she allegedly loved. Or for her pathetic brother. For all his supposed cleverness, Radu could not secure the same happy ending for himself that he had tricked his sister into.

If Lada were still here, would this plan of enforced distance be his life? Or would Lada have come up with another way to subvert Halil? A way that let Radu keep his friendship with Mehmed? A way that did not leave Radu alone every night, wondering when his future would be what he hoped it to be? Wondering what those hopes even were?

Hope was an arrow that never ceased piercing his heart.

Plans notwithstanding, Mehmed could have done things as Nazira said. He could have made excuses so he and Radu were able to speak face to face instead of via covert, hidden messages. There were many things Mehmed could do but did not, and probably never would. If Radu let himself dwell on those things, he would surely go mad.

He avoided Nazira's gaze. "It is fine. Everything is as it ever was, and as it will ever be. Once we have taken Constantinople, I will be at his side again. As his friend." Radu's voice wavered on the last word, betraying him.

"Will it be enough?" she asked.

"It will have to be." Radu tried to smile, but it was useless to be false with Nazira. Instead he bent and placed a kiss on his wife's forehead. "Give my love to Fatima. I have work to do."

Nazira stood, taking his elbow firmly. "Not without me. You need an ally."

Radu sighed. He really did. He had been so lonely, so lost.

He did not want to ask this of her. But then again, he had not asked. She had simply shown up and told him how things would be. That was her signature, he supposed. And he was grateful for it. "Thank you."

Together, they walked back into the party. It felt less like hell and more like a game. Nazira deliberately greeted the people least likely to speak to Radu now that he was out of favor. She did it to annoy them, and he adored her for it. It was delightful to watch those who had once clamored for his favor and then shunned him squirm as they tried to be polite. Radu was actually enjoying himself. *And* he had good news for Mehmed, which meant an excuse to sneak into his rooms to leave a message.

He was laughing as he turned and came face to face with ghosts from his past.

Aron and Andrei Danesti. His childhood rivals. Memories of fists in the forest, stopped only by Lada's ferocity. Radu had been powerless to face them on his own. But he had figured out another way. The last time he had seen them, they were being whipped in public for theft. He had set them up in retaliation for their cruelty.

Time had stretched them, built them new forms. Aron was thin and sickly-looking. His mustache and beard were sparse and patchy. Andrei, broad-shouldered and healthy, had fared better, though there was something wary in his expression that had not been there before Radu's trick. Radu felt a brief pang of guilt that his actions had carved that onto someone else's face. Aron smiled, and Radu saw something in the man's eyes he had never seen as a child: kindness.

But apparently time had been more exacting on Radu than

it had on his Danesti foes. That, or his turban and Ottoman dress disguised him completely. Their smiles—Andrei's guarded, Aron's kind—held no spark of recognition.

Nazira cheerfully introduced herself. Radu resisted the urge to shield her from them. Surely they were not the same bullies they had been in childhood. "Where are you from?" she asked.

"Wallachia," Andrei answered. "We are here with our father, the prince."

A noise like the roaring of wind filled Radu's ears.

Nazira lit up. "Oh, what a coincidence! My husband is—"

Radu tugged her arm. "Apologies, we have to leave." He walked away so quickly Nazira had to run to keep up. As soon as he had rounded a corner, Radu leaned against the wall, overcome. Their father. A Danesti. The Wallachian prince. Which meant that Lada was not on the throne.

And if they were here paying respects, Mehmed *knew* Lada was not on the throne.

What else did Mehmed know? What other secrets was he keeping from Radu?

For once, though, the biggest question did not revolve around Mehmed. All these months, Radu had never written Lada, because she had never written him. And because he hated her for getting what she wanted and leaving him with nothing, as always.

But apparently he had been wrong about that.

Where was Lada?

2

February 1453

IT TOOK ONLY THREE fingers smashed beyond recognition
before the would-be assassin screamed the name of Lada's
enemy.

"Well." Nicolae raised his eyebrows, once singular but now
bisected by a vicious scar that failed to fade with the passage of
time. He turned away as Bogdan slit the young man's throat.
The heat of life leaving body steamed slightly in the frigid winter air. "That *is* disappointing."

"That the governor of Brasov betrayed us?" Bogdan asked.

"No, that the quality of assassins has fallen this low."

Lada knew Nicolae meant to make the situation palatable
through humor—he never liked executions—but his words
struck deep. It was certainly a blow that the governor of Brasov
wanted her dead. He had promised her aid, which had given her
the first shred of hope in months.

Now she had none. Brasov was the last of the Transylvanian cities she had tried to find an ally in. None of the noble
Wallachian boyar families would so much as respond to her

letters. Transylvania, with its fortified mountain cities crushed between Wallachia and Hungary, was heavily Wallachian. But Lada saw now that the ruling class of Saxons and Hungarians treated her people like chaff, and considered her worthless.

But almost worse than losing her last chance at an ally was that *this* was the most they could be bothered to spare for her: an underfed, poorly trained assassin barely past boyhood.

That was all the fear she instilled, all the respect she merited.

Bogdan kicked the body over the edge of the small ravine bordering their encampment. Just as when they were children, he never had to be asked to clean up her messes. He wiped the blood from his fingers, then tugged his ill-fitting gloves back on. A misshapen hat was worn low, hiding the ears that stuck out like jug handles.

He had grown broad and strong. His fighting was not flashy but was brutally efficient. Lada had seen him in action, and had to bite back the admiring words that sprang to her lips. He was also fastidiously clean—a quality emphasized by the Ottomans that not all her men had retained. Bogdan always smelled fresh, like the pine trees they hid among. Everything about him reminded Lada of home.

Her other men crouched over their fires, scattered in groups among the thick trees. They were as misshapen as Bogdan's hat, their once pristine Janissary uniformity long since abandoned. They were down to thirty—twelve lost when they had met an unexpected force from the Danesti Wallachian prince as they attempted to cross the Danube River into the country, eight more lost in the months since, spent hiding and running and desperately seeking allies.

"Do you think Brasov is in league with the Danesti prince or with the Hungarians?" Nicolae asked.

"Does it matter?" Lada snapped. All sides were set against her. They smiled to her face and promised aid. Then they sent assassins in the dark.

She had bested vastly superior assassins on Mehmed's behalf. Meager comfort, though, and worse still that she found it only by remembering her time with Mehmed. It seemed as though anything she might look on with pride had happened when she was with him. Had she been so diminished, then, by leaving the person she was at his side?

Lada lowered her head, rubbing the unceasing tightness at the base of her neck. Since failing to take the throne, she had neither written to nor received word from Mehmed or Radu. It was too humiliating to lay bare her failure before them and anticipate what they might say. Mehmed would invite her to return. Radu would console her—but she questioned whether he would welcome her back.

She wondered, too, how close they had become in her absence. But it did not matter. She had chosen to leave them as an act of strength. She would never return to them in weakness. She had thought—with her men, with her dispensation from Mehmed, with all her years of experience and strength—that the throne was hers for the taking. She had thought that she would be enough.

She knew now that nothing she could do would ever be enough. Unless she could grow a penis, which did not seem likely. Nor particularly desirable.

Though it did make for an easier time relieving oneself

when perpetually hiding in the woods. Emptying one's bladder in the middle of the night was a freezing, uncomfortable endeavor.

What, then, was left to her? She had no allies. She had no throne. She had no Mehmed, no Radu. She had only these sharp men and sharp knives and sharp dreams, and no way to make use of any of them.

Petru leaned against a winter-bare tree nearby. He had grown thicker and quieter in the past year. All traces of the boy he had been when he joined Lada's company were gone. One of his ears had been mangled, and he wore his hair longer to cover it. He had also stopped shaving. Most of her men had. Their faces were no longer the bare ones that had indicated their station as Janissaries. They were free. But they were also directionless, which increasingly worried Lada. When thirty men trained to fight and kill had nothing to fight and kill for, what was there to keep them bound to her?

She pulled a branch from the fire. It was a burning brand, searing her eyes with its light. She sensed more than saw the attention of her men shift to her. Rather than feeling like a weight, it made her stand taller. The men needed something to do.

And Lada needed to see something burn.

"Well," she said, spinning the flaming stick lazily through the air, "I think we should send our regards to Transylvania."

—•—

It is easier to destroy than to build, her nurse had been fond of saying when Lada would pull all the blossoms off the fruit trees, *but empty fields make hungry bellies.*

As a child, Lada had never understood what her nurse

meant. But now she thought she might. At least the part about destroying being easier than building. All her time spent writing letters or standing in front of minor nobles attempting to forge alliances had been wasted. It had been nothing but struggle for the past year. Struggle to arrange meetings, struggle to be seen as more than a girl playing at soldier, struggle to find the right ways to work within a system that had always been foreign to her.

They were closer to the city of Sibiu than to Brasov. For efficiency's sake, Lada decided to stop there first. It took less time to herd hundreds of Sibiu's sheep into the icy pond to drown than it had for a servant to inform her that the governor would not be meeting with her. The Wallachian shepherds, who would no doubt be killed for their failure to save the sheep, were quietly folded into her company.

That accomplished, Lada and her men passed through the slumbering, unprotected outer city of Sibiu, harming nothing and no one. Ahead of them rose the walls of the inner city, where only Transylvanian nobles—never Wallachians—were allowed to sleep. She imagined they dreamed deeply, pampered and protected by the sweat of Wallachian brows.

They had neither the time nor the numbers to launch an attack on inner Sibiu. And they were not here to conquer. They were here to destroy. As each volley of flaming arrows arced high over the walls and down into the maze of roofs, Lada's smile grew simultaneously brighter and darker.

───◆───

A few days later, they waited outside Brasov for the sun to go down. The city was set in a valley ringed with deep green growth. Towers stood at intervals along the inner city walls, each maintained by a different guild. If she were planning a siege, it would be a challenge.

But, as with Sibiu, they did not want to keep this city. They merely wanted to punish it.

At twilight, Nicolae returned from a scouting trip. "Terror spreads faster than any fire. Rumors are everywhere. You have taken Sibiu, you lead ten thousand Ottoman soldiers, you are the chosen servant of the devil."

"Why must I always be a man's servant?" Lada demanded. "If anything, I should be partners with the devil, not his servant."

Bogdan scowled, crossing himself. He still clung to some bastard version of the religion they had been raised with. His mother—Lada and Radu's nurse—had wielded Christianity like a switch, lashing out with whichever stories suited her needs at the time. Usually the ones about naughty children being eaten by bears. Lada and Radu had also attended church with Bogdan and his mother, but Lada remembered very little from those infinite suffocating hours.

Bogdan must have carried his religion with him through all his years with the Ottomans. Janissaries were converted to Islam. There were no other options. The rest of her men had dropped Islam like their Janissary caps, but they had not replaced it with anything else. Whatever faith they had had in their childhood had been trained out of them.

Lada wondered what it had cost Bogdan to hold on to Christianity in spite of so much opposition. Then again, he had always been stubborn both in grudges and loyalty. She was grateful for the latter, as his loyalty to her had been planted young and deep in the green forests and gray stones of their childhood in Wallachia. Before he had been taken from her by the Ottomans.

Impulsively she reached out and tugged on one of his ears like she had when they were children. An unexpected smile bloomed on his blocky features, and suddenly she was back with him, tormenting Radu, raiding the kitchens, sealing their bond with blood on dirty palms. Bogdan was her childhood. Bogdan was Wallachia. She had him back. She could get the rest.

"If you are working for the devil, can you tell him to pay us? Our purses are empty." Matei held up a limp leather pouch to illustrate. Lada startled, turning away from Bogdan and the warmth in her chest. Matei was one of her original Janissaries, her oldest and most trusted men. They had followed her in Amasya, when she had had nothing to offer them. And they still followed her, with the same result.

Matei was older even than Stefan, with years of invaluable experience. Not many Janissaries lived to his age. When they had been surprised on the border, Matei had taken an arrow in the side protecting Lada. He was graying and gaunt, with a perpetually hungry look about him. That look had grown hungrier still during their sojourn in the mountain wildernesses of Transylvania. Lada valued that hunger in her men. It was what made them willing to follow her. But it was also what would drive them away if she did not do something more, soon. She needed to keep Matei on her side. She needed his sword and, in a less tangible but just as important way, she needed his respect. Bogdan she had no matter what. Her other men she was determined to keep.

Lada kept her eyes fixed on the walls of the city beneath them, watching as lights appeared like tiny beacons. "When your work is done, Matei, take anything you wish."

Brasov had sealed its gates, allowing no one in after dark. Matei and Petru led five men each to scale the walls under cover of darkness. After waiting for them to get where they needed to be, Lada lit the base of a bone-dry dead tree. It greeted the flames hungrily, pulling them so quickly to the top that she and her men had to run from the heat.

The bases of the two towers on the opposite end of the city were engulfed in a matching bright blaze. Lada watched as panicked guards ran around atop the tower nearest her and peered over the edge. "Are you Wallachian?" she called out in her native tongue.

One of them shot an arrow. Lada twisted to the side, and it glanced off the chain mail shirt she wore. Bogdan fired a return arrow. The man tipped silently over the tower's edge.

"Are you hurt?" Bogdan said, voice desperate as his big hands searched for a wound . . . around her breasts.

"Bogdan!" She slapped his hands away. "If I were, it would certainly not be a wound for you to see to!"

"You need a woman, then?" he asked, looking around as though one would magically appear.

"I am fine!"

Another man waved a piece of cloth above the edge of the tower. "Yes, we are Wallachian!" he shouted, voice quavering.

Lada considered it. "Let us in and you can run. Or you can join us."

She counted her heartbeats. It took only ten before the

tower door opened and seven men filed out. Three skulked silently into the trees. Four stayed. She walked past them and climbed the stairs to the top of the tower. It was circular, with a thick stone railing that she leaned over to view the city.

Already, panic spread like disease within the walls. People flooded the streets, women screaming, men shouting directions. It was chaos.

It was perfect.

Three days later, stray remnants of smoke still wrote Lada's anger across the sky above the crippled city. She and her men had camped brazenly close by, drunk on soot and revenge, secure in the knowledge that every man in the city was spent with the effort of saving what had not already been lost. They were also more than a little drunk on the cart full of wine that Matei had somehow managed to bring back.

It was there that Stefan slid in, silent and anonymous as a shadow. He, too, had been with Lada since the beginning. He had always been the best at gathering information: a blank and unremarkable face making him a half-forgotten memory even as he stood in front of someone. One day, Lada thought, the world would know she was deserving of an assassin such as him.

"What news from Tirgoviste?" she asked. Her throat was still raw from breathing in so much smoke, but her hoarseness did not disguise her excitement. "Did you kill the prince?"

"He was not there."

Lada scowled, hopes of announcing her rival's death to her men dashed. His death would not have meant the throne was hers—he had two heirs her own age, and she still needed the damnable boyars to support her claim as prince—but it would have been satisfying. "Then why have you returned?"

"Because he is in Edirne. At Mehmed's invitation."

Though Lada knew her internal fire should have blazed to white-hot fury at this information, she was filled instead with cold, bitter ashes. Her pride had not allowed her to ask Mehmed for help. But all this time she had held him tightly in her heart, knowing that somewhere out there, Mehmed and Radu still believed in her.

And now even that was taken from her.

3

January

MEHMED HAD NOT LEFT a letter in the potted plant where they exchanged messages. Radu always took the secret passage—the same one that Lada had run through the night of Ilyas and Lazar's betrayal. And Radu always wished that *this* time Mehmed would be waiting in the chamber where Radu and Lada had saved his life. But Mehmed was never there. Radu lived for the few brief sentences he spent in Mehmed's company. His eyes devoured the aggressive lines of Mehmed's script, lingering on the few curving flourishes. They never signed or addressed the messages. Radu would have liked to see his own name, just once, in Mehmed's hand.

But today, the dirt was as empty as Radu's life. Mehmed had to know that Radu knew about the Danesti prince. Radu had not been technically invited to that party—meeting Suleiman there had been a desperate, last-minute plan—but Mehmed had seen him. And so, rather than leaving his own message about the navy and then slipping away to wait until Mehmed decided to address the matter of Lada's fate, Radu sat. He hoped that . . .

Well, he no longer knew what to hope for. He sat, and waited.

As the sun set, Radu tried not to dwell on the horrors this room had held, but with Lada so firmly in his mind he could think of little else. He had been so certain she would take the Wallachian throne, he had not considered the possibility that she might fail. His sister did not fail. Was she even still alive? He could not imagine that Mehmed would withhold news of his sister's death.

But Mehmed *had* kept the knowledge of their father's and brother's deaths from Lada. Who was to say he was not doing the same with Radu? And if he was, what did that mean? That he was trying to protect Radu? Or that he was trying to keep him focused on their goals with Constantinople and feared what this news would do? Or that Mehmed cared so little that Lada was dead, he had not even found the time to pass along the information . . . ?

No. Radu could not believe the last one.

Unable to settle on any peaceful train of thought, Radu turned to the only solace in his life. He prayed, losing himself to the words and the motion. Whatever else was happening, had already happened, or would happen, he had God. He had prayer.

By the time he finished, a veil of peace had drifted over his harried mind. Drawing it tightly around himself, Radu opened the door and walked into the central hall of Mehmed's sprawling apartments. He could do nothing to change the past. He could only do what he felt best for the future. And to do that, he needed more information.

All the rooms were dark. Radu found a chair in the corner of Mehmed's bedchamber. He avoided looking at the bed, which threatened to tear his veil of peace.

Some time later, a girl around Radu's age came in and lit the lamps, then slid silently back out. Radu was so still she did not notice him.

Neither did Mehmed when he finally walked in. The same girl followed him. Radu would have been afraid of seeing something he had no wish to, but the girl wore the plain clothing of a servant, not the silks and scarves of a concubine or a wife. Mehmed held out his arms and she carefully took off his robes, one luxurious layer at a time. Radu knew he ought to look away.

He did not.

When Mehmed was down to his underclothes, the servant set his robes aside and slid a nightshirt painted with verses of the Koran over his head. Then, bowing, she backed out of the room. As soon as the door shut behind her, the sultan melted away. All the darkness and fear that had nestled in Radu's heart disappeared along with the sultan. There was Mehmed. *His* Mehmed, not the stranger who inhabited the throne.

Mehmed rubbed the back of his neck and sighed. Then he sat on the edge of the bed and unwound his voluminous turban. His hair was longer than Radu had ever seen it. Curling toward his shoulders, it was black in the dim light, though Radu knew it would shine with chestnut colors in the sun. Radu did not know what it would feel like to touch it, but he desperately wanted to.

"Is my sister dead?" Radu asked.

Mehmed stiffened, one hand going to his waist, where his dagger would normally be. Then he relaxed, shoulders sloping downward.

"You should not be here," he said, without turning.

"You should not be meeting with the Danesti Wallachian *prince* without telling me what happened."

Mehmed sighed, rubbing the back of his neck again. "She is not dead."

Unexpected tears pooled in Radu's eyes as he let out a sharp breath of relief—relief both that Lada was not dead and that his immediate reaction was not one of disappointment. He was not yet so evil, then, that he would begrudge his sister her life. Merely her place in Mehmed's affections.

"What happened? I thought you gave her the throne."

"I did. Apparently Wallachia disagreed with me."

"And yet you support her rival?"

Mehmed lifted his hands helplessly. He was still facing away from Radu. Radu yearned to see his face, his expression. But he could not cover the distance between them. After this long, he did not trust himself to be close to Mehmed.

"What can I do? You know I need all my borders secure. I cannot fight a war on two fronts. If we are to take Constantinople, we need peace everywhere else. Hungary looms as a threat, with Hunyadi harassing me at every opportunity. I cannot afford to lose any territory in Europe, and I cannot start a war there without risking a crusade. The Danesti prince accepted all my terms."

It made sense. It was a perfect explanation. And yet ... Mehmed still would not look at him. "Is that all? Or do you keep Lada from the throne in the hopes that she will return here in her failure?" All Radu's frustration and loneliness of the past year climbed out his throat, lacing his words with accusation.

Mehmed laughed, darker than the night pressing against the

balcony. "Do you see her here? Have you heard from her even once? If she had asked for help, Radu, I would have sent it. I would have gone to war at one word from her. But *she* left *us*. She rejected us, and I will be damned if I follow without an invitation."

Again, the explanation made sense. But none of the information felt as though it should have been withheld like a secret. "How long have you known Lada was not on the throne?"

Mehmed grunted away the question with a noncommittal sound in his throat. "Does it matter?"

"It matters to me. She is my sister. Why would you keep information about her from me?"

Finally, *finally*, Mehmed turned to him. In the dim light of the lamp, his face was thrown into sharp relief, nose and cheekbones golden, lips teased into view and then tipped back into darkness. "Maybe I was afraid."

"Of what?"

"Afraid that if you knew she struggled, you would go to help her."

Radu laughed in shock. "What do you think I could do to help her?"

Mehmed tilted his head to one side, half his face in shadow, the other in light. "You are asking sincerely?"

Radu looked at the floor, intensely uncomfortable. He longed for an answer, and feared one. What if Mehmed could think of no reasons that didn't sound like anything more than empty words?

"I was always better with a bow and arrow." Radu smiled wryly.

"Lada does not need a perfectly aimed arrow. She needs a

perfectly aimed smile. Perfectly aimed words. Perfectly aimed manners."

Radu finally dared to look back up. "Her aim in those matters *has* always been off."

"And your aim never errs. Do not devalue what you can do merely because it is not what Lada excels at. You two are a balanced pair." Mehmed stared into the space between them, eyes no longer focused on Radu. "Or you were, at least."

In that moment Radu knew Mehmed was not seeing him but the absence of his sister. "Do not keep secrets from me," he said.

Mehmed refocused sharply on him. "What?"

"When you keep things secret, it gives them more power, more weight. I assumed the worst as soon as I discovered your deception. I was willing to risk our friendship being found out simply to talk with you. Be open with me in the future." Radu paused, knowing he had spoken to Mehmed as a friend and not as a sultan. In the past he would not have noticed. But now—now there was a distance. And he wondered if maybe the pretend distance had grown into something more. Frightened of this unknown element between them, he added a gentle "Please."

"And you are open with me in all things?" There was a note in Mehmed's voice, a subtle teasing lilt that terrified Radu in a different way. *Was Mehmed asking what it seemed like he was asking?*

"I— You know I work only for you, and—"

Mehmed dispelled the terror with one raised corner of his lips. "I know. And I was foolish to doubt your loyalties to our cause. But you cannot blame me for selfishly wanting to have you only to myself."

"No," Radu croaked, his mouth suddenly parched. "Of course not." But the words that wanted to leave his mouth were *"I am yours. Always."* He swallowed them painfully.

Mehmed shifted on the bed. "Do you have further plans for this evening?"

Radu's heart pounded so loudly he wondered if Mehmed heard it. "What? What do you mean?"

Mehmed gestured toward the door. "Any idea how you are going to sneak out without being seen?"

The sweat that had broken out on Radu's body turned cold and suffocating. He was a fool. "No."

"I will go out and make certain any guards follow me to the first antechamber. You should be able to slip into the passageway then." Mehmed stood, and Radu followed. Too close. He bumped into the other man.

Mehmed paused, then turned and clasped Radu's arms. "It is good to see you again, my friend."

"Yes," Radu whispered. And then Mehmed was gone.

———— ◆ ————

A letter from Nazira waited for him on his desk. She wrote that she and Fatima would be staying in the city in the modest home Kumal kept there. And, she informed Radu, he would be joining them for regular meals.

Radu was both annoyed and pleased. She did not need to fuss over him, but it would be nice to have someone to talk with who expected nothing from him. If he imagined the perfect sister, Nazira would be close to what he would create for himself.

The guilt resurfaced. He had been able to dismiss thoughts of Lada because he assumed she had everything she wanted.

Now he knew otherwise. With a weary sigh, he pulled out a piece of parchment and a quill.

Beloved sister, he wrote. One of those words was true, at least.

Three days later, Radu walked toward an inn close to the palace, swinging his arms in time to his steps. A gathering of pashazadas—sons of pashas who were unimportant enough to still welcome him—had been talking about a foreign woman trying to be seen by the sultan. They joked she wanted to join his harem and had brought a cart full of cannons to make up for her homely face.

It was the cart that sparked Radu's curiosity. And his concern. If a foreign woman was in the city with weapons, trying to meet the sultan, Radu wanted to know why. The other men might dismiss her as crazy, but he knew firsthand that women could be every bit as violent as men.

Turning a corner, Radu ran right into a woman. He managed to catch her, but her bundle of parchments tumbled to the ground. She swore loudly and vehemently in Hungarian. It made Radu oddly homesick for his stuffy, stuttering tutor running through their lessons in the middle of a forest. And then he realized this had to be *her.* The foreign woman trying to meet Mehmed.

"Forgive me," Radu said, his Hungarian sliding into place despite years of neglect. He practiced his other languages—Latin, Greek, Arabic, anything that Mehmed had learned with Radu at his side—regularly, but Hungarian and Wallachian had not been on his tongue since Lada had left. "I was distracted."

The woman looked up, surprised. She was young, older

than him but only by a few years. She wore European-style clothing, sturdy skirts and blouses designed for travel. "You speak Hungarian?"

"Among other things." Radu handed her the parchments. Her fingers were blunt and blackened, her hands shiny with scars from old burns.

"I do not speak Turkish. Can you help me?" She said it crossly, more demanding than pleading. "No one in this damnable city will let me have a conference with the sultan."

Radu felt this wise of the damnable city. "Where are your servants? Your father?"

"I travel alone. And I am about to be kicked out of my inn for just that. I have nowhere to stay." She rubbed her forehead, scowling. "All this travel wasted."

"Are you trying to join the sultan's harem?"

Her look of murderous outrage was so sudden and severe it reminded him of Lada. He liked the woman more for it, and was also alarmed. Maybe she *was* here to kill Mehmed.

"I would sooner join his stables and let him ride on my back than join his harem and let him ride on my front."

Radu felt his cheeks burn and he cleared his throat. "Then what do you need?"

"I have a proposition for him. I went to Constantinople first, and they would not see me, either."

"You come from Constantinople?" If she was an assassin, she was a stupid one, admitting this up front.

She lifted one of the parchment rolls. "That ass of an emperor would not so much as let me show him my work. He laughed and said even if my claims were true, he could not afford me."

"Afford you for what?"

She finally smiled, showing all her fine teeth. "I can build a cannon big enough to destroy the walls of Babylon itself. I would have done it for the sultan, if he would have seen me. Now it appears I have to go home, every bit as disgraced as my father and mother said I would be." She shook her head bitterly and turned to walk away.

"Wait! What is your name?"

"Urbana. Of Transylvania."

"I am Radu. And I think we may be able to help each other." He took the bundle of parchments from her. "Go get your things, and I will introduce you to my wife."

Urbana raised an eyebrow. "I have no intention of joining *anyone's* harem."

Radu held back a laugh. It might have been misinterpreted as mean. "I assure you that is the last thing on my mind. I was born in Transylvania, and I know what it is to be a stranger in a new land. Allow me to help you as I would want someone to help my own sister."

"If you try anything unseemly, I am fully capable of blowing up your home."

This time Radu let himself laugh. "My sister would accept help in much the same spirit. Come, I will take you to my home. You are going to love my wife."

With Nazira's help, he would be able to determine whether Urbana could be trusted. If so, Radu had a creeping, joyful suspicion he was about to once again prove to Mehmed just how valuable he could be.

4

February

LADA KNEW PUNISHING TRANSYLVANIA for everything that had gone wrong in the past year did not make perfect strategic sense. But it felt better than anything else, and so Transylvania burned.

Lada was not happy, but she was busy, and that was almost the same.

"God's wounds," she whispered, trying to fasten binding cloth tightly enough around her breasts so that they would not chafe against her chain mail. It was difficult to dress herself in the woods. But this arrangement was far preferable to the one the governor of Brasov had proposed—*before* he sent an assassin after her. After agreeing to see what men and funds he could free up to support Lada's bid for the throne, he had suggested she stay with him rather than going back "where no lady belongs."

She belonged with her men. Even if it *was* freezing. She shivered behind the blanket she had hung to give herself some privacy. She nearly had the binding cloth right, but her cold fingers fumbled the knot. She threw the cloth to the ground and shrieked in rage.

"Lada?" Bogdan asked. He hovered on the other side of the blanket. "Do you need help?"

"Not from you! Leave me alone!" After a few more infuriating minutes, she finally had everything in place. She pulled on a tunic—clean, which was a novelty—and rejoined her men.

"You need help," Bogdan said, his voice low so no one would overhear.

"I do not need *help.*"

"You are a lady. You should not have to do these things for yourself."

Lada gave him a flat, angry stare. "Bogdan, when have I ever been a lady?"

He returned her angry look with a soft, shy smile. "You have always been a lady to me."

"Maybe you do not know me very well after all."

Bogdan put one rough hand out, holding it palm up to show the scar from when they had "married" as children. "I know you."

Before Lada could decide how to respond—or how to feel—Petru drew her attention.

The last caravan they robbed had been filled with fine clothing, pieces of which were strewn about their camp. Trousers hung from trees, shirts danced in the breeze. The bright colors on bare branches gave everything a festival air.

Petru wrestled with an intricately brocaded vest, struggling to get it across his shoulders. He spun in one direction and then the other. Nicolae watched, lips a single straight line but eyes dancing with mirth.

"That would fit better if it were designed for a man," Matei said as he walked by. Matei's purse was full now, but he still looked hungry.

Petru stopped spinning and ripped off the vest in horror. Nicolae burst into laughter. "You could have told me!" Petru said.

"But it set off the color of your eyes so nicely."

Petru glared murderously. Then he looked over at Lada and held the vest out. She raised a single eyebrow at the delicate colors and needlework. Muttering to himself, Petru threw the vest at Nicolae's head and walked away.

Lada wore a long tunic over trousers, all black except for a red sash tied at her waist. A thick black cloak, lined with glorious fur, kept her warmer than she had been in months. Her boots—finely tooled leather decorated with delicate patterns—were the only women's clothing she wore. She had grown accustomed to wearing her hair tied in cloth, but instead of Janissary white, she used black. Over that, she wore a fur cap.

They had all ceased wearing the Janissary caps and uniforms long ago. But some kept a few reminders of their lives as slaves: a sash here, a knife there. Bogdan used the white cloth from his cap to clean his weapons. Many of the men used theirs for much less savory cleaning.

"Has Stefan returned?"

Nicolae finished buttoning his vest, then drew his cloak closed. "Not yet. Must we wait for him before having any fun? We have plenty of men."

"Tonight is not a night for plenty. Tonight is a night for speed and secrecy."

Bogdan shifted closer to Lada. "I will come."

"Not you."

His face fell. Gritting her teeth, Lada continued, "I need to leave you in charge of the camp."

He shrugged and stomped away. She did not know if he stomped because he was angry, or simply because he was large. The truth was, she could not bring Bogdan tonight because he would object to what she had in mind. Nicolae might as well. Petru, she did not know. But Matei . . .

"Matei, just the two of us."

"What are you going to do?" Nicolae asked.

Lada sheathed her knives. One at either wrist, one at her right ankle. A large container of lamp oil hung from a strap slung over her shoulder. "I am going to visit the governor of Brasov."

"Is that really necessary?"

"He betrayed me. Why promise me aid and then try to have me killed? He must have been gathering information. And when he passed that information along, the return instruction was to eliminate me. Either he is working for Hungary or in league with the Danesti prince. I want to know which one. If it is the Danesti prince, we have nothing to fear. We already know he wants us dead. If it is the Hungarians, we have a new problem."

"How are you going to get to him? The city will be well guarded."

Lada met Matei's eyes. He nodded grimly. He would be up for the task. And Lada knew she was up for anything, always.

———— ·‡· ————

They slid through the night-black streets of the Wallachian section. It was a rambling warren of shacks pushed up to the very edge of the walls. Some of the homes were built against the wall itself, using the stones as an outer wall. A few times Lada and Matei heard patrols, but it was a simple matter of altering course to avoid detection.

The shacks built against the wall provided a benefit. Bracing against two homes within spitting distance of each other, they pushed their way to a roof. Matei boosted Lada up onto the wall itself. After a few tense breaths to make certain she was undetected, she lowered a rope so Matei could follow.

Within the walls of the inner city, even the air felt different. Cleaner. Wealthier. More privileged, with fewer desperate mouths pulling at it. But the scent of charred wood lurked beneath everything. It filled Lada with something like peace.

Lada knew exactly where to go, but it took two hours for them to make a journey of a dozen streets. They skirted the now-cold ruins of the homes that had burned, hiding in them when necessary. It was good that Lada had dressed in black, because the char would have ruined anything else.

Patrols tromped through the streets with aggravating consistency. Finally making it close to the governor's house did not simplify things, though. Three guards were stationed at the door, while others ringed the perimeter. Lada had counted on breaking in through a first-floor window, but that was not possible.

Matei waited in silence, but she could feel the question pulsing off him. *What now?*

Lada raised her eyes to the night sky to curse the stars, but the lines of the roofs caught her attention. The houses were built close together, elbowing each other for space. Sometimes the alleys between them were so narrow one had to turn sideways to make it through.

She did not need to break into the governor's house. She just needed to break into one of his less-protected neighbors' homes.

"How do you feel about churches?" she whispered.

Matei frowned at her in the dark.

"Did you notice how, in the countryside, all the churches are fortified? They provide shelter for everyone during an attack. But here in the heart of the city, the church is beautiful and cold. They do not let any of the Wallachians in to worship. I think we should warm up the church." She held out her container of oil. Understanding lit Matei's face as he took it from her.

He disappeared into the darkness. Though Lada had more men now, she always trusted her first few above all others. Matei would do the job. Nicolae and Bogdan might have balked at setting fire to a holy building, but how could something be holy if it was denied to Wallachians?

She slid from her shadowed nook and raced through an exposed alley. Four houses from the governor's was a three-story home with large windowsills, perfect for flower boxes in the spring.

Lada stepped onto a windowsill and pulled herself up to the second story, then the third. The roof had an awkward angle and jutted out too far for her to catch hold. Above her, tantalizingly out of reach, was a small attic window that would give her easy jumping access to the next roof.

The window in front of her was not sealed shut. One corner was lifted enough to slide a knife in. Lada worked it open, each tiny creak or protest of the wood making her certain she would be discovered. When it was wide enough, she pushed herself in feetfirst.

A girl sat in bed, staring directly at Lada. She could not be older than ten, her hair pinned beneath a cap, her nightshirt white.

"If you scream," Lada said, "I will murder your whole family in their sleep."

The girl was solemn—and silent—in her terror.

"Show me how to get into the attic."

The girl climbed out of bed, shivering, her small feet soundless on the wood floor. She eased open the bedroom door, looking both ways before gesturing for Lada to follow. At the end of the hallway was another door. Lada braced herself to face a foe, but the room was empty save for a jumble of old furniture and a ladder.

The girl pointed up.

Lada put one hand on the ladder, then paused. She turned back to the girl, who watched her in the same wide-eyed silence she had maintained since Lada first entered her bedroom.

Lada reached into her boot and pulled the small knife free. She turned it hilt out and bent down. "Next time someone comes into your room in the middle of the night, you should be prepared. Here."

The girl took the knife, staring at it like it was a puzzle. Then she gripped the hilt and nodded.

"Good. I am leaving now. Go back to sleep." Lada climbed up the ladder and eased open the trapdoor to the attic. The attic window, though, would not open. Cursing her luck, Lada grabbed a chair with a broken leg and smashed the window. She hoped Matei's work had begun in earnest, distracting anyone who might raise an alarm.

After pushing the jagged remnants of glass free, Lada climbed out and crouched on the sill. Beneath her the night waited, dizzying and dark. She jumped.

The roof slammed up to meet her faster than she had anticipated, and she nearly rolled off before she caught herself. Then she ran. Up and over the peak, gaining momentum before launching herself across the void yearning to claim her. Another roof. This one was angled the opposite way, and the roof after that was several feet higher. Lada ran along the peak, put on a burst of speed, and jumped.

Her hands found the edge of the next roof. Her legs dangled, her weight threatening to drag her down. Swinging from side to side, she hooked a knee onto the roof and pulled herself up.

One more.

This time she crept carefully across the tiles. Though the air was icy, her body itched with sweat. The governor's roof was higher than the one she was on, but it was not her goal. She prowled along the edge between the houses until she found what she was looking for—a window with a small ledge beneath it. She had planned on breaking in, but luck was finally on her side.

The casement window was flung wide, and a balding head leaned out, looking down toward the city center and the shouts echoing from that direction. There was a faint glow, and the distant sound of shattering glass.

For the eternal space between one breath and the next, Lada paused. He looked old and soft and vulnerable in his baggy nightshirt. He was a husband. A father. Then he cleared his throat with that same phlegmy rattle he had made while promising to help her and already planning to betray her.

Lada jumped the distance, slamming into the governor. They rolled together into the room. Lada recovered immediately and knelt on his chest, her knife to his throat.

"Who wanted me dead?"

He trembled, eyes crossing when they tried to focus on the knife.

She pressed her knife, drawing blood. The governor whimpered the words to a prayer.

"God is not here tonight," Lada said. "It is only you and me and my knife. Who wanted me dead?"

"The prince!" he said. "The prince of Wallachia."

"Why?"

"Because you are a threat."

Lada smiled. She knew that should not please her, but it did. The prince thought her a big enough threat to warrant an assassin. She still had a chance. Where there was fear, there was power.

She withdrew the knife and placed it next to the governor's head. He did not move. "A gift for the *prince*. Tell him I send my regards, and I will see him soon. And tell your god to make less flammable churches."

Lada slipped out the window, followed by the relieved sobs of the governor. She carried them with her like a gift as she ran across the rooftops, away from the center of Brasov and toward her men.

5

February

URBANA WAS A DECIDEDLY odd houseguest. In the week she had been living with Nazira and Fatima in Kumal's city house, she had not stopped talking.

"If she is a spy," Nazira said, sitting with an exhausted sigh next to Radu in the garden, "she is the worst spy that ever lived. How can she gain any information if she never lets anyone else talk?"

"What does she talk about?" Radu had made himself scarce at the house, wary of drawing too much attention before he was certain the risk was worthwhile.

"Her horrible cannons. Nothing else. She pulls sticks from the stove to draw diagrams—on the walls, Radu, the lovely white walls. And then she expects Fatima to wash them, because we have to pretend that Fatima is nothing but a servant."

"I am sorry." Radu knew it was asking much of the two women to let someone else into their private life.

Nazira waved a hand. "I do most of the cleaning after Urbana retires for the night. Fatima understands."

"So what do you think?"

"I think Urbana is insane, but she may also be a genius. I know nothing of cannons, but no one could fake what she is doing. And she is not lying when she says she will build them for anyone willing to fund her. She has been pursuing this her whole life, and rejected at every turn. Her only loyalty is to creating the most stunningly large and effective means of killing people the world has ever seen."

Radu tried to temper his excitement. "So you think I should move forward?"

"She is an incredible find. She may even prove invaluable."

Radu could not help his delighted smile. If Radu brought Mehmed something—someone—invaluable that he had found on his own? If Radu was the reason that Mehmed finally realized his dream of Constantinople?

Nazira put a hand on Radu's cheek. "Where are you right now?"

Radu shook his head. "Sorry."

"What about the navy? How is that progressing?"

"As well as can be hoped. Most of the galleys are built and Suleiman has found sailors to hire. I thought it would be difficult, but the men flocked to him. They foam at the mouth for the riches of Constantinople." Radu sighed. "I hear it among all the soldiers when Constantinople comes up. The golden apple at the center of the city, held by the statue of Justinian. The churches bricked in gold and decorated with jewels. They care nothing for our destiny to have the city, as declared by the Prophet, peace be upon him." Radu frowned. He also heard much darker talk that focused on the wealth and spoils to be found among citizens of the city. Right now it was spoken half in jest, as no one knew Mehmed meant to go for the city immediately. But it left a bad taste in Radu's mouth.

"But that is not why we have to take the city."

Radu had not really spoken with Nazira about Constantinople before. He was surprised that she had an opinion. "What do you mean?"

"People think it is prophesied because it will bring us wealth and fortune. But why would God care about that? I think the city will be ours because we need it to be. As long as Constantinople exists, it will draw crusades. More people who come into our land and kill us simply for being Muslim. I think Constantinople's fall will bring safety and protection. God will give us the city so we can worship in peace."

Radu closed his eyes, lifting his face to the sun. He had been so focused on *how* to help Mehmed take the city, he had stopped thinking about *why*. Nazira was right. This was not just for Mehmed; this was holy work. He would do it to help protect the faith that had given him so much.

"What is the timeline?" Nazira asked, pulling him back to the present.

"We are getting close. Everything is nearly in order. But Mehmed will not move until he is certain of all his borders. Hungary still troubles him. Hunyadi is a threat."

"And the Italians?"

Radu was glad he had opened up to Nazira. It was such a relief to discuss this openly with someone who understood all the pieces in play and who reminded him of what the actual purpose was. "They are too busy quarreling with each other to defend a city with as much history of animosity as Constantinople. Once we secure the waterways, they cannot send aid even if they decide to."

Nazira sighed. "I know it must be done, but I do not look forward to the day that will claim both my brother and my husband for their destinies at the walls of Constantinople. I fear the outcome."

Radu drew her close. "You know I will make certain you are taken care of. No matter what."

Nazira laughed sadly against his chest. "There you go again, assuming I am worried for myself. You never account for others loving you for *you*, Radu, rather than what you can do for them. It is my greatest prayer that someday you will know enough of love to recognize when it is freely given."

Radu had no answer. Sometimes Nazira offered *too much* insight. "I am going to speak with Urbana, then. Thank you." He kissed Nazira's hand.

As he walked inside, he passed Fatima. "Thank you for enduring this," he whispered. "Nazira is in the garden, and I will be occupying Urbana for the next few hours. Go spend some time with your wife."

She briefly met his gaze, a grateful smile shaping her kind face. "Good luck," she said.

"Your wife may be infertile," Urbana said as she and Radu sat down for a midafternoon meal.

Radu choked in surprise. "What?"

"You have been married more than a year. How often do you copulate?"

Radu raised his eyes to the ceiling, searching for answers

there as he felt his cheeks burning hotter than the furnaces of the foundry. "Are you also an expert in these matters?" he asked, trying for a teasing tone.

Urbana frowned. "No. But I wonder about the practicality of continuing on a course that is yielding no results. What about the maid?"

Radu panicked. Apparently they had underestimated Urbana's perceptiveness. "Fatima?" he asked, stalling. How would he explain this? What if she told someone?

"She is your servant. I am not unaware of customs here. If she bore you a son, he would be an acceptable heir. And it would be a nice thing for her, too. She would have legal status and you would not be able to sell her to someone else. I like Fatima. You should consider it."

Radu's voice came out strained, both with relief that Urbana did not realize the truth of his marriage and embarrassment that this was a conversation she thought appropriate. "I prefer to remain faithful to my wife."

"Is that why you have not tried to join my bed? I would have rebuffed you, violently if necessary, but it has puzzled me."

"I want to talk about your cannons!" Radu said, desperate to wrestle the topic away from babies and beds.

Urbana's face fell; then she brought her thick eyebrows together as though bracing for pain. "If you would just let me talk to your sultan, I can—"

"I want you to make them."

Her eyebrows lifted in surprise. "What?"

"I want you to make them. All of them. Your Babylon crusher, yes, but also every cannon you have time and dreams for. I want you to create the greatest artillery the world has ever seen."

Urbana's delight quickly shifted to tired disappointment. "I want that, too, but neither of us has a foundry or materials or the money to acquire them."

"Can you keep a secret?"

She licked her lips, pulling them thoughtfully between her teeth. "No, not really."

Radu laughed drily. Urbana might become invaluable, but not if he was unable to keep her hidden from Halil Vizier. Nothing could be easy in his life, apparently. He rubbed his forehead beneath his turban. "Well, that is a problem, then. Tell me, would it be possible to create these cannons without drawing a lot of attention?"

"Not with the amount of ore we will need. And we will need men—lots of men. I cannot do it alone. And I cannot do it just anywhere. That is why I came here—Edirne and Constantinople have the only foundries big enough for me to make my cannons in."

Radu had too many secrets. They were overflowing. And he did not know how he could build an artillery without being noticed. Besides which, the weight of secrets was wearing on him. He doubted everything now. Even Mehmed, which hurt. If Mehmed hid his dealings with the Wallachian prince, hid Lada's plight, what else might he be keeping from Radu?

Secrets gave everything more power, more potential for devastation and destruction.

Radu stood and walked to the window. Nazira and Fatima lay on a blanket in the garden, whispering and laughing. If he had seen them without knowing the truth of their relationship, he would have assumed they were very dear friends. No one questioned why Fatima was always with Nazira, why they were happy to live out in the countryside with no one else around.

They hid their love in plain sight.

"Urbana," Radu said, an idea forming that he liked the shape of, "how do you feel about parties?"

"I hate them," she said.

"What if I said that going to a lot of parties is the price you will have to pay to make your cannons?"

Her voice was flat but determined. "What should I wear?"

6

February

THE TREK BACK FROM interrogating the governor of Brasov was a frigid and lonely one. Lada looked for Matei on the way to camp. At every sound she whipped around, expecting to find him.

He did not appear.

She was nearly there, the fires in the distance promising rest and warmth, when a horse whinnied in the darkness to her right. She dropped into a crouch, cursing her generosity with the little girl that left her with only one knife out of the three she had brought. Why had she felt compelled to give the brat one?

The daughter of Wallachia wants her knife back.

She shuddered at the distant memory. Her father had given her a knife, and it had changed her life. She only hoped her own gift would change that little girl's life, because Lada might very well die for the gesture.

"Quiet, boys," a man whispered exaggeratedly, his voice carrying through the night. He spoke Hungarian. "We seem to have found a small predator. They are very dangerous when cornered."

Lada backed up against a tree so at least she could face whatever was coming. Her muscles were tight with the cold. She flexed her hands rapidly, trying to work some blood back into them.

She heard someone dismount. He made no attempt at hiding his footfalls as he approached. He sat close enough for Lada to see him, but too far for hand-to-hand combat. She would not throw her last knife. If she missed, she would be weaponless.

With a groan, he picked up a rock from beneath him and tossed it to the side.

"I have been looking for you, Ladislav Dragwlya. You are terrorizing the Transylvanians. It is in very poor taste."

Lada lifted her chin defiantly. "I owe them nothing."

"You were born here."

"And will I die here?"

The man laughed, pulling something from his vest. Lada tensed, but he leaned forward, striking flint until it caught on a pile of tinder. He fed the fire a few sticks pulled from the frozen forest floor. As the flames grew, the face of her enemy revealed itself. The face of the man who had driven her father from Tirgoviste and into the arms of the sultan, where he had abandoned his children. The face of the man who had returned to kill her father and her older brother.

Lada leaned back. She did not relax her grip on the knife, but it was an odd relief to have a connection to the man who would be her undoing. "Hunyadi."

His auburn hair gleamed as red as the fire. His forehead was broad, his eyebrows were strong, and his nose bore the evidence of multiple breakings. He did not seem to have grown older since Lada had last seen him in the throne room at Tirgoviste. He was around the same age her father would have been, if Hunyadi had not killed him. It was not fair that Hunyadi had remained unchanged when his actions had altered Lada in unimaginable ways.

Hunyadi dipped his head in acknowledgement. "What mischief have you been up to tonight?"

Lada saw no advantage to lying. "Arson. Threats of death. Gathering information."

Hunyadi sighed. "You have had a very full night. What did you burn?"

"The cathedral."

He coughed in surprise. "I paid for the new altar."

"It was a poor investment."

He snorted. "I suppose so. I was vaivode of Transylvania for a few years. I have never been so happy to be relieved of power. *Saxons.*" He shook his head, breath fogging the night in a silent laugh. Then he put an elbow on one knee, reclining to the side. "Tell me, what did burning the church give you?"

Lada touched her index finger to the point of her knife. "Distraction so I could accomplish my task. And satisfaction."

"Hmm. Somehow I doubt that anything here is going to satisfy you. I know you were sent for the Wallachian throne. Are you still in league with the sultan?"

Lada twirled her knife. "Does it look like I serve the Ottomans?"

"So you are not sending updates to him on where you are and what you are doing?"

Lada was glad the firelight covered her flush of humiliation. Write to Mehmed and admit her failures? Never. "No."

"He has been keeping track of you." Hunyadi held out a thin sheaf of parchment. It was crowded with spidery writing. One corner was blotted and darkened with a few large splashes of ink.

Lada squinted. Not ink. Blood.

"We found this on a wounded man following you. It is a letter to the sultan, detailing everything you are doing."

"Matei," Lada said. So that was why he had not caught up to her. He could not. She breathed something as close to a prayer of relief as she was capable of that she had left Bogdan behind. It surprised her, how glad she was that he was safe. She did not dwell on it. "What did you do with my man?"

"He fought. We killed him."

Lada nodded numbly. Matei was dead. Wounded in Brasov, finished by Hunyadi. And carrying a letter to Mehmed. How long had he been updating Mehmed on her? How much did Mehmed know? And whom should she be most angry with—Mehmed, for spying on her, Matei, for betraying her, or herself, for trusting Matei?

Or herself, for having so many miserable failures to write of?

Matei's betrayal cut deep, though. She had chosen Wallachians precisely because she assumed they would be as eager as she was to sever their Ottoman ties. But apparently Matei's hunger had extended beyond what Lada could provide. "I did not know he reported to Mehmed."

"I thought as much from the contents of the letter. So you are not working for the sultan. But you call him by his name. You know him, his temperament, his tactics."

This felt both dangerous and promising. "Better than any-one."

"In that case, I have another letter for you." Hunyadi dropped Matei's letter in the fire. Lada's fingers reflexively stretched toward it. She wanted to know how her life would read when being looked at by Mehmed. But it was too late.

Hunyadi reached into his vest and withdrew an envelope. He tossed it in front of Lada.

Puzzled, she picked it up. The seal was broken.

"We got this one off a Turk asking around for your where-abouts. It is from your brother." Hunyadi spoke as pleasantly as if they were discussing the weather over a meal. "He wonders how you fare, and fears for your safety. He even suggests re-turning to Edirne. He says they are having the most wonderful parties under Mehmed's rule."

Lada snorted. "He says that only because he knows nothing could keep me farther away than the promise of parties." Still, Lada tucked the letter into her shirt, against her heart. Beneath the necklace Radu had given her. Did he know everything, too? Were none of her humiliations private?

Hunyadi stood, holding out a gloved hand. He was close enough to strike. One quick thrust of her knife and she could avenge her father. And her older brother Mircea. Blood for her blood.

For his betrayal, Matei could go unavenged.

"Come," Hunyadi said. "I have an offer for you."

Lada's knife paused. Her father had died doing what he al-ways did—running—and she had never cared for Mircea any-way. She took Hunyadi's hand.

7

February–March

EVERYONE WHO MATTERED IN Edirne was around the massive table: valis, beys, pashas, viziers, and a smattering of their wives. Even a few daughters, hopeful of catching the eye of someone important. One such daughter had been trying to attract Radu's attention all evening. But he knew her father was already firmly in support of Mehmed, so there was no reason to be cruel and indulge her.

Salih, too, was here. Halil's second son. The only person Radu had ever kissed. But Salih had long since given up trying to speak to Radu. Radu could not even look at him without feeling a sick twist of guilt, and so he had gotten very good at letting his eyes pass over the other man's head.

They all reclined on pillows, a sumptuous spread laid out in front of them. Next to Radu, Urbana kept shifting, trying to get comfortable in her stiff European clothing. She stood out terribly, scowling and muttering to herself in Hungarian. If she caught anyone's eye, it was definitely not in a flirtatious way. She looked like she wanted to strangle someone. It made Radu miss Lada.

"Sit still," Radu whispered, looking toward the head of the table. He was seated far from where Mehmed lounged on a higher level than anyone else. A servant fanned the sultan, while behind him lingered the lonely stool attendant. And on the sultan's right, Halil Vizier.

Radu waited, anxious to the point of giddiness.

"What is this?" Urbana complained, dipping a finger in one of the cool, creamy sauces for the meat. "I am tired of these parties. Why do I have to be here when I could be working?"

Radu hushed her as Mehmed stood. "My friends," Mehmed said, extending his arms to take in the entire room, "this is a night for celebration! Tonight, I honor three of my greatest advisors. Their wisdom gives me strength. Their guidance builds my legacy. And tonight, I dedicate that legacy to the world. Zaganos Pasha. Sarica Pasha." He nodded at the two men to his immediate left, men Radu knew to be deeply loyal and committed to the cause of taking Constantinople. Kumal was gone, already on-site. "And my most important advisor, Halil Vizier."

Halil flushed a deep red, his expression that of a child who has gotten away with some feat of naughtiness. He bowed his head and put a hand over his heart.

"To honor you, my three wisest, I am building a fortress with a tower named for each of you. Your might will reach up to the very sky. Your wisdom will watch over our land forever. You three will be my towers of strength, my sentinels."

The three men bowed even deeper.

"For this honor, I would pay everything I own," Zaganos Pasha said.

Mehmed laughed brightly. "Well, that is good to hear,

because you will each be in charge of financing and constructing your tower. I would not trust your legacies with anyone else."

Halil Vizier looked slightly less pleased, but displeasure marred his visage only briefly. This was a tremendous honor, and further proof that his hold on Mehmed was tighter than ever. That Mehmed announced it in front of every important person in the empire doubtless did not escape Halil's notice. Halil nodded. "Of course, my sultan."

"Yours will be the most vital tower, and the largest." Mehmed took Halil's hand, squeezing it warmly. For him to touch another man was a gesture of the highest regard. Halil swept his eyes across the room, exulting in the moment.

Mehmed released Halil's hand and sat. His tone became less formal. "We begin construction immediately. The fortress will be called the Rumeli Hisari."

Halil's eyebrows drew together. "Rumeli Hisari. Like your grandfather's fortress on the Bosporus Strait, the Anadolu Hisari."

"Yes, precisely!" Mehmed gestured to a servant to refill his glass. "I have already moved the men into place, and the stones are being brought in as we speak. Kumal Pasha is there to direct construction."

"Where—" Halil wiped at his forehead, where sweat was beginning to bead beneath his turban. "Where will the Rumeli Hisari be built?"

Mehmed waved dismissively with the flatbread in his hand. "Across from the Anadolu Hisari."

"Across— But that is Constantinople's land."

Mehmed let out a burst of laughter. "It belongs to a few

scrappy goats. There is nothing there. Yet. But soon the foundation of a fortress honoring you will displace those goats! The fortresses will wink at each other from across the water of the Bosporus Strait. Their cannons could meet in the middle, I think." Mehmed laughed again. "We will have to try it out after your tower has been built."

This time, the deep flush on Halil's face was not one of pleasure. His mouth opened and closed as he struggled to find a way out of the trap Radu and Mehmed had set.

But it was too late. He had agreed to the fortress in front of everyone, had shown nothing but support. He had even agreed to pay for it. If he backed out now, he would have to say why. And he could not challenge Mehmed on Constantinople outright. He had no solid proof that Mehmed meant to attack, and he had to keep his own connections to Emperor Constantine secret.

Halil's options were dwindling, and would dwindle further when his allies in Constantine's court heard that a tower built on their land bore Halil's name.

Secrets made information more powerful and suspect. The best way to keep the fortress safe from Halil's machinations was to make him intimately—and inescapably—involved in its construction. It was the same method Radu was applying to the artillery, inspired by Nazira and Fatima's relationship. Hiding in plain sight.

"What is so funny?" Urbana said, scowling. "I did not understand any of that. Why are you smiling?"

"Because I am pleased with tonight's events."

She sighed, picking at the bones of the unfortunate fowl on

her plate. "I still do not understand why I have to be here. We never even speak to the sultan."

"You are here so that everyone sees you are my special project. I want the whole city gossiping about how foolish I am, hiring a woman to make the largest cannon in the world to try to impress the sultan. I intend to subject us both to ridicule."

Her scowl deepened. "Why would you do that?"

"So that no one pays any attention until we succeed."

For the first time that night, Urbana smiled. She snapped a bone off the chicken.

Radu nudged her with his elbow. "Imagine how surprised they will be when the sultan has the most advanced artillery in the world, built by a woman and the most handsome and useless foreigner in the empire." He stood. "Come. I need to introduce you to everyone, and tell them how we are designing a cannon so big it could puncture a hole in the bottom of the Black Sea and drain it dry."

Urbana grimaced but nodded. "Lead on."

———◆———

Later that week, Radu pulled aside the tapestry to leave his update on Urbana's progress and the navy's readiness. He was so shocked to find Mehmed sitting in the room that he barely stifled a cry.

"Radu." Mehmed grinned. "You are very late."

"I— What is wrong?"

"Nothing. I have something for you." Mehmed held out a letter.

It was addressed to Radu in a hand like someone had taken

a blade and dipped it in ink. The part of his heart that was permanently vacant hurt as it beat again. He turned the parchment over to find it had been sealed by a knife tip pressed into wax.

"Lada," he whispered, running his fingers over the red seal.

"It arrived this morning." Mehmed's voice was carefully neutral. "Did you write her?"

"Yes, after I found out she was not on the throne. I had given up hope that the messenger would ever find her."

Radu would have preferred to read privately, but he could not bear to leave this gift of time with Mehmed. But the way Mehmed's eyes were fixed on the letter, like a starving man on a circle of bread, hurt. All this time they had spent apart, all these times he had never been waiting for Radu.

Mehmed was here only for Lada.

He was still in love with her. They never spoke of her, but it was inescapable. Perhaps, since she left before Mehmed could claim her, he would long for her forever. The same way he was fixated on Constantinople, simply because it was not his but he felt it should be.

According to Islam, though, Mehmed could not consummate his relationship with Lada. It was forbidden outside of marriage or official concubines. Lada had been inside Mehmed's harem, though, which legally made her part of it.

There was always a way forward for Mehmed and Lada.

Radu hung his head. What did he hope his future would be? To stand forever at Mehmed's side, beloved friend, trusted advisor? He had told Nazira it would be enough. It would never be enough.

Mehmed put a hand on Radu's shoulder. The jolt of the

touch went so much deeper than the light pressure of his fingers. "Are you well, my friend?"

Radu cleared his throat, nodding. He tore open the letter with more force than was needed. It was addressed, in typically sentimental style, to *My only brother, Radu.* It had been more honest than his greeting to her.

"What does she say?" Mehmed asked, perfectly still. He may as well have been bounding around the room, for all his stillness hid his anxiety.

Radu read aloud, his voice flat from the exhaustion of his emotions.

"I was surprised to receive your letter. I am sorry to report that the messenger you sent is dead. I did not kill him. I suppose, in a way, you did, for sending him here."

Radu paused, narrowing his eyes in annoyance both at Lada's words and at the fact that she might have a point. Had he sacrificed a life simply to send a letter to his sister?

"She teases you," Mehmed said. "I am sure the messenger is fine. Go on."

"In turn, I will surprise you by telling you I am with Hunyadi. He found me in Transylvania and we declined to murder each other. I wondered if I was being disloyal to our father and brother, but they are dead and so cannot complain. He invited my company to join his.

"I do not know his motives, but I accepted. I will finally have an ally worth something. If I can convince Hunyadi to support me, I can take the throne. I know it. But after that, I do not have the skill for nobility. I am a blunt weapon. I need a surgeon.

"I am tired of being the right hand to powerful men. I want you as my right hand. I have seen you move among nobility as easily as a hawk cuts

through the air. Cut through the boyars for me. Come home, Radu. Help me. Wallachia belongs to us, and I will not be complete without you."

Radu paused, shocked. "And then she signs her name." He did not say how she signed it.

Lada, on the ice and in need of your hand this time.

With one line she had dragged him back to his helpless childhood, when he had needed rescuing after going out too far on the ice. And—he could not quite believe it—she was asking him for help.

She recognized that he was good at something she was not. Mehmed had been right. Lada needed him to secure her path to power. For a few silent, painful moments, he considered it. She was his sister. She had never asked him for anything. She had expected him to come along initially, because she thought he should, not because she wanted him to.

Now, though . . .

"Will you go to her?"

Radu looked up, surprised. Mehmed's voice was as quiet as his own had been, as carefully devoid of emotion. But Radu knew his friend's face better than anything on earth. He had studied it, worshipped it. And Mehmed could not hide his fear and anguish.

It was balm to Radu's soul, such a tremendous relief that Radu let out a shaky laugh. Lada was not the only Dracul who mattered to Mehmed.

"No. No, of course not."

Mehmed's shoulders relaxed, the tension draining from his face. He again put a hand on Radu's shoulder, then took the letter from him.

And Radu was happy, standing there with his friend. Because as much as it meant to be valued by his weapon of a sister, it was not where he belonged. She wanted him to achieve *her* goals. But, as always, she discounted his feelings. He had worked too long and hard here to abandon it all in pursuit of her dream. It had never been his dream.

Lada would be hurt by his decision. The thought made him feel oddly powerful. He hated that about himself, but he could not avoid it. Lada wanted him, *and* Mehmed wanted him. He would choose Mehmed. He could not do anything else.

Mehmed tapped his finger against the page. "It is very interesting that she is in Hunyadi's inner circle. After everything he did to your father and brother."

Radu was surprised, too. But it made a sort of sense. "Lada only holds grudges that are useful to her. In a way, our father's death freed her. She might even be grateful to Hunyadi. Regardless, if she can learn from him and use him to gain power, she will forgive him anything."

"Hmm," Mehmed said. His finger traced Hunyadi's name.

Radu wanted the letter back. He wanted to read again how he could do things his strong, vicious sister never could. He wanted to hold the letter and remember the fear on Mehmed's face when he thought Radu would choose to leave. That fear was enough to give Radu hope.

He might have his own dream yet.

8

February

A WEEK INTO LADA'S TRAVELS with the Hungarians, Hunyadi rode along the edge of camp where her men had set up. He shouted a command in Hungarian to pack up. No one responded. He looked to Lada.

They had not spoken much, and Lada was beginning to question her rashness in sending Bogdan to find someone to carry a letter to Radu. Maybe she had written too soon of Hunyadi as her ally. And if anything happened to Bogdan, she would never forgive herself. He was the one piece of her childhood she had managed to hold on to. She could not bear to lose him, too.

The absence of Bogdan reminded Lada of the absence of the other two men who mattered most to her. But soon Radu would receive her letter and join them. The other man she chose not to dwell on.

Hunyadi shouted the order again. "Why do your men not obey?" he asked.

Lada raised an eyebrow. "They do not speak Hungarian."

He shouted the same command in Turkish. As one, the men looked at him. No one moved.

Lada narrowed her eyes. "And they do not answer to Turkish."

Hunyadi frowned, tugging at his beard. "Then how do I command them?"

"You do not. I do." In Wallachian, she commanded her men to pack up. Immediately they sprang into efficient, well-practiced action. Hunyadi watched, his expression thoughtful. Lada rode with more cheer after that. She would prove herself to him yet.

Later that day, Hunyadi found Lada riding next to Stefan and Nicolae near the back of the company. Stefan veered his horse away, giving Hunyadi space.

"Your men are very disciplined," Hunyadi said, scratching his beard. He toyed with it constantly. Lada wondered if it was because as a young man he had not been allowed a beard. He had fought long and hard to move from being the son of peasant farmers to one of the strongest leaders on the borders of the Ottoman Empire. She supposed he had every right to be amused by and affectionate toward his beard.

Or perhaps beards were just itchy.

"We were well trained," Lada answered in Wallachian.

Hunyadi responded in the same language. "I always prefer fighting spahis to Janissaries. Janissaries are so much fiercer."

Nicolae smiled wryly. "That is one of the benefits of a slave force that can have neither possessions nor families. It is easy to be fearless when you have nothing to lose."

Hunyadi grunted. Pointing to Nicolae's prominent scar, he

asked, "Where did you get that?" His Wallachian accent was so bad that it hurt Lada to hear him speak.

Nicolae's smile broadened, stretching his scar tight and white. "At Varna. From a Hungarian. Right before we killed your king."

Lada's hands went to her wrists, ready to defend Nicolae. To her surprise, Hunyadi laughed. "Oh, Varna. That was a disaster." He shifted back into Hungarian. "Set me back a few years. We still have not recovered from the loss of our king. Our new one, Ladislas Posthumous, is not exactly ideal." His expression grew faraway and thoughtful. "He could be replaced."

Lada pounced on his tone before she could think better of it. "You?" Hunyadi had been a prince of Transylvania. He was beloved by his people, and a fearsome military force. If he were king—and her ally—

The path to the throne of Wallachia opened before her, bathed in golden light.

Until Hunyadi laughed, puncturing her hopes and bringing darkness crashing back down. "Me, king? No. I have tried a throne. It turns out I am not fond of sitting, no matter what the seat may be."

Lada slouched moodily in her saddle. Hunyadi would still be a strong ally. But a king was better. "Your people would be fortunate to have such a man as their king."

Hunyadi clapped a hand on her shoulder. "I am a soldier. I am not made for politics and courts. My son Matthias, on the other hand, has been raised in them. He will go far, and do greater things than I ever could." Hunyadi beamed. "He is my greatest triumph. And he is very handsome."

Lada frowned, unsure what that had to do with Matthias's merits. She had seen, though, how many doors opened for Radu because of his face. "I am sure that will be useful to him."

"He needs a strong wife. Someone who can temper his . . . extravagances. Help steer him."

"He will need a good alliance." If Matthias wanted to continue to rise within the Hungarian courts, he would have to bring some sort of power with him. Hunyadi had no family name, no history. He had land and wealth, yes, but they were new. And newness was not something to be proud of in the world of nobility.

Hunyadi patted her shoulder again. "I am less concerned with alliances. Those come and go. But strength of character— that cannot be valued enough."

Hunyadi rode away, with Lada staring at his back in confusion.

"Does he want me to find his son a wife?" she asked, turning to Stefan, who had been leaning over to Nicolae and whispering. Stefan pretended not to speak Hungarian, but he understood it.

Nicolae's face was purpling from the effort of holding something back. Finally, it escaped in a strangled, airy laugh. "Lada, my darling dragon, he wants you to *be* his son's wife."

"The devil take him," she snapped. Anger and humiliation washed through her. All this time Hunyadi had been viewing her as merely a womb. How could she make the world see her as she saw herself? "And the devil take his son, too." She rubbed her forehead wearily. No wonder he had tried to command her men. He probably already viewed them as his own, some sort of dowry. "Where exactly are we?"

Nicolae pulled closer to her. "Near Bulgaria."

Staring bleakly at the winter-dead trees around them, Lada did not know what to do. Kill Hunyadi and move on? Marry his son for a chance at the Hungarian throne? Would that bring her closer to Wallachia, or take her even further away? It was the same choice she had faced before, the only choice ever given to her: take what little power you can through a man.

If she had known this would be her fate, over and over, she would have stayed with Mehmed. At least with him she had that spark, that burning. If Matthias was as smart and handsome as his father said, he would have no use for a wife such as her. And she did not want to be a wife.

Never a wife.

She had left behind love and ridden off to a future devoid of power. "I have nothing," she whispered.

Nicolae nudged his horse even closer to hers, until their legs brushed. "You still have us," he said, his voice soft with understanding. "We will figure something out."

Lada nodded, trying not to let her despair show. How much longer could she hope to keep Nicolae? Stefan? Petru and the rest of her men? Would they choose to stay loyal to her over someone with a reputation and power like Hunyadi's? Not if they remained with him for much longer.

"We break from Hunyadi at the first opportunity." She did not know how he would react, but he had more men than she did. She would not risk their lives against him. Until the right opportunity came up, she would grit her teeth and dodge all talk of marriage.

At camp two days later, Hunyadi huddled with three of his men. Though Lada had been avoiding him, the intensity of the men's conversation hinted at something new. It might be an opportunity for her men to make an exit. Or it might mean she was in trouble.

Lada marched over and shouldered her way in. "What is happening?"

Hunyadi looked up, surprised. "There is an armed force of Bulgars coming our way. They are in a canyon. If we let them get out, they can spread and form ranks. Our best option is to ride and meet them."

"But you do not have enough time to plan."

"Attack is my favorite form of defense."

Lada let the phrase turn over in her mind. It reminded her of something. Tohin—the Ottoman woman who had taught her how to use gunpowder in combat. She had spoken of the need to constantly be on the attack so that other countries did not invade Ottoman lands. Push out so no one can push in. *A dealer of death,* that was what Tohin had said one must become. Deal enough death elsewhere to keep it away from your own home.

"What kind of force?" Lada asked.

One of Hunyadi's men let out a dismissive huff of air at Lada's inclusion in the conversation, but Hunyadi answered. "Mounted, heavily armored."

Hunyadi had some armored men who could meet such a force head-on. But Lada's men wore light mail, unsuited to direct combat. Hunyadi must have followed her thoughts. "This is not a battle for your Janissaries. I will keep them in the rear."

Lada bristled. She knew her men were worth twice

Hunyadi's. He would know that, too, were he not so focused on her as a marriage prospect. But she bit her tongue before she could argue. If Hunyadi was engaged in a canyon, and her men were in the rear, it was as good an opportunity as any to flee.

She sighed, feeling these new threads to the throne snap one by one. She was left, as always, with her only thread of power: herself.

They rode fast through flat, open farmland until they came to the threat. Canyon walls rose before them, a narrow gash through a leagues-long line of rocky, steep hills—the only easy passage for mounted troops.

Lada saw immediately why Hunyadi needed to stop the Bulgars before they exited the canyon. Once through, they had a straight shot to anywhere in Hungary they wanted.

Shouts drifted to Lada on the sharp breeze. Hunyadi was riding his horse back and forth in front of his men. A scout appeared, his horse heaving and frothing. Lada saw Hunyadi's shoulders tense as he listened to the report. He said something, then pointed at her. The scout nodded.

Raising a fist, Hunyadi roared. His men roared in response and charged after him into the canyon.

Had he told the scout to make certain she did not leave? Lada smiled grimly. She would welcome that. She rode to meet the scout. He trembled atop his trembling horse.

"What is it?" she demanded.

"Hunyadi asks that you watch. If Bulgars begin to come through, ride hard for the nearest village and get the people out." He pointed to the east, where Lada could see hearth smoke lazily marking the village's location.

"Does he expect the Bulgars to break through?"

The man shrugged wearily. "More men than we thought. Too many."

"Why did he go in, then?"

"If they get through, they will burn the village and take all the winter stores. The people will starve."

Lada frowned. "But it is one village."

The man smiled bleakly. "It is *his* village, though. He grew up there."

Lada rode her horse slowly back to her men, the information nagging at her. They could leave. No one could stop them. But Hunyadi could have left, too. Regrouped elsewhere. Let one small village fall.

"Damn his honor," Lada grumbled, staring back into the canyon. Hunyadi's forces had already disappeared around a bend. It would not be long before they met the enemy. Both would be trapped and constricted by the canyon. It would be a slaughter on both sides.

It was not her problem.

But her eyes went to the rim of the canyon. It would be impassable for heavily armored mounted soldiers. But that did not mean it was impassable for everyone.

She needed an ally. She needed more threads of power. And if she could prove to Hunyadi what she was capable of, then maybe she would have them. She could run—again—or seize this chance.

Lada jumped off her horse and grabbed her weapons. "Dismount! Take everything you can easily carry. Nicolae, take men up the other side in case this one is impassable."

"What are we doing?" Petru asked, already following her lead.

"We are going to take a look."

They ran up the hill, scrambling between trees and boulders. Everyone found a different path and fanned out. Lada led the way, running and sliding and climbing. It was not easy going, but they made good time. The sound of men and horses screaming drew them closer to their goal.

Finally, scraped and sweating, they reached the rim of the canyon immediately above the fighting. Both sides had bottlenecked, leaving only a few men in front to fight. When those men died, the next went at it. Lada looked down the Bulgar line. It stretched too far. They could push harder and longer.

Hunyadi was not far beyond the front line. Everyone there would die. He had to know that—had to have known it going in.

But he had left Lada's men behind. If she had been in charge, she would have sacrificed someone else's men to wear down the other side. Instead, he had kept them out of the battle with a charge to protect the village if his efforts failed.

Hunyadi had killed her father and brother. Before that, he had been the reason her father ransomed her to the Ottomans. And he had invited her to join his troops with only a marriage in mind. She had every reason to let him die, even if she was grateful he had protected her men. But Wallachia called to her, and she had to answer. How could she win this for him?

"They will all be killed," Petru said, frowning.

Lada and her men were too high up for accuracy with arrows and bolts. And the Bulgars wore heavy armor. They would waste all their ammunition with very little effect.

But . . .

"Have you ever heard the story of David and Goliath?" Lada remembered that one. She only really cared for the old stories, the ones about battles and lions and armies. She had no use for Jesus with his parables and healing. She liked the wrathful god, the god of vengeance and war. She picked up a large stone, tossing it in the air a few times.

Lada looked across the canyon at Nicolae. She hefted the rock, then pointed at the rear of the Bulgar line. There was an area of the hill that spoke of years of rockslides—no trees, dirt recently churned up—and at the canyon's rim a collection of boulders waited patiently for time and the elements to free them.

Lada mimed pushing, then let the rock fall from her hands. Nicolae looked at the boulders. He waved an arm, then ran with Stefan and several men toward the boulders.

Lada waited, Petru crouching next to her. The sound of the battle beneath them was terrible. She had never seen one this big, this close. She watched, fascinated. It was not what she had expected. Her only experience with hand-to-hand combat had been with assassins or in practice. She saw how Hunyadi directed his men, how even from the ground he acted as though he had an aerial view.

She also saw how, in spite of his intelligence, he would lose. He had chosen honor instead of practicality. He should have sacrificed her men to slow the Bulgars, then regrouped elsewhere, ignoring the threat to his village.

But he had not counted on her.

A clatter that shifted to a rumble snapped Lada's attention back to Nicolae's work. The boulders crashed down, accompanied by a huge plume of dust. The fallen boulders were not enough to fully block the canyon, but they were enough to make it impossible to get more than one man at a time back the way they had come.

Hunyadi looked up. Catching sight of Lada, he shouted something, gesturing angrily toward the rocks. Lada laughed, knowing what it looked like. They had just guaranteed that the Bulgars could only go forward, into Hunyadi.

Lada picked up a rock, so heavy she had to use both arms. Then, with a loud whoop, she threw it.

The rock sailed downward, landing with a metallic *thunk* on the helmeted head of a soldier in the middle of the Bulgar ranks. He slumped in his saddle, then slid to the ground.

On either side of the canyon, Lada's men set to work. There was no shortage of rocks. The Bulgars were packed in so tightly that there was no need to aim. Throw a rock, hit something. It was as simple as that.

The Bulgars started to panic, trying to shift out of the way, but there was nowhere to go. Their horses screamed. Soldiers dismounted and tried to climb up the sides of the canyon. They were met with rocks. A few kept their wits and pulled out crossbows, but the distance was too great and Lada's men had too much cover.

The Bulgars in front made a desperate push, but Hunyadi had grasped that his role was to block them. He set up a firm line impervious to the chaotic attacks of the Bulgars, and then waited.

By evening, Lada's arms screamed with weariness as she tossed a last rock down. Then, exhausted, she sat. Nicolae and her men on the other side of the canyon followed suit. There were so few Bulgars left, it would be easy for Hunyadi's men to pick them off with crossbow bolts. It looked as though a careless god had passed through, tossing bodies aside like refuse. Men and horses clogged the path, broken and tangled together.

When Lada and her men stumbled down from the hills, they were greeted with roaring fires and waiting food. Hunyadi's men cheered, welcoming them with open arms. Hunyadi pushed through to Lada. He picked her up and spun her in a circle. "That was brilliant!" he shouted, laughing.

She waited until he put her down. Then she met his gaze with an unsmiling and unflinching one of her own. "Yes," she said. "It was. You are no king, and I am no wife. I am a leader and a ruler, and I want your support."

Hunyadi nodded solemnly, his fingers once again disappearing into his beard. "You have much value outside of marriage." He did not say it jokingly or dismissively. Lada could see in his eyes that he considered her differently now.

She stood a little straighter. She had done something good. She had secured an ally through her own merits. And she would use him however she could to destroy her enemies.

9

March

IT WAS A FESTIVE day in the port city of Bursa.
Ribbons adorned everything, whipping gaily in the perpetual wind that blew from the Sea of Marmara and through the streets. Children laughed, darting through the press of people. Vendors called out their goods—mostly food, and most of that fish—over the noise of the crowds.

Radu let the crowd pull them along. Nazira pointed out a young girl carrying a screaming toddler nearly as big as herself. The toddler managed to wriggle out of her arms. The little girl grabbed his wrist and dragged him on determinedly.

"Does that make you miss your sister?" Nazira asked.

Radu shook his head. "Lada would never have been so tender."

"I wish I had gotten to know her better."

"No, you do not."

Nazira stopped, looking into Radu's eyes. "Yes, I do. Because she is important to you, and you are important to me, so she is important to me."

Radu shifted away from acknowledging Lada's importance

to him. He tried not to think about it, or whether he was actually important to her. He had made his choice. Again. "You would not like her. And she would not like you."

Nazira sniffed, lifting her nose haughtily. "*Everyone* likes me. Just because you could not make your terror of a sister be civil does not mean I would have fared so poorly. I am the sweetest person alive. Or have you not heard?"

Radu laughed, taking her hand and rushing through a brief opening in the square. "I have heard, and received ample evidence to support the rumor."

After a few stops for Nazira to purchase ribbons for waving, they reached the docks. It took some time to find a spot to stand, but people tended to make way once they noticed Radu and Nazira's fine clothing. Radu still dressed the part of a frivolous member of the court, with bright robes and as much jewelry as he owned. Nazira wore her status with the easy grace of one born to it.

The day was brilliantly sunny, the warmth cut through by the wind. Light reflected off the churning water, and small waves slapped at the dock they stood on.

Out on the water were Radu's ships. Well, the empire's ships. But Radu felt a flush of pride looking at them. He had visited the construction docks under the pretense of going to his country estate with Nazira. Suleiman was ambitious but practical. Under his hand, everything went according to schedule. And now, before them, were the fruits of their labors.

It was a glorious sight to behold.

Nazira pointed out the different types. "Three of the big ones! What are they called?"

"Galleys. The largest ships the empire has ever owned, all brand-new."

"And those five medium ones?"

"Also galleys. Three are older, two are new."

Nazira sniffed in disappointment. "They should really be cleverer with naming than that. Big galleys and medium galleys. What about the smaller ones moving between them?"

Radu laughed. "You are going to be disappointed."

"Galleys?"

"Yes."

She scowled crossly. "I should have been consulted. Still, it is amazing! Look at them all! How can the water hold that much weight? Oh! They are moving."

Sails unfurled. Though the ships were too far out for Radu to see their decks, he knew the sailors would be scrambling to tie things off and adjust the sails to capture the wind. There would be even more men on benches manning the long, heavy oars for navigating rivers.

The boats danced on the water, cutting through the waves or skimming on top of them, depending on their size. Every time a boat maneuvered particularly well, the crowd cheered. After a few minutes, all the galleys lined up near the shore and stopped there, close enough for the onlookers to see the flurry of on-deck activity. And then the cannons fired across the water, away from the bank.

Though the ships could not bear the load of too much heavy artillery, the sound was terrible and impressive. Babies and children cried in fear and surprise. Everyone else clapped and waved their ribbons in the air. Never before had the Ottomans had such a navy. Never before had any of them seen such a demonstration.

Radu smiled, because he knew the truth: this was only half of their fleet. The other half was hidden in a boatyard on a little-used section of one of the tributary rivers.

"There he is." Nazira's quiet voice broke through the noise. Radu turned to see Mehmed, standing on a balcony. He wore deepest purple, with a red turban and a blindingly white cape. Nazira and Radu were not the only ones to notice him. Much of the crowd turned to cheer and wave their ribbons at him. Radu was too far away to be sure, but he thought Mehmed smiled.

Radu pretended that the smile was for him, and joined the cheering.

———— ·❦· ————

"We should take more holidays together," Nazira said, leaning back in their carriage. "Fatima does not like to go to new places. It was all I could do to persuade her to stay in Edirne for this long. She loves familiar things, routine." Nazira smiled fondly. "She has settled in nicely there, though. As long as she does not have to go out among crowds."

"I did not know she had such a hard time with them." Radu watched the countryside pass by. He tried to hold on to the happy pride of seeing his work dance on the water. But the same scene kept playing out in his mind. Instead of being on the dock with Nazira, he had been on the balcony, at Mehmed's side. As Mehmed watched the triumph of Radu's planning, he shifted closer and closer. And then their hands, at their sides, brushed.

Instead of pulling away, Mehmed's fingers linked with Radu's, and they stood like that, watching the ships, together.

"Yes," Nazira said, puncturing Radu's fantasy. Which was just as well. It was poisonous, dwelling on such things. "Fatima does not— You see, when she was very young, she—" She paused, frowning. "I do not think it is my story to tell."

"I understand." He took Nazira's hand, which felt nothing like Mehmed's had in his imagination. "I wonder if anyone gets through childhood without being broken. I certainly did not."

"Oh, I had a wonderful childhood! Our parents died when I was too young to understand it. Kumal made certain that my life was filled with love and joy. And then, when I discovered Fatima shared my feelings, I had even more love and joy. And then, when you married me, even more. I sometimes think I am the most blessed woman in all of creation. I pray God gives me an opportunity to repay all the kindness He has shown me."

They had entered the city. The buildings rose around them like guests at a party—familiar, all of them, but hiding so much.

Radu squeezed Nazira's hand. "You have nothing to repay. Your life is filled with the goodness you attract because of your own goodness."

Nazira laughed, then grew solemn. "I do wish to do more, though. *Be* more. Maybe, someday . . ." She looked down, blushing, holding her stomach.

"Are you feeling ill? We have been in the carriage too long." They had left Bursa earlier than anticipated. They were back in the city a full day before planned. He was heading straight for the foundry to check in on Urbana.

She looked up, blinking rapidly. "Ill? No. No, I am well. Radu, I wondered . . ." She paused, sucking in her round lips. "Would you join us for a meal, a special family meal, next week?"

The carriage stopped in front of the narrow street leading to the foundry. Radu gave Nazira a quick kiss on the cheek. "Of course. Give my love to Fatima."

"And give mine to Urbana?"

Radu laughed. "Urbana would not care in the slightest for your love, unless it came with extra supplies of bronze, or a new furnace."

Though Radu did not like the intense heat of the foundry, he visited as often as he could. And it was a good thing he had come back when he did. Urbana was screaming in Hungarian at several confused workers. Radu jumped in as translator, though he left out most of what she said. He did not think telling the workers that they were "more useless than the rotting carcasses of a thousand dead dogs" would help morale.

Later that afternoon, he leaned against the entrance and watched a small caravan approach. Urbana had told him they were expecting a delivery, but Radu did not anticipate the grizzled woman who showed up with the gunpowder.

She climbed down from her cart, her back arched like a crescent moon. Radu moved to help her, but she waved him away. "I can manage, you young fool."

A bit stung by her dismissiveness—older women usually loved him—he directed two men to begin unloading the bar-

rels of gunpowder. The woman watched warily. Another cart
pulled up behind hers. A man jumped out to aid the unloading process.

"How many, Mother?" he called.

"All of it." She shook her head. "That ass cannot keep a
number greater than three in his head."

Radu frowned at her lack of maternal softness. She turned
her critical eye on him, taking in his robes. He had taken to
wearing jewel tones lately, bright and bold colors to combat
how he felt on the inside.

"Who put you in charge of so much gunpowder?" she
asked.

Radu tried on his best smile, but it slid off his face. It would
make no difference with this woman. "We are building the
largest cannon in the world. It could take down the walls of
Babylon itself."

The woman snorted. "Nothing quite so useful as an imaginary cannon to defeat a city that no longer exists. I can see all
my work and travel has been useless. One of these days I will be
asked to do another stupid thing, and I will finally hit my limit
on idiocy. I have a husband and three sons, so my limit is very
high, but even I cannot bear all things. And on that day, there
will be an explosion to take down the walls of every *actual* city
in the world."

Radu shifted on his feet, wishing the men would hurry up
so this horrible woman would leave.

"You are not Turkish," she said.

Radu shook his head. "Wallachian."

She nodded, toying with several long white hairs on her

chin. "Not a lot of Wallachians in the empire. Too stupid to be useful. But I met a good Wallachian a few years ago. Made an impression on me. I never forgot her."

With a shock like a cannon burst, Radu tuned in to the woman's words. "'Her'?"

"Mean little bitch." The woman smiled with tenderness, an emotion that looked out of place on her. "Clever as anyone. It was out in— Where was it? I forget."

"Amasya," Radu said softly.

"That was it. You know her?"

"Lada. My sister."

Her gaze grew even more critical as she looked him up and down. "You do not seem like siblings."

Radu smiled tightly. "I am aware of that."

"Well. I always wondered what she might do, a bright, vicious mind like that. And those men followed her without question. She made me feel younger."

A sprig of affection rose in Radu's chest. It was strange, talking to someone who had known Lada and admired her. Not in the way Mehmed admired her. That did not ever make Radu happy. But this gnarled old woman's memories made Radu miss his sister.

"Where is she now?" the woman asked.

"In Hungary, I believe."

"What is she doing there?"

"That is anyone's guess."

"Well, whatever it is, it will not end well for anyone who gets in her way. The world will destroy her in the end. Too much spark leads to explosions." She patted a barrel of gunpowder that had not yet been unloaded. "But your sister will destroy as much as she can before she goes out."

The old woman's eerie prophecy rubbed at Radu like an ill-fitting collar. "Perhaps she will find a balance."

"No. She will go down in flames and blood." The woman smiled fondly. "If you write her, tell her Tohin sends her regards." Then, her eye catching something else, she shouted at her son, "Timur! Did you check the way they are storing them?"

"Yes, Mother," Timur said.

Tohin stomped toward the storage building. Timur shook his head, giving Radu a long-suffering smile. "I have three children of my own, and she would still dress me if she could. You know how mothers are."

Radu's return smile was reflexive. He did not, in fact, know how mothers were. But he knew what it was to have someone watching out for him. He stared at the remaining barrels, wondering. Lada was already playing with fire, taking up with Hunyadi. She might respect the man, but he had never shown kindness to their family. Who knew what purpose he had in taking her in?

Radu had been flattered and angry when she demanded he come help her. But perhaps he should have been afraid. For Lada to ask for help, surely she was teetering on the edge of the destructive end the old woman saw for her. And though she had never asked for Radu's help growing up, he had helped her. He had worn away her edges, talked their way out of trouble she would have welcomed. Maybe . . . maybe she had always needed him. And he always chose Mehmed.

Someone shouted his name, and he hurried back to his duties.

His duties to his God. His duties to the Ottoman Empire. His duties to Mehmed. Lada would have to figure it out on her own. He owed her nothing.

But the promise of the guilt he would carry if she died without his help clung to his skin like a shadow.

10

February

Lada tracked a group of fifty Janissaries. They were a long-range frontier group, used for enforcing the empire's will in vassal states. Hunyadi had no particular reason to attack the Janissaries, but he demanded no reason to kill Turkish forces.

Up until now they had only fought more Bulgars, brief flashes of blood and screaming and swords breaking up monotonous riding, camping, sleeping outside.

Lada was proud of her men. They were as good as or better than any that Hunyadi rode with. And he noticed. After their canyon victory, Hunyadi frequently consulted with Lada and asked her advice.

She had studied his tactics, but only on paper and in theory. Watching him in the field was something else entirely. He always thought three days ahead—food, water, defensible locations. But he was not so set on plans that he could not respond with lightning-fast force to an unexpected threat or opportunity.

This Janissary group was one such opportunity. Lada looked uneasily at Nicolae next to her.

"What do you think?" she asked.

"I think they could have been me."

She looked back at the men they stalked. He was right. They were the same—boys stolen and turned into soldiers who served another land and another god.

"We let them go, then," Lada said. She could not help imagining Nicolae on the other side of the meadow. Or Bogdan. Or Stefan, or Petru, or any of her men. She did not want to feel this companionship with the Janissaries, but it could not be avoided.

The Janissaries came to a sudden stop. Lada tensed, fearing they had discovered her ten men tracking them. Instead, they shifted direction and started heading straight for Hunyadi's camp.

Lada gestured sharply. Her men ran, silent and low to the ground. She pantomimed drawing crossbows. Still running, they fixed their bolts. If the Janissaries did not already know the camp was there, they would in a few minutes. Hunyadi would be caught unaware. Lada gestured to her men to head back to the camp.

"Go warn them," Lada whispered to Nicolae.

"What are you going to do?"

"Delay them, idiot. Now go!"

Nicolae disappeared into the woods. Lada stood. "The sultan is the son of a donkey!" she shouted in Turkish.

The Janissaries turned as one, arrows already nocked to bows and pointed in her direction. She had cover, but it would not take them long to find her. She darted to another tree. "I am sorry. I should not have said that about the sultan. It is an offense to donkeys, which are perfectly serviceable creatures."

Lada peeked around the tree. Their weapons still at the ready, the Janissaries were searching the dense foliage for threats. Lada laughed loudly, the sound ringing through the trees. "Are you Janissaries? I have heard that Janissaries are not fit to lick the dust from spahi boots."

"Who is there?" an angry voice shouted, while another cursed her. Their leader barked an order for them to be quiet. Then he called out, "Show yourself, woman!"

"Why do Bulgars make terrible farmers?" she answered.

There was silence. She peered from behind the trunk, amused to see the Janissaries trading confused looks. Most of them had lowered their bows when no attack came.

"What?" the commander shouted.

"I said, why do Bulgars make terrible farmers?"

One of the Janissaries in front sheathed his sword. "I do not know."

The commander barked at him for silence, but the Janissary shrugged. "I want to know."

"So do I," another called. Most of them nodded, a few grinning at this odd forest interlude.

"Because they confuse the pigs for Bulgar women, and cannot bear to slaughter their wives."

A chorus of snickering laughs broke out.

"Who are you?" one of the men called. "You should not be in these woods. It is not safe."

A volley of arrows rained from the sky onto the men.

"I know," Lada said, coming from behind the tree and letting her shaft join the others.

After, when the work of killing was done, Lada took no pleasure in the white-capped bodies on the ground. Stepping over the corpses, Hunyadi found her and clasped her hand in his. "How did you think to distract them like that?"

She lifted a shoulder as they walked back toward camp. "They are soldiers. They depend upon routine, and anything out of the ordinary will give them pause. And they are men. They hate to be insulted, but they love to hear others mocked. And they are fools, because they cannot imagine that a woman alone in the woods would be a threat."

Later, around a campfire, Lada sat next to Hunyadi. Nicolae was on her other side. The men traded stories like coins, each trying to make his the most valuable, the brightest. Petru mimed being struck through the eye with an arrow so dramatically he nearly fell into the fire.

Lada remembered a time not so long ago when some of these same men had come back from fighting and she had been forced to listen to stories she feared she would never be part of. Now she was at the center, truly belonging.

"How did you find your men?" Hunyadi asked. He spoke Turkish around her men as a courtesy, since most of them did not speak Hungarian and his Wallachian was dreadful.

"*We* found *her*," Nicolae said, beaming proudly. "Or I did, at least. It is a funny story. When Lada was this small . . ." He held his hand close to the ground, then squinted at her. "Well, she is still that small."

Lada punched him in the shoulder. Hard.

He rubbed it, grimacing. "When Lada was not the towering giantess of a woman that she is today, she was in Amasya as the playmate of the little zealot. Back then no one knew he would be sultan. He was just a brat."

Lada nodded, then quickly erased the wistful smile threatening to break through her expression.

"She was spying on us while we trained. We caught her. Then when she beat up poor Ivan—" Nicolae paused. "Whatever happened to Ivan?"

"I killed him," Lada said without thinking.

"You—you *killed* him? I thought he was moved to a different city! Why did you kill him?"

Lada realized the low, steady hum of conversation around them had died. All eyes were on her. Most of her men had never known Ivan. She wished she had not, either. He had been stupid and cruel, had always hated her. In the end, he had tried to force himself on her as proof she was nothing but a girl. Something he could take. Something he could break.

She lifted her chin. "That is none of your concern."

Hunyadi laughed. "Spoken like a true leader," he said in Hungarian.

She met his gaze and he gave her a slight nod, something fierce and proud in his eyes. She saw how he sat straight, even while relaxing with his men. He was still in charge, still slightly apart. She mimicked his posture. She was their leader. She did not owe them explanations. Especially not for traumas of the past.

"Wait," Petru said, concern pulling down his features and making him look like a puppy. "Did you kill Bogdan, too? Is that why he is gone?"

Lada sighed in exasperation. "No, I did not kill Bogdan.

But I might kill you if you act out that stupid arrow-through-the-eye death one more time."

* — *

Bogdan found them.

How he tracked them down Lada did not know. But the next week he walked into camp with a grin so giddy she could not understand how his blocky features managed it. Lada ran to him.

Her first impulse was to throw her arms around him. Her second was to hit him for taking so long. Instead, she stood in front of him, glaring at his beloved stupid face and his beloved stupid ears and his beloved stupid self. "Where have you been?"

"I brought something you need."

"More men?" She looked behind Bogdan, but only one person followed him. And that person was not a man. She walked with solid assurance. Her long hair trailed down her back in a braid, showing off two ears sticking out like jug handles.

"Lada!" her old nurse said, rushing forward and embracing her. Lada's arms were pinned to her sides by the woman's hug. How Bogdan had found his mother, Lada could not begin to fathom. But he was Bogdan. He stayed loyal to the women in his life.

Lada looked at him. "*Why* did you bring her?"

"To help," he said, shrugging. "You needed someone who could help you with . . . girl things." He paused, blushing. "Woman things."

Lada clenched her jaw, grinding her teeth together. "I do not need anyone's help with anything."

"Where is your brother?" the nurse asked. "He should be here. I thought you would take better care of him."

Anger flared. Who was this woman to tell Lada how to take care of Radu? The nurse had not been there in Edirne. She had not seen what they had gone through, what Lada had had to do to survive. "He is coming," Lada said through still-gritted teeth. She extricated herself from her nurse's arms.

"Let me brush your hair," the nurse said, reaching for Lada's snarls.

The sensation made Lada feel like a child again. She stumbled back, flinging her hands up to deflect the woman's touch. "I do not need a nurse!"

"You said the same when you were five. But at least your hair was presentable then."

"Take yourself to the devil," Lada snapped.

Bogdan looked hurt, but her nurse just laughed. The woman's eyes shone with something. Mirth or affection, neither of which were tolerable to Lada. Worst of all, Hunyadi was sitting nearby, watching the whole encounter.

"Where is my cloak?" she snapped, yanking clothes out of her saddlebag.

"Let your nurse help you find it," Nicolae teased. He and Petru were sitting at the campfire. Had no one missed this spectacle? What had Bogdan been thinking?

"She is not my nurse!"

Petru shrugged. "You are lucky. I wish I had someone to take care of me. Maybe I should find a wife."

"Maybe you could marry the nurse," Lada spat out.

Giving up on the cloak, she threw herself onto her horse and left camp. They had moved from the location of the slaughtered Janissaries and were working their way toward the capital. The increasingly frequent sections of frosted farmland made Hunyadi's hands twitch. When asked where they were going, he would merely shrug. "The castle." It sounded like a foreign word when he said it.

Today, though, they were in a heavily forested section of the countryside. They had not seen another soul all day, but that did not mean they were alone. Lada scanned the trees as a matter of habit, one hand always on her sword.

The trees were as bare and cold as the air. The sun was overhead, but all it did was blind her. How could something be so bright and give so little warmth? After so long in the temperate climate of Amasya, she had forgotten what winter felt like.

Right now, she wanted nothing more than to be back there. *No!* she screamed at her traitorous heart. She did not mean back in the empire. She meant back at camp. Around a fire, with her men.

The nurse would be there, lingering, hovering, much like a fly that buzzed incessantly, but at least a fly Lada could swat. She did not need another woman. She did not need to be taken care of. That woman was not her mother. Her own mother had fled to her home country of Moldavia when Lada was four. That was what mothers did. Nurses, apparently, were more dependable. And embarrassing.

Hunyadi pulled his horse alongside hers. "It might be good to have someone to help."

"I do not see your nursemaid following you around, combing your hair."

Hunyadi ran his fingers through his thick auburn locks. "I

would not object!" His tone softened. "All leaders need help. Let someone do the mundane tasks so you can focus on the bigger ones. Surely Mehmed does not do anything himself."

Lada rolled her eyes. "He has a man whose only role is to follow after him carrying a stool."

"Does he even clean his own ass, I wonder?"

Lada grimaced. "Why would you put such an image in my mind?"

Hunyadi laughed loudly. Then he settled more deeply into his saddle, sighing happily. "This is a beautiful part of my country."

"It reminds me of the forests outside Tirgoviste. I used to make our tutor take us out there to study. The castle was an oven in the summer and an icebox in the winter. I always suspected the architect was a cook."

"Do you miss it?"

Lada frowned as she followed the trail of a dark bird across the pale blue sky. "Miss what?"

"Tirgoviste."

"I never cared for Tirgoviste. I prefer the mountains."

"But you still want the throne."

"I want Wallachia."

Hunyadi huffed a laugh. "Is that all?"

"It is far less than what Mehmed—" She stopped, biting off the rest of the sentence. How dare he slip out of her mouth uninvited.

Hunyadi leaned closer to Lada, his horse following the movement and nearly brushing its flanks against her legs. "So he does mean to go for Constantinople, then."

Lada had avoided talking about Mehmed's plans. It felt

disloyal, which made her angry. He had shown no loyalty to her by entertaining the usurper Danesti prince.

Hunyadi pressed on. "The general opinion is that he is young and easily swayed. More interested in lavish parties and well-stocked harems than expansion."

If Lada flinched at the mention of the harem, Hunyadi pretended not to notice. He continued. "Everyone has solidified advantageous treaties with him. No one fears him. Murad's death was seen as the end of Ottoman expansion. But I wonder. I think the sultan is settling us all down so his way to Constantinople is clear."

The word *harem* still rang in Lada's ears. Obviously Mehmed was not loyal to her. He spied on her. He supported her rivals. She owed him nothing, and would cut this traitorous impulse to protect him out of her heart. "Constantinople is his only desire. Everything he does, however innocent seeming or counterintuitive, is to achieve that goal and that goal only. He will not stop until it is his capital, until he is both sultan of the Ottoman Empire and Caesar of Rome."

Hunyadi breathed out heavily, slumping in his saddle. "Do you think he can do it?"

"If any man can, he will."

"I feared as much." He rubbed his face, tugging on the ends of his graying mustache. "When do you think he will move?"

"As soon as possible. This spring or next."

"That changes everything. We will head to Hunedoara tonight. I have letters to write and a crusade to plan."

"You would defend Constantinople?"

"Of course."

"But it is not your city, not your people. And it is no closer to Hungary's borders than the Ottomans already are, so there is no increased military threat."

Hunyadi smiled. "I am Christian, Lada. It is my duty to rally to Constantinople's cause. It is the last we have of the mighty Roman empire. I will be damned if I let the Turks take it." He pulled his horse to a stop, then paused before turning. "I would be honored if you were at my side. I think together we could hold off the very forces of hell."

Lada was glad he was not facing her. The warm flush of pride at his words was something she wanted to keep private.

11

Late March

"WHEN WILL IT BE ready?" Radu demanded, the air shimmering with heat.

"When it is ready!" Urbana wiped sweat from her forehead as she used giant bellows to adjust the temperature of the flames in the nearest furnace.

"I need it now!"

She laughed, a sound like a hammer ringing against an anvil. "You need it now? I have needed it my whole life! The Basilica is *my* legacy, my genius. I will not risk blowing us all up with a faulty cannon so your schedule can be maintained!"

Radu wiped the sweat that was dripping into his eyes. "Can you at least show me? We have both invested so much in it."

Huffing, Urbana led him to the back of the sweltering building. She pointed to a pit of sand that stretched more than four times longer than Radu was tall. "There it is."

"When will it be cool enough?"

"Two days." Urbana leaned against the wall, staring at the sand as though she could succeed by sheer force of will. "If there are no cracks or fissures—if, God willing, it actually worked this time—we can demonstrate it for your precious sultan in two days." She patted a six-hundred-pound stone cannonball with the tender affection of a mother.

"It will work," Radu said. It had to. It would prove, once and for all, that he was the better Dracul sibling. The more valuable. The more deserving of love. And it would prove to himself that he had made the right choice in staying.

———◆———

The ambassadors from Constantinople arrived the next day. Radu no longer stood next to Mehmed in the receiving hall, but near the back and off to the side.

Normally, Radu would have liked to see the ambassadors squirming. Mehmed was still acting the silly, spoiled sultan. But it was all so tiresome. He was ready for this interminable waiting period to be over. Constantinople needed to fall. When they marched, then everything would be better. Everything would be revealed. Radu would reclaim his place next to Mehmed. They would take the walls together.

And Lada would be nowhere near, either physically or in Mehmed's thoughts. When Constantinople fell, Mehmed would have what he wanted most. He would forget the girl who had left them behind. He would know who had been with him, helping him every step of the way.

He would finally see Radu's whole worth.

Radu refocused on what was being said. Though the ambassadors kept trying to steer the conversation back to the fortress Mehmed had built on their side of the strait, Mehmed could not be trapped.

"We should have a feast! A party." He smiled distractedly,

leaning over to whisper to a man taking notes, "Fish. No, lamb. No, fish. Both!"

The lead ambassador cleared his throat. "But we must discuss the matter of the land. You killed citizens from a nearby village."

Mehmed waved dismissively. "Our men defended themselves against attack. It is nothing. Tell me, do you like dancing? What style of dance do they favor in Constantinople now?"

The lead ambassador, who wore a blue coat that was open to reveal a bright red vest, shifted from foot to foot. "At the very least, we must demand payment for the land you took." The other five ambassadors remained perfectly still.

Mehmed's smile chilled even Radu. "Yes. Payment. We would say a great deal is owed Constantinople. Very soon every debt will be erased."

A silence as thick as blood had descended on the room.

Mehmed laughed, suddenly the bright, happy young sultan again. He clapped his hands. "A party! Tonight. You can show us how they dance in Constantinople. We will make you all dance."

Mehmed leaned toward Kumal, engaging him in conversation and effectively ignoring the ambassadors. They stayed where they were, shuffling their feet or clearing their throats. Mehmed had not dismissed them, so they could not leave. Radu could not see their faces from where he stood, but he did not imagine they looked happy.

Then one, the nearest to him, turned. It was the ambassador with the gray eyes who had delivered a gift—a book—to Mehmed upon his coronation. Radu was surprised at how easily he recognized the young man after more than a year. And it appeared the ambassador recognized him as well. His eyebrows lifted in shock, and then he smiled grimly, shrugging his shoulders toward the throne.

Radu answered with a similar smile.

To Radu's surprise, the ambassador took it as an invitation. He left his companions and made his way to Radu's side.

"You stood next to the sultan before," the ambassador said without preamble.

"Things change."

"They do. I am Cyprian."

"Radu."

Cyprian clasped Radu's hand, holding on for a few seconds more than seemed necessary. Radu was always deeply aware of touching, nervous to do anything out of the ordinary. As though someone might figure out he was not normal by the way he lingered in a hug, or drew too close while standing. Cyprian did not seem to have this same worry. He leaned in close, his unusual eyes piercing Radu. They were the color of the sea on a stormy day, and had a similar effect on Radu as that of stepping onto a boat. The floor swam beneath him for a moment, until Cyprian looked away.

"Tell me, is there somewhere we could get a meal outside the palace?" the ambassador asked. "It is far colder here than I remembered."

It was, in fact, quite warm in the room in spite of the season. But Radu did not think Cyprian referred to the temperature.

"I am sorry." Radu found to his surprise that he actually was. "We have a party to prepare for."

"I will find you there, then." Bowing his head, Cyprian smiled, his eyes crinkling until they nearly disappeared. Radu thought Mehmed's smile the best in the world, but he could not deny that something about Cyprian's transformed his whole face in a way that made Radu feel some hope for the first time in days.

As Radu was changing for the party, a knock came at his door.

Opening it, he was shocked to find Mehmed standing there. Exactly as he had hoped and dreamed. "Mehm— My sultan?" Radu bowed low.

"Stay here," Mehmed said to the Janissary guards who always accompanied him. He brushed past Radu and waited for him to close the door.

Radu's heart raced, so loudly that he again wondered if Mehmed could hear it. "What is it?"

Mehmed paced the small length of Radu's receiving room. His hands were clasped behind his back, his brows drawn tight. "I have an idea."

"Oh?" Radu watched him. His presence filled the room. Mehmed did not talk further. Radu needed him to talk, needed to keep him here. "I have good news! Urbana said we can test the Basilica tomorrow. I wonder if we should make a demonstration of it. We could even invite the ambassadors. Let them run back with tales of your astonishing artillery."

Mehmed's gaze was on the floor, and though he nodded, he did not seem to have really heard Radu. "I sent forces into the Peloponnese today. They will keep the emperor's brothers from going to his aid in Constantinople. As soon as our troops set up a line there, we have effectively declared war. But I think I will do it sooner."

Radu wished there was enough room to pace by Mehmed's side. He would burst if he had to remain by the door. "The cannon demonstration would be the perfect moment!" He could see it playing out. Everyone lining up, watching. The shock and awe of the court. The fear of the ambassadors. Mehmed looking at him with secret, joyful pride. And it was all Radu's doing. Without him, no one would have helped Urbana. The cannon was his project alone. Radu's triumph would be used to declare war, and they could finally end this pretense at distance.

Mehmed stopped. He narrowed his eyes at Radu, expression unreadable. "I saw that ambassador seeking you out."

"I— What?"

"The young one. He sought you out the first moment he could. Why?"

Radu scrambled to adjust the trajectory of his thoughts. "I do not know, actually. He wanted to take a meal together."

"Was that all he said?"

"He remarked on the difference in my post from last time, when I stood at your side."

Mehmed smiled. It had none of the warmth of Cyprian's smile. "That was what I had hoped. Radu, I need you to do something. Something I can trust no one else to do. Something only you can do for me. For the empire. For the cause of our God."

Radu's heart beat even faster. Something only *he* could do for Mehmed. "Yes. Anything. You know I would do anything."

"At the party, seek out the ambassador. Tell him you want to leave me. Tell him you want to aid Constantine with your knowledge of my plans. Tell him you wish to be a traitor."

Radu could not process what was being asked. "But ... then I will be *in* the city. How will I get back in time to join you?"

"You will be more valuable to me behind the walls than any man on my side of them."

Radu could not pick which path of thought to follow. Happiness that he would be the most valuable man in the world to Mehmed? Fear of what he was being asked to do? Or disappointment that after all his planning and work, he would not stand with Mehmed at the wall?

"How will I convince them? And if I do, what do you want me to tell Constantine?"

"Tell him anything you wish. In fact, tell him the truth. Tell him I am better prepared than anyone who has led forces against the wall. Tell him of my navy, my cannons, my legions of men. Tell him Constantinople will fall. Or, tell him that he has hope still. Either way, give him verifiable information and tell him you wish to fight at his side against the people who kidnapped you and stole your childhood."

"But I do not think that!"

Mehmed put his hands on Radu's shoulders, steadying him, forcing Radu to meet his eyes. "I know. But he does not. You will be my eyes and hands behind the wall."

"I wanted to be with you." Radu heard the longing in his own voice, but could not hide it. The idea of another separation— for a length of time no one could predict—was as cruel as a knife in his chest.

"I need you elsewhere. Do you think you can do it?"

Radu nodded, his head bobbing almost of its own volition.

"The ambassador will trust you. He seemed to . . . like you."

Radu came back to himself sharply. He searched Mehmed's face for a hint that there was something behind his words. Mehmed leaned closer, so close Radu could feel the other man's breath on his own lips. "Do not forget where your loyalties lie. Promise me."

It would be only a matter of leaning in to kiss. Radu managed to whisper, "I could never forget."

"Good." Mehmed pressed his lips against Radu's forehead. Radu closed his eyes and resisted tipping his face up. Mehmed's lips were so close to his own. Would it be so bad? Would Mehmed resist, be surprised? Or would he answer with his own lips in a way Radu never dared allow himself to imagine?

And then Mehmed pulled back. "I know you will accomplish this. Visit the cathedral of the Hagia Sophia for me. I will see you inside the walls of Constantinople."

"Inside the walls," Radu echoed hollowly as Mehmed released him and left as quickly as he had come.

12

Late February

IF LADA HAD TO endure this torture, the least her tormen-
tor could do was pretend not to be so happy about it. Her
nurse hummed and sang tunelessly as she finally got her way
with Lada's hair.

"I could kill Bogdan for finding you again," Lada said.

"It was not easy. My boy is cleverer than he looks." Her
nurse paused. "But not by much."

Lada snickered. Then she cursed as her head was yanked
sideways, hair caught on the comb. "If he wanted his mother,
that is fine. But I do not understand why you are still pretending to be my nurse."

"You silly child, Bogdan did not bring me for himself. He
had barely greeted me before telling me that you needed someone to take care of you while you 'saved Wallachia.' Which he
absolutely believes you will do. Ever since you could talk, he has
belonged to you. He would do anything for you then, and he
will do anything for you now."

Lada did not have a response to that. She had taken Bogdan's loyalty for granted as a child. When they found each other again, falling back into the same patterns had been effortless. But she knew now, after Matei, that loyalty was not a given. "I did not ask him to find you."

"Well, Radu was the one who loved me. But I love you enough for both of us." The comb caught on another snarl.

"God's wounds, Nurse, I—" Lada paused, gritting her teeth against the pain. "I cannot keep calling you Nurse. What is your name?"

The nurse paused, her fingers on Lada's temple. She stroked once, so lightly Lada wondered if it had been intentional. "Oana."

"Fine. Oana, when will you be finished?"

The nurse—no, Oana—laughed. She had lost most of her teeth in the years since they had parted. Lada had always thought her old, but now she realized Oana must have been a very young woman when she began taking care of her and Radu. In truth, Lada could not believe the woman was still alive. In Lada's mind, she had ceased existing once they were taken to Edirne. But Oana was strong and sturdy, as capable as ever.

Tonight, Lada both loved and hated her for that.

"It is easier to destroy than to build," Oana said. "And you have been destroying your looks for a long time now."

Lada could not enjoy the irony of hearing her nurse's— Oana's—favorite phrase used in relation not to the burning of Transylvania, but to the styling of hair.

"What does it matter? I am swearing loyalty to a foreign king as a soldier, not as a girl."

"These things matter, little one. Now hold still." Oana smacked the hard wooden edge of the comb against Lada's temple. Lada was certain it had been intentional.

The tiny room they had been given in the castle at Hunedoara had no fire. The stones themselves seemed to have been carved out of ice. Twice Oana had had to break the frozen top layer of the water bowl. Lada shivered violently, but not as violently as her thoughts were turning under the continued assault of the comb.

Finally satisfied, Oana helped her dress. The replacement king, Ladislas, had gifted her with a dress. Lada knew it would be disrespectful and even dangerous to reject it. Still, it was a good thing the room had no fire. Otherwise the dress would be feeding it.

Lada slapped Oana's hands away when she tied the underclothes too tight. Oana slapped Lada's hands away in return. By the end, they were both red-faced and sweating, having fought a more intense battle over getting Lada into the dress than Lada had ever endured.

"I cannot breathe in this damnable thing." Lada tried to lift her arms, but the sleeves were not made for her broad shoulders or thick arms. She could barely move. Oana had had to let out the waist some, and Lada's breasts still spilled out from the top of the bodice. Oana tucked extra fabric in there, trying to cover the soft mounds.

"This weighs more than my chain mail." Lada tugged at the layers of material that made up the skirts, and something stiffer sewn in to keep their shape.

"Think of it as armor."

Lada's lip curled in a sneer. "What could this possibly protect me from?"

"Mockery. Ridicule. Your men are used to you, but this is a court. You have to do things a certain way. Do not mess this up." Oana yanked on one of Lada's curls as she tucked it back into the elaborate style. A lacy kerchief went over the top of it all.

"Radu should be here." Lada stared down in despair. "I do not know how to talk to these people."

"He was always better at that. How did he fare when you left? I worried for him. I thought they would kill you, and break Radu's heart." There was a wistful tenderness in Oana's voice.

Lada took a deep breath. Or tried to—she could not manage it in this abomination of a dress. She and her nurse had not really spoken of Radu since Oana had asked where he was. The truth was as cold and brittle as the ice in her water bowl. "He grew into a new man. Smart. Sly. Too handsome. And, eventually, into a stranger to me." She had had no word from Radu, no news. She wanted to tell Oana that Radu was coming, but it had been so long. What if he was not? "When I left, he chose the Ottomans. So you were wrong. I survived, and Radu grew a new heart."

"Did you have nothing in common, then?"

A strangled laugh escaped the prison of her bodice. "Well, one thing." Lada wondered, yet again, whether her absence had granted Radu the portion of Mehmed's attention and love that he so desperately craved.

And, yet again, she forced herself not to think on it.

Lada tugged at the bodice, trying to shift it to make it more comfortable. She missed her Ottoman finery. At least those draped layers of tunics and robes were comfortable. "I am going to give the wrong impression, wearing this."

"You mean a good impression?"

"Yes, exactly."

Oana surveyed her with a critical eye, then threw her hands up in surrender. "This is the best we can hope for, at least as far as your looks. As far as everything else, tonight, pretend you are Radu."

A small pang hit just above Lada's heart. Did Oana wish that it were Radu and not Lada she had been reunited with? Everyone always loved Radu best. And now Radu and Mehmed had each other, and all Lada had was this woman who wielded a comb as a weapon.

Well. Lada could be Radu for one night. She grimaced, then smiled broadly and opened her large eyes as wide as she could. It was her best imitation of him.

Oana recoiled. "That is terrifying, girl. I was wrong. Be yourself."

Lada let her hooded eyelids drop low. She had never been able to be anyone else.

———◆———

The castle at Hunedoara was small compared with anything in Edirne, but bigger than Tirgoviste. A moat surrounded it, with a hill on the back side of the castle that dropped off steeply. Lada liked looking out over the wall at the winter landscape stretching into the hazy distance. She pretended she could see Wallachia from there.

But tonight there was no time for that. She left her tiny room and traversed the back tower's serpentine stairs. For a few terrifying moments she thought the dress would actually be the death of her, but she managed to make it to the bottom. Stefan met her there. He was the only one of her men who spoke Hungarian—though no one else knew it. He would gather information as he always did, snatching pieces and organizing them into a whole for her.

They walked across the open courtyard in the center of the castle, then through a massive wooden door into the throne room. The floor was brightly tiled—though no tile was impressive to Lada here. After Edirne, everything except churches seemed drab. The walls of this castle were whitewashed and hung with elaborate tapestries and gilded, framed paintings of mournful-looking Hungarian royalty.

Lada had gotten used to large, lovely windows during her time in Edirne. She had forgotten that castles elsewhere were not for ornamentation, but rather for defense. To compensate, chandeliers dripped with light, and two fireplaces roared cheerily.

If her room had been freezing, the throne room was stifling. Lada had always thought it weakness when women fainted, but now she understood. It was not their bodies—it was their clothes.

She was not the only thing on the schedule for the evening. After interminable droning speeches in Hungarian, it was finally her turn. Kneeling in front of the king was a relief, if only to get off her feet. As she knelt, there were some tittering laughs and shocked whispers. The man who went before her had knelt.

What was she expected to do instead? To her horror, she realized there was nothing she *could* do. In her dress, she could not get up again on her own. Her face burning, she looked up at the king.

Ladislas Posthumous, the painfully young replacement for the previous monarch, trembled. At first Lada had thought him cold or frightened, but the trembling continued unabated. He was stricken with some sort of palsy, his illness showing in his every movement. Lada did not have to be ruthless to see that this was a king who would not last.

Younger than her, physically weaker than her, and still he was more important than her. So she bowed her head and murmured the words. She vowed to protect the Transylvanian frontier—no one objected that she had come directly from terrorizing it—and to keep the borders safe from the Ottoman threat. Finally, she swore her fealty to him and the crown of Hungary.

The crown that was nowhere to be seen. Certainly not on Ladislas's trembling head.

When Lada had finished, she stayed where she was, utterly humiliated. She could not get up, and she could not ask for help. A hand at her elbow rescued her. Stefan smiled wanly at her as he steadily guided her back to her feet. Hoping her expression hid her relief, she nodded at him as gracefully as she could manage. They walked back to their position at the rear of the room.

After the official business ended, everyone remained. Apparently there was always an informal reception afterward. Lada leaned against a wall for support. Every part of her hurt from being held in an unfamiliar position by her dress. No one spoke to her. She knew she should try to strike up conversations, try to gain allies, but she could not smile. She was gritting her teeth too hard to manage it. She was as likely to kill anyone who talked to her as she was to make a friend.

No. She was *far* more likely to kill someone than to make a friend.

Only when she could not place her source of vague disappointment did she come to a horrible realization. She had thought if she looked like a noblewoman, men would talk to her. Of course she would have rejected their flirtations, but she had been preparing herself to do that.

She had not prepared herself to remain utterly invisible while wearing a dress and with her hair combed. Or maybe she was so unbelievable in a dress, or had humiliated herself so completely by kneeling, that no one would ever believe she belonged among nobility.

Lada was taken back to Mehmed's wedding. Standing alone, always alone, without a place and without worth. She drew a ragged breath. This was not the same. She was not that person. She had more than just Mehmed and Radu now.

But she did not have *them* anymore. Tonight, she felt the full weight of that loss. The loss of a brother who would have stood at her side and fought this battle of manners and politics for her. The loss of a man who would have laughed at her dress and her hair but also been desperate to be alone so he could undo it all for her.

Perhaps she had never stopped being that girl lost in a place where she could never have power.

It took Lada several minutes to realize Stefan had returned from his rounds. "What did you find?" she asked, relieved and grateful for a familiar face. Even one as anonymous and blank as Stefan's.

"The crown," he said, nodding toward where Ladislas spoke with several priests and a tall, confident-looking older man. The rest of the royalty revolved around two men and a regal woman. The woman was glorious, Lada had to admit. She truly wore her elaborate clothes as armor, not something to wilt under like Lada did. The way she commanded the attention of everyone around her, shooting frequent sharp glances at the king, reminded Lada of Huma, Mehmed's mother. Huma had been so sick when Lada left, surely she was dead by now. The thought of Huma's death made Lada oddly mournful. The woman had been a threat, and a murderer, too. But she had been so *good* at everything she did.

The woman in layered, gold-embroidered finery briefly met Lada's eyes. Lada felt herself weighed and summarily dismissed. It stung.

"Where is the crown?" Lada asked, glad Stefan was here to distract her.

"After Varna, the Polish king took it for safekeeping. But no one can truly be king of Hungary without the crown. Elizabeth is trying everything she can to secure it."

"Elizabeth?"

Stefan nodded toward the glittering woman. Suddenly it all made sense. "She is his mother?" Lada asked

"She is the true ruler of Hungary. But she does not have the money to buy the crown back. And until Ladislas has it, his rule is illegitimate. The man next to him is Ulrich, his regent. Between him and Elizabeth, this country is run."

"I suspect Ladislas's rule will be as short in stature as he is."

"No one speaks outright of killing him. They do not speak of him at all. He does not matter. Elizabeth is the throne."

"And Ulrich?"

"The most likely successor. The connection to the royal line is distant, but there. He is modest, just, and well liked."

"How do you know?"

"I spoke with his servants. It is the best way to get a sense of a man. And the other—"

They were interrupted by silence, which was followed by a wave of noise. Lada followed the crowd's eyes to a doorway in which Hunyadi stood. The day before, he had ridden out to the Transylvanian border, to respond to a problem there. Judging by the riding cloak he wore on his shoulders and the weariness on his face, he had only now returned. A chorus of cheers filled the room as he smiled and lifted one hand. People surged forward to speak with him. Elizabeth watched with narrowed eyes. Then the crowd parted for her, and she greeted Hunyadi with a lingering embrace.

"He could have it all," Lada said.

Stefan shook his head. "He will not take it. But he controls the soldiers, which means he has more power than anyone else in this castle."

It was similar in Wallachia. The prince was allowed no troops of his own, permitted no fortresses or defense. He was entirely dependent on the boyars, each of whom kept his own soldiers at the ready. It did not make for powerful leaders.

King Ladislas waved to Hunyadi. Hunyadi did not see it. Lada pitied the king then, but more than that, she hated him for being weak. This was his country, and he let another man have all the power. He deserved to lose everything. Lada did not understand why Elizabeth depended on a feeble son rather than taking the throne herself.

Huma had played the same game, and in the end it had seen her banished. Power through sons was no more secure than power through husbands.

"You said there was another contender for the throne?" Lada asked Stefan.

One man had not moved forward to greet Hunyadi. He stood alone, dark eyes calculating as he watched everyone who mattered in Hungary clamoring for a moment of Hunyadi's attention. Though he was far leaner than Hunyadi and dressed in more finery than Hunyadi would ever wear, Lada saw the same determined jaw, the same confident brow. But where Hunyadi's eyes were bold and honest, his son's were calculating and secretive.

"Matthias," Stefan said.

———————

Lada watched Matthias throughout the evening. He never so much as glanced her way, so she had ample time to study him without fear of being caught. He wore a smile as ostentatiously as he wore the gold chain at his neck and the jeweled pins on his vest. It was ornamentation, meant to dazzle. But always his eyes were narrowed and shrewd as he spoke to this person or another or, in many cases, did *not* speak to them.

Hunyadi had been drawn into a corner, trapped by an impassable wall of dresses. Lada did not envy him. He was a widower, and the most powerful man in the country. The fact that he had no family name paled in comparison to his wealth. She wished he could break free so they could speak. Of what, it did not matter. But he was her only ally here, and she might as well have been alone.

Nicolae sidled up to Lada. He had secured some clothes nice enough to gain him access. She did not know where or how he had obtained the clothing, and she did not care. It was a relief to see him.

"You should dance. Or at least speak to someone," he said.

Lada shook her head. "It will do no good. I belong here as much as a pig in a dress does, and everyone will know as soon as I open my mouth."

"I actually saw several pigs in dresses as I came in. Not a single one got past the door. You are definitely doing better than they are."

Shaking her head, Lada let Nicolae lead her away from the wall. "Look, no one is speaking to the king." Nicolae nudged her in that direction. "Talk to him."

"No one speaks to him because he does not matter. I have pledged my loyalty for nothing."

Something in Lada's tone must have warned Nicolae, because he immediately turned them both around and steered Lada out of the throne room and into the freezing night air of the courtyard. He smiled and nodded to everyone they passed, quickly taking them through the gate and across the bridge. Lada leaned heavily against one of the stone pillars.

"I knelt in there and swore fealty to another king—a foreign king—for nothing, Nicolae. He will not help me get my throne. He cannot even get his own crown. What have I accomplished?"

Nicolae took her hands in his. "You do what you must. It is no different from what the little zealot does, making treaties and creating alliances that mean less than the paper they are written on. Your brother would have done the same. You must survive, and Hungary has welcomed you. Take advantage of it. Hunyadi is a powerful ally. In spite of your best efforts, he cares about you. This is a good situation. It is certainly better than hiding in the woods, picking on Transylvania."

"But it is not what we came for."

Nicolae shrugged, stamping his feet against the cold. "I came to get away from the Ottomans. We all did. You gave that to us."

"Matei was spying on me," she said. She had told no one, holding the information close out of shame, anger, and, perhaps, a bit of guilt over his death. "He was reporting to Mehmed."

Nicolae uttered a sad oath, his breath fogging into the night air. "Matei was a fool, then. I will keep a sharper eye on everyone. But I know this—you have done many things for us already. We are in a good position. You fight at Hunyadi's side. Foreign kings accept your allegiance. Your men respect and are loyal to you." He smiled. "That is quite a bit for a little dragon from Wallachia."

Lada knew he was trying to help her, and she was comforted that her men were satisfied. She had gotten them out of slavery. Led them successfully in battle. Earned the respect of one of the greatest men of her time.

She stared numbly into the night. The Hungarian night. Not the Wallachian night.

It was not enough.

Never enough.

13

Late March

Radu had only an hour before the party, before he would need to persuade Cyprian that he was ready to betray Mehmed and join Emperor Constantine's cause. He hurried to Kumal's house. Kumal was not there, but he was not whom Radu needed to speak with.

"Nazira?" he called, bursting through the front door. "Fatima? Nazira?"

Nazira rushed into the front room, Fatima close behind her. Nazira held a cloth in her hands, dripping water along the floor. Concern pinched her face. "What is it?"

"I am leaving. For Constantinople."

"They march already? So soon?"

"No. No. I—" Radu paused, looking around the room. "Are we alone?"

"Yes, of course."

Radu sat, suddenly exhausted. He looked down at his hands. "Mehmed has asked me to defect. I am to convince an ambassador that I wish to aid Emperor Constantine. If all goes to plan, I will run tonight."

Nazira covered her mouth with the wet cloth, then dropped it. "Tonight?"

"Yes."

"But what if they find out you are still loyal to Mehmed?"

"They cannot. I have to pretend to want a new life with them. They must think I am never coming back. I do not know what Mehmed will tell Kumal, but I wanted you to know the truth. I will not be able to write or communicate in any way."

A sudden determination hardened Nazira's face. "That will not be a problem. I am coming with you."

"What? No. You cannot!" Radu stood again in disbelief.

"I can, and I will. You have taken care of us all this time. Now it is my turn to repay you. It is too much to bear this secret alone. I will go as your wife."

"It is too dangerous! If they discover me, they will kill us both!"

"Which is exactly why I need to come! Why would a man put his beloved wife in that much danger? My mere presence will sell your loyalty in a way nothing else could. Besides, I have spent all these years studying Greek. It is about time I got to use it."

Radu shook his head, aghast. He turned to Fatima for support. "Tell her this is insane."

Fatima looked as though she wanted to cry, but she shook her head instead. "Nazira is right," she whispered. "It is the best way to keep you safe. We will come."

"But you hate to travel!" Radu looked back at Nazira, triumphant. "You cannot ask Fatima to come."

"I am not." Nazira turned to Fatima, cupping her face gently in her hands. She put her lips to the other girl's ear, whispering something Radu could not hear. Then she said, "You understand?"

Fatima shook her head, silent tears streaming down her face. "I can come," she whispered. "I want to be wherever you are."

"And I want to be wherever you are. But I need you to be safe." Nazira regarded Fatima with a tenderness that hurt Radu to see. "I can weather this storm for both of us, but only if I have the shelter in my heart of knowing that my Fatima is well."

Fatima shook her head again, then nodded, crying.

"I will come back to you. Always." Nazira closed the distance between their mouths in the exact way Radu had imagined Mehmed doing with him. But this kiss was infinitely more sweet, more intimate than any Radu had ever managed to dream of. He looked away, unwilling to intrude on the two women's love and heartbreak.

Nazira cleared her throat. Radu turned back to find her still holding Fatima close. Fatima hid her face in Nazira's shoulder, but Nazira's face was ferocious. "When do we leave?"

———◆———

Cyprian was waiting outside the grand doors to Mehmed's party. Though the ambassador had carefully composed himself, his nerves showed in the way his fingers tapped unceasingly against his blue-clad leg. Radu did not care for the styles out of Constantinople. He found the deliberate exposing of multiple layers of clothes to be gaudy and vain. But unlike that of the other ambassadors, Cyprian's layers were coordinated and less jarring. Radu supposed he himself would be wearing clothes like that soon.

He did not realize he was running his fingers along his turban until they caught in one of the folds.

And prayer. When would he pray? Being cut off from prayer with his brothers would be like being cut off from sleep. He could already feel his soul wearing thin and tired simply from contemplating it. He would find a way to pray. He had to. Even if he could only pray in his heart, God would understand.

Light and music spilled from the doorway, a jarring accompaniment to Radu's bleak thoughts. There was no use in delay. He crossed the hall to Cyprian, whose visage flashed a brief look of happiness before worry claimed it once more.

"You came," Cyprian said. "I had begun to fear you would not."

"We are all of us slaves to the whims of the sultan." Radu hated the way the words flowed smoothly out of his mouth, as though they belonged there. "Cyprian, this is Nazira, my wife."

A momentary twist of confusion distorted Cyprian's face as he finally noticed Nazira at Radu's side. "Your wife?" With movements formed by years of habit, Cyprian reached out and took her hand, bowing and kissing it.

"Hello," Nazira said, her voice strained. She looked over her shoulder constantly. Radu did not know how much of it was nerves, and how much was acting to sell their deception to Cyprian.

"I—I did not expect you to have a wife." Cyprian frowned, then shook his head. "I mean, you are so young. My age."

Radu smiled tightly. "When you find someone like Nazira,

you do not wait." He looked past Cyprian toward the party, and then back down the hall. "Can we speak in private?" he asked in a low voice.

"Of course." Cyprian followed them out into a side garden. The same side garden Radu had come to so many times to read and then destroy Mehmed's secret notes. In the face of what he was moving toward, he longed to have even that level of closeness again.

As soon as they were far enough into the garden, Radu turned to Cyprian. "We want to leave."

"What?"

"Right now. We cannot pretend to support Mehmed anymore. His father kidnapped me, tortured me, stole my entire childhood. I cannot stand by and watch as Mehmed takes Constantinople the same way."

Cyprian wilted. "So he does mean to attack."

"As soon as he is ready. Can you get us to the city, to the emperor? I will do whatever I can. I grew up with Mehmed and served him; I am familiar with his true temperament and many of his plans. I can help you."

Cyprian nodded. Mehmed had been right. Cyprian must have planned to try to get information from Radu. Why else would he be so quick to trust them? "We should leave right now," he said.

"We are ready." Radu pulled his and Nazira's traveling bags from behind a stone bench.

"She is coming?" Cyprian's surprise was confirmation of what Nazira had said. No one turning spy would risk the life of an innocent woman. *Please*, Radu prayed, *please let Nazira come through this safely.* It was one thing to gamble with his own life for Mehmed's cause. He felt sick knowing he was also risking Nazira's.

"Radu is my husband." Nazira gripped his hand. Some of Radu's fear was soothed. It was selfish to draw any amount of happiness from her sacrifice, but he could not help it. "Where he goes, I go."

"Very well." They followed Cyprian to the guest stables, where he found one of the ambassadors' servant boys. The boy was small, with intelligent eyes and black hair thick and tangled like thatch. After a quick, whispered conversation, the boy saddled three horses.

Though Radu knew perfectly well they would not be followed, Cyprian's paranoia was contagious. Radu found himself glancing over his shoulder as they rode through the city. His last view as they crested the hill outside Edirne was the same as the first he had ever had of the empire. Spires and minarets were black points against the starlit sky.

He bid them a silent farewell, praying that they would watch over the city in his absence.

14

Early March

LADA WAS NOT CERTAIN which was more surprising: that she had been invited to one of Hunyadi's inner-circle councils, or that his son Matthias had not.

Hunyadi sat at the head of the table, with several similarly grizzled men around him. At the opposite end of the table sat two priests. The seat next to Hunyadi was empty. He stood and gestured for Lada to sit there. The sting of invisibility that had plagued her in the week since swearing her loyalty disappeared as she sat at Hunyadi's right hand. As soon as she was settled, he leaned forward, slamming a fist against the table.

"Constantinople!" he roared. "Once again it faces a threat. Perhaps the greatest threat it has ever known. We cannot let the heart of Christendom, Rome of old, fall to the infidels. If Constantinople succumbs to the Muslim plague, what is to stop them from spreading over the whole world?"

One of the priests nodded vehemently. The other remained impassive. A few of the men were engaged, but several leaned away from the table as though distancing themselves from the topic.

"What are you suggesting?" the excited priest asked.

"We crusade, as we have before. We gather the righteous until we swell around the walls like God's own wave, to forever drown the infidel threat."

The other priest smiled drily. "I believe the last successful Christian crusade actually *sacked* Constantinople."

Hunyadi huffed, waving away the words with his hands. "Italians. They have no honor. If we let the Muslims take Constantinople, the heart of Eastern Christendom, what is next? Transylvania? Hungary? Long have we stood between Islam's expansion and the rest of Europe. As defenders of Christ, we cannot ignore the plight of Constantinople."

Lada watched, trying to figure out Hunyadi's angle. The Ottoman Empire already surrounded Constantinople. If the city fell, it gave them a virtually impregnable capital, but it did not move them any closer to Hungary or the rest of Europe. The threat was merely spiritual, not physical. It would be demoralizing to lose the great city, but not damaging. At least not to Hungary.

"You have led us against a sultan before," said one of the men, his head shiny and bald, but his beard still dark. "We fought with you at Varna. We lost. We lost our king. Hungary still suffers the consequences and will continue to until the crown is once again stable. Why would we risk that again for Constantinople?"

"It is not about Hungary. It is about Christianity. Have you heard of the priest who led peasants—ordinary peasants!— against the Ottomans? They drove them back with the ferocity of their faith! They won a decisive and shocking victory, because Christ was on their side."

"Yes," the bald man said, rubbing his face wearily. "And then the priest caught the plague and most of the peasants froze to death."

Lada watched as Hunyadi tugged on his beard, trying to impose his intensity on the other men. He had no angle, she realized. There was no political advantage for him, personally, at Constantinople. If anything, he stood to lose all he had worked so hard to build here for himself and his son.

Listening to him talk and argue, Lada could not help but be stirred. He was passionate and charming, utterly adamant in his belief that defending Constantinople was the right thing to do. She weighed it against Mehmed's fervent desire for the city. She knew others thought he did it for gain—even his own men wanted the city only for the rumored riches—but that was not what moved Mehmed. Mehmed felt the weight of prophecy and the burden of his god on his shoulders. That would not disappear until he took the city or died trying.

Lada wondered how the world could survive with men such as Mehmed and Hunyadi on opposite sides. Or perhaps that was how it did survive. If they served the same purpose, she could not imagine any nation not falling before their combined might.

Each god, Christian and Muslim, had champions, keeping the other at bay.

Whose side would she fall on? Could she join Hunyadi?

Could she go against Mehmed?

That evening Lada walked, Stefan at her side. He did not have much to report, other than that the king's mother did not like Hunyadi and was trying to either subvert or marry him.

"What do you think about Constantinople?" Lada asked, looking up through the bare branches at the twilight sky.

"Hunyadi does not have enough support to go fight, but he will. The king's mother is encouraging him. She hopes he will die there, and solve some of her problems. She will make certain he has the forces and the funding he needs."

"I mean you. What do you think? What do the men think? If I asked them to march with Hunyadi and defend the walls . . . would they?"

Stefan was quiet for a long time. Then he lifted his shoulders. "I think they would."

"But it is not our goal. It is not what has kept us together."

"Goals change," he said simply. "If you ask, most will follow."

"Will you?"

A ghost of a smile disrupted the blank space of his face. "I do not know."

Lada nodded, looking back up at the sky. "That is fine. I do not know, either."

———

Two weeks after the council about Constantinople, Hunyadi invited Lada to dine in the castle. She always ate with her men, so this was unusual. Against her better judgment, she agreed, but only after Hunyadi said she did not have to wear a dress. She would not put herself through that again.

She entered the dining room with her back as straight as a sword, hair tied in a black cloth in defiance of the elaborate styles of the Hungarian court.

She need not have worried so much. Dress or trousers, curls or cloth, she was still invisible.

As dishes of food were passed by servants, Lada tried to listen to the conversations around her. Her dinner companions spoke of people she did not know, of matters that did not concern her. Nowhere was there anything for her to contribute to or even enjoy. The familiarity of it all exhausted her. It was the same as what she had grown up with: circles of gossip, words and favors traded for power, deals made for which the nobility would see none of the work and all of the benefit.

Since she had nothing to offer anyone, no one paid her the slightest mind. Hunyadi fared better. He was wildly popular, regaled with requests to tell stories of his conquest. But his otherness was inescapable. He was a soldier, through and through, and though he was undeniably charming, there was a gruff directness to him that was out of place here. The nobles deferred to him with a certain patronizing arrogance. The king's mother, Elizabeth, asked him for story after story, each circling back to his childhood.

Lada realized with a spike of anger what it was: Hunyadi was their pet. They were proud of his accomplishments, boastful of what he had done, but they would never, ever see him as their equal. And Elizabeth made certain no one forgot where he came from.

He was worth more than every glittering waste of a person in this whole castle.

Though Hunyadi never drank when they were campaigning or riding, Lada watched as he downed glass after glass of wine. She revised her previous thought that he was doing better than she. He was miserable. As the meal broke up and people stood in groups to talk, Hunyadi suggested dancing several times. Lada had seen him dance—he was a wonderful dancer—and she understood his need to do something with his body. Movement was freedom. But there were no musicians, and his suggestions were met with laughter, as though he jested.

Lada stomped across the room and took his elbow. "I need him," she snapped at the courtesans polluting the air with their aggressive perfume. They pouted, protesting mildly that he had not finished his story, but as soon as Lada removed Hunyadi they filled the space as though he had never existed.

"Thank you," Hunyadi said, swaying slightly. "These people are more terrifying than a contingent of Janissaries."

"And far more ruthless."

Lada guided him toward the door, but he stumbled to a stop, a smile of true joy parting the haze of alcohol on his expression. "Matthias!"

Matthias, his own auburn hair oiled and carefully styled, unlike his father's mane, paused in his conversation with several other men. Lada knew he had heard Hunyadi, but he continued as though he had not.

"Matthias!" Hunyadi barreled over, clapping his hands on the young man's shoulders. Matthias's answering smile was as carefully styled as his hair.

"Father."

"Matthias, I wanted you to meet Lada Dracul." Hunyadi turned back to her and gestured at Matthias with unabashed pride. Matthias's answering whisper of a sneer made Lada wish to run her sword through him.

He gave her a perfunctory bow. "So you are the feral girl of Wallachia he has taken under his wing." The men around him laughed. One made an obscene gesture behind Hunyadi's back.

Their opinion of her relationship with him was evident. Lada sensed that Matthias had never been privy to his father's idea of marrying them.

"Lada single-handedly defeated a whole Bulgar contingent. Saved my life. And she grew up with Sultan Mehmed. Invaluable insight. Very clever." Hunyadi smiled at Lada with the same level of pride as he had shown for his son, and something inside her broke.

"Is that so?" One of the men leaned forward, leering. "Tell me, is it true what they say? That he has one thousand women in his harem, and another harem made up entirely of boys?"

Lada felt the familiar stab of anger that always accompanied mention of the harem, and a brief spike of fear. A male harem? Was such a thing possible? Was Radu ... She shoved those feelings down with an unexpected defensiveness on her brother's behalf. How must Radu, already tormented by the impossibility of his love, feel when he heard such insinuations used as slander?

Besides, these men did not know Mehmed. How dare they speak of him this way? She raised an eyebrow coolly. "If you are so interested in male harems, I can introduce you to the sultan. Though you are not quite pretty enough for his tastes."

The man's face turned a dangerous shade of red. Hunyadi let out a barking burst of laughter and clapped Matthias on the back. His son cringed, then carefully reset his face. "I believe Elizabeth would like to speak to you," he said to his father.

Hunyadi groaned.

The leering man spoke again. "I believe she would like to do more than speak with you." Matthias pretended outrage, but it was all in jest. Hunyadi was embarrassed. Response was impossible. He could not impugn Elizabeth's honor, nor did he want to criticize Matthias's friends.

Lada could bear no more. "The room is too warm. Will you see me out?" Hunyadi nodded graciously, offering his arm. She steered him once more toward the door and grabbed a bottle of wine on their way. She handed it to him wordlessly. They walked through the center courtyard, then over the bridge, descending the bank to a bare weeping willow. Hunyadi slipped several times, nearly taking them both down.

Lada's thoughts were on Mehmed. It was so strange, hearing accounts of the Mehmed that the world saw—seemingly infinite versions of the same person, each distorted and exaggerated. But she knew the real him.

Or did she?

He had spied on her. He had sent her to Wallachia with his support, and then supported her rival. He had married and fathered children, all while professing his love for her. And through it all, he had never taken his sights off Constantinople. He would not, could not. Not even for her.

Could she really consider fighting for Constantinople, knowing it would be going directly against Mehmed and everything he had been to her? She did not think she could raise a sword against him. As much as she loved Hunyadi and hated the Ottomans, it would not be the Ottomans she would truly be fighting. It would be Mehmed.

She remembered those warm nights together, cocooned in her room, plotting and planning the attack on the city. It had felt like playing pretend. But it had never been pretend for Mehmed. Constantinople was his dream, the one thing he would not give up. Everything was to that end. Including supporting her rival on the Wallachian throne. He had sacrificed her dreams for his.

Maybe she *would* go to defend the walls.

"Did you see him?" Hunyadi said, once they were sitting.

Lada startled out of her thoughts. "Mehmed?"

Hunyadi laughed. "No! My son! He looks like a king."

Lada thought that was not a thing to be proud of. She weighed her next words as judiciously as she could. "He is nothing like you."

Hunyadi smiled, nodding. "I know. I do not understand him. But I have worked with blood and sweat my whole life so he could have access to everything that I never could. My sword has cut a way to the courts for him. He never has to do what I have done. I gave him that." Hunyadi lowered his head, closing his eyes. "I think he has a chance at the throne. Can you imagine? I am the son of peasants, and my son could be king. Everything I have done, all that I have lost, all the struggle and death. It was for him."

Lada remembered the look of pride he had given her. Matthias did not deserve Hunyadi. "I wish you had been my father," she said. If Hunyadi were her father, everything would be easier. She would jump at the chance to crusade with him, to fight at his side.

If Hunyadi were her father, she would never have known Mehmed, never had her loyalties twisted and tugged into strange new shapes. And her heart would not have to constantly shield itself from the part that missed Mehmed so desperately.

Hunyadi would have protected Radu, too. And Radu would have appreciated him in a way Matthias was incapable of.

Hunyadi patted her arm with his heavy hand. "Do not wish away what you are. If you were my daughter, I would have extinguished your fire long ago. I would have given you the best tutors and the finest clothes and made you into a pretty doll to be traded away in marriage. I did the same with my son; I made him into someone I do not know, and it fills me with both pride and sadness. That is the best we can do for our children—turn them into strangers with better hopes than we ever had. Your father was a fool and a coward, but his choices shaped you into the fearsome creature you are. I do not want to imagine a world in which you are not you."

For years Lada had nurtured only hatred for her father, to take away the pain that loving him had left her with. But that night in her tent as she drifted to sleep, she let some of it go. Because she, too, was grateful for who she was. She would not wish any part of herself away.

Which meant she was still left with the question of what to do with the parts that loved Mehmed and the parts that wanted to fight at Hunyadi's side.

15

Late March

THREE HOURS AFTER LEAVING Edirne, Radu, Cyprian, and Nazira heard a horse galloping madly toward them. They pulled their horses to the side of the road. Cyprian drew his sword, and Radu copied him, though he could not imagine who might be pursuing them. Certainly not Mehmed's forces. Perhaps one of the ambassadors had somehow discovered their deception, and was riding to warn Cyprian?

The horse, lathered and shivering, was drawn to an abrupt stop in front of them. "He has killed them!" the rider shouted.

"Valentin?" Cyprian sheathed his sword. It was the thatch-haired boy who had helped them in the stables.

Valentin tried to dismount, but fell roughly to the ground instead. "He killed them!"

Cyprian jumped from his horse, grabbing Valentin. "What do you mean? Why are you here?"

"He killed them! At the party. The sultan killed them. He killed them all."

Cyprian looked up at Radu and Nazira in horror. "Did you know?"

Radu shook his head, numb with shock. He had not known. This, then, was Mehmed's declaration of war. Radu knew that lives would be lost—of course they would, that was the price of a siege—but this felt so personal. So . . . excessive. It felt more like murder than war. He had no doubt Mehmed had his reasons, and if Mehmed could explain them, Radu would understand.

Unbidden, the image of the ambassadors lying on the gleaming tile floor, blood pooling around them, came to Radu's mind. Sour acid rose in his throat, threatening to come out. Surely there had been a reason. "I did not know," he whispered.

Cyprian cradled the boy, still looking up at Radu and Nazira. "Your timing saved my life. I owe you everything, and will call you friends to my dying day."

Nazira and Radu looked at each other as the full weight of what they were in the middle of finally descended on their shoulders.

Three days later, Radu's assumption that Nazira would require a lot of help on the road was heartily disproved. She had packed not only her essentials but also provisions. Radu had not even thought of it, a fact that was not lost on Nazira. She batted her eyes slyly at him as she started a fire effortlessly and pulled out food from a saddlebag. "We wives are very useful things to have around," she said.

Radu huddled close to the fire, grateful for the heat and for Nazira's skills. "And all this time I thought you were merely decorative."

Cyprian gave a small laugh, while Radu and Nazira traded

a secret smile over how true her decorative role actually was. It was good to hear Cyprian laugh. He had understandably been in a pall since receiving news of the murders.

Assassinations, Radu corrected himself. Political, not personal. That made them assassinations, not murders. Which he found easier to stomach, though neither was pleasant.

"How much farther to the city?" Radu asked.

"We should be there tomorrow." They had taken a wandering route, fueled by the servant Valentin's terror and Cyprian's fear of pursuit. Radu and Nazira could not very well assure their traveling companions that Mehmed wanted them all to arrive safely, so they toiled along little-used roads and through backcountry.

Nazira dished out soup and then settled in next to Radu.

"You even remembered spices?" Radu said. The soup was deliciously hot on his tongue.

"You married extremely well, Radu." She leaned against his free arm. Radu looked up to see Cyprian watching them with a forlorn, wistful expression.

Nazira noticed it, too. "Are you married, Cyprian?"

He shook his head as though coming out of a daze and looked down at his bowl. "No."

"I wondered if you were going home to a wife. Did you grow up in Constantinople?"

He nodded, soaking the now-stale flatbread in the soup to soften it.

Nazira continued asking questions, pumping Cyprian for information. Radu was both proud of her and sad that it was necessary. "Do you have family there still?"

"Yes. Sort of." Cyprian's smile twisted and did not touch his eyes. "My father is Demetrios."

"The despot?" Radu asked, surprised. Constantine's two brothers, Demetrios and Thomas, ruled other areas in the Peloponnese. They were often at odds with each other, enemies as frequently as they were allies. Radu could not understand why one of them would allow his son to be an ambassador. It was a job of dubious prestige, thankless and, frankly, dangerous. Ambassadors were as likely to be killed by foreign courts as their own if they brought back undesirable reports.

Cyprian nodded. "I am, unfortunately, a bastard. My mother was his mistress. So I am not as valuable as his legitimate sons. Constantine took me in and gave me a position in his court as a favor to my mother."

"Was she from Cyprus?" Nazira asked.

Cyprian's expression softened. "She named me after her island. She always said I was her home wherever she was."

Nazira sighed prettily. "I like her very much already. Have you ever been to Cyprus? I hear it is beautiful."

"No. My mother died four years ago. I have meant to go and see her birthplace, but Constantine's need has been greater than my whims."

"Is he so demanding, this uncle emperor of yours?" Nazira's tone was light and teasing. Radu leaned back, wondering how else Nazira would prove he had drastically underestimated her.

Cyprian laughed. "No. That is what keeps me at his side. I would fear for my soul if I had it in me to repay all his kindness by abandoning him in his time of greatest need." His expression turned dark once again. "I worry for how he will mourn if news of the ambassadors' deaths reaches him before we do. He will think me murdered, and will blame himself. It was not his fault. I requested to go."

Radu frowned. "Why would you do that?"

Cyprian took a moment to drain his soup, looking into the bowl like he could make more appear. "I liked my first visit. Edirne seemed to me very beautiful and . . . intriguing. I did not anticipate how things would have changed." He looked back up, another attempt at a smile moving his lips but not changing the sad shape of his eyes. "Besides, I had taken all that time to learn Turkish. It seemed a pity to waste it."

"If I had known, I would have warned you all." Even as he said it, Radu knew it was not true. He would have wanted to warn them. But he would not have gone against what Mehmed thought best.

Cyprian leaned forward as though he would grasp Radu's shoulder. Then he sat back. "It is for the best you did not. It would have alerted the sultan to your disloyalty, and you would have died with us. No, it is better this way. I will mourn my companions, buoyed by the hope that you have brought us."

The soup had turned sour in Radu's stomach.

16

Early March

"AMBASSADORS ARE HERE. FROM EDIRNE." Stefan had hardly finished speaking when Lada ran from their camp to the castle. Radu would be with them. She had a lot to speak with him about, and she anticipated with delight presenting Oana to him.

She pushed toward the throne room, trying to see over heads of others trying to get in. Two guards would not let her past. Hunyadi found her there, arguing with them.

"My brother will be with the ambassadors," she said.

Hunyadi shook his head. "No, they are all Turkish. But they brought this." He held a letter addressed to her. Unlike last time, he gave it to her unopened.

Lada clasped Hunyadi's hand, trying to hide her disappointment and frustration. "It is from Radu. I asked his aid. If there is news of value, I will bring it to you."

He nodded, smiling. "I know."

She took the letter and retreated beneath the bridge, where the heavy weeping branches of willows cocooned her and she could pretend to be far from the poisonous castle. There were many reasons why Radu might not have come. He was ill. He was delayed. He was dead. Or he finally had what he wanted, and nothing could tempt him to leave.

Lada only marginally preferred the last option to his death.

She split the seal and opened the letter. It took her a moment to process that it was not from Radu, telling her whether he would join her in her quest for Wallachia.

It was from Mehmed.

Her face flushed as she read and then reread the first few lines, horrified.

I dream of her neck, slender and unadorned as the gazelle,
I long to see her tresses, draping a cloth between us and our nakedness,
Her breasts like smooth mirrors, her legs like slender reeds bent by the
water,
At eventide she lightens the shadows, a lamp against the night,
And I will not forswear that fire nor the passion it alights in my body,
Swift and taut as an arrow at the ready, with her, my target.

"What has he shat out on this page?" Lada muttered, scowling at the words. Mehmed had tried to read her poetry before, and she always stopped him. It was a waste of words and breath. Who had ever looked with lust upon a gazelle? And her breasts had nothing like the mirror about them.

She skimmed the rest of the poem. When he had finally finished comparing her body to various objects and animals, he moved on to business.

I know you have not been successful in your attempts at the throne. I wish I could help. However, I have a proposition.

Lada scowled. He did not wish that he could help—he had very clearly demonstrated he wished no such thing. She braced herself for his suggestion that she return to him.

Do whatever you must to persuade Hunyadi to stay out of Constantinople, and I will be able to part with enough men to give you the strength you need to reclaim your throne. Send word back with my ambassadors. Once I have it, I will wait for you in the south of Transylvania, where it meets Serbia and Wallachia.

Lada dropped the letter in her lap. Whatever she had thought Mehmed might write, whatever sly attempts to lure her back or to remind her she had made the wrong choice, they were not there.

She did not know if that disappointed her. But she had found something she had not expected. Support. He wanted her to succeed. And he was offering her help.

Her way to the throne had opened up again. All she had to do was betray Hunyadi.

It was dark by the time Lada walked in a daze back to camp. Her men still lived outside, with no room for them in the barracks. It suited them fine, and it suited her as well. She preferred a tent to the stone prison of Hunedoara.

When she entered her tent, she found Oana sitting on the rug next to a lamp, mending in her lap. As a child, Lada had sometimes wondered if her nurse came with sewing supplies permanently attached. Lada collapsed onto her bedroll with a sigh. "What are you doing in here?" she asked Oana.

"Bogdan snores. This is my reward for carrying his great weight for nine months and nearly dying bringing him into the world. My beautiful little boy turned into a great hulking man who sounds like a dying pig when he sleeps."

Lada could not help laughing. "Have you walked the camp at night? An army of boars would make less noise than my men do."

Oana nodded, squinting, then set aside her work. "It is too dark for my old eyes."

"Sleep." Lada stripped some of the furs from her bedroll and tossed them at Oana. "Or, if you want, I can probably get you a bed in the castle."

"Lada, my dear one, you got me my Bogdan back. You do not need to get me anything ever again." The nurse sounded dangerously close to crying. "Though," she said, her voice turning gruff, "I would very much like to get out of Hungary. They all have marbles in their mouths. I cannot understand one word in five."

"You may get your wish soon enough."

"Back to Wallachia?"

Lada let out a breath heavy with the weight of the future. "No. Hunyadi plans to defend Constantinople."

"Why would we go there?"

"Because he thinks it is the right thing to do."

The nurse made a derisive sound. "The devil take Byzantium and all its glory. It never did anything for us."

Lada listened as the nurse lay down and shifted around, making all the small noises tired bodies make. It was annoying, but there was also something comforting about having another woman present. Someone she knew cared for her.

"Which way is the wrong way?" Lada asked. "How much should I give if it means getting back to Wallachia?" She could lie to Mehmed, tell him she had persuaded Hunyadi to stay out of Constantinople. He would not discover her duplicity until she already had the troops. There would be hell to pay after, though, and her castle was already filled with enemies.

Hunyadi's love and trust was a valuable thing; it meant more to Lada than she had thought possible. But he could not get her the throne. And she did not feel the pull of Constantinople that all the men in her life seemed to. Hunyadi, she cared about. Constantinople was only a city.

Wallachia, though. Wallachia was everything.

As though hearing Lada's thoughts, her nurse echoed, "Everything. There is no cost too high for your people, for your land."

"Even if it means betraying someone who trusts me? Or making deals with the empire that took your son from you?"

"You brought him back. You brought yourself back. Wallachia needs you, and you deserve Wallachia. Let your loyalty be only where your heart is. Everything else can fall by the road and be trodden underfoot as we pass to our home." Oana patted Lada's arm. "My fierce little girl. You can do anything."

Lada did not know if it was permission or prophecy, but she believed it either way.

Though manipulating people was Radu's area of expertise, Lada found the opportunity to do so handed to her with all the poetic grace of a gazelle's neck.

Hunyadi paced in front of her. He had called her to the meeting room in the castle, but this time only the two of them were present. "What about Serbia?" he asked.

Lada shook her head. "I know for a fact Mara Brankovic, one of Murad's wives, made a new treaty for Serbia. If you go to Constantinople, you will fight against Serbians, not with them." Lada wondered briefly what Mara Brankovic was doing with her cleverly purchased freedom. Mara had taken an offer of marriage from Constantine himself and used it to forge a deal between Mehmed and her father, the Serbian prince—creating a new, permanently single life for herself.

"Damn." Hunyadi leaned back with a sigh. "What do you think of the Danesti prince? I know you hate him, but will he aid us? Maybe he will die at the wall, which would be very convenient for you."

Lada dragged a knife along the tabletop, scoring the wood deeply. "He is a worm. And not long ago he was in Edirne, delivering his loyalty to Mehmed in person."

"How do you know?"

"Because I had someone in Tirgoviste trying to kill him at the time."

Hunyadi shook his head, but his expression was more amused than shocked.

"Besides," Lada continued, "he cannot commit troops without the boyars giving him support. They will bide their time and twiddle their thumbs until any usefulness has passed, and then they will send their condolences."

"The Wallachian boyars like me, though."

"Yes, and they fear Mehmed. Which do you think will be a stronger motivator among that pack of cowards?"

Hunyadi nodded grudgingly. "I have some support, though. Elizabeth encourages me to go. And I have you and your men. It will be good for you to have something to do."

Lada already had something to do. She respected Hunyadi, but he could not give her the throne. Mehmed could. He could also take it from her afterward, if she failed to uphold her end of their bargain.

"Elizabeth is exactly why you need to stay," Lada said, working her knife back and forth along the gash she was carving into the table.

"What do you mean?"

"Hungary is in turmoil. Ladislas will not live long, and Elizabeth knows you are a threat to her power. Matthias has a chance at the throne. Your son could be *king*." She paused, letting the word hang in the air between them. "He will never have a better chance at the throne. If you go to Constantinople, Elizabeth will maneuver him out of the castle. You *must* see how much your strength and reputation buoy his popularity. All your toil and blood will be wasted if you shed it for misplaced loyalty to the emperor of a dead land."

The lines in Hunyadi's face deepened. "But I go for Christianity."

"Serve Christianity here. Protect the borders. Keep Mehmed from pushing farther into Europe. He will not be satisfied with taking Constantinople. As soon as the city falls, his eyes will turn toward Hungary. You cannot leave it under a weak child king and his conniving mother." Lada paused, as though thinking. "Besides, you will not make a difference at the walls."

She knew that was false. If Mehmed was willing to trade troops for the promise that Hunyadi would stay out, he understood that Hunyadi's experience and reputation were both weapons that could tip the city out of Ottoman reach forever.

Hunyadi would absolutely make a difference to the defense of the city. And Lada could not let that happen.

"But the infidels—"

"If even the pope does not see this as a threat to Christianity, I hardly think you need worry about it. Cities fall. Borders change. God endures." Lada finally dared look at Hunyadi, and what she saw nearly destroyed her resolve.

He looked older than he had when he began speaking, and infinitely more tired. "I already told Emperor Constantine I would fight for him. He depends on my aid. Matthias can manage without me."

Lada saw her opening, and she struck deep. "Then you are no better than my father. He sold our future for his own selfish desires, just as you would sell Matthias's to satisfy your soldierly pride."

Hunyadi held his hands apart, palms up, and looked down at them. They were thick and callused hands, with knotted joints. Then he dropped them to his sides, his shoulders drooping. "You are right. It is selfish of me to seek glory elsewhere. My duty is here."

Lada wanted to embrace him. She wanted to offer him comfort. She wanted to confess that she cared nothing for Matthias or Constantinople, but that she did care for Hunyadi. And she had manipulated him anyway.

Instead, she let him walk away, alone. Then she drafted her letter to Mehmed. His ambassadors were leaving the next day and would carry it to him. They would deliver her betrayal— and her future—to Mehmed.

Wallachia was waiting.

17

Late March

THE NEXT DAY THEY passed Rumeli Hisari, Mehmed's new fortress. Radu strained his neck to see as much as he could from the road. The fortress loomed, three soaring towers watching over the Bosporus. Cyprian regarded it with sad, solemn eyes. Valentin spat in its direction. They paused as a series of stakes came into view. Lining the banks of the Bosporus, decapitated bodies stood sentry.

"What happened?" Nazira whispered.

Cyprian's gaze darkened. "Someone must have tried to get through the blockade. This is the sultan's warning that the strait is closed."

They rode on, silent and disturbed. Radu remembered all too well his first lesson in Mehmed's father's court. He and Lada had been forced to watch as the head gardener had impaled several men. It was the beginning of many such lessons in the absolute rule of law. Radu had been able to forget them—mostly—since being taken under Mehmed's wing. But apparently Mehmed had received the same tutelage.

It was not long before they saw the patrol riding from

Rumeli Hisari. One of the ironies of a secret mission was that Radu was as liable to be killed by his own side as he was the enemy.

Cyprian drew his sword.

"No," Radu said. "Let me talk to them. I think I can get us past."

He scanned the soldiers' faces desperately as they got closer, but he knew none of them. Radu sat as straight and commandingly on his horse as he could manage after three days on the road. They were not in open war with Constantinople yet. He could make this work.

He had to.

"Who is your commander?" he asked, his tone both lazy and imperious, as though he had nothing to fear and every right to make demands.

The men slowed, fanning out to surround the small group. Their horses trotted a slow circle around them. "What business do you have in the city?" asked a man in front. Missing teeth beneath his clean-shaven lip gave him a lisp. Under other circumstances, it might have struck Radu as funny. But the man had his sword drawn, which dampened any humor.

Radu lifted an eyebrow. "I bring a message to Constantine from our glorious sultan, the Hand of God on Earth, the Blessed Mehmed."

"What message?"

Radu curled his upper lip, channeling Lada. "I was not aware you had been made emperor of Constantinople."

The man jutted out his chin angrily. "How do I know you are telling the truth?"

"By all means, detain me and take the time to send word to

the sultan. I am sure he will look kindly on you interfering with his express wishes."

The soldier looked less sure of himself and pulled his horse back sharply. "Who are you, then? I will send a message that we have seen you."

"My name is Radu."

The man frowned, then a mean smile revealed all the gaps in his teeth again. "Radu the Handsome? I have heard of you."

Radu pretended he was not surprised by this unusual title. "Then you know you should get out of my way."

The man gestured to the other soldiers, and they moved to the side. The gap-toothed soldier spoke in a low, ugly tone as Radu rode past, "Are you sure you are not a gift for the emperor? Maybe he has a taste for pretty boys, too."

The soldiers laughed, the sound hitting Radu's back like blows. But he did not cringe and he did not turn around, riding straight and steady toward the city.

"Well done," Cyprian said, alongside him. "I thought we were all dead."

"There are some benefits to being notoriously handsome, after all," Nazira said. She tried to pass it off as a joke, but Radu heard the strain beneath her voice.

He was more troubled by the soldier's insinuation. How had he heard of Radu? And what did he mean, that the emperor might have a taste for beautiful boys, *too*? The implication was that Radu had been the beautiful pet of another man.

He could think of only one man this rumor might be directed at. He tried to shake the thought off, but it lay heavier across his back than his winter cloak.

"Look," Nazira said, pointing. "Ships." The road curved and a view of the Bosporus strait opened up. Seven large, beautiful ships were sailing at a brisk clip toward the twin fortresses. Radu wondered where they were going, and envied the sailors' obvious skill. He had not seen such masterful maneuvering among their own navy. It planted a seed of doubt deep inside.

Cyprian cried out. "No!"

"What? What has happened?" Radu whipped around, certain his lie had been revealed and the gap-toothed soldier was coming for them. But the road was empty. Cyprian looked out at the water.

"Those are Italian ships. They must have hundreds of men aboard. They flee the city." Cyprian's shoulders fell, his head hanging heavy. "They abandon us. News of war has outpaced us. Come. We must hurry to console my uncle."

They spurred their tired horses forward. The wall, so long at the forefront of Mehmed's mind, and therefore Radu's, was . . . anticlimactic. Miles and miles of stone, worn and patched with jumbles of mismatching rocks, cut through farmland. Radu could not fathom how anyone was able to man the wall. It was too long. But it was also too high—easily five times taller than him. Any advance could be seen and met. There was nowhere to hide, no point more vulnerable to attack than any other. And behind the outer wall was another one.

"Stop gaping so," Nazira said, elbowing him. "You look like a slack-jawed boy from the country." Her smile was a tight warning. He had been scanning the walls as an invader. He was fortunate Cyprian focused only on the path ahead.

Radu had waited so long to be here, but he had never anticipated being escorted through a gate with a salute from soldiers
posted there. Just like that, they were within the outer walls.
Radu risked one look back as the gate closed behind them. He
did not know when—or if—he would leave again.

He glanced at Nazira, who rode tall and proud on her horse,
a hopeful smile pasted onto her face. He copied her confidence.
Cyprian was far enough ahead that he dared speak. He leaned
closer to her. "How are you so good at this?"

She lifted a hand in the air, gesturing toward herself. "When
you spend your whole life learning how to show people only
what you want them to see so your truest self remains safe,
you become quite adept at it." She smiled sadly at Radu. "You
understand."

He nodded. She was right. He knew how to do this. It
would work. "I am glad to have you with me."

She laughed. "Of course you are. Now put on a sorrowful
but curious expression, and let us go see the city that is our
sultan's destiny."

Radu faced forward again as they drew closer to the smaller
wall that barred the way into the city. It felt like his whole life
had been leading him here. If this was not how he had expected
to enter, well, he would simply make the best of it. After all,
Constantinople was the greatest city in the world.

———◆———

Constantinople was not the greatest city in the world.

Compared with Edirne, it was a city of ruins. A city of
ghosts. More than half the narrow, crowding houses they passed

had an air of dereliction about them. Refuse filled the streets and pushed against foundations. Doors hung askew on some houses or were missing altogether from others. They passed entire blocks without seeing a soul. Unless scraggly stray cats and mean-looking mangy dogs had souls, in which case they passed many souls.

As Radu's group moved from the outskirts, things improved slightly. More of the homes appeared lived-in. A few stalls with vendors popped up here and there, the men halfheartedly soliciting them as they passed. Women hurried through the streets, dragging children and darting furtive glances at their mounted procession.

Radu had expected more soldiers patrolling, especially if word of war had already reached the city, but they had seen no one aside from the guards at the gates.

And he had seen nothing of the fabled wealth of Constantinople. He had always known, rationally, that the streets were not paved in gold, but he had expected something more. Even Tirgoviste had glittered brighter than this.

Finally they came to a quarter that showed more life. They pulled to an abrupt stop as a priest crossed their path, swinging a censer and trailing scented smoke in his wake. He sang hauntingly in Greek. Behind him was a parade of people. It took several minutes before the citizens, eerily silent save for the singing priest, finally passed and their way was clear again.

"What was that?" Radu asked.

"A procession." Cyprian looked troubled. "There is no small amount of internal strife. Most of it centers around Orthodoxy versus the Catholic Church. I will explain later. Come."

Bells tolled, their clanging echoing through the city. Cyprian looked up, then sighed. "I had forgotten the day. My uncle will be in the cathedral. We cannot speak with him there. Come, I will get you settled. I have a home near the palace."

"We cannot intrude," Nazira said. "Surely there is some-place else?"

Cyprian waved her worries away. "I have many bedrooms and only one me. We could all live there and never see one an-other. Much like this city, my home is in need of a much higher population."

Cyprian's house was not far. It was a handsome, well-maintained building. The houses in Constantinople practically shared walls, narrow gaps between them sometimes disappear-ing where the roofs met. He pulled out a key and opened the front door. They were greeted with a wall of frigid air.

"Valentin, go start the fires." The boy nodded and ran in-side. Cyprian frowned. "I have a maid. Where is that girl? The main room should have a fire going already. Maria? Maria!" There was no response. "Well, come in. It will warm up soon enough." He led them to a small sitting room, where Valentin had already succeeded in lighting a fire.

They heard footsteps on the stairs. "Maria?"

"Just me," Valentin called out. "No one else here."

Cyprian looked troubled. Nazira put a hand on his. "Your home is lovely. Thank you so much. I hope you know your kindness is not unappreciated."

"Of course!" Cyprian covered her hand with his other hand. "I am sorry. I have been so caught up in my own worries and fears, I have scarcely thought how you must be feeling. You have left your home, your country, all your possessions." He turned to Radu. "Both of you have."

Radu thought of what Lada might have said in response. "Edirne was my prison, not my home. Nazira's is the true sacrifice."

She nodded, looking down. "I will miss my garden. But I no longer recognize the landscape of the empire under this new sultan. And I do not think I belong there anymore." She stood straighter, brightening. "And I have my Radu."

Radu tried to imagine what Fatima must be doing right now, alone in the home that she shared with Nazira. How she must worry. If his separation from Mehmed was agony, how much worse to be separated from someone with whom you shared everything, including your heart?

He held out his arms. Nazira met him, resting her head against his chest. Cyprian watched them with the same look of longing Radu had seen before. Then he cleared his throat. "I will see to some food and send a message to the palace to find out when the emperor can meet with us."

He left them alone. Radu stroked Nazira's back one last time, and then they sat, side by side, staring into the fire.

"I like him," Nazira said, and it sounded like a eulogy.

"Me too," Radu echoed.

18

Late March

LADA'S MEN HAD NEARLY finished breaking camp when Hunyadi rode up. His horse pranced and shifted beneath him, picking up on his agitation.

"You have heard, then?" he asked Lada.

She paused in tightening her saddle straps. "Heard what?" she asked, careful not to reveal anything by her tone.

"Rumors of Ottoman troops massing in Belgrade, with designs on our Serbian border. You were right about Serbian loyalties. Housing the infidels in their own capital!"

Lada whipped around. How had Mehmed been this stupid? They were to meet in southern Transylvania. Surely he would not have come close to the Hungarian border. She had accepted that she needed Mehmed's help, but she would be damned if she let Hunyadi know what she had done.

"Are you certain?"

Hunyadi shook his head. "One report. And the scout saw nothing himself. But I cannot risk this. Not with Matthias so close to the throne. You were wise to counsel me to stay." He smiled at her, his eyes sad. "My duty is here. I cannot turn my back on Matthias for Constantinople. When will your men be ready to ride?"

Lada was seized with a sudden need to recheck every strap on her saddle. "You want us to ride into Serbia?"

"No. I want you in Transylvania. Protect the passes in case the Ottomans try to go through Transylvania and come into Hungary that way."

Hunyadi had aided her yet again, giving her the simplest way to disguise her true goals: Mehmed and Wallachia. She nodded. "We will go to Transylvania. But after, we are not coming back. We will continue on when the way is clear." She let her words imply that she would continue after the Ottomans were gone, though she meant she would continue once the Ottomans had cleared a way for her. "We go to Wallachia."

Hunyadi put out his hand to stop Lada's frantic tugging on an already-tight buckle. His voice was soft with concern. "What awaits you there?"

"I do not know what will happen. But I know that it is my country. I spent too many years in exile. I cannot continue to exile myself. We go back to whatever fate holds for us. Live or die, I want it to be on Wallachian ground."

"Give me more time. Let me secure our borders, address this rumor of a threat. Once Matthias is on the throne, we can help you."

Lada shook her head. Though a few weeks ago she would have clung to that offer, now she knew better. A promise of help that might never materialize was worth less than a sultan already waiting with troops. She had to do this. For Wallachia.

Her thoughts lingered on Mehmed. Her Mehmed, waiting for her. She pretended that was not a factor in her desperation to go, but her heart knew her to be a liar of the worst sort.

"*Wallachia,*" she whispered firmly to herself.

Before she could think better of it, she threw her arms around Hunyadi. "Thank you," she said, "for everything."

He patted her back. "Be careful, little dragon. You and I were made for battlefields, not royal courts. Do not start fights you have no weapons for."

He kissed her forehead, then got back on his horse. "May God be with you."

Lada smiled, and this time it was genuine. "God only sees me when I am in Wallachia."

Hunyadi laughed. "Give him my regards, then." He turned his horse and rode away, much slower than he had come. Lada watched him go, her smile disappearing. Her nurse, carrying their bedrolls, caught her eye and gave her a sharp nod.

It was time to go home.

19

Late March

CYPRIAN RETURNED, CARRYING A basket of bread and cheese and a skinny chicken with its neck already snapped. He motioned them to follow him into the kitchen. Radu and Nazira had been sitting in silence in front of the fire, both consumed with private strife. Radu had no doubt Nazira's revolved around thoughts of Fatima, but his was an endless cycle of worrying over what Mehmed was doing and how Radu could prove his worth to him.

Nazira gently edged Cyprian out of the way. "Show me where the dishes are and make a fire in the stove."

Cyprian nodded and gave her a tour of the kitchen. It appeared to be his first tour as well. "Oh, look! That is a lot of pots. Why do we need so many pots?"

Laughing, Nazira pointed at the table. "Go sit, you oaf. I can figure it out better on my own anyhow."

Cyprian did as he was told. "I solved the mystery of my missing maid. Apparently word of my death has spread far and wide. She considered it notice of termination of her employment, and fled not only my house but also the city. So many have. I hope she will be all right." He sighed, rubbing his face wearily. "I will try to find a replacement, but I do not think it will be easy."

"We can manage quite well," Nazira said. She smiled at Valentin, who had materialized and was helping stoke the fire in the stove. "Valentin is more than capable, and I am not unfamiliar with kitchens. I think we will do very nicely without extra bodies in the house." She caught Radu's eyes. She was right, of course. The fewer people watching them in close quarters, the better.

"Thank you," Cyprian said. His relief was visible, a relaxing of the tightness around his eyes and the strain in his shoulders.

There was a knock at the door. Valentin left and then returned, accompanied by a liveried servant wearing a vest with the double-headed eagle crest of the emperor. "The emperor wishes to see you immediately."

Radu stood. "I am at his disposal. We will go at once."

Radu and Cyprian fastened their cloaks as they stepped out into the chilly afternoon. The servant walked at a pace so brisk he was almost running.

"Is there anything I should know before I go in?" Radu asked, seized with nerves. This first meeting was the most important. If he could gain the emperor's trust now, he would be positioned perfectly. If he could not . . .

Well, that would be a much more unfortunate position.

Cyprian put a hand on Radu's shoulder. "You have nothing to fear."

Radu could not agree with that.

Constantine, just like the city he ruled, was not what Radu had expected. He was older, nearer to fifty than forty. His hair had thinned on top. In place of an elaborate crown, he wore a simple metal circlet on his head. Though every other man adhered to the fashion of layers, the emperor did not follow suit. His white shirt and purple breeches were simple, even austere. He seemed utterly devoid of pretense.

What a luxury honesty was.

Radu and Cyprian stood at the back of the crowded room. Constantine paced near the front, his tall, thin body leaning into the movement so that his head led the way with every step. With a start, Radu realized the emperor's feet were bare. He stifled a surprised laugh at the absurdity of the emperor of Rome walking around without even stockings.

"What of the Golden Horn and the seawall?" the emperor asked.

"We have nothing to fear there," a man said, waving dismissively. He was tall and broad, his body a blunt instrument of war. "A handful of poorly trained ships against my Italian sailors is nothing. We are perfectly safe on the seawall."

Radu saw his opportunity. Telling Constantine the truth, and about something easily confirmed, would solidify his status. Knowing what they faced would not magically replace the seven ships that had already fled, or line their walls with men that were not coming.

"You are not safe there," Radu said. Every face turned to him with curiosity. "When I left, Admiral Suleiman had six large galleys. Ten regular. Fifteen small. Seventy-five large rowboats for transporting men and navigating small spaces. Twenty horse transports."

The change in the air was palpable. "Who are you?" the Italian man demanded.

"Radu of——" Radu paused, again not knowing what name to give himself. "Radu most recently of Edirne, where I served at Mehmed's—the sultan's—side these last several years. Most particularly overseeing the secret development of his navy."

Cyprian put a hand on Radu's shoulder. "This is the man who saved my life, Uncle."

Constantine pointed at a man near the door. "Send word to the governor of Galata. Tell him we are drawing the chain across the horn to block all entry." No one moved. "Now!" he shouted.

The man stood, bowing, and ran from the room.

"Is that to be his main point of attack, then?" Constantine asked.

Radu shook his head. "He means to press you on all sides. If he can get through on the seaward side, he will. But his focus is the land walls."

"The walls will stand," a priest said. "They have always stood. They will always stand."

"They have always withstood attacks before, but attacks change," Radu said. "The sultan spares no expense on new methods and weapons. He has studied the walls, has even been here in person. He means to focus on the Lycus River Valley and the section outside the palace."

A man near the front frowned. He wore clothes closer in fashion to the Ottomans than to the Byzantines. "Those are obvious choices. We already know this."

"Orhan is right," the Italian man said. Radu startled, looking closer at the oddly dressed man who had just spoken. Orhan was the false heir to the Ottoman Empire—a man whom Constantinople had used to threaten Mehmed's rule since before it began. Even now, Mehmed had to send money periodically or else Constantine would send Orhan into the empire to stir up civil war.

Orhan had been and was an actual, active threat to Mehmed's life. Anger flared in Radu's heart. He wanted something to hurt these people, to make them feel the fear they should. "He has artillery."

"We have seen artillery!" a portly man shouted. "So he throws some stones. Our stones are bigger." Laughter echoed through the room. Encouraged, the man continued. "The Ottomans have never had stones as big as ours."

Radu offered a tight smile in response to the man's dirty bravado. "They have a cannon four times my height that can shoot a six-hundred-pound ball over a mile."

No one laughed at that, though several scoffed visibly. Constantine sighed. "We may as well bring in food. And I hope someone is writing all this down?" He gestured for Radu to take an empty seat nearby.

Radu sat. He was in, for good or ill.

Constantine looked at the ceiling as though an answer were there. "What if we relinquish Orhan's claim?"

Radu looked at the pretend heir. Orhan stared down at his hands, which were soft and pale. Not warrior's hands, like Constantine's or the Italian's. Orhan nodded.

Constantine reached out and squeezed the other man's shoulder. "We release any threat against Mehmed's legitimacy.

We graciously decline payment for the land the Rumeli Hisari is built on. We increase our payments to him."

Radu wondered if he should encourage that. Perhaps Mehmed would want it. But he would still attack. And everything here would be Mehmed's in the end, so it did not matter. Radu would tell the truth. "His mind is set on the city with a singular focus. He has spoken and dreamed of little else since he was twelve. I do not think anything will deter him now. You can offer, but short of surrender, you should prepare for siege." Radu dared to hope that after hearing his tales of men and cannons, they *would* surrender. He could deliver the city, unharmed, directly to Mehmed!

Constantine turned to the Italian, eyebrows raised expectantly. "Giustiniani?"

Giustiniani's Greek was heavily accented, but he spoke with a command and even a joviality that demanded confidence. "We are nearly settled, your grace. We stretched your purse as far as we could. All the food and water is stored. We have enough to last for a year, with minimal supplementation." He smiled bitterly. "There are advantages to so many leaving, after all."

Radu wilted inside. No easy surrender, then.

Giustiniani continued. "We may be outmatched in artillery, boats, and men—overwhelmingly outmatched in men—but rest assured, Constantinople is still the best-defended city in the world. It will not fall easily. Tell me, Radu: do you think we can outlast Mehmed?"

Radu weighed the truth. Surrender was not on their minds yet. And they were right to make an effort. Even speaking the words felt disloyal, but acknowledging reality would not change it. "If you can draw out the siege long enough, you have a chance. The Ottomans have come against Constantinople before, and they have always failed. They are superstitious; they will see portents of doom in any delay or failed initiative. Mehmed will be fighting time and morale. He is better prepared than anyone who has ever come before, but he is betting his throne and his legacy on this single assault. If you can outlast him, he will never be able to amass the support to make another attempt."

"So if we do this, the city is safe from him."

Radu nodded. "I do not doubt that if Mehmed fails at the wall, he will not live long afterward. There are too many powerful men who do not like him." The thought terrified Radu. Halil Vizier was still with Mehmed, working against him at every possible turn. How could Radu protect Mehmed from here?

Constantine stared blankly at the floor, his expression far away. "All we have to do is outlast him, then."

It was as simple and as impossible as that.

20

Late March

"WHERE ARE YOU GOING?" Bogdan asked.

Lada whipped around, knives in her hands. Taking a deep breath, she put them away. It was near midnight. She had thought her furtive exit from camp would go unmarked. She should have known Bogdan would mark it, as he did all her movements. He had a way of tracking her, watching her without watching. His childhood loyalty had grown as broad and strong as he had. Usually Lada found comfort in that. But lately it felt far more serious, like he was not only looking for her but also looking for something *from* her.

She had been deliberately vague about their purpose on the shared border of Hungary, Transylvania, and Wallachia. None of her men had questioned her disobeying Hunyadi's directive and leaving the Transylvanian passes they were supposed to guard.

Lada did not know how her men would feel about taking up with the Ottomans yet again. Some harbored less ill will toward their onetime captors and benefactors; others hated them. Doubtless some would prefer to fight for Constantinople than at the sides of Ottomans. But she was their leader. They joined her to take back Wallachia, and she did not need permission to make decisions. If they did not like it, they were welcome to make their own way.

Her way was forward, to the throne, however she got there.

"You are supposed to be patrolling on the other end of camp," she snapped.

Though she could not see his face, she could practically feel Bogdan's blunt smile. "You did not answer my question."

"Because I do not have to. I am leaving. I will be back. That is everything you need to know."

"Something is wrong."

"Nothing is wrong!" All day she had been on edge, knowing how close Mehmed was. She was not certain of the precise location of his camp, but she knew it was within a few miles of where she stood now. Mehmed was within a few miles, not separated by rivers and countries and the year that had come between them. She thought she had hidden her agitation well, but apparently not.

"I will go with you."

"No!" Not Bogdan. Anyone but Bogdan. Lada could not face him if he found out what she was doing. Admitting it felt like asking permission, and she refused to do that. Besides, she remembered Bogdan's thinly veiled distaste for Mehmed. She did not want to bring that along with her. "I must go alone."

"Why?"

"Get back to your patrol."

Bogdan stood, unmoving, for five eternally long breaths. Then he walked off into the night.

Lada hurried through the dark, knives back in both hands. She had a lot of ground to cover. It would have been easier on a horse, but that would have drawn even more attention to her departure. Still, after an hour crisscrossing through the terrain, looking for signs of a camp, Lada found herself slowing down. She wished she could enjoy walking alone—solitude was not a luxury she had much of lately—but she knew what awaited her.

Who awaited her.

And she did not know how to feel about seeing him again after so long apart. She had not been able to sort through her feelings, to separate what was real and what was merely a re-action to the circumstances of her childhood. What if she saw Mehmed and felt nothing? Worse, what if she saw Mehmed and felt everything as acutely as she had when they were together? It had been a hard thing, leaving him. Would this reopen the wound?

Before she could settle her emotions, she saw the familiar white cap of a Janissary. It glowed in the moonlight. Annoyance flickered through Lada. They should know better than to wear those white caps at night. If she were an assassin, this sentry would already be dead.

A slow, vicious smile spread across her face. She had planned on walking into the camp and announcing herself. She was not expected tonight—Mehmed had merely said where they would be. There had been no specific time to meet established.

It was a night to play "Kill the Sultan."

She generously decided not to hurt any sentries. They would

probably be punished for their failure to detect her, but they deserved that. The first was easily skirted. The second and third announced their approach with a cacophony of snapping twigs. Closer to camp, the going was more difficult. The tents were packed close, and under cover of trees. Between the trees and the darkness, Lada could not get a sense for how many men Mehmed had brought. It did not seem like enough. He probably had them spread out, though. That was what she would have done.

She pressed into the deeper darkness behind a tent as two Janissaries walked by, talking in quiet voices. She had an odd stirring of something that felt like nostalgia at hearing Turkish again. Scowling, she gripped her knives harder.

Mehmed's tent might as well have had his name painted on it. It was the largest, made of sumptuous cloth in what she assumed would be red and gold in the sunlight. That was another mistake. If she were in charge, he would be sleeping in one of the small, anonymous tents. Make an assassin look through every tent, rather than boldly advertising the target.

He really did make this too easy.

Lada peered around the edge of a soldier's tent from which gentle snores emanated. The entrance to Mehmed's grand tent was manned by two Janissaries, both awake and alert. Lada slipped around to the back of the tent, which was guarded only by her friend darkness.

She darted forward, not hesitating as she stabbed a knife into the tent and dragged it down. With only the barest whisper of material, she had her own private entrance.

Inside, it was dim, a coal brazier in the corner giving only a faint glow. Lada wondered who had to carry the furniture

Mehmed traveled with: a desk, a stool, a full table, an assortment of pillows, and a bed. No bedrolls for the sultan, whose body was too precious for the ground.

And whose body was in that bed, breathing softly.

Lada crept forward with her knife raised. And then she stopped, looking down at Mehmed.

She had forgotten the thick sweep of his black lashes. His full lips were turned down at the corners, as though his dreams troubled him. His hair, so often covered by turbans the past few years, was draped on his pillow, one strand lying across his forehead. Lada was filled with a sudden tenderness. She reached out and brushed the hair from his skin.

He awoke with a start, grabbing her wrist. His eyes were wide, body tensed for a fight. Lada leaned closer. She had never seen this ferocity in his face. She wanted to taste it.

Mehmed kept his painful grip on her wrist. "Lada?" he asked, blinking rapidly.

"I have just killed you. Again."

He pulled her down, meeting her lips with desperate hunger. She dropped the knife. She had forgotten what it was to be kissed, to be desired. She had thought she did not need it.

She had been wrong.

Mehmed moved from her lips to her neck, his hands in her hair. "When you left, you took my heart with you. Kill me, Lada," he said, with so much longing she could not keep her own hands off him. He rolled so she was beneath him. His hands explored her body, alternating between rough greediness and softness so gentle it nearly hurt her.

He put his mouth against her ear. "I have learned some things," he said, voice teasing, "about pleasure."

Before she could wonder where he had learned those things—things she had accused him of not caring about aside from his own satisfaction—he moved down her body. Her back arched as his hands slid under her tunic and up her torso. She grabbed his hair, not knowing whether she wanted to pull him away or draw him closer. She feared if he continued, she would lose control. She had never let herself lose control before.

His hands found the space between her legs and she cried out with the shock and intensity of it. He responded with greater eagerness, kissing her stomach, her breasts. He pulled her tunic up higher, and, impatient with his clumsiness, she tugged it off herself. They had done this much before, but absence had made every sensation stronger. This was where she had always stopped him, where she had always drawn the line so that she stayed in charge of what they did. So that she remained hers, and hers alone.

She did not stop him.

He pulled off his own nightshirt. He wore nothing underneath.

He unlaced her trousers and pulled them off. She thought he would try to put himself inside her, and thought—maybe—she wanted him to.

Instead, he lifted her legs and kissed her, and kissed her, and kissed her where she had never imagined being kissed. Lada's control fled on the wave of pleasure, and she did not miss it. She cried out like a wounded thing, but Mehmed put a hand over her mouth as he shifted on top of her.

She let him.

21

Late March

"HOW MANY ANGELS CAN dance on the head of a pin?" a man shouted, a sneer deforming his pockmarked face.

Another man jabbed his finger into the first man's chest, screaming something about the Father and the Son. The pockmarked man threw a punch, and then they were wrestling on the muddy street, biting and kicking.

Cyprian did not even pause as he steered Radu around them. "People here are very . . . religious?"

Cyprian laughed darkly. "To all our downfall. There she is." He pointed. With nothing else to do for the day, Radu had asked to see more of the city. He wanted to see the fabled Hagia Sophia cathedral in particular. Mehmed had told him to visit. It had been his only actual instruction. And until Constantine called for him again, there was not much he could do besides wander with his eyes and ears open.

The street led to a courtyard, where the massive cathedral loomed. It was darker than Cyprian's laugh. Everywhere they had passed churches with bells ringing, a near-constant stream of people going in and out. But the Hagia Sophia, the jewel of Constantinople, the church so magnificent that stories said it had converted the entire population of Russia to Orthodoxy, sat cold and empty in the late-afternoon rain.

"Why is no one here?" Radu asked. They walked up to the gate, and Cyprian pushed experimentally against the door. It was locked.

"We had Mass in Latin here a few weeks ago."

Radu knew that Orthodox services were conducted in Greek, but he did not follow Cyprian's meaning.

A dog ran past them, followed by a young boy with bare feet. "Rum Papa!" he shouted. "Stop, Rum Papa! Come back right now!"

"Did that boy call his dog the Roman pope?"

Cyprian rapped his knuckles against the beautiful lacquered wood of the Hagia Sophia door. "Yes. Half the dogs in the city are called that. While my uncle appeals to the pope for help, people curse his name. My uncle pushed for union between the two churches, and even held Mass here to celebrate the official reunion, the ending of the schism between East and West. And now the most beautiful church in Christendom is silent and abandoned because it was tainted by watered wine, Catholic wafers, and worship in Latin." Cyprian sighed, resting the palm of his hand reverently against the door. "And for all her sacrifice, the Hagia Sophia brought us nothing. The pope sends no aid." He shook his head. "Come. We can see some relics. That is always fun."

"You and I have different opinions of fun."

Cyprian laughed, this time a bright sound at odds with the

dreary, wet day. "We take our relics very seriously in this city. They protect us." He winked.

"Do you really believe that?"

"Does it matter? If the people believe it, then it gives them strength, which gives the city strength, which means the relics worked."

"That is very circular."

"We Byzantines love circles. Time, the moon, arguments, and, most of all, coins. All good things are circular."

They passed another empty section of the city. As they walked, Cyprian cheerfully gave the history of this pillar or that crumbling foundation. The whole city was steeped in heritage, and falling down around them.

They were almost to another church when the ground rumbled beneath their feet. Radu stumbled, and Cyprian caught him. A sliding noise came from above. "Run!" Cyprian shouted, tugging Radu away from the walls of a house next to them. Slate crashed down with shattering force where they had just been standing. The two men dove onto the muddy street.

Radu breathed heavily, his arms tangled up in Cyprian's. Cyprian's eyes met his own, black pupils nearly swallowing the gray. Then he shook his head and stood. They brushed as much of the mud from their clothes as they could, but it was a lost cause.

"Thank you," Radu said. "Your quick instincts saved us both."

Cyprian smiled shyly, reaching out to flick away some mud on Radu's shoulder. "Consider it partial payment against the debt I owe you."

Guilt seeped the color from the world. Radu swallowed,

turning away. "Does that happen often? The earth shaking like that?"

"More and more lately. We have also had unseasonable storms, and a miserable winter and a torturous spring. You can imagine how much that boosts the morale of people looking for signs and portents in everything around them."

They heard someone shouting up ahead. Radu wondered if it was another fight, but the cadence suggested a performance. They made their way toward the voice, crossing a couple of streets until they found a crowd gathered around a man standing on the wall outside a shrine.

"Wretched Romans, how you have been led astray! You have trusted in the power of the Franks, rather than the hope in your God. You have lost the true religion, and our city will be destroyed for your sins!" The man, who wore rough-woven brown robes, lifted his arms to the cloud-laden skies and tipped his head back. "O Lord, be merciful to me. I am pure and innocent of blame for the corruption of this city." He snapped his head upright to stare down at the crowd and swept a hand over their heads. "Be aware, miserable citizens, of what you have done by betraying your faith in God for the promises of the pope. You have denied the true faith given to you by your fathers. You have accepted the slavery of heresy. In doing so, you have confessed all your sins to God. Woe to you when you are judged!"

Women cried out, beating at their chests. Men held children up, begging for blessings. Vicious, ugly shouts against Constantine, the pope, and all of Italy tore through the air.

Cyprian made a rude gesture, then took Radu's arm and pulled him away. "That fool hates the pope more than he hates the sultan. He would love nothing more than to see the city burn, welcoming hell with open arms as proof that he was right all along."

"How can they hate Constantine for doing whatever he must to protect them?"

Cyprian rubbed his face wearily, then looked down at his still-muddy hands. "This is Constantinople. We are more concerned with the purity of our souls than the survival of our bodies. Come. There is nothing left worth seeing here."

———•———

After they had washed, and eaten dinner with Nazira, Cyprian excused himself to attend to his uncle. Constantine's main duties seemed to be an endless campaign of letter writing, his weapon the pen, his ammunition empty promises and desperate pleading. Radu wished that Cyprian had invited him to come along.

"Patience," Nazira reminded him, squeezing his shoulder as he cleaned the dishes. "You will find ways to help. The best thing we can do now is become a part of the city."

Radu turned to see her wearing clothes in the style of the women in Constantinople: a stiff and structured bodice, with tight sleeves and excessive skirts. He raised his eyebrows. Twirling in a circle, she smirked. "Do you like it? I feel like a flower in the wrong petals."

"You always look lovely. Are you going somewhere?"

"Oh, yes. I met the wife of one of Emperor Constantine's advisors today in the market. She felt very sorry for me when I confessed I did not know how to cook with the food here. I am invited to supper with her."

"But we just had supper—and it was very good."

Nazira's smirk grew. "But she does not know that. And at this supper, I will meet all the other wives of important men, and they will gossip about all the mistresses of the important men, and in such a way I will soon have a larger net than you."

"I did not realize it was a competition."

Nazira laughed, rising up on her toes to kiss Radu on both cheeks. "It is. It is a competition to see who can find out the most the fastest so that we can go home."

She said it lightly, but Radu could hear the longing in her voice. Nazira never spoke of Fatima, and he was too ashamed of having separated them to bring her up. But if he missed his aching, one-sided relationship with Mehmed every day, how much more must she miss the woman who loved her back?

"I would place all my bets on you and your gossip, then. You are a terrifying creature."

Curtsying prettily, Nazira left. Radu was restless and itchy with anticipation. Alone for the first time since he had come to the city, he slipped out of Cyprian's home and into the evening-dark streets. He drew his cloak close against the bite of the cold drifting up from the stones beneath his feet.

Terrifying thoughts nipped at his heels. Nazira already had plans in motion. All Radu had was one meeting with Constantine in which he had merely told the truth. The fear he had been avoiding wrapped itself around him even tighter than his cloak.

He had no idea what he was doing.

This whole thing had been a mistake. Even if he got crucial information, pulled from Cyprian or Constantine, he had no way of communicating it to Mehmed. They had no code, no ways of trading messages. Unless Radu found some brilliant form of sabotage within the city, his being here as a spy was almost pointless. He did not want to fail Mehmed, but he could not shake the worry that Mehmed had failed him. Why had he sent Radu here with so little instruction, so little preparation? Radu would have been much better used at his side.

Or maybe that was simply what Radu was desperate to believe, because Mehmed's side was the only place he wanted to be. Was he really so expendable?

Or ... had Mehmed suspected Radu's true feelings, and deliberately sent him far away? Radu knew he should not feel the way he did about another man. There were many things that could be justified. But he did not know of anything that allowed for what he wanted from Mehmed.

Would this love separate him both from the most important person in his life and from the God that brought him solace in his loneliness?

He had meant to wander and get a better idea of the lay of the city, but he found himself back at the dark Hagia Sophia. Even now, he followed Mehmed's requests without conscious thought.

No one was in the streets. Radu removed some tools from a secret pocket in his vest and carefully picked the lock. After a few patient minutes, he was rewarded with a click. He slipped inside. It took his eyes some time to adjust to the darkness. He jumped at a rustling noise, fearing discovery, but it was the clacking of pigeon wings. They, too, had come to the empty church to worship.

Releasing all his exhaustion and fear with a long exhalation, he prayed. He had not been able to fully pray since arriving in Constantinople. Going through the movements was more comforting than slipping into a warm bath, and equally cleansing. He released everything he had been holding. His focus was singular, his faith a bright point in the dark building.

Reluctant to leave when he was done, he climbed the stairs to the gallery where the women would stand during services. Eventually, he found a small door that led to another flight of stairs, and then to a ladder. Pushing against the trapdoor at the top, he emerged onto the roof. Constantinople unfolded beneath him. He could see the palace, a hulking structure where Constantine worked into the night.

It would be enough to be here, waiting. He would get close to Constantine, and trust that a way to help Mehmed would reveal itself. He would trust that Mehmed had a plan for him. He would trust that God would help him in this mission.

Radu tried to draw that trust closer than the fear. Looking out over the city, he wondered at each of the lights. Who lived there? What were they thinking? Were they, too, praying for peace? For direction? For protection?

And whose god was listening?

He sat on the edge of the roof, his feet dangling in the void beneath him. It echoed the one that had opened up inside him. He felt close to falling—or to flying. He did not know which it would be, but had no doubt time would tell.

22

Early April

MEHMED LAY WITH AN ease so complete he seemed like a different person. Lada wondered . . . No, she would wonder nothing. Think about nothing. If he could exist in this space like he needed nothing more in the whole world than what he had just had, she could do the same.

That lasted about two minutes. She squirmed, pushing him away from her. "Do you always sweat this much?"

He laughed, pulling her close and nuzzling his face against her neck. His hand found somewhere else. "Would you like me to make you sweat more?"

She shrieked, half from delight, half from the shock of his wandering fingers, and pushed him. Before she could realize her mistake in making so much noise, the tent's front flap opened and two Janissaries rushed in. Mehmed shifted so that Lada was hidden behind him.

"Leave," Mehmed said, his voice coldly imperious and so different from the one he had been using moments before.

"We heard—"

"Leave."

The Janissaries bowed. One paused. "Your grace, we have reports of a skirmish, with Hunyadi, on the Serbian-Hungarian border."

"Reports that can wait until the morning! Do not come back in here for any reason."

The Janissaries nearly fell over as they bowed low and backed out in a rush.

Lada propped herself up on an elbow and drew the blanket up over her bare chest. "You do have troops there, then?"

Mehmed tried to pull her back down. "You are letting all the cold air in."

She scooted farther away. "Why do you have men on the Hungarian border?"

There was a studied casualness to Mehmed's voice that made the hairs on the back of Lada's neck rise. "As a reminder to Hunyadi that he is still needed in Hungary."

"But I persuaded Hunyadi to stay out of Constantinople. I told you I had. Do you not trust me?"

"Of course I trust you! But I cannot risk anything. It was extra assurance, is all."

It made sense, Lada supposed. But the fact that he felt he had to double up on work she had already done bothered her. And she worried for Hunyadi's safety. He was one of the few people in the world she considered family.

Family. Lada had not even thought to ask about Radu yet. "Where is Radu? Did he come?" He had not come with the ambassadors, but where Mehmed was, Radu would be, too.

Mehmed stopped trying to coax her back down. He flopped

flat onto his back, raising an arm over his face as though tired. "No, Radu did not come."

"He did not come," she repeated, her voice flat with disappointment and shock. She needed her brother. He had a way with people like the boyars. Hunyadi had been right—she did not have the weapons for that kind of combat. Radu did. How dare he reject her again. "Did he say why?"

Mehmed shook his head.

"Where is he now?" What was important enough to keep him away from both Lada and Mehmed?

Mehmed shrugged. He was avoiding answering her. She grabbed the arm that covered his face and pulled it down so he could not hide his expression from her. "Where is my brother, Mehmed?"

He looked at the ceiling of the tent. "Constantinople."

"The siege has already started?" The siege had started, and Mehmed was here. With her. She was warm with pleasure over finally outranking that stupid city.

"No."

Her pleasure fled, leaving her cold. "Then what is he doing in Constantinople? Did you make him an ambassador? You know how dangerous that is!"

"I needed someone there, inside."

Lada sat up, the blankets dropping. He had not answered her question about Radu being an ambassador. He had dodged it with something that sounded like an answer, but obviously was not. Not an ambassador, then. "You sent him as a *spy!*"

"I needed someone I could trust absolutely."

"I do not care what you needed! He was supposed to be

here, with me! Or at the very least at your side during the siege, where he would no doubt be perfectly safe."

Mehmed sat up, too, eyes flashing dangerously. "What do you mean by that?"

"I mean that wherever you are during the siege will be the safest place in the world. Which is where my brother should be as well! How could you throw him into so much danger?"

"It was the best choice."

"For him, or for you?"

"For the empire."

"Oh, for the empire! Well, that makes everything better." Lada threw back the blankets and got out of bed. She began tugging her discarded clothes on.

"Radu will be fine. He is smarter and stronger than you have ever given him credit for," Mehmed said.

Lada jabbed a finger against his bare chest. "Do not dare tell me you know my brother better than I do."

Mehmed laughed. "But I do."

Words she knew she would always regret saying halted on the tip of her tongue. If Mehmed did not know how Radu felt about him, he would not learn of it from her. "You ask too much of him."

"I ask only what he is willing to do. Nothing more."

"Then I do know him better, you fool. Radu would do *anything* for you."

Mehmed looked away, a dark flush spreading across his cheeks.

"You know . . ." Lada's eyes narrowed to thin slits, her fists clenched so tightly they ached. "You know that he is in love with you."

Mehmed tilted his head to the side, as though brushing something off his shoulder. "Your brother is very important to me."

"But he will never be as important to you as you are to him. Mehmed, release him. You must release him from this false hope he carries."

He shook his head. "I cannot. I care for Radu. And I need him."

"But you will never love him the way he loves you."

Mehmed stood, reaching for Lada's fisted hands. "How could I? I love you."

Lada closed her eyes against the way his words struck her. Radu felt like a ghost in the room, looming in the whisper of a breeze against the back of her neck. She had what he wanted, and she did not even know what to do with it.

"Bring him back. He could die."

Mehmed released her hands. "I have no one else better suited to the task. It is a risk, yes. But it is an acceptable risk. He knows the dangers, and he agreed. He cares as much as I do about Constantinople."

Lada let out a harsh bark of laughter. "No one cares about anything so much as you do that accursed city."

"You care about Wallachia that much."

"Because it is mine! What claim do you have to Constantinople that justifies risking Radu's life?"

Mehmed shook his head. He sat on the edge of the bed, shoulders curved inward as he ran his fingers through his hair. "I promise Radu will come out unharmed. And then we will all be together."

"You cannot promise that. And how will we be together? He will always choose your side over mine."

"Not if my side is your side as well." He smiled up at her, exhaustion pooling in the hollows beneath his eyes. "I cannot do this alone. You were right to leave before. I did not know your value, and I would have left you behind. But I know now." His smile turned tender. "And you know now, too. I need you with me. I *want* you with me. Stand by my side at the walls. Help me claim my destiny. And then ... rule it. With me. As empress of Rome."

Lada took a small step back, overwhelmed. "Empress."

Still naked, Mehmed stood before her, completely open and vulnerable, with his hands out, palms up. "Take the city with me. Take the crown. Take *me*, Lada."

A memory long since forgotten played out in front of her. Huma, Mehmed's terrifying mother, telling her the story of Theodora. The actress, the prostitute, the powerless woman who found the love of the emperor and rose to be emperor with him. Saving him and the city, changing everything to her vision of how it should be based only on her strength.

And the strength of the man who loved her.

Could Lada be that woman?

But Mehmed had not said *emperor*. He had said *empress*. Emperor consort. She would still owe her power and her position to a man. And she was no lowly prostitute, no actress. She already had a birthright of her own.

"What about Wallachia?"

"Forget about Wallachia! Why be vaivode of a worthless country when you can be empress of the greatest empire in the world?"

She stepped back from him. "Because if I do not lead Wallachia, no one will."

Mehmed brushed a hand through the air. "We will make certain Wallachia is always taken care of."

Lada shook her head slowly. The offer was tempting. But she was so close to Wallachia. She could feel it nearby, just as she had Mehmed. She could not turn her back on her country now. "Where are the troops? I can—we can discuss this after. When I have Wallachia secured, and you have Constantinople, then . . . then, I do not know. Maybe there will be a way for us. After we have accomplished what we need to."

Hurt reshaped Mehmed's face into something younger, softer. "Is that the only reason you came?"

"Of course it is!" Lada snapped.

His vulnerability was replaced with cold, stony features and imperious brows. He grabbed his nightshirt and pulled it over his head. "There are no troops."

"What do you mean?"

"I need every man I have. I cannot spare them to destabilize a country I already control. I have a treaty with the Danesti prince."

Lada staggered back. "But you could spare men to harass Hunyadi. You did not need to do that. You could have trusted me and given me those forces instead. Were there ever any troops? Did you ever mean to help me?"

"I *am* helping you! You are destined for bigger things! With me." He stepped toward her and she put her hands up.

"You did not write me. Not once, not until after I wrote Radu about having Hunyadi's trust. You saw an opportunity, and you used me. I betrayed Hunyadi for you." In all her life, Lada had never felt as small and miserable as she did then. She had sold Hunyadi's kindness for nothing. All her justifications and rationalizing amounted to nothing. She was no closer to Wallachia in spite of all her sacrifices. "You tricked me."

"I did you a favor! Even if I sent you the troops, even if you took the throne, you could never keep it. They would never follow a woman as prince. Abandon this delusion, Lada. It will destroy you. Come with me. Fight at my side. I trust only you with my life." He pointed at the slit in the tent wall. "I could die without you."

Lada raised an eyebrow. "I suppose that is an acceptable risk."

Mehmed threw his hands in the air and started pacing. "I am offering you so much more. I am offering you the world. I am offering you myself." He pointed angrily at the bed. "You were happy enough to accept it a few minutes ago."

"That was different! You promised me soldiers."

Disgust squeezed his words. "Was this merely a transaction for you?"

Lada slammed her fist into his stomach. He doubled over, and she spoke right into his ear. "Do not *ever* talk to me that way." But his words had struck too close to home. Angry tears filled her eyes. She had not sold her body to him, and she hated him for thinking she had used it to manipulate him. But she *had* sold her determination to gain the throne on her own, as well as her relationship with Hunyadi. All for the false promise of a few hundred men.

Mehmed caught her hand and pressed it against his cheek. "Whatever else you believe, know that what I did, I did out of love. I love you. I have always loved you. Will you still choose Wallachia?"

Lada yanked her hand away and retrieved her knife from

the floor. "You betray my brother with your feigned ignorance of his feelings. You betrayed me. But I will never betray Wallachia." She lifted the knife, pointing it at him. "If you set foot on Wallachian soil again—*my* soil—I will kill you."

Ignoring Mehmed as he shouted her name, she left the tent through the same cut she had entered it. This time it seemed much deeper.

23

Early April

IN THE CLAMMY MORNING fog, Radu sweated. He leaned against the stone steps for a few breaths, then continued climbing. The awkward shape of the tombstone chunk he held made his fingers cramp. When he finally reached the top of the wall, he staggered to the mound of stones and added his own.

"Funny, using tombstones of the dead to repair the walls."

Radu looked up into the well-worn but cheerful face of Giovanni Giustiniani, the Italian man from his first, and so far only, meeting with Constantine. Giustiniani was tall, broad-shouldered, even powerful in the way he moved. A deep line between his brows made them look set in a permanent scowl, but all his other wrinkles told of smiling and laughter.

Radu wiped his forehead with the back of his arm and straightened. He was only a couple of inches taller than the older man. "Well, it is the least those citizens could contribute to the city's defense."

Giustiniani laughed, a sound like a cannon shot. He clapped

a hand on Radu's shoulder. "I remember you. You brought us news of the infidels' preparations."

Radu nodded. It was always jarring to hear the Ottomans referred to as the infidels, since that was what they called the Christians. "I wish I had come armed with better tidings."

"All information, good or bad, helps us." Giustiniani sighed and turned toward a group of men shouting at each other. "The dead contributing their tombstones may yet do more than the living who cannot stop fighting with each other." He strode away, toward the fight.

Radu leaned over the edge of the wall and looked out onto the plain beneath. It had been cleared of anything that could hide the Ottoman forces. In front of them was a fosse, a large, deep ditch meant to slow down attackers and make them easy to pick off. Constantinople's defenses of a fosse, the outer wall where Radu stood, and an inner wall had repelled all attackers for more than a thousand years.

But none of those attackers had been Mehmed.

"Radu!" The voice triggered a wave of happiness even before Radu realized who had called to him.

Radu turned to find Cyprian walking next to the emperor. Radu bowed deeply, trying to look surprised, as though he had not overheard Cyprian saying that he would be touring the walls with Constantine today, as though Radu had not deliberately stationed himself at one of the weakest points of the wall, knowing that the two men would end up here sooner rather than later. Cyprian had been so busy that he and Radu barely saw each other, even living in the same house.

But going out of his way to run into the other man was

tactical. It was not because he was lonely for conversation with anyone outside of the bedroom he shared with Nazira. She, too, was frequently gone, making social calls and leaving Radu with far too much time to think.

"Have you seen Giustiniani?" Cyprian asked.

"You only now missed him. There was a fight, and he went to see about it."

Constantine leaned out over the wall, itching at his beard. "If the Italians send us nothing else but Giustiniani, they have still done more to help than anyone. I cannot keep the Genoese from fighting with the Venetians, who fight with the Greeks, who suspect the Genoese, who hate the Orthodox, who hate the Catholics. Only the Turks under Orhan seem to get along with everyone." He smiled wryly at Radu.

"Orhan is still here?" Radu was surprised that he had not fled the city in advance of the siege.

"He has nowhere else to go. And I am glad for his help, and the help of his men. He is no Giustiniani, but no one is. Except perhaps Hunyadi."

Radu was eager to contribute to a topic he knew something about. "I had never heard of Giustiniani before, but if he is anything like Hunyadi, the Ottomans will fear and hate him."

"They fear Hunyadi that much?"

"He is a specter that haunts them. Even their victories against him count for little when stacked against how much he has cost them. His name alone would cause problems for Mehmed."

Constantine nodded thoughtfully. "He should have been here by now. I am afraid we have lost him."

"But you have more Venetians?" Radu hoped it sounded like he was trying to be positive rather than fishing for more information.

"Only a handful. We hope more are coming. Galata, our neighbor, will send no men. They are too afraid of being caught in the conflict. They are everyone's allies, and thus no one's. It was all we could do to make them attach the boom across the horn."

The giant chain that closed access to the Golden Horn bay was strung from Constantinople to Galata. Sitting along the swift water leading to the horn, Galata lacked Constantinople's natural defenses. If Mehmed attacked the city, it would fall. But he did not want to waste resources on Galata. If he took Constantinople, Galata would effectively be his.

During the day, people walked freely between the cities, but at night both closed and locked their gates. Radu wished everyone in Constantinople would walk across the bay to Galata and stay there. He did not understand why they stayed in Constantinople. When Mehmed arrived, Radu hoped they would finally see the futility.

"There," Constantine said, pointing. Cyprian was taking detailed notes. Radu moved closer, following the direction of Constantine's finger. "We need as many men as can be spared on the Lycus River section."

Though Constantinople was on a hill, there was one section of the wall that did not command high ground. The Lycus River cut straight through it, making a fosse impossible to dig, and lowering that section to a dangerously accessible level. Radu knew all this from Mehmed's maps, but it was still a strange thrill to see it in person, and from this side of the wall, too, where he had not expected to be until after the siege.

Constantine detailed which men and commanders should be stationed where. Radu committed it to memory, secreting it away with all the other information he heard. Everywhere they went, Constantine stood straight and confident, complimenting the men on the work in progress, giving suggestions for further improvements. He may have been jeered in the streets, but among the soldiers it was apparent that he was deeply respected—and returned the respect.

"Here," he said, stopping again. They had come to a patch-work section. Where the other walls were shining limestone with a red seam of brick running through, this one had a haphazard look to it. And, unlike the rest, there was only one wall, rather than two. It jutted out at a right angle, the palace where Constantine lived rising behind it.

"Why is this section so different?" Radu asked, though he knew the answer.

"We could not leave a shrine outside the walls." Constantine's tone hinted at annoyance, but his confident smile never left. "We are better protected by one wall and a holy shrine than by two walls without one. Or at least, that was the reasoning a few hundred years ago when they built the wall out to encompass the shrine."

Constantine noted several weakened and crumbling points as he talked with a foreman directing repairs. Finally, the three men descended the stairs and went back into the city through a sally port, a heavily guarded gate used to let soldiers in and out during attacks. "Tell me, Radu, what do you think of my walls?" Constantine asked.

"I think they deserve their tremendous reputation. They have stood for this long for a reason."

Constantine nodded thoughtfully. "They will protect us yet."

They had lasted a thousand years of unchanging siege warfare. But Mehmed was not the past. Mehmed was the future. He brought things no one else had yet imagined, and that no walls had yet seen.

Constantine spoke again, his thoughts apparently on the same man as Radu's. "I hear the sultan is repairing roads and bridges all over my lands. It is very generous of him to perform maintenance while I am busy. Do you think he would spare some of his men to help us repair the walls while he is at it?"

Radu laughed weakly. "I am afraid I am no longer in the position to make that request."

Constantine's face turned serious so quickly that Radu feared he had betrayed something. The emperor's hand came down on his shoulder, but instead of a blow, it was a reassuring weight. "I know why you fled. Everyone has heard of his depravity, his harems of both women and men. You are safe here, Radu. You never have to go back to that life."

Several moments passed while Radu worked through Constantine's words and tone. He looked at Cyprian, who was staring determinedly up at the palace. And then everything made sense. The sneering guard they had passed at the Rumeli Hisari. Everyone's willingness to accept that Radu would so easily turn from Mehmed. Eyes filled with scorn or with pity.

"I— Yes, thank you. I have to— Excuse me." Radu turned and walked stiffly away. When he had rounded a corner and was out of sight, he sank against the wall, pushing a fist into his mouth in horror.

Was that the rumor, then? That Mehmed had a male harem? And that Radu had been the jewel of it? *Radu the Handsome.* Someone else had called him that recently, before the soldier. Halil Vizier, back in Edirne. Was he the source? Was this another tactic of his to demean Mehmed, to make him seem evil?

Radu did not know which filled him with more despair—that everyone had heard this rumor except him, or that the mere suggestion of Mehmed loving women and men was seen as evil. His feelings for Mehmed had never felt evil or wicked. They had been the truest of his life, bordering on holy. To hear his love so casually profaned made him sick to his stomach.

And then another, more horrible thought occurred to him. Mehmed must know about these rumors. Surely he knew. Was the ruse of Radu's distance from Mehmed not simply for their enemies? The way Mehmed had jumped on the chance to send Radu away, too, with so little preparation or aid. Mehmed had been eager to take the opportunity without any information or guarantees. Radu had thought it was because Mehmed trusted him. Now he wondered.

Did Mehmed know the rumors *and* Radu's true feelings, and had he sent Radu here to end both of them?

———◆———

Radu collapsed into bed next to Nazira. He had spent a long day helping repair the walls. The irony of being sent behind the walls to undermine them while physically repairing them was not lost on Radu's aching muscles.

Sighing heavily, he put an arm over his face. "You first."

Nazira shoved him onto his stomach, then began kneading

the muscles in his back. Radu sank deeper into the uneven mattress, not caring about the feather spines that jabbed into him. Simple human contact with someone who cared about him did more healing than Nazira's small hands ever could. He realized how little anyone had actually touched him over the last few years. Lada had never been physically affectionate, unless he counted her fists. Lazar had frequently *accidentally* touched him, but Radu tried his best not to think about his dead friend. He could remember every moment of physical contact with Mehmed, but each was too short, too formal, never enough.

And then there had been the horrible kiss with Halil's son, Salih, a kiss that still filled Radu with self-loathing for how much he had liked being wanted, even when he did not return the feeling.

So this friendly intimacy with Nazira had its benefits. Of course, the downside to being married was that they were given the same room, and same bed, to share. Sometimes Radu woke up from dreams—aching, desperate dreams in which his mind somehow knew the sensations his actual body had yet to experience—in a state he *really* did not want Nazira to witness. Frequently, in spite of his exhaustion, he could not fall asleep for fear of what he might dream about while lying next to her.

Nazira worked on a tender knot and Radu grimaced. "Let me think of what I heard today," she said. "Mehmed is the Antichrist."

"Yes, I heard that one, too."

"Did you hear about the child who dreamed that the angel guarding the city walls abandoned his post?"

"No, that is a new one. I heard about a fisherman who drew up oysters that dripped blood."

"Good thing I never cared for oysters. And fish! So much fish in this city. If I never eat fish again when we leave, I will be happy. What else. Hmm. Oh! Helen, one of my new friends, is very bitter. Apparently the first emperor of the city was Constantine, son of Helen. And now this emperor is Constantine, son of Helen, which means the circle of history is closing and the city is doomed. It also means the name Helen is deeply unpopular, and she is taking it quite personally."

"Why are you friends with her?"

"She is currently entertaining one of the Venetian ship captains, a man named Coco. She talks about him constantly."

"Well done," Radu said, wincing as Nazira hit another particularly sore area of his shoulders. "Word from the walls is that with the relic of the true cross in the city, it cannot be taken by the Antichrist. On the other hand, they do not like the patterns of birds flying in the skies. However, Mary herself is protecting the city. Unfortunately, someone's uncle finally decoded the secret messages scrawled on a thousand-year-old pillar that declares this the last year of Earth. But the moon will be waxing soon, and the city cannot be taken on a waxing moon, so there you have it. The city is both utterly doomed and cannot possibly fall."

"These people are insane," Nazira said sadly.

"At least it saves us the trouble of trying to foment chaos within the walls. They need no help with that."

"How are you doing with getting close to Constantine?"

Radu shrugged, rolling back over. Nazira lay on her side,

propped up on an elbow. He had not told her the real reason why Constantine accepted his loyalty without question; he was too humiliated to speak it aloud. "I see him only in passing. He is everywhere in the city, constantly on the move to inspire people."

"I have seen him a few times. Helen hates him. I think he looks nice. What about the other important men?"

"Right now they are trying to organize, and waiting for further aid before they decide where to commit. I do not see much of them. I never knew waiting could be such a wearying task."

"What about Cyprian?"

Radu shifted uncomfortably. "He is close to Constantine. He takes notes for him. I am sure he knows most of the organization of the city. But . . ."

"But what?"

Closing his eyes, Radu rubbed his face. There was a bigger issue where Cyprian was concerned, a nebulous one, the contours of which Radu had not yet traced out. He did not know if he wanted to or even could. "We are living with Cyprian. We eat meals with him, sleep next to his room." And they liked him. Nazira had not said it, but Radu could see in the smiles she gave Cyprian, the easy way she laughed at his stories over meals. Radu was not the only one with complicated feelings toward their enemy. But he rationalized them anyway. "It would be dangerous to abuse any information we get through him. Too immediately suspicious."

"True." Nazira drew the blanket up to her chin and snuggled into Radu's side. "We carry on, then."

Radu patted her arm, waiting for her breath to go steady

and deep. Then he rolled away, sitting on the edge of the bed with his head in his hands.

The only thing coming here had accomplished was getting Radu far away from Mehmed and the rumors spread about them. Radu knew if that was what Mehmed needed, he should be glad. He should be willing to sacrifice himself to protect Mehmed's vision, to protect his reputation. But he could not—would not—be willing to sacrifice Nazira.

He would stay the course. He would make something of their time here. And he would get her out alive, no matter what.

24

Early April

OANA—THE ONLY ONE WHO knew about Lada's meet-ing with Mehmed—said nothing as Lada commanded her men to pack up camp the next morning. Lada was grateful to her for that. She could not have handled questions about the soldiers she should have returned with.

Bogdan stayed closer to her side than ever. He never asked where she had gone. At least his unquestioning acceptance of her actions had not changed. But even if he asked, she would never tell him.

Or anyone.

Lada's mind chased itself in angry circles. Mehmed—whom she had always trusted—had deceived her. And he thought she would choose Constantinople after that? How little he knew her.

The next night, though, lying on the frozen ground, her mind betrayed her. Images of being empress next to Mehmed haunted her when she closed her eyes. It was the worst part of everything, knowing that, on some level, she wanted that much power, even at that cost.

She awoke, gasping and aching. No. The worst were dreams of Mehmed at her side in an entirely different fashion.

She made her men move before dawn. Sleep was not her ally. She drove them hard toward Hunedoara, reassuring herself that at least she had done some good for Hunyadi. Constantinople would fall—of that she had no doubts, whatever else she might now doubt and hate about Mehmed—and Hunyadi would have died there. Her duplicity had spared him his life. She could take comfort in that.

"I hate Hungary," Petru grumbled, riding abreast of Lada, Nicolae, and Bogdan. "And that lord or noble or prince, Matthias? Whenever he is around me, he holds a handkerchief to his nose." Petru ducked his head to smell under his arms. "I smell nothing."

Nicolae leaned close, then feigned fainting. "That is because your sense of smell has killed itself out of despair."

"Matthias is not a prince," Lada said. "He is Hunyadi's son."

Petru's expression shifted in surprise. "How did Hunyadi's seed produce that weak politician?"

Nicolae's cheerful voice answered. "The same way Vlad Dracul's traitorous seed produced our valiant Lada!"

Lada stared straight ahead, numb. In that moment, she realized she was *exactly* like her father. Hunyadi had cautioned her not to discount the man who made her the way she was. Apparently her father had done his job well. She, too, had taken someone who trusted her and leveraged that trust for Ottoman aid—aid that benefitted her nothing. And she had been stupid enough to make it personal with Mehmed.

She was a fool.

"Lada?" Bogdan asked, his low, grumbling voice soft with concern.

She pushed her horse forward, outpacing them all so they could not see the first tears she had cried since she was a child.

Oana caught her, though. Lada wiped furiously at her face. "What do you want?"

"Where are we going?"

"Back to Hunyadi. He is my only ally."

Oana made a humming noise. "Not your only ally. You have other family besides your father."

"Mircea is dead, too. And none of the boyars are more closely related to the Dracul line than to the Danesti or Basarab."

"Not that side. Your mother. Last I heard, she was alive in Moldavia. And she is still royalty there."

Lada turned her head to the side and spat. "She is nothing to me."

"Be that as it may, you might not be nothing to her. Blood calls to blood. You could yet find your path to the throne through the support of her family. If nothing else, it is a place to rest and regroup. You need some rest."

Groaning, Lada rubbed her forehead. "I do not want to see her." There was a reason appealing to her Moldavian relatives had never crossed her mind. Her mother had ceased existing for her years ago. The idea of welcoming that woman back into her life, even if it got her the throne . . .

Oana leaned closer. "It cannot cost you more than whatever happened with the sultan."

"God's wounds, woman, very well." Lada ignored Oana's pleased smile as she turned her horse around. "New plan," she said when she rejoined her men.

"New plan?" Petru asked.

"Where are we off to now?" Nicolae asked.

"Moldavia."

"Moldavia?" Petru said.

"Is there an echo here?" Lada glared at Petru.

Though he ducked his head and blushed, excitement animated his voice. "Are we burning Moldavian cities? Like we did in Transylvania?"

Lada had not forgotten Matei and the waste of his death, traitor or not. She would not lose men to petty vengeance again. Only to vengeance worth taking. She shook her head.

"What, then?" Nicolae asked.

"We go to appeal to my blood. We go to see my—" She paused, feeling the edges of the next word sticking in her throat, threatening to choke her. "My mother."

———————

"She is so beautiful," Petru whispered, peering through the hedge they hid behind. "You look nothing like her."

Nicolae cringed. "And that, Petru, is why your line will die with you."

Lada did not—could not—answer as her mother rode elegantly toward them down the dirt path of her country manor.

The only clear memory Lada had of the woman was one of lank hair hanging over her face, sharp shoulder blades, bowed back. Crawling. Weeping. She had expected to come here and find the same broken creature. She had not been able to picture her mother standing, much less riding.

This woman was small and fine-boned like a bird. Her hair, pinned elaborately beneath her hat, shone black with hints of silver threaded through. Her back was straight, her chin lifted, a veil of lace over her face.

Lada had been apprehensive about trying to leverage her connection to her mother to get help from the Moldavian king, her grandfather. But it had been easier to think of her mother that way, as a stepping-stone. Someone to climb over.

Here her mother was not on the ground. She was higher than Lada.

"We should leave," she said. "This was a bad idea."

"We should at least talk to her," Nicolae said.

"I do not even know if that *is* her. I have not seen her since I was three. Perhaps we were misdirected. My mother might be dead."

Bogdan pushed Petru aside, taking over his vantage point. "That is her."

"How do you know?"

He shrugged. "I was older than you when she left."

"By a year!"

He blinked at Lada, expression intractable. "I remember everything about our childhood." He said the word *our* with uncharacteristic tenderness. It made Lada feel unsettled, even more than she already was.

Lada crossed her arms over her chest. "Well, what are we supposed to do? Jump out of the hedge and scream, 'Hello, Mother!'"

Nicolae shook his head. "Of course not. She is not *our* mother. Only yours."

"She is barely even that. She will not recognize me." Lada would have to prove her identity to the woman who had fled when she was a child. She had no way of doing that.

"We could bring my mother," Bogdan said. "She was your mother's companion for many years."

They had left Oana at camp with the rest of the men, hidden along the mountain pass where they had crept into Moldavia. The whole journey Lada had longed to turn around, to flee, to go back home. But she could not. She needed help.

She *hated* needing.

"Fine." Lada stood and pushed through the hedge. She struggled out from it right as her mother's horse passed.

"God's wounds!" Vasilissa shouted, using Lada's father's favorite curse. "Where did you—" She stopped, her fingers going to her mouth, pressing at the veil.

"You should travel with guards." Lada wore her anger as armor against this woman. "We could have been anyone."

Vasilissa moved her trembling hand to her heart.

"We are not going to rob you." Lada sighed. "We are here to speak with you."

"Ladislav," Vasilissa whispered. "My little girl."

Lada had been prepared to be humiliated by introducing herself. She had not thought about what she would do if her mother knew her. She stepped back as though struck, her vision narrowing to a tunnel. Every muscle tensed, waiting for attack.

Vasilissa leaned down as far as she could from her horse. Her voice was barely discernable over the rush of blood in Lada's ears.

"Ladislav." She reached one tiny, gloved hand toward Lada's hair. Then she cleared her throat, looking Lada up and down in a way that made her feel naked. "Come. We will get you a bath and some new clothes." Her mother turned the horse back toward the manor and set off at a brisk pace.

"I have men with me!" Lada shouted, finally regaining her voice.

"No," Vasilissa said, not turning around. "Only you. No men."

At a loss, Lada gestured to Petru, Nicolae, and Bogdan, who watched her from the cover of the hedge. "Just . . . stay, for now. I will come back for you."

"Are you certain you will come to no harm?" Bogdan asked, narrowed eyes tracking Vasilissa's hasty exit.

Lada was certain of the opposite. But she did not expect the type of harm Bogdan feared. "Wait here."

When she got to the manor, the front door was closed. Barren ivy climbed over every surface, its tangled brown masses swallowing the angles and shape of the house. In the summer it would be green and lovely, but not now.

The least her mother could have done was wait for her. Lada laughed bitterly. No, her mother was skilled at doing far less than the least she could do for her daughter. Of course she would make Lada knock. Lada pounded her gloved fist against the door. It opened with such speed, the maid behind it must have been waiting there.

The girl curtsied awkwardly. She wore a shapeless brown dress and an ill-fitting black cap. "Welcome, mistress. My lady has prepared a room for you."

Lada frowned. Who else was her mother expecting? "I only met her just now on the road."

The girl cleared her throat, keeping her eyes on the floor. "My lady has prepared a room for you. Please come with me."

"Where is my moth—where is Vasilissa?"

"If you will come with me, I will show you your room and draw a bath for you. Her ladyship receives visitors after supper."

"But she already knows I am here. And I have my men waiting outside."

The maid finally looked up. Her eyes pointed in slightly different directions, one drifting to the left. She whispered, "Please, mistress, do not speak of the men to her. We do as she wishes. It is for the best. Allow me to take you to your room, and she will see you after supper."

Exasperated, Lada flung a hand out. "Fine. Take me to my room."

The girl flashed a quick, grateful smile, and led Lada into the house. The deeper they got, the more Lada's stomach clenched in fear.

There was something very wrong here.

25

Early April

CHRIST STARED MOURNFULLY DOWN at Radu. No matter how Radu shifted or where he looked, the round eyes of Jesus followed him.

"Are you well?" Cyprian whispered out the side of his mouth, leaning close.

Radu stopped fidgeting under the giant mosaic. "Yes. Just tired."

In front of them, standing behind a giant wood postern, a priest ran through liturgy after liturgy. Radu's Greek was good, but he could barely understand the antiquated phrasings and words. Even if he could, he would not care. Being in this church made him feel like a child again. Radu had not enjoyed his childhood, and it was deeply uncomfortable to be reminded of it.

Everything was larger than life in the church. Though it was not as big or beautiful as the Hagia Sophia, gilt covered all possible surfaces. The priest wore elaborate robes, stitched and embroidered with pounds of history and tradition. A censer filled the room with scented smoke that made Radu's eyes water and his head spin.

On the raised dais next to the priest, Constantine sat on a throne. Radu envied him a seat. All the other men stood, packed in too tightly, still and listening. Radu yearned for the movement of true prayer, for the simplicity and beauty and companionship of it.

The liturgy continued, as cold and uncaring as the murals of various saints meeting violent ends that decorated the walls. Lada would like those at least. Radu smiled, remembering when they had visited a monastery on the island of Snagov in Wallachia. Lada had been chastised for laughing at the gruesome death scene of Saint Bartholomew. An elaborate painting of him with half his skin already off adorned one of the monastery walls. Radu could never look at that mural without shivering in fear. Lada had told him to think instead of how cold poor Saint Bartholomew must have been without any skin on.

He wished Lada were with him now. But even if she were, she would be up in the gallery with Nazira and all the other women. And she would be blisteringly angry about it.

Radu avoided Jesus's gaze yet again and found himself staring at an equally mournful mosaic of Mary. Her head was tilted down and to one side, a miniature Christ child solemn and staring on her lap. *Will you protect your city?* Radu silently asked her. He knew there was one God. But in this city of mysticism steeped in so much religious fervor, he could not escape the fear that the other god, the god of his childhood, lurked in the mist and the rain and the tremors of the earth. Radu was trapped behind these walls, separated from who he had become. With his tongue he cursed Muslim infidels and with his heart he prayed for constant forgiveness.

Surely the true God, the God of his heart, knew what Radu was doing here. Even if Radu himself did not.

When the liturgy finally ended, Radu wanted nothing more than to go back to Cyprian's house and sleep for a day. But Cyprian grabbed his arm and pulled him toward a group that was milling about near Constantine.

"I wanted to introduce you to—ah, here they are!" Cyprian clasped hands warmly with two boys who shared the round-eyed, mournful faces of the mosaics around them. Radu half expected them to tilt their heads and lift their hands in various saintlike poses. Instead, they smiled shyly.

"This is John, and his brother, Manuel. My cousins. Their father was John, the emperor before Constantine."

The older boy looked to be around eight, the younger five. They wore purple robes and gold circlets. The clasps of the chains securing their robes glittered like jewels, but as Radu looked closer, he saw they were made of glass.

Radu bowed. "I am Radu."

The younger boy, Manuel, perked up, his round eyes growing even rounder. "From the sultan's palace?"

"Who told you about me?" Radu asked, with a puzzled smile.

"Cyprian has told us all about you!"

Cyprian cleared his throat. "Not all about you. Just . . . that you saved me."

Manuel nodded. "Is it true what they say about the sultan?"

Radu smiled to hide the pit that had opened up in his stomach. Had even this small boy heard that Radu was the sultan's shameful plaything? Why would Cyprian have told him that? "They say many things. I am afraid you will have to be more specific."

"That the sultan kills a man before every meal and sprinkles his food with the blood to protect himself against death."

Radu was so relieved he had to choke back a laugh. He covered it by pretending to cough. "No, unless things have changed dramatically since I left. He prefers his food without blood, like most men."

"I heard he is so wealthy that he had all his teeth replaced with jewels." John, the older boy, said it with a studied casualness, but he leaned forward just as intently as his brother.

"That would make eating all his blood-sprinkled meals quite a task! But no, that is not true, either. Though he does sometimes wear a turban so large it nearly brushes the ceiling!" That was an exaggeration, but both boys nodded in wonder. "He has fountains of clear water in all his rooms, and his fingers are so heavy with jewels that he cannot sign his own name without removing his rings first."

Manuel scowled. "I do not know why he wants our dumb city, then."

John elbowed him sharply in the side. "You are just jealous because I am the heir to the throne and you are not."

Manuel stuck out his tongue. "Not if you die first!"

Cyprian put a hand on both their shoulders. "No talk like that, boys." They deflated, looking shamefacedly at the floor. "And I am going to have a word with your nurse about the rumors she is letting you hear."

John looked up first. He lifted his chin bravely, but it trembled slightly. "Is the sultan as cruel as they say?"

Radu wanted to deny it, but he had to remember he was playing a part. "He is . . . very smart, and very focused. He will do whatever it takes to get what he wants. So, yes, he can be cruel."

John nodded, then set his jaw determinedly. "Well, it does not matter. The walls will save us. And even if he gets past them, an angel will come down from heaven with flaming swords before they can pass the statue of Justinian. The infidels will never have my city."

A loud, deep laugh sounded next to them. Constantine ruffled the boy's brown curls, skewing the circlet to the side. "Your city? I am fairly certain it is still mine."

John smiled, blushing. "I only meant—"

"Have no fear, John. I will take good care of it until it is your turn."

They turned their smiles on Radu. The combined weight of their love and hope with the heavy gaze of Jesus above them nearly knocked Radu to the floor. He bowed to cover his feelings, then straightened.

"Will you join us for a meal?" Constantine asked. "It will be nice to have someone else to answer their infinite questions for once."

"I would love to," Radu said, still exhausted but with a spike of excitement. This was his first personal invitation to spend time with the emperor. It was a good thing. A step in the right direction. A way to feel like he was actually accomplishing something, even though he feared there was no point.

Then a tiny hand slipped into Radu's own, and he looked down into the saintly eyes of Manuel. The little boy beamed up at him, and Radu felt his soul wilt as he smiled back.

Everything had been so *normal* at dinner. Even Radu had managed to relax, enjoying the food and laughter and stories. All his hopes to hear something useful were dashed in the middle of bread and meat and preserved fruit.

And that was when he had his idea.

Mehmed might have sent him in without a plan, but he could destroy the city's chances at surviving a siege before the Ottomans ever got to Constantinople. If food made them feel normal, allowed them to continue on as though their city were not under imminent threat, the absence of food would finally make it clear they could not survive.

It would be an act of mercy, destroying the food supplies. People would be forced to flee. Even if it did not lead directly to surrender, at least it would empty the city of innocent citizens.

Orhan, the pretend heir to the Ottoman throne, proved the key to discovering the location of one of the major food supplies. Because his men were not allowed at the wall—for fear soldiers would confuse them for Turks loyal to Mehmed—they had other assignments throughout the city. And one of those assignments was patrolling and checking all the locks on a warehouse. Radu could think of no reason for its protection other than that it housed food.

It had been a simple enough task for Radu to shadow the

men and find his target. But now the bigger question: how to eliminate it?

Lada would burn it down. Radu did not doubt that. But the warehouse was in the middle of a relatively populated section of the city. If he set the building on fire, the fire would spread. He could end up killing innocent citizens—and part of his motivation in doing this was to save them. He could not live with collateral damage.

Poison would have the same effect, because they would not know the food was poisoned until people were dead. And Radu had no real means of obtaining large quantities of poison, much less doing so in secret.

He was in the kitchen tearing apart bread, pondering the problem of the food, when Nazira shrieked in terror from their bedroom. He raced upstairs to find her standing on the bed. "A rat!" She pointed to a corner where a large, mangy rat seemed equally terrified of her. "Kill it!"

Radu sighed, looking for something large enough to smash the rodent. And then he stopped. A smile lit his face. "No. I am going to catch it."

———•———

Though rats were in plentiful supply in the city, catching a significant number of them was no small task. Or rather, it was many, many small, wearying tasks. And because Radu could not risk being missed at the wall, he had to sacrifice sleep. Nazira loved the plan, but was physically incapable of interacting with rats without screaming. Screaming did not lend itself well to secrecy.

So Radu spent all night, every night, catching rats. It was a far cry from his life at the side of the sultan, but not so far from what his role had always been. Sneaking around, gathering supplies, building toward an ultimate goal.

It would have been thrilling if it did not involve so many damned rats.

"What happened to your hands?" Cyprian asked a couple of mornings into the rat adventures. He and Radu were eating together on the wall, shoulder to shoulder as they looked out on the empty field that was filled nonetheless with the looming threat of the future.

Radu looked down at his fingers. "Vermin cemetery residents do not like sharing gravestones with trespassers."

Cyprian set down his bread and took Radu's hands in his own. He carefully examined them. Radu's stomach fluttered. It felt like something more than fear of discovery, but he could not say what.

"Be careful," Cyprian said, running a finger as soft as a whisper along Radu's palm. "We need these hands." Cyprian looked up and Radu found himself unable to bear the intensity of his gaze. Cyprian released his hands, laughing awkwardly. "We need all the hands we can get."

"Yes," Radu murmured, still feeling Cyprian's finger tracing his palm.

—◆—

That night, Radu had enough rats. Any more and he would not be able to carry them in secret. He waited for Orhan's men to finish their patrol past the back doors of the warehouse. They never went inside, only checked the locks. He crept silently across the street, a wriggling, repulsive burlap sack filled to bursting slung across his back. He set the sack down and picked the lock, cursing his bitten fingers for their slowness. Cyprian had been right. They needed these hands.

Finally, shivering with nerves, Radu got the door open. Slipping inside, he made his way to the center of the vast space. Crates and barrels loomed like gravestones in the darkness. Everything smelled warm and dusty. He had guessed right about the contents of the warehouse. He used the metal rod he had brought to pry open lids, then he dumped rats into crates and barrels until his sack held only the rats that had not survived captivity. But he had managed to hit barely a third of the containers. He would have to do this every night for weeks to actually destroy all the supplies.

Burn it, Lada whispered in his mind.

"There's always another way," Radu answered. Thunder rumbled overhead as though agreeing with him. The city was prone to torrential downpours. Radu would need to hurry home to avoid getting caught in one. He looked up at the ceiling—

And he had another idea.

Back out in the night, he examined his options. The buildings in Constantinople were old and built close together. He hurried down the alley, looking for what he needed. Three buildings over, he found it: a ladder. The first drops of rain hit him as he climbed onto the building's roof. Taking a deep breath, he ran as fast as he could and jumped over the alley, slamming into the next roof so hard he nearly slid off. Lada would be so much better at this. But she also would not have bothered. Everything would already be burning.

Steeling himself against thoughts of his far more capable sister, Radu ran for the next roof and sailed over the alley. Landing softly this time, he collapsed onto his back and laughed as rain pattered down around him. Beneath him, warm and dusty and dry, was the city's food.

He clambered to the peak of the shallowly angled roof. The key was to pry enough shingles and thatch free to make small holes, but not so many that the damage would be noticed until it was too late. The shingles were heavy and tightly nailed down. He used his lever to pry them up. He focused on areas where it was obvious water had pooled in the many years of the roof's life.

The rain began pouring in earnest. The shingles were slick; Radu clung to them carefully. He could afford neither discovery nor injury. He allowed himself a few moments of quiet triumph as he watched water stream from the sky onto the roof and through the holes he had created.

Tearing up as many shingles on his way as he could, he crawled to the far end of the building. But he had a new problem.

He could not run to gather momentum. With the roof this slick, he would certainly slip and fall to his death. The drop to the ground was far—three times his height—and if he crashed down with any speed he did not like his chances.

There was a narrow ledge along the edge of the roof. Rain poured around him; the storm was picking up speed and force. He left the lever on the roof and grasped the ledge. Then he lowered himself, hanging on by only his fingertips. Praying silently, he dropped. When he hit the ground, he collapsed, trying not to let any one part of his body absorb too much of the impact. It was a trick he had learned long ago, running and hiding from his cruel older brother, Mircea. He had had to jump from many windows and walls in his childhood.

Mircea was dead now, and Radu did not mourn him. But

as he stood, checking his body for injuries, he was momentarily grateful for the lessons. One ankle was complaining and would be sore in the morning. It was a small price to pay. Radu pulled his hood up over his head.

"Hey! You!"

Radu turned in surprise. It was too dark for them to see his face, but Orhan's men had circled back on their patrol. And Radu was standing right next to the door of the storage warehouse. If they looked inside, all his work would be for nothing.

He quickly pulled a flint from his pocket and dropped it. Then, cursing loudly in Turkish, he ran.

"He was trying to burn the food! Spy! Sabotage!" The cry went up behind him, followed by the pounding of footsteps.

Radu ran for his life.

Bells began clanging the warning, chasing him with their peals. Radu cut through alleys and streets. He jumped over walls and kept to the darkest parts of the city. Soon he was in an abandoned area. But still he heard the sounds of pursuit. It was like a nightmare: running through a dead city, pursued in the darkness with nowhere to hide.

Desperate, Radu considered the outer wall. If he could make it to the wall, he could make it outside. He could find Mehmed.

But if he disappeared the same night a saboteur had been spotted in the city, it would not take much thought to connect the events. Nazira would be left in harm's way. Radu turned and ran into an empty stable. Rain poured in from the collapsed roof. He huddled in the corner of a stall.

Once, he had hidden with Lada in a stable. She had promised no one would kill him but her. *Please*, Radu thought, *please let that be prophetic.*

After he had waited for so long that his heart no longer pounded and he shivered with cold rather than fear, Radu stood and crept through the night. The rain was tapering off as he slowly found his way from the abandoned section of the city back to a part with life. He left his long black cloak on a washing line and combed his hair into a neat ponytail. Then he walked, unhurried, hunched against the rain.

His hand was on the doorknob when someone grabbed his shoulder roughly from behind. He was spun around—and embraced.

"Radu!" Cyprian said, holding him tightly. "I have been looking everywhere for you. There is a saboteur in the city. They caught him trying to light a fire. I was so worried about you."

Radu took a deep breath, trying to calm his voice. "I heard the bells and went out to see what was wrong. I feared the Ottomans had finally arrived. But why would you worry about me?"

Cyprian lingered in the hug, then pulled back, his hands still on Radu's shoulders. "If the sultan's man had discovered you ..." His eyes were wrinkled with concern. "I feared for your safety."

Radu embraced Cyprian again, both because it was warm and comforting against the weariness of this long night, and because it was the only way he could hide how touched and sad he was that Cyprian's first fear had been for Radu's traitorous life.

26

Early April

A CLOUD OF DUST HUNG in front of the window, where musty drapes had been hastily tugged aside. The room was in the back of the house, on the second floor. Lada could see across a fallow field to the hedge where she had watched for her mother. But it was not clear enough to make out where her men waited for her.

She hoped they were still waiting for her. She felt so cut off. What if they left her, too? Radu was lost to her. Mehmed was a traitor. She had separated herself from Hunyadi. She could not lose her men.

The maid cleared her throat. Lada expected the girl to leave, but she just stood there next to the steaming bath she had filled.

"Well?" Lada snapped.

"I will help you undress?"

"No!"

The girl recoiled as if struck. "I am supposed to."

"You are *not* supposed to."

"But—I was to wash your hair, and plait it for you after, and help you into one of her ladyship's dresses." The girl frowned worriedly, looking at Lada's thick waist and large chest.

Lada laughed, the absurdity of it all finally getting to her. Here she was, seeing her mother for the first time in fifteen years, and her mother wanted to brush her hair and dress her up. No—her mother wanted someone else to do it for her. That made sense. At least Oana was not here. She would have been thrilled to volunteer.

"You may stand outside the door so that she thinks you are still in here. And then you may take a message and some food to my men outside. You will see their campfire."

The girl squeaked in fear. "Men! I could not. It is forbidden. Oh, please, do not ask it of me. If she knew, if she found out—"

Lada held up her hands. "Very well! They will last until I go back to them. Get out."

The girl nodded, wringing her hands, and slipped out the door. Lada followed, putting her ear to the door. She could hear the rapid, panicked breaths of the girl immediately outside.

What went on in this house?

Lada took a bath. Over the last year on the run, she had learned never to turn down a bath or a meal. But she did not wash her hair, or make any effort to tame it. She dressed again in her traveling clothes—breeches, a tunic, and a coat, all black. A red sash around her waist. When she was done putting her boots on, she opened the door. The maid was so close their noses nearly touched.

"Your hair?"

Lada shook her head, expression grim.

"I found some of her ladyship's old dresses. I could let out the seams, and . . ." The girl trailed off, hope dying on her face as Lada's expression did not change.

"When is supper?" Lada asked.

"She has already eaten."

"Without me?"

"Our schedule is very specific." The maid leaned forward, looking to either side as though fearful of discovery. "I will bring you some food from the kitchens later tonight," she whispered.

Lada did not know how to respond. With gratitude? Incredulity? Instead, she pushed forward with her goal. "If supper is over, I can see her now."

"Yes! She will be waiting to receive visitors in the drawing room."

"Does she receive many visitors?"

The maid shook her head. "Almost never."

"So she is only waiting to see me."

"After supper, she waits to receive visitors. You are a visitor. So you may see her now."

Lada followed the girl through the hall and down the stairs. She would much rather be facing a contingent of Bulgars, or a mounted cavalry. At least those she would understand.

Mehmed's mother, Huma, suddenly came to mind. Huma had been ferocious and terrifying. She had wielded her very womanhood like a weapon, one Lada did not understand and could not ever use. Was that what her mother was doing? Throwing Lada off guard to gain the upper hand? Huma had been able to manipulate Lada and Radu by forcing them to meet on her terms. Her mother must be doing the same thing.

It was comforting, in a way, girding herself to meet a challenge like Mehmed's formidable mother. Huma was a foe worth having. A murderer many times over, who had even had Mehmed's infant half brother drowned in a bath. Lada shuddered, the back of her hair wet against her neck. Was there a darker reason the maid had tried to insist on staying during Lada's bath?

She regarded the tiny, trembling thing ahead of her with new suspicion. Flexing her hands, Lada dismissed the notion. Though Lada *was* certain that if her mother wanted her dead, she would make someone else do it. This waif would have to resort to poison or murdering her in her sleep. She was glad she had missed supper, after all.

But everything Huma had done, she had done to further her son's place in life. What would Vasilissa stand to gain by killing Lada? And why did Lada find it more comfortable to think of Vasilissa as a potential assassin lying in wait than as her mother?

Before Lada could settle her mind, the maid opened a door to a sitting room. It was like being greeted by an open oven. The air was too close and heated past any reasonable degree. The windows were shuttered tightly, and a fire roared in a fireplace too large for a room this size.

The maid practically tugged Lada inside, closing the door as quickly as possible behind them. It took a moment for Lada's eyes to adjust to the dim room. Her mother sat in a high-backed chair, hands folded primly in her lap, voluminous skirt hiding her feet. Her hat had been replaced with a long veil pinned at the top of her head that completely obscured her face. She was not wearing the same dress as before. This one was white, with a ruffled neck so high it looked as though her veiled head sat on a platter. All the dress's folds and pleats nearly swallowed her whole.

"Oh," she said, an entire discourse in disappointment contained in that single word. "You did not change."

Lada longed to draw her knives, sheathed at her wrists. "These are my clothes." She took the chair opposite her mother without being invited. It sank under her weight, the stuffing worn and the velvet threadbare.

"Would you like something? Tea? Wine?"

"Wine."

Vasilissa nodded toward the maid, who poured two glasses and handed one to each of them. Lada took a sip. Or rather, she pretended to take a sip, preferring to wait until her mother drank first. Huma was too recently on her mind to risk otherwise. So far her mother was nothing like Huma, though. Huma had filled the space around her, no matter how large the room. Even in this small room, Lada's mother seemed to blend into the furniture.

Vasilissa lifted her veil and took a dainty sip. Lada followed suit. Her mother's eyes were large, like hers, but there was more of Radu in her face. It was startling, seeing her brother reflected in the face of a stranger. Lada could not place the exact similarities; they had something delicate and beautiful in common. But her mother's face was worn and broken at the edges. Was that what would happen to Radu, too? Would he fade with time, become a withered shadow of himself?

Lada longed for Radu at her side yet again. If he were here, she could focus on protecting him. Having only herself to protect made her feel so much more vulnerable.

"Tell me," her mother said, keeping a hand in front of her mouth. "What brings you to the countryside? It is not so lovely this time of year, I am afraid. Much nicer once spring has taken hold."

Lada frowned. "I am here to see you."

"That is sweet. We do not have many visitors." She lowered her hand, smiling with tightly shut lips. Then she simply stared. Lada wondered if her own large, hooded eyes were that disconcerting.

Lada had never been good at the games women played, the battles fought and won through incomprehensible conversations. So she pushed ahead. "I assume you have had news that my father is dead. So is Mircea."

Vasilissa lifted her hand to her mouth again. Lada thought it was in horror or mourning, but Vasilissa's tone was conversational. "Do you ride? I find a brisk ride in the afternoon settles my nerves and rouses my appetite. I have three horses. They have no names. I am so terrible with choosing names! But they are all gentle and sweet. Perhaps you can meet them tomorrow."

"Why are you speaking to me of horses?" Lada set aside her glass and leaned forward. "You have not seen me in so many years, since you abandoned us. At least do me the courtesy of speaking to me as an equal. Your husband, my father, is dead."

Her mother made a wounded face, a flash of truth breaking free. Her lips parted in an animal way, and Lada had a glimpse of a mouth full of broken teeth. Not rotted teeth— Lada had seen plenty of those—nor the gaps indicating lost teeth. Vasilissa's mouth was a graveyard of shattered teeth. Lada did not know what could have caused such damage.

Her mother, crawling away, weeping.

No. She *did* know what could have caused such damage.

Lada lowered her voice. "He is dead. Gone."

If her mother heard her, she did not indicate it. She drew her veil back down, making a repetitive clicking noise with her tongue. "Tell me, do you hunt? I find it abominable, but I have word that all the fashionable ladies do it now." Her laugh was high and trilling, like the panicked flight of a startled bird. "If you would like, I can have word sent to your cousin. He has an excellent falconer. I am certain he would give you a demonstration, should you wish it. He visits every summer. He has to stay in town, of course, several leagues away, but he always stops by when I receive visitors! We can expect him in a few months."

"I will not be here then. I am not here for a visit. I need help."

Vasilissa laughed again, the same terrible noise. "I should say so! But my maid works wonders on hair. We will have you settled in no time. Do you like your room?"

Lada stood. "I need to speak to your father."

Vasilissa shook her head. "He is— He has— I believe he is dead?"

With a defeated sigh, Lada sat back down. "Who leads Moldavia?"

"Your cousin, I think. Oh." Vasilissa wrung her hands in her lap. "Do you suppose that means he will not come this summer? I am sorry. I promised you a falcon demonstration."

"I do not care about falcons! I need men. I need alliances." Lada shook, a wave of unacknowledged anger and grief overwhelming her. Her father had given her a knife, and her mother had left her with nothing. She desperately wanted something to hold on to. Or, barring that, something to fight against. "I need you to ask me where I have been the last fifteen years! I need you to ask where your *son* is!"

Her mother stood, her dress-draped frame trembling. "It is time for me to retire for the night. The maid will see to you. Your room is the nicest in the house. You will be happy. And you will be safe; this is a very safe house."

Vasilissa held out a hand. The maid rushed to her side. Lada saw, for the first time, that her mother walked with a pronounced limp. One of her feet, when it peeked from beneath her skirts, was twisted at an odd angle. The way Vasilissa moved without cringing spoke of it as an old, permanent injury. Lada did not know what to say, how to talk to this strange, ruined creature. Her impression of Vasilissa on the horse had been wrong. Her mother was exactly the same person who had left them behind. The only difference was that she had found a safe place to hide.

Perhaps Radu would feel tenderly toward her. Lada knew he would urge compassion.

She felt only rage.

"You never came back for us," Lada said. "He sold us. To the Turks. We were tortured. We were raised in a foreign land by heathens. Radu stayed behind. They broke him."

"Well." Vasilissa reached out as though she would pat Lada's arm as she passed. Her hand hovered in the air, then moved back to the maid's arm for support. "You are welcome to stay forever. We are all safe here."

"I belong in Wallachia."

Her mother's voice was as harsh as Lada had ever heard it, finally filled with true emotion. "No one belongs there."

The maid was loath to part with any information, but as far as Lada could determine, her mother was mad. They had lived together in this house, far away from everyone and everything, for the last ten years. Vasilissa had been given the manor by her father, who doubtless could not stand the broken shell of a woman she was.

Every day was the same. The maid smiled as she described it, saying over and over how pleasant it was, to be safe and to always know what to expect. This was what Lada's mother had chosen. Safety. Seclusion. The woman had abandoned her children, utterly and completely, to live in pampered isolation instead of dealing with the harsh realities of life.

The harsh realities of her own children's desperate attempts to survive without anyone to aid them.

Lada did not say goodbye. She stopped in the kitchen and stole as much food as she could carry. Then she closed the front door behind her and walked along the dark lane to where the campfire of her men—her friends—called to her. She sat next to them, drawing heat and strength from their shoulders. Bogdan shifted closer and she leaned against him.

"Well?" Nicolae asked.

"She is mad."

"Then you do have something in common after all!"

His attempt at levity met with no reaction from Lada. His voice got quieter. "Will there be any aid from Moldavia?"

"None that she can provide. We can go to the capital and appeal to the new king. But I do not think these people will help us. She is just like all the nobility, the boyars. They are sick with the same disease. They lock themselves in finery and wealth, and they refuse to see anything that might jeopardize their comfort." Lada paused, remembering her mother's teeth, her mother's foot. Perhaps she should not begrudge the small measure of comfort a powerless woman had managed to find in a cruel world.

But she would absolutely begrudge her mother the failure to empower herself. Running and abandoning those who needed her was the weakest, lowest thing possible. Lada would not do that. She could not. Whatever else she was, Lada was nothing like the class who could go on living after turning their backs on those who depended upon them.

"What, then?" Nicolae asked. "Do we try to convince more boyars that you are a tame princess and not a warlord prince?"

Lada picked up a canteen of water and poured it on the flames, watching them sizzle and die. "I do not know. I have tried—" Her voice caught. She had tried everything. She had pledged loyalty to foreign kings, she had betrayed an ally, she had trusted that love was the same as honesty. "I have tried everything."

"The little zealot was always unlikely. None of us blame you for looking for help there, though."

Lada sat up straight, alarmed. "What do you mean?"

Nicolae's expression was without reproach. "We are all *very* good soldiers and scouts, Lada. Did you really think we would fail to notice the sultan camped within miles of us?"

She hung her head, the weight of her shame pulling her down. "I told you I was freeing you. But when he offered help, I leapt at the opportunity."

"We do not care," Petru said.

The way Bogdan sat perfectly still next to her indicated that he, perhaps, did.

"We know you fight for us. For Wallachia." Nicolae shrugged. "The little zealot was a means to an end. It did not work. So we find more means for the same end."

Lada held out her hands. "I have exhausted my means. I am sorry you have followed me this far."

"We still have Hunyadi," Bogdan said.

Nicolae rubbed his beard, leaning back with a thoughtful expression. "No, Hunyadi is not our best option. We have our own Hunyadi in Lada. What we need is someone who can work new angles of power. What we need is Matthias."

"He is the same as all the other leaders," Lada said, shaking her head.

"That is precisely the point." Nicolae smiled, the fire illuminating his face in the midst of the darkness. "He is the same as them. So if we get him . . ."

Lada took a deep breath filled with smoke. It seared her lungs. She wanted nothing to do with Matthias, and knew his help—if she could get it—would not be without a price. How much more of herself would she have to lose to get where she belonged?

"For Wallachia," Bogdan said.

Lada nodded. "For Wallachia."

27

April 4–6

A THICK FOG OVER THE city muffled all life: muting church bells, softening footfalls, cloaking the streets in a layer of damp and stifling mystery.

Radu turned from staring out his window into the blank white that had settled over the distance like a sickness coming ever closer. Taking a deep breath, he knelt on the floor facing Mecca. Letting go of his fear and questions, he hoped his prayer could find its way out of the fogged-in city even if nothing else could. He was so lost in the ritual he failed to notice an increase in the frequency and number of church bells until his door burst open.

For a split second, Radu froze. He was upright on his knees, so he clasped his hands in front of himself like he had been caught in an acceptably Christian form of prayer. Cyprian, breathing hard, had been scanning the room at eye level. By the time he looked down at Radu, Radu was *almost* certain everything appeared as it should.

"What is it?" Radu asked, standing.

"The Turks." Cyprian steadied himself against the door-frame. "They are here."

Without a word Radu pulled on his cloak. Nazira was in the kitchen preparing the afternoon meal with anemic vegetables and some lumpy bread. "While you are out, try to buy some meat!" she called as they rushed by.

"The Turks are here!" Cyprian shouted. Nazira was at their side as they ran out the front door. She wore only slippers and a layered dress. Radu unfastened his cloak and threw it around her shoulders. She held it shut, keeping pace with the two men as they raced through the streets toward the walls.

If Cyprian had not been with them, Radu was certain they would have gotten lost. The fog changed the character of the city, obscuring landmarks, leeching the already faded colors. With no church steeples visible, bells rang out as though from the world of spirits, their metallic warnings hanging lonely in the air.

"When did they arrive?" Radu nearly slipped on a slick portion of road. Cyprian grabbed his elbow to steady him.

"I do not know. I only now heard word of it."

By the time they bypassed several religious processions and made it to the walls, Nazira was winded and Radu was exhausted. They were allowed through a postern, one of the gates between the walls that let soldiers in and out of the city. Pulled down by the weight of fear, fog had settled heavily in this no-man's-land, curling and pulsing like a living thing. Radu kept brushing at his arms, trying to rub it off.

They were not the only ones who had come running. They had to wait several minutes before there was an opening for them to climb a narrow ladder to the top of the outer wall. As he searched for a good position for them, Radu bumped into Giustiniani. The Italian nodded, shuffling to the side to let them squeeze in.

There, shoulder to shoulder with their enemies, Radu and Nazira looked out on their countrymen. Tents had sprung up out of the mist like a growth of perfectly spaced mushrooms. Movement stirred the white tendrils of fog, offering glimpses of men who were then swallowed again.

"We are beset by an army of ghosts," Cyprian whispered.

"Do not let anyone hear you say that," Giustiniani said, his tone sharp. "We have more than enough superstition to contend with."

"When did they arrive?" Radu asked. He leaned forward and squinted, even though he knew it would not magically help him pierce the moisture-laden air. Knew he would not see what—who—he wanted to. But he tried nonetheless.

"It must have been in the night," Giustiniani said. "The damn fog has been so thick we did not even see them. I got reports of strange noises, and then it finally cleared some."

"What should we do?" Cyprian asked.

"Wait until we can see something. And then we will start collecting information."

Giustiniani had been right—visibility was poor, but sounds hung in the dead air. At times the noises were muted, as though coming from a very great distance. And sometimes they broke through with such startling clarity that everyone spooked, looking around in fear that the Ottomans were already behind the wall.

"Shovels," Nazira said, pointing toward the camp. "You hear that rhythmic scraping?"

Giustiniani nodded. "They will be digging their own moat, a protective line for themselves. Building up a bulwark to hide their lines behind. And generating material to try to fill in our fosse."

Another sound cut through the air. Radu had half turned before he realized what he was doing. The call to prayer, and Radu could not answer. He had prayed too early. Nazira's hand found his, gripping tightly. They stood, frozen, until it was over.

"Filthy infidels," a man to Giustiniani's right said, spitting over the wall. "The devil's own horde." Then the man straightened, brightening. "You hear that? Christians! I know that liturgy. We are answering them! I—" He stopped, his eyebrows drawing low. "Where is it coming from?"

"Outside of the wall," Cyprian said, his voice as heavy and blank as the fog.

"Mercenaries?" Giustiniani asked.

Radu realized the Italian had been addressing him. "Probably men pressed into service from vassal states: Serbs, Bulgars, maybe even some Wallachians. And then anyone who came willingly when they heard of the attack."

"Why would Christians come against us?" The soldier's face was twisted with despair. He turned to Radu as though he held all the answers.

It was Giustiniani who spoke, though. "For the same reason they sent us no aid. Money." This time he spat over the wall. "How will he organize?"

Radu leaned against the wall, turning his back on the Ottoman camps and staring toward the blank white bank of fog. Only one thing rose up high enough to pierce it—the spire of the Hagia Sophia. The cathedral the city left dark. "Irregulars and Christians at the fronts on most areas of the wall. Places he thinks are less important. He does not trust anyone who is here solely for money. Janissaries and spahi forces at the weakest points—the Lycus River, and the Blachernae Palace wall section."

"So he will be weak where the other forces are weak. If we sallied out, broke through—"

Radu shook his head. "He will have enough men to spare to make certain the irregulars maintain as much order and discipline as possible. There will be no breaking point in his lines. He will concentrate his attacks on your weaknesses, but he will have no weaknesses vulnerable to direct attack."

Giustiniani sighed. "So we wait."

"So we wait," Radu echoed.

———◆———

The next day dawned bright and clear. From the looks on the soldiers' faces, they wished it had not.

Radu was once again at Giustiniani's side, along with Cyprian. Nazira had stayed home. Her parting embrace had been too tight, her whispered caution tucked around him. Radu had to be more careful than ever.

Giustiniani handed him a spyglass. He pointed toward the back of the camp, in a corner where smoke was billowing upward. "What are they doing there?"

It took a moment for Radu to focus, and another few moments for him to train the glass on what he was trying to find. Familiarity warmed him, and he hid his affection behind a grim look. "Forges," he said, handing back the glass.

"What do they need forges that big for?" Cyprian asked.

"Cannons."

"They are going to make cannons on the battlefield?" Cyprian laughed. "Are they also planning on a brick kiln? Building a wall of their own while they are at it?"

"I think it is to repair cannons, mostly."

"They would need a tremendous amount of supplies." Giustiniani frowned. "The logistical aspects would be a nightmare. Do you think they could actually do it?"

"I do. Mehmed—" Radu cringed, and started over. "The sultan is organized and methodical. He has resources he can pull from two continents. If he needs it, it is already here or on its way. I have been in an Ottoman siege before, under the sultan Murad. This will be even bigger, cleaner, more efficient. Mehmed watched and learned. He will have enough supplies to last as long as he needs. The men will be limited to one meal a day to preserve food. He will keep things meticulously ordered and clean to prevent sickness."

Giustiniani pointed toward the rows of tents. "By my estimations, there are almost two hundred thousand men out there."

Cyprian let out a breath, as though he had been hit in the stomach. "That many?"

Radu nodded. "But roughly two men in support for every one man fighting."

"That still leaves sixty thousand? Seventy thousand?"

Cyprian covered his mouth with his hand. Radu was shocked to see tears pooling in his gray eyes. "So many. What could Christianity accomplish with a mere fraction of the unity Islam has? How can our God ever withstand the ferocity of this faith?"

"Do not blaspheme, young man." Giustiniani's tone was sharp, but it softened when he spoke again. "And do not despair. The odds are not so against us as they look." He patted the stone in front of them with one thick, callused hand. "With a handful of men and these walls, I could hold back the very forces of hell itself."

"Good," Cyprian said, his voice hollow as he looked back over the Ottoman camp. "Because it looks like we will have to."

Giustiniani left, but Radu and Cyprian stayed where they were. Cyprian waved his hand in disgust. "Look at those animals in that pen. That one, there. Those are not even war animals! That lord brought those to show off!"

Radu's eyes never left the red and gold tent in the center— Mehmed's. "A pasha, probably. Or a ghazi from the Eastern regions. They do not see each other often, so they would want to use this as a show of wealth and strength."

Cyprian laughed. "They do not even care about scaring us. They are here to impress each other." He sighed, finally turning and sinking down to sit with his back against the stones. Radu knew Mehmed was not here yet, that the tent was empty. Still, it was all he could do to look away and sit next to Cyprian.

"If they have all that—if they can do this much on a *military campaign*—why do they even want our city? That camp is nicer than anything we have in here."

Radu sighed, resting his head against the cold limestone

that stood between him and his people. "They think Constantinople is paved in gold."

"They are two hundred years too late. How can the sultan not know that?"

"He knows." Radu was certain of it. Mehmed was too careful, too meticulous not to know the true state of the city. "He lets them believe the city is wealthy so they are willing to fight. But he wants the city for itself. For its history. For its position. For his capital."

"And so he will take it."

Radu nodded, echoing Cyprian. "And so he will take it."

"What is life like under the Ottomans? For the vassal states and conquered people?"

Radu closed his eyes and saw a red and gold tent in the darkness. Saw the face of the man who would be there, so soon. Saw himself, where he should have been, in the tent next to Mehmed.

To impress his loyalty on Cyprian, he should probably talk of horrors. But the look of despair in Cyprian's eyes haunted him. There was comfort in the truth, so Radu extended it. "Honestly? It is better than many other things." Radu blinked away the images of what would not be, focusing on the city on a hill in front of him. "The Ottomans do not believe in the feudal systems. People are far freer under their rule. Industry and trade flourish. They let their vassal subjects continue to worship how they wish, without persecution."

"They do not force conversion?"

"Christians are free to remain Christians. The Ottomans actually prefer it, because they have to tax Muslims at a lower rate."

Cyprian laughed, surprising Radu. "Well, that is very . . . practical of them."

Radu smiled grimly. "I do not know if it will comfort you, but when I compare the people in Wallachia to the people in the Ottoman Empire, the Ottomans have it better."

Cyprian swallowed, his throat shifting with the movement. He looked down at his hands, which were clasped in front of him. "But it was not better for you."

Radu turned his head away as though struck, remembering what they thought he was to Mehmed. What shame and pain they must think he carried over what he was rumored to be. What he would gladly have been, had Mehmed so much as hinted that it was a possibility.

"No," Radu said, his voice a cold shadow in the clear sunlight. He stood just in time to see Mehmed's procession arrive, the walls of the city the least impossible barrier between Radu and his heart's desire. "Not for me."

28

Mid-April

LADA STOOD, PARALYZED WITH rage and grief, next to the bed where Hunyadi lay dying.

Three weeks ago when she left him, he had been robust and thick with power. Now he was a wasted shadow of himself.

Mehmed had managed to kill him after all.

Hunyadi wheezed a laugh. "He sends any men with the plague to the front lines. It is clever, really. He could not get me with a sword, but he got me with—" His words were cut off as he struggled to breathe, gasping.

Lada had never before felt so powerless. She wanted to kill something.

She wanted to kill Mehmed.

"Where is Matthias?" she asked the girl attending Hunyadi in the dark, cramped room in a humble home a good distance from the castle.

The girl kept her eyes averted, tending the fire as though keeping it alive would do anyone any good. "He does not come."

"His father is dying. Send someone to fetch him."

The girl shook her head, locks of hair falling in front of her face. "He will not come."

"It is better," Hunyadi said, finally able to speak again. He smiled. His gums were pale, his lips cracked. "I was gone when my father died. Too busy fighting to watch a sick old farmer die. And now my son is too busy in the castle to watch a sick old soldier die. It is good."

Lada hated this talk. She wanted more time with Hunyadi. She wanted back the time she had squandered that had cost them both so dearly. She could still learn so much from him. She helped him sip some water, then adjusted his pillow. "How did you manage it? How did you come so far from such a humble start?"

"I always chose the path of most resistance. Did things no one else was willing to. Took risks no one else dared take. I was smarter. More determined. Stronger." He lifted one shaking hand in the air and wheezed a laugh. "Well, some things change. But I was always brutal. I was the most brutal. When you start lower, you have to fight for every scrap of space you occupy in the world." He patted Lada's cheek, his palm too warm, and thin like parchment. "Even starting from nothing, I had more luck than you. If you had been born a boy, the whole world would tremble before you."

Lada scowled. "I have no wish to be a man." Then she cringed, the memory of Mehmed's hands and tongue and lips on her body. She had never been happier to be a woman than she had been in that falsely precious space. Her body had not felt like a stranger to her then. She wanted to reclaim that feeling.

Hunyadi's eyes narrowed thoughtfully. "No. You are right.

I think if you had been born a boy, perhaps you would have been satisfied with what the world offered you. That is how we are alike. We saw everything that was not ours, and we hungered. Do not lose that hunger. You will always have to fight for everything. Even when you already have it, you will have to keep fighting to maintain it. You will have to be more ruthless, more brutal, more *everything*. Any weakness will undo everything you have accomplished. They will see any crack as evidence that they were right that a woman cannot do what you do."

Hunyadi knew what he spoke of. Her merits, her accomplishments, her strength would never speak for themselves. She would have to cut her way through the world, uphill, for the rest of her life. She showed all her small teeth in a vicious smile. "I will make you proud. No one will be more brutal than me. No one will be more ruthless. And I will never stop fighting."

Hunyadi laughed, wheezing and gasping until he was so pale he looked dead already. Lada helped him drink. He choked, spitting most of the water out, but managed to swallow some. Finally, he closed his eyes. "No rest for the wicked. But this wicked soul will have some now, I think."

"Sleep." She wanted to give him assurances that he would get better, but she could not bring herself to lie to him. Not again.

"Promise me," he whispered. "Promise me you will watch out for my Matthias. Be his ally."

"I swear it." She did not mention that she already intended to be just that.

"Your father is dying," Lada said as she sat in a private room with Matthias. It came out as an accusation, though she knew Matthias was not to blame. *She* was, at least in part.

"I never understood him," Matthias said, toying with a goblet of wine. "I never even really knew him. He sent me away as soon as I could talk. When he visited, he watched me with this look—this look like he could not believe I was his. All I heard of him was stories of his conquests, his bravery, his triumphs. And when he visited, I recited *poetry* for him. I asked him, once, to teach me to fight. He had never lost his temper with me, never been around long enough to, but that day I feared he would strike me. He told me he had not fought his whole life so his son could learn to swing a sword." Matthias touched a worn hilt at his side. "Now I have his sword and no idea how to use it. That is his legacy to me."

"You do not need a sword. All you need is to work with people who know what to do with them." Lada leaned forward, forcing him to meet her eyes. "You want to be king."

Matthias smiled slyly. "I am loyal to our blessed king, long may he rule."

Lada brushed his false sentiment from the air with a wave of her hand. "If I wanted shit, I would have visited the privy, not asked for an audience with you."

Matthias laughed. "I think you have been living with soldiers for too long."

"And I think you and I have something to offer each other. You want Hungary. I want Wallachia. I will do whatever you need to secure your throne. And, once you have it, you will help me to mine."

Matthias raised his eyebrows. "Will I? Tell me, why would I want that?"

"A strong Wallachia means a more secure Hungary. We both know the current prince has given the sultan rights to move through the country. They walk straight to your borders without so much as a blade to bar their way. If you help me gain Wallachia, I promise no Ottoman army will make it through alive."

Matthias's hand traced the air above his head, lingering on something Lada could not see. "Do you know, Poland has the crown? They took it for 'safekeeping.' No one can be a legitimate king of Hungary without that crown."

"What does that matter? It is an object."

"It is a symbol."

"Dependence on symbols breeds weakness. If you are king, you do not need a crown."

"Hmm." Matthias dropped his hand and looked Lada up and down in a way that made her feel more like livestock than a person. "My father has left you in charge while he is on the mend."

How little did Matthias know of his father's condition? Lada was not equipped to break the news gently to him. He should have already been told. "Your father will never mend."

Matthias shook his head. "No, that will not do. My father is in seclusion for his health, but while he rests, he has entrusted you with his most private concerns and important charges."

Lada caught his meanings like the beginning of a cold. "Yes," she said. "He has left me in charge."

"And he tasked you with rooting out threats to the throne. Such as treason."

"Treason." Lada had expected to argue with Matthias, to

convince him of her utility. She had underestimated his willingness to grasp at any advantage.

"Yes. It would appear that Ulrich, the protector of the king and my chief rival, has been committing treason. You and your men will go to his home and find all the evidence you need." Matthias smiled, teeth stained dark with wine. "And then you will execute him on behalf of my father."

Lada raised an eyebrow. "Without trial?"

"You are Wallachians. Everyone knows how vicious you are." He watched Lada for her reaction. Balking at being asked to commit murder. Taking offense at being called vicious. He would get no such reactions from her. She met his look with a hint of a smile. He seemed to think she would dislike her people being spoken of this way. Instead, it filled her with pride.

Satisfied with her lack of objections, Matthias continued. "After Ulrich is dead, the king will need a new protector and regent."

Lada nodded. It was simple enough. "And then?"

"And then the king will succumb to his weaknesses, and the protector will be the most obvious choice for king. A king who can connect you with those who will secure your own throne." Matthias held out his hand. It hung in the air between them like a chain. The chain was weighted with the deaths of two innocent men. Ulrich, whom Lada did not know, but whose reputation was one of fairness and morality. And the child king, who had done nothing wrong but be born to power he could not wield.

Two deaths. Two thrones.

Lada took his hand.

29

April 9

RADU CREPT INTO THE kitchen, a knife in his hand. The noise that had awakened him in the middle of the night was revealed by a candle, which threw the room into sharp relief. A few golden glows, a multitude of black shadows.

One of the glowing points was Cyprian's face, but it did not have its usual light. "What is wrong?" Radu crossed the room to him and felt his forehead, fearing Cyprian was ill.

Then he smelled the alcohol, and Cyprian's malady was explained. "Come on." Radu took Cyprian's elbow to steady him. "You should go to bed."

"No. No! I cannot sleep. Not now. I fear what dreams will dance before me after tonight's meeting with my uncle."

The withered part of Radu that still hoped to make some difference jolted alert. "Then we should go for a walk. The night air will help sober you."

Cyprian mumbled assent. Radu found the other man's cloak discarded on the floor and helped Cyprian fasten it. Cyprian stayed close to Radu, one hand on his shoulder. The weight of it suggested Cyprian could not quite stay upright without Radu's support. "What about Nazira?"

"She will not miss me." Radu opened the door and helped Cyprian navigate the short distance to the street. They walked in silence for some time, Cyprian leaning against Radu for support. The night was bitterly cold and as still as the grave.

"You love Nazira," Cyprian said.

"Yes."

"Like a sister."

Radu stopped, causing Cyprian to stumble. Radu forced a quiet laugh. "You have never met my sister if you think I could ever adore her as I do Nazira."

Cyprian gestured emphatically. "But there is no passion."

Radu began walking again, his mind whirling. Cyprian saw too much. They should never have agreed to live with him. If someone suspected Nazira was anything other than his beloved wife, they were in more danger than ever. She had come to sell his story beyond doubt. But if people doubted the marriage itself . . . "She is my wife, and my concern. And now you are my concern, too. What is wrong? I have never seen you like this." In the weeks that they had known him, Cyprian had never been drunk. Even when he had learned of the deaths of his fellow ambassadors, he had remained focused and collected in his grief. Something must have happened tonight to effect such a change.

"Eight thousand," Cyprian said, his voice a whisper.

"Eight thousand what?"

"Eight thousand men. That is all we have."

Radu paused, causing Cyprian to stumble again. Radu

caught him and held his arms. "Eight thousand?" That was fewer than Radu had suspected. He had seen how bleak the city was, but not even that was enough to indicate just how few men they had to call on.

"Eight thousand men for twelve miles of wall. Eight thousand men against sixty thousand."

"But surely more help will come."

Cyprian shook his head, listing to the side with the movement. "My uncle holds out hope, but I have none. The Turks are already here. You told us they have a navy on the way. Who will send aid? How will they get here? Who will look at the hordes at our gates and dare stand with us?"

"But you heard Giustiniani on the walls. You are still fighting from a place of strength." Radu did not know whether he was trying to press Cyprian for more details on the city's defenses or to comfort him. "You were able to repel that attack yesterday!"

Mehmed had sent a small force against one of the weaker sections of the wall. It was a sudden, ferocious attack. But after a couple of hours, two hundred Ottomans were dead and only a handful of defenders had been lost. It was a huge victory for Giustiniani, evidence that his claims of being able to defend the city had some weight.

Or at least, that was what was being said. Radu suspected that Mehmed had been playing, like a cat with its prey. Because what no one knew, what they did not take into account, was that throwing men at the walls was not how Mehmed meant to break them. The cannons had not arrived yet. Until then, he was content to bat at the walls and watch the mice scramble.

Radu saw a familiar building in front of them. He steered Cyprian toward the Hagia Sophia and propped him against the wall while he picked the lock. The door clicked open. Radu grabbed Cyprian and pushed him into the church. Cyprian stumbled, looking up at the ceiling instead of at his feet. "Why are we here?"

"Because it is quiet."

"Have you come here before? You picked that lock very easily."

Radu smiled, because Cyprian could not see it in the dark. "It took me forever to pick the lock. You are too drunk to remember. You fell asleep in the middle."

"I did not!"

Laughing, Radu guided Cyprian toward a corner, where the drunk man slid down against the wall and leaned his head back. Radu sat next to him, mimicking his posture.

"I am so sorry," Cyprian said.

"For what?"

"For bringing you here. I condemned you to death. I should have— I thought of taking us somewhere else. To Cyprus. I should have talked you out of this madness. Now you are trapped here, and it is all my fault."

Radu put a hand on Cyprian's arm, hating the anguish in his friend's voice—no, not his friend. He could not view him as a friend—would not. He quickly pulled his hand back. "You saved us from Mehmed. Do not apologize for that. We came because we wanted to help the city. We would not have accepted running and hiding, just as you could not bring yourself to do it."

"You call him Mehmed."

Radu turned toward Cyprian, but the other man was staring straight ahead into the darkness. Radu could not make out his expression. "What do you mean?" he asked, his voice careful.

"The sultan. You try not to, but when you are not being careful, you call him Mehmed. You were close to him."

Radu searched the shadows around them for the right way to answer. Cyprian spoke before he could, though. "It was not all bad, was it? Being with him?"

Now Radu was fully alert. Could Cyprian's drunkenness have been an act to lull Radu into security, to get him to reveal something he should not? Was this a follow-up to the prying questions about Radu's relationship with Nazira? He chose his words with as much care as he had ever given anything. "The sultan was kind to me when we were boys. I looked up to him. I thought he had saved me from the pain we endured from his father's tutors. He was all I had."

"Your sister was with you, though."

Radu laughed drily. "Again, you have never met my sister. She responded to our torments by getting harder, crueler, further away. It made her stronger, but it was breaking me. So when Mehmed—the sultan—offered me kindness, it was like someone had offered me the sun in the midst of the longest, coldest winter of my life." Radu cleared his throat. He walked as close to the truth as he could, so that his lies would be masked in sincerity. "But as we grew older, he became different. More focused. More determined. The friend and protector I thought I had was not mine at all, and never had been. I valued him above everything else, and he— Well. Everything in the empire belongs to him, and he uses people as he sees fit."

Radu knew Cyprian would think he was referring to being part of a male harem. But the sadness in his voice was not hard to place there. Mehmed had used him—sent him away on a fool's errand. He would rather have been a shameful secret than a banished one.

"But did you love him?"

Radu stared hard at Cyprian. Cyprian, in turn, stared only at the frigid marble tiles beneath them, tracing his finger along a seam. The question sounded oddly earnest, not as though he were teasing or trying to provoke Radu.

Radu stood. "It does not matter, because I betrayed him. He never forgives betrayal." Radu held out his hand, and Cyprian took it. He pulled Cyprian heavily to his feet, and they both lost their balance and stumbled. Cyprian held on to his collar, his face against Radu's shoulder.

"I would forgive you," he whispered. There was a moment between several breaths where Radu thought, maybe, perhaps—

Then Cyprian bent over, hands on his stomach, and ran for the door. Radu followed, then wished he had not as Cyprian vomited into the street just outside the Hagia Sophia.

Confused and cold, Radu closed and locked the door behind them. *I would forgive you* echoed in his brain, sticking where it should not.

Would he really? If he knew?

Radu turned to help Cyprian, whose wretched retching noises were the only sound in the dark. A movement caught his eye. Across the street, in the shadows of a pillar, stood a boy. Radu peered through the darkness and then inhaled sharply with surprise.

It was Amal. The servant who had spied for him while

Murad died. The servant who had raced through the empire to bring word to Mehmed so he could claim the throne before it was taken from him. The servant who had most definitely been in the palace at Edirne when Radu left.

The boy smiled at Radu. Checking to make sure Cyprian was otherwise distracted, Radu hurried across the street. He whispered troop locations, numbers, and any other details he could recall that Amal would be able to remember. To take to Mehmed.

His Mehmed.

Then Radu went back to Cyprian and helped the other man home, his burden lifted by excitement and hope.

Radu paced, the candle in his hand throwing his shadow on the wall behind him. Nazira sat on the bed.

"He did have a plan for us! That was why he told me to visit the Hagia Sophia. He always meant to send a scout to find us there. Amal is the perfect choice! The passage between Galata and Constantinople is open during the day. He can easily slip back and forth, meeting Mehmed's men beyond Galata and carrying information. Oh, Nazira, he did have a plan for us."

Radu finally sat, overcome with exhaustion and relief. Nazira got off the bed and knelt in front of him, placing the candle on a table and taking Radu's hands in her own. "Of course he had a plan for us. Did you really think he sent us here for nothing?"

"I feared it. I thought he wanted me gone. I was so scared. I thought I had risked your life without any purpose."

She tutted. "I would never do anything so foolish. And I would never accuse Mehmed of being wasteful with resources. Of course he would not fail to take advantage of you. We will have to be careful with Amal and not put him in any danger. But it is a good method."

Before Radu could stop himself, tears streamed down his face. He and Nazira would be useful. They would help Mehmed. And Mehmed would know and be glad. "He did not abandon me," Radu said, lowering his head onto Nazira's shoulder. "I can still help him."

Nazira patted his back, then lifted his chin so he looked her in the eyes. "We can help the empire. That is why we are here. To fulfill the words of the Prophet, peace be upon him, and to secure stability for our people. We fight for our brothers and sisters, for their safety. Do not lose sight of that. We are not here as a favor to Mehmed." She paused, her voice getting softer but cutting deeper. "He will not love you for what you do here."

Radu jerked back from her words. "Do not speak to me of it."

"You carry too much hope, and it will canker in your soul like an infection. Serve Mehmed because through serving him, you serve the empire. But do not do it out of some desperate hope that it will make him love you the way you love him. He cannot."

"You do not know him!"

Nazira raised an eyebrow. Radu lowered his voice, hissing instead of shouting. "You do not know him. Besides, I do not wish anything more from him than his friendship."

"You are welcome to lie to me, but please stop lying to

yourself. Whatever your hopes are with him, I promise they will never be realized."

"*You* have found love."

"Yes. With someone who could return it. But you refuse to let go of this festering love for a man who is incapable of loving you."

Radu blinked back tears. "Do I not deserve love?"

She put her hand on Radu's cheek. "Sweet Radu, you deserve the greatest love the world has ever seen. I simply do not think Mehmed is capable of loving *anyone* the way you love him."

"He loves Lada."

"I have met your sister, and I have met Mehmed. They love themselves and their ambition above all else. They love what feeds their ambition, and when it stops feeding that, the love will turn to hate with more passion than either could ever love with. You love with all your heart, Radu, and deserve someone who can answer that with all of theirs."

Radu's buoyant happiness was now a leaden weight, dragging his soul lower than it had ever been. "But Mehmed is all I have ever wanted. He is the greatest man in the world."

"I agree. He will be the greatest leader our people have ever seen. And he will do great things. He is more than a man—which also makes him less. He has nothing to offer you."

Radu stood, pushing past Nazira. He felt hemmed in on every side, claustrophobic and desperate for air. "It does not matter anyway! I cannot have the love I want under any religion. It is wrong."

Nazira grabbed his arm, spinning him around to face her. She was livid. "Do you think my love of Fatima is wrong?"

He held up his hands. "No! No."

"God encompasses more than any of us realize. The peace I feel in prayer is the same I feel when I am alone with Fatima. The clarity of fasting is the same I have when we work side by side. When I am with Fatima, what I feel is pure and good. I cannot imagine a god who hates anything that is love, any way we find to take tender care of each other. I want you to find that same love, and I never want you to hate yourself for any love that is in you." She pulled him close and he let her, wondering if it was possible for him to ever have the clarity and purity of love that she had.

Knowing that with Mehmed, it was not possible.

But how could he let go of the man written onto his very soul?

30

Mid-April

THEY SPREAD THROUGH THE manor like fire. Servants awoke to the sounds of crashing furniture and breaking glass. Some tried to fight. Lada had instructed her men to kill no one. It was not difficult to subdue half-asleep, unarmed people.

By the time they reached Ulrich's bedchambers, he had dressed and was waiting for them. His back was straight, his shoulders broad, his face impassive. There was no one else in the bedchamber. Lada was grateful his wife was not there to weep and beg, to bear witness. It was cleaner this way.

Ulrich had a sword sheathed at his side. He made no effort to draw the weapon.

"What is the meaning of this?" he asked, voice calm and assured.

Lada knew his fate already. She did not wish to engage with him. With no witnesses, she did not have to playact and accuse him of things they both knew he had not done. Watching him greet his end with such stoic resolve filled her with a measure of shame. He was a strong man. Possibly even a great one, according to Stefan's information.

So she said nothing. She walked past him, drawing the letter from Mehmed out of her vest. The seal was still intact, his elaborate signature unmistakable. She took tongs and pulled a coal from the fire. With a small thrill of vindictive pleasure, she burned away her own name and the poetry Mehmed had written with his false fingers. When she was finished, the only things that could be seen were Mehmed's signature and his promise to meet in Transylvania with a gift of men.

She held out the letter to Nicolae. "We found him trying to burn this."

Nicolae took it, an uneasy look shadowing his face. She had not told her men everything, merely that they were raiding the house on behalf of Matthias and Hunyadi. This alliance had been Nicolae's idea, after all. He had no right to question where the road he had set them on would lead.

Lada turned back to Ulrich. Now, at last, emotion shaped his warm brown eyes. But he did not look angry or afraid as she had expected. He looked sad. "He could be an excellent king, you know."

Lada wondered why Ulrich was talking about Matthias. But then Ulrich continued. "He is a good child. Smart. With a genuine kindness to his soul that is uncommon in anyone, much less royalty. If he is allowed to grow long enough to reach manhood, he will be a fair and just king. The type of king Hungary needs and deserves."

"I am sorry." And, to her surprise, Lada *was* sorry. She had been so focused on getting Matthias's bidding done, she had not stopped to think how it would feel. Securing the throne of Hungary for someone else was not so simple as she had imagined.

She shook her head. "But I cannot put the needs of Hungary over the needs of Wallachia."

The tears that pooled in Ulrich's eyes caught the light of the fire. He lowered his head, whispering a prayer. Then he held out his arms to either side. "Remember that he is a child. Give him a gentle death."

Lada's knife paused. She looked down at it as it trembled in her hand. This was the first time she would kill a man outside of battle. It was not a reaction to save her own life. It was a choice. She could let Ulrich—a good man—live. He would take this attack as proof of Matthias's treachery and use it to drive him out of the castle. The young king could grow into a man shaped by the strength of his genuine protector.

Lada looked up into Bogdan's face—the face of her childhood. It held no judgment. He simply watched her, waiting. The locket around her neck pressed heavy against her heart.

Wallachia.

She took a deep breath. When she plunged the knife into Ulrich's heart, her hand was steady.

—◆—

The "evidence" was enough to justify Ulrich's death with only moderate outcry. And since Elizabeth had chosen him as the king's protector, her decisions were suspect as well. She was removed to a far distant castle, to be kept there in seclusion. Matthias was named regent—and heir, should the king die without issue.

Lada did not doubt that would be the case, and sooner rather than later. When she watched Matthias put a hand on the trembling child's shoulder, Lada remembered Ulrich's request.

"Kill him gently," she said when Matthias met her in a quiet hall of the castle that would be his. Lada hated Hunedoara, hated this castle, hated her ally. She needed to be free of Hungary.

Matthias laughed. "Are you giving me commands now?"

"It was Ulrich's last request."

"I will do as I see fit." He handed her a letter, sealed with his coat of arms, in which a raven figured prominently. That morning, Lada had seen a raven pull a pigeon from its own nest in the castle eaves, tearing it apart methodically and efficiently.

"This is an introduction to Toma Basarab. He will instruct and help you on your way to the throne. No one knows the Wallachian boyars better than Toma."

"And men?"

Matthias shook his head. "I have no men better than the ones you already possess, and besides, I cannot part with any. If my men were to accompany you and you failed, it would destroy relations between Hungary and Wallachia."

Lada smiled tightly. "So regardless of whether I win or if I die, you still have an ally on the throne." Matthias was born to this. The young king might have a core of kindness, but Matthias knew what it took to gain and keep power.

"You understand perfectly," he said. "I do hope you succeed, Lada Dracul. I am very curious to see what you can do. I look forward to a long and fruitful relationship."

Lada wanted no such thing from him. But he had given her another knife, and she would use it to cut her way to the throne.

She inclined her head, unwilling to bow or curtsy. "I will pay my respects to your father before I leave."

Matthias's expression turned briefly wistful before resuming its usual sharpness. "He is dead. His final act was rooting out the traitor Ulrich. I do not expect you to stay for the funeral."

Lada flinched. She had betrayed Hunyadi to his downfall, and then she had falsely betrayed a good man in his name. This was the thanks she gave Hunyadi for his love, for his trust, for his support.

She clutched the locket around her neck so tightly her knuckles went white, drained of blood.

"You are a strange girl," Matthias said fondly.

"I am a dragon," she answered. Then she turned and left the toxic castle for what she hoped was the last time.

31

April 12–19

As Radu and Nazira prayed in their room in the pre-dawn light, the end of the world began.

They felt the rumblings beneath their knees, cutting off their prayer. The church bells began pealing with all the urgency of angels ushering in the end of times. Radu heard screaming in the streets.

"The cannons." He turned to Nazira. "The cannons are here."

"Go," she said.

Radu yanked on his boots, nearly falling over in his haste. Before he had finished fastening his cloak, there was pounding on the bedroom door. Radu opened it to find Cyprian, as pale and worn as the limestone walls. "The cannons," he said, shaking his head. "We are finished."

"We must go to the walls." Radu grabbed Cyprian's arm and turned him around. "Have you been yet? What has fallen? Are the Ottomans in the city?"

"I do not know what has happened since I left. I was with

my uncle and Giustiniani. They have requested you. I think they finally believe your account of the Turks' guns."

Radu almost laughed as they raced out of Cyprian's home and through the streets. They had to push past several mobs that had gathered outside churches, everyone trying to press in at the same time. Concussive blasts shook the whole city, bursts that punctuated the still-clanging bells and the desperate wailing.

"You!" Cyprian grabbed a monk by the collar. The man looked at Cyprian as though he were the devil himself. "Where are you going?"

"To the church!"

"You will do no one good there!"

The monk's conviction that Cyprian was the devil solidified. He glared, aghast. "That is the only place we *can* do any good!"

"Gather citizens, have them haul stones and material to the walls. We will need everyone's help if we are to survive the night. You can pray while you work."

The monk hesitated but nodded at last. "I will spread the word."

"That was good," Radu said as they continued their sprint toward the walls.

"It will not be enough. Promise me that if they get through, you will run."

"I must get Nazira first."

Cyprian nodded. "Go to Galata, if you can. You may be able to slip out undetected."

"What about you?"

"I will stay with my uncle."

Radu stopped. The walls were in sight. They could see plumes of smoke, and the dust of shattered stone hanging in the air like a vision of the future. "You do not owe this city your life. It is not even *your* city."

Cyprian stopped, too, and they stood side by side, chests heaving from their run. "My uncle has shown me every kindness."

"And you should be and are grateful. But if it comes to staying and dying, or running and living, choose the latter. He would want that for you."

"Would he?"

"If he does not, he should. The city will stand or fall depending on the whims of fate. It would be a tragedy if you fell with it." Radu realized as he said it how true it was. He could not bear the thought of Cyprian dying with the city.

Cyprian's gray eyes shifted from troubled to thoughtful. Then his smile, the one that nearly shut his eyes with its exuberance, the one Radu had not seen in some time, erased everything else. Cyprian shook his head as though trying to physically shift the smile into a more appropriate expression, but it lingered. "Thank you," he said. Radu had never really noticed Cyprian's mouth before, but for some reason he could not look away from it now.

With all the clanging and shouting, Radu was disoriented. His head felt light, and his heart was beating far faster than the run here should have made it.

The sound of a stone ball smashing against a stone wall shook him out of his stupor. Cyprian guided Radu through the chaos to where the emperor and Giustiniani waited. They stood beneath a tower, gesturing emphatically. The barrel of a very large cannon stuck out of the tower, pointed toward the Ottoman troops.

"No!" Radu shouted, sprinting toward them.

A cracking noise rendered him momentarily deaf. As though it were happening from a very great distance, he watched the unanchored force of the cannon shoot it backward. The heat and movement of the blast were too much for the gun. As it hit the back of the tower with shattering force, both gun and tower exploded. Radu turned and tackled Cyprian to the ground beneath them, covering his head as rubble rained down on them. Something slammed into his shoulder.

When only a fine shower of dust was left falling around them, Radu rolled off Cyprian, clutching his shoulder.

"Are you hurt?" Cyprian leaned over him, searching him for a wound.

"Look for the emperor! He was closer."

Cyprian stood, dodging around the remains of the tower. "Uncle? Uncle!"

With a pained groan, Radu pushed himself up to a seated position. The tower was gone. Only its stone base was left. Several broken bodies were half buried in the rubble.

"Over here!" Cyprian shouted. Radu grimaced as he tried to stand. Cyprian must have found the emperor. Or his body. Radu knew he should feel relief or even joy that the emperor had been killed this soon—and by his own men's folly, no less. But it made him sad.

"Oh!" he exclaimed, looking up in wonder as Constantine held out a hand to help him stand. "I thought— You were so close to the tower!"

"Giustiniani heard your shout and we jumped free. How did you know it would come down?" Constantine looked toward the remains with murder written on his face. "Is my weapons master a traitor? Did he sabotage us?"

Radu grabbed his shoulder as though that could ease the pain pounding through him. "Not a traitor. Simply a fool. You cannot fire a cannon that large without padding all around it. The force of the blast pushes it backward. He packed too much gunpowder, too. I told you I knew of the sultan's guns. Urbana, the engineer who made them, was from Transylvania. She was my friend. We spoke often."

"Let me see," Cyprian said. He turned Radu around and gently peeled Radu's shirt free from his injured shoulder. His fingers were as light as a promise where they traced Radu's skin. Radu shivered. "You are not bleeding. There will be a lot of bruising. But if you can still move your shoulder, it is probably not broken." Cyprian's fingers lingered for a few infinite seconds longer; then he replaced Radu's shirt. That sense of breathlessness was back.

Giustiniani cleared his throat, spitting. He had so much stone dust in his hair he looked as though he had aged thirty years. He considered Radu thoughtfully. "Are you an expert in cannons, then?"

"Not an expert. But none of these towers are equipped for cannons. They are not strong enough, and there is not enough room to support the guns. You will have to figure out another way to use them."

"We thought if we could fire back at the sultan's cannons, we could—"

"Too small a target. By the time you used enough shots to

get the range right, they would move their guns. You have seen their camp. If you managed to destroy even one cannon, they have the means to repair and cast new cannons. I am certain Urbana will be with them. No one is better than she. And I am guessing they have dug in and are firing from behind a bulwark."

Constantine nodded grimly. "That first shot at the Saint Romanus Gate—even I thought the world was ending. But it has not been repeated. Maybe the cannon broke?"

Radu tested his shoulder. He could move it, but the pain was excruciating. "The Basilica." He almost smiled, thinking how delighted Urbana would be. "It has to cool between firing, so it's limited to several shots a day. It was more to prove they *could* than for any practical use. It is the number of guns you should fear, not the size of one. Are the walls holding?"

Giustiniani shook some of the grit from his hair. "So far there are no holes big enough to threaten us. They fire wrong. They should fire in sets of three, one on each side and then one in the middle, to bring a whole section down. Instead, they fire at the same spot over and over again. They are doing damage, but not enough."

Giustiniani leaned out, watching without flinching as a massive ball shattered against the wall some ways down from them. The sound was louder than any Radu had ever heard, like thunder smashing against thunder.

"We cannot absorb these blows. The fragments from the wall are as likely to kill our men as the cannon shot itself." Giustiniani was silent for a while, deep in thought. "We cannot answer their cannons, nor can we trust the strength of the walls." He smiled grimly. "It is time to become more flexible."

Because of Radu's shoulder injury, he helped Cyprian with organizing rather than going to fix the walls. All day they ran, directing men to dump mortar paste down the walls to strengthen them. They attached rope to bales of wool and lowered them to absorb impacts. The palace was raided of all tapestries, the elegant stitching and bright depictions of the past now draped over the walls in a desperate attempt to secure a future.

By nightfall, everyone in the city was wide-eyed and trembling from the ceaseless bombardment. But they were ready. As soon as it was dark, Giustiniani sent the supplies up. At each significant breach in the wall, they put down stakes with stretches of leather hide nailed tightly between them. Into the space between the hides and the remains of the wall they dumped stones, timber, bushes, brushwood, and bucket after bucket of dirt.

A few stakes to save a city.

"Will they burn?" Radu asked Cyprian as they oversaw a patch along the Blachernae Palace wall.

"The hides will not light easily. But we will need to station guards with crossbows to keep men away, regardless." Cyprian paused to shout directions to men rolling large barrels packed with dirt toward them. "Along the top so we have something to hide behind!"

The men had only just finished placing the barrels when a stone ball came sailing out from the blackness. Radu did not have time to hold his breath as he watched it smash directly into the makeshift wall.

The loose materials held by the skins absorbed the cannonball's impact, and the ball rolled harmlessly to the ground.

The men around them cheered. Many dropped to their knees in prayer. Cyprian whooped joyfully, throwing his arms around Radu in a hug. Radu cringed at the pain in his shoulder, and at the shout of joy that had escaped his own lips before he realized he was cheering for the wrong side.

The next five days brought no rest, no change. The cannons fired, the sound of stone shattering stone so constant Radu stopped noticing it. The acrid scent of smoke was everywhere. When he came home to sleep for a few hours, Nazira made him dump water over his hair outside to try to rinse some of it away.

But as soon as sleep claimed him, the noise from the wall would jar him awake. He stopped trying to go home, instead slumping in the shadow of the inner wall for a few minutes of rest. The hours blurred, only the sun or the moon marking the passage of time. Even those were so obscured by smoke that they were hardly visible.

In addition to the ceaseless bombardment, Ottoman troops threw themselves against the walls at random. They used hooks to pull down the barrels of earth protecting the defenders. The Ottomans were packed so tightly that a single shot of a small cannon could kill several, yet still they came.

That was the part Radu wished he could block out, the acts that made him certain he could never wash the scent of the wall from his soul. Because he had to be on this side, and he had to play his part. And so, when the Ottoman soldiers—his brothers—ran up to try to retrieve the bodies of their compatriots, he sat on top of the wall with the enemy and picked them off one by one.

The first time he hit a man, he turned and vomited. But soon even his body was numb to the horror of what he was doing. That felt worse. With each shot he prayed he missed, and with each hit he prayed the walls would fall soon and spare them all.

On the sixth day of the bombardment, an explosion cracked through the air, echoing off the walls. It was notable only because it had not come from the walls—it had come from the Ottoman camp.

Radu ran to the top of the wall, leaning over. Black smoke billowed from the bank of earth that hid the Basilica. The location of the cannon had been identified on the first day, but Giustiniani had not been able to destroy it. They had not needed to, apparently.

Even from this distance the devastation was obvious. The gun must have finally succumbed to the heat and pressure of so many firings and exploded. Radu wiped furiously at his face, his hands leaving more grit than they cleared away. He had no doubt that Urbana had accompanied Mehmed to take care of her precious artillery. Had her greatest triumph been her end?

An exhausted and ragged cheer rose around him, but this time he could not even pretend to join in. The Basilica was gone. The wall still held. And his friend was more than likely dead.

Cyprian found him sitting with his back to the barrels, staring blankly at the city on the hill. How much more would this damnable city cost them all before the end?

"Come. Giustiniani is at the Lycus River Valley section of the wall. He is guaranteed to have some food worth eating." Cyprian led Radu down the line to the Italian. He ate the offered food in numb silence as the sun set, realizing too late that he had not even remembered to pray in his heart.

"You should go rest," Giustiniani said, his tired smile kind. "We have had a victory today, through no merit of our own. But we will take it."

Radu felt as though he could sleep for years. That was what he wanted. To fall asleep and wake up with the city already the Ottoman capital, everything changed and settled and peaceful once more. Because he still believed Constantinople should be and would be Mehmed's. The Prophet, peace be upon him, had declared it.

But Radu did not want to see anything more that happened before the city fell.

That was when a rhythmic pounding broke through the smoke-dimmed quiet of the night air. It was followed by the clashing of cymbals and the calls of pipes. Finally, the screams of men joined the chorus, a chilling cacophony promising death. The hair on Radu's arms stood. He had been on the other end of this tactic before, at Kruje, exhilarated to join with his brothers in a wall of noise.

He had never been on the receiving end. He understood now why it was so effective, to hear what was coming and be unable to flee. Flares bloomed to life in the valley beneath them. With a wave of noise, thousands of men surged forward to crash against the wall.

Radu followed Giustiniani's screamed commands. Men raced from other sections of the wall to help. Radu fired arrow after arrow, switching to a crossbow when his injured shoulder became too much.

Still the Ottomans came.

Where they breached the wall, Giustiniani was waiting. At

some places the bodies were piled so high they formed steps nearly to the top. Ottomans scrambled on top of Ottomans, clawing their way to the death that waited for them. And then their bodies became stepping-stones for the men behind them.

Everything was smoke and darkness, screaming and drums, blood and fire. Radu stared in a daze. How could these be men? How could this be real?

"Radu!" Cyprian shouted. He grabbed Radu's arm, spinning him out of range of a sword. Several Ottomans had breached the wall next to him. Radu wanted to tell them they were not enemies. But their blades were raised, and so Radu met them. Cyprian pressed his back to Radu's. A sword flashed toward Cyprian. *Not Cyprian* was Radu's only thought as he hacked off the arm holding the sword. It was then that he finally saw the face of the man. He looked at Radu, all rage draining away. He looked like Petru, that stupid Janissary Lada kept around. He could have been, had Lada not taken them to Wallachia. Then the man tipped off the edge of the wall and fell into the darkness.

Radu did not have time to think, to feel, because there was another sword and another arm. These were his brothers, but in the chaos and the fury, it did not matter. It was kill or be killed, and Radu killed.

And killed.

And killed.

Finally, the attack that had started like a wave receded like one, quietly fading back into the night. Giustiniani limped past Radu and Cyprian. "Burn the battering rams. Let them gather their dead."

Radu did not know how long it had lasted, or what it had cost them, but it was over. He did not realize he was crying until Cyprian embraced him, holding him close. "It is done. We did it. The wall stands."

Whether Radu was crying in relief or despair, he was too tired to know. He had had no choice—had he? He had kept Cyprian alive, and he had stayed alive. But it did not feel like a victory. Together, they stumbled from the wall and into the city, collapsing in the shadow of a church and falling into a sleep not even the angry increase of bombardment could disturb.

When Radu awoke, his head was resting against Cyprian's shoulder. A deep sense of well-being and relief flooded him. They had done it. They had made it.

And then horror chased away the relief. He had fought at this man's side, rejoiced in their survival, knowing full well that every Byzantine who survived was one more Mehmed had to fight to win. Knowing that every day the walls held, more of his Muslim brothers died.

Where was his heart? Where was his loyalty?

Radu staggered away from the still-sleeping Cyprian. He wandered, dazed and in mourning, once again finding himself at the Hagia Sophia. A small boy was curled into himself, asleep at the base of the building. Invisible in the midst of so much darkness.

Radu walked over to Amal, his steps heavy. He leaned down and shook the boy awake.

"Tell Mehmed he is firing the cannons wrong."

32

Mid-April

LADA RAN TO MEET the solitary form of Stefan making his unhurried way through the canyon toward them. He had shaved. Facial hair had helped him blend in at the castle in Hunedoara, but out here where only landed men could have beards, a bare face made him more invisible.

"No gossip precedes us," he said. "We should make camp this afternoon, and travel the rest of the way in the morning."

Lada sighed. "I would set up camp with the devil right now if it meant getting out of the cold."

"I believe the devil quite likes flames."

Lada started, narrowing her eyes. "Stefan, did you make a joke? I did not think you knew how."

His face betrayed no emotion. "I have many skills."

Lada laughed. "That, I already knew."

The path they took followed the Arges River, retracing the route Lada had taken with her father so many summers ago. This time Bogdan rode at her side instead of in the back with the servants. And Radu was lost to her, as was her father and any tenderness she might have held for him.

Radu would survive. He would be fine. He could not die at the walls of Constantinople, because he belonged to her and she would not allow it. Just like Wallachia belonged to her and she would not allow anyone else to have it.

"Why do you keep looking up at that peak?" Nicolae asked, following her line of sight. "You are making me nervous. Do you expect an attack?"

Lada glared. "No."

She had considered slipping out and making her way toward the ruins of the fortress on the peak. She wanted to stand at its edge to greet the dawn and feel the warmth of her true mother, Wallachia, greeting her and blessing her.

But the too-recent encounter with her other mother pulled at her, tearing at the edges of her certainty. What if she remembered the fortress wrong? What if she climbed up and the sun did not come out? What if it did, but it felt the same as any other sunrise?

She could not risk tainting that precious memory. She clutched the locket around her neck, the one Radu had given her to replace her old leather pouch. Inside were the dusty remains of an evergreen sprig and a flower from these same mountains. She had carried them with her as talismans through the lands of her enemies. Now she was home, and still in the land of her enemies.

She would climb that peak one day, soon. When it was all hers. She would come back, and she would rebuild the fortress to honor Wallachia.

They paused at the peak's base, refilling their canteens and watering the horses. Lada dismounted. She scrambled through a jumble of dark gray boulders, following a trickle of water that met the stream. Hidden behind the rocks was a cave. She ducked inside, where the frigid temperature dropped even lower. She could not see far, so she felt along the rough edges of the cave. But then something changed under her fingers. These were too smooth, no longer the natural shape of rocks. Someone had carved this out of the mountain. Which meant it was not a cave.

It was a secret passage.

Lada pushed forward blindly until she hit the end. There were no other tunnels, no branches. Why make a passage that led nowhere? Had someone been cutting to the heart of the mountain just like Ferhat in the old story, only to find that mountains have no hearts?

A drop of water fell on her head and she tipped her chin up. She shouted. The sound echoed upward, disappearing into the noise of frantic bats disturbed in their slumber. Lada flinched, but none came down toward her.

Which meant there was another way for them to escape. She felt the wall again until she found handholds carved into the stone. There was only one place this tunnel could lead: straight to her ruined fortress. Which meant it was a secret escape, a way to be free when all other ways were closed.

Wallachia always found a way.

—◆—

Though it was spring—bitterly cold, but still spring—Lada saw more fallow fields than ones ready for planting. The land they traveled through had an air of stagnation.

Finally they reached farmland that was being used. Decrepit hovels with smoke rising from their chimneys dotted the edges of fields. On the horizon, the Basarab manor soared, two stories and large enough to house all the peasants in all the hovels they had passed. Lada and her men made no attempt to hide their approach. Matthias had promised to send notice. If he had betrayed them, they were going to have to fight regardless.

A child sat on the side of the road. His head was too big for his rail-thin body, which was visible through his rags. It was too cold to be out in anything less than a cloak. He watched them approach, listless.

Nicolae paused in front of him. "Where is your mother?"

The boy blinked dully.

"Your father?"

When there was no response, Nicolae held out a hand. "Come with me," he said. The boy stood, and Nicolae easily lifted him onto his horse.

"He is probably crawling with bugs," Petru said, frowning. "Leave him be."

Nicolae gave Petru a dangerous look, all his good humor gone. "If being infested disqualified someone from our company, you would have been out years ago."

Petru sat straighter in his saddle, hand going to the pommel of his sword. "I tire of being the butt of your jokes."

"If you do not want to be the butt, try to be less of an ass."

Petru's expression turned ferocious. Lada moved her horse between them. "If Nicolae wants to pick up strays, that is his choice."

Bogdan, next to Lada as always, nodded toward their party. "We are doing a lot of that." Behind the mounted men, straggling back for half a league, a weary but determined group of people was catching up.

In addition to her thirty remaining Janissaries, Lada had picked up more than two dozen young Wallachian men from her time in Transylvania and Hungary. They carried staffs, pitchforks, clubs. One had a rusty scythe. None of them had horses, but they marched in as near a formation as they could manage. Lada knew those men. But behind them were the fringes of the camp—women organized by Oana to run things, men too old to fall in easily with the eager young ones, even a man and his daughters who had followed them from Arges rather than take the dangerous roads alone.

"This is absurd," Lada said. "Why do they stay with us?" Her men, she understood. They had nothing better, nowhere else to go. They were loyal to her, and to the hope that perhaps she would find them a place in the world. They were soldiers, too, used to travel and hardship. But these people, they . . .

They had nothing better, nowhere else to go. They were loyal to her, and to the hope that perhaps she would find them a place in the world, too.

<hr />

An hour later Lada sat in a pleasantly furnished room, drinking hot wine, and warm for the first time since her mother's stifling sitting room. Bogdan was on one side, Nicolae the other. Petru and Stefan stood at the door, casually intimidating. Against the opposite wall, Toma Basarab's guards stood with snide confidence.

"The letter I received from Matthias Corvinas was . . . interesting." Toma Basarab's hair and beard were silver. He wore velvet and silk as dark as his wine, his buttons shining silver beacons that matched his hair.

"I want to be prince," Lada said.

Toma Basarab laughed, his mirth as bright as his buttons. "Why would you want that?"

"Our princes fail Wallachia. They are too busy appealing to foreign powers, pandering to boyars, desperately going over their own coffers. Meanwhile our country rots around them. I will change that."

Toma leaned back, tapping his fingers on his glass. "The system is what it is. It has worked for this long."

"Worked for whom?"

"I know you have big dreams, little Draculesti. But Wallachia is as Wallachia was and will ever be. What can you offer it?"

Lada understood immediately his true question was "What can you offer me?" She wished Radu were here. He would have this old fox eating out of his hand. Lada fixed a cold glare on him. "Your mistake is in thinking I care one whit about *offering* anything. The system is broken. I am going to change it."

"People who agitate for change end up dead."

Lada bared her teeth at him in a smile. "We will see who is dead at the end of all this."

Toma smiled, a slow spread of his mouth and ending with his dark eyes. "I think I see what you have to offer, then. Matthias was right to send you here. You have much potential. I will advise you. There are many boyars I can sweep into your support. A few will need . . . aggressive persuasion. But I suspect you excel at that. Under my guidance, you will get your throne in Tirgoviste. I would be proud to be at your side, serving a Draculesti prince." He held out his hands in offering, the fire in the hearth burning behind him.

Lada remembered her joke about making camp with the devil, and a sudden revulsion seized her. She did not want to have his help, or anyone's. But she needed it.

"Thank you." The words grated against her teeth like sand.

"My men will show yours where they can stay. Let us take a meal while we discuss the surrounding regions. Many of these boyars have done simply horrendous things to their people." He clucked his tongue in pity, but his eyes looked like they were tallying encouraging financial ledgers as he considered Lada.

33

April 19–21

RADU'S INFORMATION HAD LED to more successful cannon fire, and he paid the price. Every day he watched as the adjusted bombardment targeted the walls with more devastation, and every day he stumbled home, exhausted from trying to fix the holes. His aid to Mehmed put his own life in constant danger. Did Mehmed worry about that? Was he sorry?

Nazira's work was equally exhausting, but in other ways. "Helen cries constantly," she said in the morning, the only time they saw each other. "I have to spend half our time reassuring her that Coco, the Italian captain she is mistress to, really does love her and that when this is all over he will leave his wife in Venice for her. It is all I can do not to slap her and tell her she is wasting her life. The other women mostly spend their time in church praying. And when they are not there, they are complaining of how hard it is to get food and how they had to donate their tapestries to the walls. How is your work?"

Radu pulled on his boots. They were caked with dust from the walls. "The bombardment is going better, but there have been no gaps big enough for a full-scale assault yet. Mehmed sends skirmishing troops to harass the forces and make certain no one is able to rest. I wonder if we can do anything more."

Nazira sat next to him on the bed, leaning her head on his shoulder. "It is wearisome work, for both souls and bodies. If you want to leave, I will be at your side. But do you feel that if we fled the city and joined the camp, we would be able to say we had done everything we could? I know you will not be satisfied with anything less. Nor will Mehmed."

Radu sighed, running his hands through his hair and pulling it back at the base of his neck. He missed wearing turbans. They kept his hair out of his face and provided protection from the sun. There was something soothing, too, in wrapping one around and around his head in the morning. All his comforting rituals were taken from him here.

"You are right. We will stay."

Nazira patted his hand. "But I did hear something that will make you happy. Word is spreading that the Ottoman navy is approaching, with doom in its terrible wake. Our friend Suleiman will be here soon, and maybe that will signal a quick end."

Radu allowed himself a weary smile tinged with hope. It would do his soul good to see those boats. And it would not even hurt that he was not on them, because the sea was the one place he wanted to be even less than on the wall.

"I have been looking everywhere for you!" Cyprian said, joining Radu at the wall overlooking the Golden Horn. Radu had avoided Cyprian ever since that night they fought side by side.

It was easier this way. Though he still caught himself watching the men for Cyprian's way of walking, with shoulders leading, arms swinging wide.

"You leave so early and are never there at mealtimes. I miss you." Cyprian looked out over the water and tugged at the cloak around his neck. "Nazira is good company, but it is not the same without you."

It had been three days since Nazira brought news of the approaching fleet. Every spare moment Radu had, he spent at this wall looking for the ships.

Today, his long wait was answered. He wished Cyprian were not here, were not leaning close. It made it so much more difficult to be truly elated. The massive chain held, an impassable barrier stretching between Constantinople and Galata. In the horn, Constantine's ships loomed, ready to repel any attempt at destroying the chain. They were Venetian merchant ships, mostly, far taller and wider than the swift Ottoman war galleys. They were also armed to the teeth and well practiced in repelling pirates.

On the other side of the chain, just outside of firing range, Radu's fleet made the water look like a forest of masts. His heart swelled with pride to see it, and he shifted guiltily away from Cyprian. The fleet had arrived the day before, but this had been his first chance to come and see it in person. He wondered which boat Suleiman was on, wished he could see the admiral in full command of the finest navy in the world.

Cyprian looked on, devastation marring his face. "So many more than we had planned for. You were right, as always. Where did they find sailors?"

"Greek mercenaries, mostly."

"We will be our own undoing yet."

Radu hoped that was true, but still wanted to extend some comfort to Cyprian. It was an impulse he could not deny, and he thought again how this would all have been easier had Cyprian abandoned them to their fortunes once they had reached the city. His insistence on friendship made everything tight and aching in Radu's chest.

Radu again opted for truth as a way to avoid lying. "But the Ottomans cannot get past the chain."

"And neither can anyone else. Which means we are cut off from help. Men, weapons, supplies—nothing more is coming. What we have now is what we will have at the end, whatever that may be."

"Still, the seawalls are safe. Even if the Ottomans get past the chain, launching an assault from this side is nearly impossible. The sultan knows that. He means to press from all sides to wear you down. But you will not have to spare too many extra men to guard this wall. The Lycus River is his avenue in."

Cyprian considered Radu wryly. "You still think more like an attacker than a defender."

Radu blushed, his sheepish expression unfeigned. "I spent many years looking at maps over Mehmed's shoulder."

"What is he like? As a person, not as a sultan."

"This past year the sultan and the person have become inseparable." As Radu had seen Mehmed grow into himself and his power, he had also seen Mehmed grow further away. He was both proud and dismayed. "Before that? Focused. Driven. He had a burning intensity that did not slacken no matter what area of his life he directed it toward. He saw something unobtainable, and that was the only thing he wanted."

"Like you?" Cyprian's tone was soft and without accusation. It was merely curious, as though he was trying to fill in parts to a story he had heard only a few passages of.

Radu shook his head, keeping his eyes fixed on the water. The skies were leaden above them, making the sea the same color as Cyprian's eyes. But the sea was safer to look at. "No, it was the other Draculesti sibling who was the challenge."

"Your sister? She was part of his harem?"

"No." Radu grinned ruefully, finally looking at his companion. "That was precisely the problem. She was not, and she never would be, and so he wanted her more than anything else."

"What happened?"

"She left."

"She should not have left you."

"I wanted her to. I pushed her toward it. I thought that if she was gone, Mehmed would finally see—" Radu bit off the end of the sentence. It was so easy to talk to Cyprian. Too easy. He should not be admitting these things, not to him, not to anyone.

Cyprian filled in the rest of the sentence for him. "But Mehmed could only see the things he did not have. He is blind."

Radu cleared his throat and looked away. "Well. She left me, and she left him, too. And because of that, I think he will always love her. Or at least want her. He cannot abide failure."

"She was his Constantinople."

Radu smiled, having entertained the same thought before. But it was not quite right. "I am afraid Constantinople is his Constantinople. Nothing could ever overtake this city in his heart."

A shout from the tower next to them drew their attention back to the water. The Ottoman ships had broken formation and were turning away from the chain. Radu could not understand why, until he saw four huge merchant ships, barreling through the water toward the horn.

And directly toward the Ottoman navy.

"Those are Italian ships!" Cyprian said, leaning out over the wall. "They are making a run for the horn!"

The ships safely in the horn edged closer to the chain, uselessly firing cannons at the Ottoman fleet. They were too far away to make a difference. Radu could almost feel the desperation from here. Everyone could see the Italian ships, but no one could help them.

"It is four ships against more than a hundred. They will never make it through."

Cyprian smiled grimly. "Do not discount them. They are born on the water. If the wind stays with them, if luck is on our side . . ." Cyprian's lips moved silently, whether in prayer or something else, Radu did not know.

Together they watched the battle play out from above. Radu did not even have to pretend to be emotionally invested in the other side—he could look on with the same intensity as everyone else, and no one would know his hopes were with the Ottoman navy.

It did not look promising. He had assumed the numbers would give them the advantage, but the tall, heavy merchant ships cut through the water as though it were nothing. The smaller galleys struggled to navigate the choppy sea, their inexperience showing immediately. They fired cannons at the Italian ships, but no cannons large enough to be effective could be placed on the lightweight galleys.

The four ships barreled straight through the middle of the entire might of the Ottoman navy.

Cyprian cheered with the crowd that had gathered on the wall. Excited chatter around them made it feel more like a sporting event than a battle. Radu was devastated to see that it was *not* anything like a battle after all. His navy was useless.

Then he realized the wind was no longer flinging sea air in his face. Everything had gone still around them—and around the merchant ships. As fast as they had been slicing through the water, they now drifted directionless.

And the galleys had oars.

Suleiman wasted no time. The larger galleys pulled in close, the smaller galleys edging between them to get right next to the merchant ships. With no wind, the ships were at the mercy of the water—which was causing them to drift, slowly but surely, across the horn to the Galata shore, where Mehmed already had men waiting.

But the Italian sailors would not go down easily. They lashed the four ships together to prevent them from being separated and picked off. So many of the Ottoman vessels had converged it looked like a sailor could walk from one end of the sea to the other without ever touching water.

The first small galleys to reach the merchant ships never had a chance at boarding. Large stones and barrels of water were dropped by the on-deck loading cranes, damaging some of the galleys and sinking others. The sounds of the battle—the snapping of wood, the shattering of stone, and the clash of steel against steel—rang through the horn.

And always, a sound Radu heard even in his sleep, the screams of men. There was a quality of voice, some subtle shift, that allowed him even at this distance to pick out which screams were screams of killing, and which were those of dying.

When the Ottomans managed to throw ropes up, the ropes were cut down. Hands were sliced off when they tried to find purchase. Burning pitch was thrown, and Radu watched as men fell into the water to be extinguished or onto their own boats, lighting them on fire with their bodies.

The Italians had the advantage of height and weight, but the Ottomans kept coming. For every galley sunk, two more pushed into its place. It was exhausting to watch. The sun, too hot for once, had shifted overhead, marking the endless passage of time. The crowd around Radu and Cyprian had gone quiet except for the occasional prayer or gasping sob. Though the Italians fought bravely, the outcome was inevitable. They drifted ever closer to the shore, where the Ottoman cannons would take them out if the galleys did not manage to first. It was only a matter of time.

Radu closed his eyes in relief as a breeze cut through the sun battering his face. And then he opened his eyes in horror. A breeze from the south that turned into a stiff wind. A ragged cheer went up along the wall as the Italian ships' sails caught. They plowed through the galleys around them, pushing them aside like branches, moving forward as one. Their escape was unavoidable, unassailable.

Radu looked to the Galata shore and his heart sank. There, astride a beautiful white horse, a tiny figure watched as his navy—more than a hundred ships, the best in the world—was bested by four merchant boats.

Radu's project. Radu's navy. He hung his head with shame. Against all odds, they had failed. Mehmed's horse reared, then he turned it and rode swiftly away. All along the wall the citizens cheered and jeered, ebullient with the miracle of the Italian boats. The chain had been slipped free to allow them through. No galleys could catch up to take advantage before the chain was closed again.

It was over.

For once, Radu was invited to a meeting with the emperor. But this one he wished he could avoid. The humiliation of his navy's defeat settled in his chest like a sickness. It was a kindness, then, that he was not with Mehmed. He could not bear to think of what Mehmed would say, how disappointed he would be. He had trusted this task to Radu, and Radu had failed utterly.

Though Radu knew he should not, he took some small comfort in Cyprian's coming with him. He was unmoored, worn down by time and failure. At least with Cyprian he would have to pretend to be okay. That was a good reason. That was the only reason. He would not allow any other reasons to crave Cyprian's smile or a touch of his hand.

In Constantine's meeting room, Radu and Cyprian joined Giustiniani, the pretend Ottoman heir Orhan, the Italian commander Coco (whom Radu knew only through Nazira's stories of the unfortunate Helen), and the emperor. Constantine moved with more lightness than Radu had seen. He was again barefoot, pacing with joyful energy. "Grain, arms, manpower. Two hundred archers! But that is not the true strength. They have brought us hope. More can come. More will come. That wind was the hand of God, delivering a blessing to this city. The first of many."

Coco nodded, unable to avoid Constantine's infectious joy. "One good Italian ship is worth a hundred infidel boats."

Giustiniani laughed, clapping Orhan on the back. "So you see, we Italians can do good things. I hear the sultan is furious. The admiral will pay for his failure."

"Suleiman?" Radu spoke before he thought better of it. He tried to shift his face into impassivity, but it was impossible. "I knew him. Is he— Will he be killed?" A gentle hand on his back startled him, but he did not turn around. Had Radu's grief been that obvious to Cyprian?

"He lost an eye in the battle. That alone probably saved him, as testament to how hard he fought." Giustiniani snorted. "For all the good it did him. Our scouts report he was flogged and stripped of all rank and authority. One of the pashas is in charge of the boats now. Not that it matters. We have nothing to fear from the sea."

"But do the Venetians know that?" Cyprian asked. "They must have heard of the size of the Ottoman navy. How can we get word to them that they are guaranteed safe passage to the horn?"

Radu wished desperately that Lada were here. She would not be sad; she would not let this failure derail her. She would figure out a way to turn it to her advantage. She would use the enemies' strength and confidence against them. Just as she had when they snuck into the palace under Halil Pasha's nose, putting Mehmed in place to take the throne when his father died.

A flicker of delight lit Radu's soul as he remembered that night, all Lada's fierce Janissaries dressed in veils and silk robes, trying to walk like women so they could sneak past the watching guard. And then he knew exactly what Lada would do.

"Do you have any Ottoman flags?" he asked.

Everyone turned to him, puzzled. Orhan, a quiet, delicate man who wore a turban along with his Byzantine styles, nodded. "I have a supply of them."

"What about uniforms?"

Constantine spoke. "We have over two hundred prisoners. They have no use of their uniforms in our dungeons."

"Send out three boats tonight under cover of darkness. Small, unthreatening ones. I will teach their crews a few common greetings in Turkish. Have them fly the Ottoman flag and sail as close to the Ottoman galleys as they can."

"Slip by in disguise." Constantine tugged at his beard thoughtfully.

"Three small boats could get out where one large ship cannot. Task them with finding the aid we need, and then they can return, heralding the ships that will follow so we can be prepared to welcome them."

Giustiniani stretched in his chair, leaning back. "It is a good plan. Coco, select the men. They leave tonight."

The Italian captain nodded. Orhan excused himself to get the flags, and Giustiniani went to find suitable uniforms.

"Well done." Cyprian beamed at Radu.

Radu could not meet that smile full on, so he looked at the floor. He would not have time to send word to Mehmed. He did not need to, though. He *wanted* the boats to escape. Because if they could escape, they could return.

And when they did, Radu would have first warning of a Venetian force. Then he could warn Mehmed, and find some sort of redemption.

34

Mid-April

THIS TIME, STEFAN DID not return alone from scouting. He walked with a peculiar guilt, slinking back into camp with a girl.

"What is this?" Lada barely glanced at the girl. "You were supposed to bring information on Silviu's land and men." Toma Basarab had sent them here first. Silviu did not have much in the way of soldiers, but he was a Danesti and in the path of all their future goals. They could not leave a close blood relative of the prince behind. Lada was to negotiate his support. If that was not possible, she was to place him under house arrest and leave precious men here to watch him. Toma Basarab would hear no arguments against it.

"Well?" she demanded.

Stefan shrugged, clearing his throat at the same time, as though he could force the words out. Lada had never seen him like this. Fear seized her—was he injured? She looked him up and down, but he did not appear harmed.

His face flushed a deep red. "She caught me."

Lada finally looked at the girl. She was Lada's height, perhaps younger than her, but not by much. She met Lada's stare with a bold, unflinching one of her own. Her narrow jaw was set and her dark eyes burned. Rough cloth wrapped her hair, and her clothes seemed made for someone else. They hung all wrong on her body, loose in the shoulders and pulled tight across her stomach, which—

"Oh," Lada said, frowning.

The girl's hands jerked instinctively in front of her pregnant belly. Then she deliberately moved them away. "Caught your man spying. Told him I would turn him in unless he brought me here."

Lada raised her eyebrows at Stefan. He shrank farther into his cloak. No one ever noticed him. He drifted invisibly, a weary traveler no one wanted. That was his entire purpose.

"Well." Lada turned her attention back to the girl. "Here you are. What do you want?"

"You are that woman, right? I thought you would be taller. And older. You are very young."

Lada gave her a heavy look. "I assume there are many women in this country. You will have to be more specific."

"I heard rumors. You are staying with Toma Basarab. Took in men for soldiers. Peasants talk."

Lada shifted uneasily. Thanks to Toma's men—both his trained soldiers and the farmers they had conscripted—her ranks had swelled to over one hundred men. The peasants were poorly trained and poorly fed, but they had a gritty eagerness that could not be undervalued. And they did not eat much, which was good.

The girl leaned forward, burning with intensity. "Are you going to do that in more places? Take men for fighting the prince?"

"Yes," Lada said.

"Good." The girl's hands fisted over her stomach. "I want the Danesti dead."

It was a dangerous sentiment to voice aloud. Lada wondered at her daring. "Does your husband want to join? He should have come himself."

The girl let out a harsh laugh, a burst of bitterness more than humor. "I have no husband. Tell her what you saw, Stefan."

To Lada's surprise, he followed the girl's order without question. "Lots of girls. In the fields. Most—" He paused, then nodded toward the girl's stomach. "Most like her."

"And between us not a single husband. A few years ago we had a nasty bout of plague. Killed most of the boys. There weren't enough men to work the fields. None to marry daughters to. So our loving Danesti boyar decided he would take care of us himself." The girl paused, as though waiting for something. When Lada did not respond, she spoke again. "No husbands." The girl glared at Lada for her stupidity. "No husbands, but all our babies are bastard cousins."

Clarity finally caught Lada in its horrible grasp. "Oh."

"So you will not find many men here to swell your ranks. Our boyar worm Silviu will agree with whatever you want because he is a coward, but he will betray you to the prince at the first opportunity. And he has nothing to offer. You should kill him. If not, then leave. These lands are a waste of your time."

Lada felt anger rising within. "Why?"

"I told you, we have no men."

"No. Why did you let this happen? Why did all of you let this happen?"

The girl's face purpled with rage. "*Let* it happen? What choice did we have? We give ourselves or our families starve. What choice is there in that?"

"Does Silviu work the land?"

"No, of course not."

"Does he tend the animals?"

"No."

"Does he do a single thing that directly feeds you or your families?"

The girl looked as though she very much wanted to hit Lada. "He owns it. He owns it all."

Lada paused, weighing her options. Then she shrugged. She would negotiate her own way. "Not anymore."

They marched straight through the fields, past more than a dozen girls in the same condition as Daciana. The girls stood watching as the men passed. No one said anything.

Daciana walked next to Stefan's horse. Lada could tell the girl made him nervous, which she found perversely delightful. She had once seen Stefan slit a man's throat without blinking. That this pregnant slip of a girl could unnerve him when that had not was odd. Daciana talked softly to him. No one noticed Stefan until it was too late. But this girl had seen him, and would not stop seeing him.

Lada liked her.

An older woman ran from the middle of a field and caught up to them. She grabbed Daciana's hand and halted her. Daciana leaned close, whispering. Apparently satisfied with Daciana's explanation, the woman fell into step.

Silviu's manor was tucked into the side of a hill overlooking the farmland. Ten guards stood in front. Their helmets were slightly askew, swords and spears clutched so tightly they shook. Lada stopped her horse directly in front of them, well within striking distance. She remembered Hunyadi riding into an enemy city, broad-shouldered and armed with unassailable confidence. She wrapped the same around herself.

"I am here to see Silviu."

The guards looked at each other, at a loss.

Lada had seventy men at her back. The guards knew as well as she did that what she wanted, she would get. "Tell him I will receive him here. And then you are welcome to join my men, or to flee. Any other course of action will not end well for you."

The shortest man, broad-chested and of middle years, gave her an ugly sneer. "I do not take orders from women."

"My men do not have a similar problem." Lada lifted a hand. The man fell, a crossbow bolt sticking out of his chest.

A harelipped guard jumped away as though death were contagious. Which, in this case, it was. "I will go fetch him, Miss! Um, Madam. My lady. I— Right now!" Two of the guards turned and ran. The rest began edging toward Lada's men, hands far from their weapons.

"Hello, Miron," Daciana said. She stepped forward, blocking the path of one of the guards. There was something verminous about his face and his beady eyes that darted around. "You remember when we used to play together as children?"

He did not look at her. She held her hand out to the older

woman next to her. "You remember when my mother gave you some of our milk because you were starving?"

His lip curled in a snarl, but still he did not respond.

"You remember when I screamed and screamed, and you stood outside the door and did nothing? You remember when he offered you—what did he call them, 'seconds'? You remember what you did?"

The man had the gall to finally meet her gaze. He shrugged, face set in cruel indifference. He shoved his shoulder into her, to push her out of the way.

"I remember that, too," her mother said as she brought her hand between them. Lada's view was blocked by the soldier's body. He made an odd noise, twitching. Then he stumbled backward, blood-soaked hands tugging ineffectually at the rough wooden handle of a knife protruding from his stomach. He sank down against the stone wall of the house. His ratlike eyes looked up in shock and pain at the girl and her mother.

"And now we will never remember you again." Daciana turned her back on him.

Stefan pulled a handkerchief from his vest and offered it to her. She passed it to her mother, who wiped the blood from her hands.

"What is the meaning of this?" A portly man, face veined and splotchy with age and alcohol, stumbled out of the manor. He wore a velvet vest with a gold necklace, and a black cap on his large head.

"Silviu?" Lada asked. "I am here to negotiate your support." Lada drew her crossbow and shot him in the chest. One of Toma's men shouted in surprise.

Lada turned her horse. "That went well. We have the full support of this estate now. It is yours." She pointed to Daciana.

Daciana nodded, a dazed expression on her face. Her mother finished cleaning her hands and gave the handkerchief back to Daciana. "I will tell the men."

"No," Lada snapped. "I did not say the land was theirs. Or any of the fathers of this land. They forfeited their rights when they sold their daughters for food. Why did you let them live?"

Daciana's mother met Lada's gaze without shame. "I have three other daughters. I could not sacrifice myself without sacrificing them. Until today."

Lada wanted to argue, to chastise. Then she realized that this woman had come directly from working in the fields, where she had no need of a knife. How long had she carried it? How long had she treasured it in secret, waiting for the right moment? This woman was smart. She saw an opening and she took it.

Though why more people had not done this sooner, she did not understand. If the Wallachians could see past titles and velvet, they would see that the true strength of the land—the true power—was theirs. All they needed was a knife and an opportunity.

Lada would be both for them.

"You are in charge," she said to the old woman.

"You cannot do that," Toma's man said. "We need a boyar."

"Are you a boyar?" Lada snapped.

The man opened his mouth to argue further.

"I am the only royal blood here." She stared at him until he bowed his head and looked away. Then she pointed at the body of the murdered soldier and addressed Daciana's mother. "I trust you. Treat your daughters and granddaughters better than their fathers have treated them."

Daciana's mother nodded slowly, a determination settling around her eyes and replacing the shock. "What do we do when the prince finds out our boyar is dead?"

"Do what you have always done. Work the land. Let me worry about the prince."

The woman nodded, then dipped her head in a bow. "We owe you everything."

Lada smiled. "Do not forget it. I promise I will not."

35

April 21–28

"THERE YOU ARE!" CYPRIAN said brightly, in defiance of the weariness painted on his face in dust and soot and traces of blood.

Radu paused on the doorstep, trying his best to meet Cyprian's smile. He had just returned from a long night on the wall. A night of black punctuated by burning orange and darkest red. It was a relief to see Cyprian again. It was always a relief, because with the wall, reunions were never guaranteed.

Cyprian leaned past him to open the door, gesturing excitedly. "I found fruit preserves. I will not tell you what I had to do to get them, but—"

"Turks! Turks in the horn!" a boy screamed, running through the street.

Cyprian and Radu shared a look of confusion and concern. Radu was too tired to know whether this feeling was excitement or dread. He sprinted after the boy, caught his sleeve, and dragged him to a stop. "The chain has broken?"

The boy shook his head, eyes wide with excitement and fear.

"They sailed their ships over land!" The boy wriggled free and darted away, shouting his news with no further explanation.

Cyprian raised his eyebrows, concern overpowered by curiosity. He started walking in the direction of the seawall. Radu followed.

"Do you have any idea what he is talking about?" Cyprian asked.

"Maybe they were able to sneak in the same way our boats slipped out past them?"

"That worked because of the chaos. But there is no chaos on our side of the chain. No one sleeps. Watch is kept at all hours. There must be something else going on."

Radu trudged after Cyprian. He could not find the energy in himself to run anymore. He had spent half the night cutting down hooks that the Ottomans threw up to try to dislodge the barrels of earth that protected the defenders. It was wearying work. Even arrows singing past his ears barely registered after a few hours on barrel duty. But at least all he had done was remove hooks. He had not had to kill any of his brothers last night, which made it better than most.

His mind was on endless barrels of earth as they climbed to the top of the seawall and looked over.

"God's wounds," Radu whispered. Nothing had prepared him for this. The Ottomans were, in fact, inside the horn. And just as the boy had said, they were sailing their ships over land.

Three medium-sized galleys floated in the water, their crews laughing and waving their oars. Coming down a road of greased logs on the hill behind the horn, another galley slowly made its way toward the sea. The men aboard rowed their oars through the air, perfectly in sync. Oxen pulled from the front, and hundreds of men held ropes to control the descent. Cresting the hill behind the galley was yet another boat.

A striped tent had been set up overlooking the boats' progress. Radu could not see clearly from this distance, but he suspected it shaded Mehmed himself. Surrounding the tent, a Janissary band played music more suited to a party than to war. The bright brass notes drifted across the horn to Radu and Cyprian.

As the lower galley slid off the bank and into the sea, a cheer went up among the Ottomans.

"Why do our ships do nothing?" Cyprian asked. Radu pointed to a row of cannons set up along the shore, aimed at the chain where Constantine's fleet floated, useless. A few ships were edging closer, apparently debating whether or not to risk the cannon fire.

Without warning, a huge stone flew over the top of the city of Galata and came splashing into the water between the Byzantine fleet and the Ottoman galleys. It was so close to the nearest merchant ships that they bobbed in the waves from the impact.

Mehmed had also solved the problem of how to fire from Galata. He could not, under treaty, place cannons in the city. And so he had engaged the trebuchets from bygone years. They sat behind the city and flung rocks over into the water.

A crash and a plume of dust from the middle of Galata proved that the trebuchet aim was not perfect. Or perhaps it was deliberate, a warning to the people not to interfere. Radu was astonished at Mehmed's brilliance.

In the meantime, yet another galley had slipped into the water, with two more on the way.

Cyprian did not look at Radu. "This plan had to be in the

works for months. With all the supplies they would need, the logistics of it all ... Did you know?"

Radu's chest was heavy with the weight of failure. Not only had he failed Mehmed with the navy, Mehmed had anticipated the failure. He had made plans without Radu, plans to circumvent everything. How could Radu hope to offer such a man anything?

"I had no idea." Radu shook his head, the music from across the horn mocking him. "I fear there may be even more plans I was not privy to."

Cyprian put a gentle hand on his shoulder. "If Mehmed suspected a hair of his beard knew his secrets, he would pluck it out and burn it."

Radu refused the comfort. "I cannot help anymore."

He could not help anyone.

———————◆·◆———————

Nazira picked out worms from the little grain they had left. "Do you suppose we could eat these?"

Radu grimaced. "If it came to it, we could. But if the siege lasts that long, Mehmed will have already lost. It is taking too long as it is."

"I wish your escapade with ruining the food stores had been less successful." Nazira gave him a wry smile.

"There is still food enough in Galata, though no one has the money to buy it. My sabotage has not ended the siege, only made it more miserable." Radu leaned forward, resting his head on the table. He was due back at the wall in the evening. His last few shifts had been uneventful. Lonely, too. And

Cyprian was gone more often than not by the time Radu returned home.

Evidently, Nazira was thinking of their host as well. "We could try to get more information from Cyprian."

Radu did not lift his head. He would not go there. Not yet. "Too dangerous."

Nazira sounded relieved. "I am glad you agree. Also, it feels . . . wrong. To use Cyprian any more than we already are."

"He is a good person, and I— Sometimes I cannot bear to even look at him, knowing what we are doing here. I cannot bear to look at any of them. Constantine is a good man, too. Giustiniani. All of them. The longer we are here, the harder it is to remember why it was so important that we take the city. I have fought alongside them, I have bled with them, I have stood shoulder to shoulder as we killed my Muslim brothers. How—" Radu's voice cracked, breaking on the last question. "How do we go on?" he whispered.

Nazira put a hand on his cheek. "You should ask to join Orhan and his men. They are kept away from the walls. You would not have to kill anyone. You should never have been put in that position. Your heart is too big for this work, Radu." She leaned in and kissed his forehead. "I cannot imagine what you have been forced to see and do. No one could have clear eyes in the midst of that."

"What does it matter? I have done no good."

"You have. And we may yet do more. The kindest thing we can do for both sides is hasten the end of this siege. The longer it carries on, the worse it will be for everyone." Nazira stood, pulling on her cloak. Though the days were warming up, the evenings were still cold. "I am going to meet with Helen. She complains that the last three days Coco has been even more on edge than usual, snapping at her and pacing incessantly."

Radu's interest was piqued. "He is their most important captain."

"Precisely. Something is in motion for the sea. I do not know what, though."

Radu stood, too, glad for something to do. "I will send Amal to Galata. I can signal him from the roof of the Hagia Sophia if something might be coming, and he can signal the galleys. I will watch Coco's house through the night."

"It may be nothing."

Radu smiled grimly. "Then it will fit in perfectly well with all my other contributions so far."

———·—·———

Radu settled into the shadows of a stoop three houses down from Coco's. Amal had sprinted away to make the crossing to Galata before the gates closed for the evening. He knew of a tower with guards under Mehmed's pay where he could watch for a signal.

It would probably amount to nothing, but it was better than being on the walls. Anything was better than being on the walls.

Radu let his mind drift, his thoughts punctuated by the distant beat of the bombardment. It never ceased, but in the heart of the city it was merely background noise. The scent of smoke and burning, too, drifted as afterthoughts. And there was no scent of blood. Merely the constant memory of it.

Because Radu did not want to think—not about Mehmed,

not about boats, not about Cyprian—he recited sections of the Koran, lost himself to the beauty and rhythm of them. There was still some peace to be found there.

He was interrupted two hours before dawn. The door to Coco's house opened, and several cloaked figures stepped out, hurrying through the streets. Toward the horn.

Radu ran in the opposite direction. The lock to the Hagia Sophia was as easy to pick now as though he had a key. He raced to the roof, where he pulled out a lantern. Three sides were polished metal, while the fourth was a pane of clear glass. He lit the wick inside, then pointed it toward Galata. He released a prayer of gratitude like a breath. The night was clear enough for the warning to be seen.

Just as Radu began to fear that Amal had not made it, a light answered him. It flashed three times in quick succession, then went dark. Radu blew his own light out. He did not know what, if anything, he had accomplished.

Then a shooting star, burning brightly, moved slowly across the sky. It left a trail of light in its wake, like a signal to him from the heavens themselves. Radu lifted a hand toward it, remembering that night so long ago when he had watched stars fall with Mehmed and Lada. He closed his eyes, gratitude and warmth filling him. Perhaps the superstitious city was finally getting to him, but he could not help but see this as a sign. He had done a good thing. He had helped Mehmed.

He went to the wall near the Romanus Gate, sliding among the men as though he had been there all night. He made certain to say a few words to some of them, taking a place in their memories. Although he faced out toward the Ottomans, all his thoughts were focused on the horn at his back and the city between them.

The bells began ringing an hour before dawn. Radu acted as surprised as everyone, looking up and down the wall as though he, too, suspected the attack was on this side.

As soon as relief came, Radu joined the other men heading to the seawall. Brief flashes of cannon fire illuminated the end of a battle. A small galley burned. Radu's stomach dropped. But as the galley drifted slowly in the water, its flames revealed one of the big merchant ships half sunk and listing heavily. The merchant ship dragged itself away, flanked by two others.

"What happened?" Radu asked a guard on the wall. "Did they try an attack?"

The man shook his head. "We did. Somehow they knew we were coming, started firing before our ships had gotten close enough to surprise them. They sank one of our small ships."

Radu could have laughed with relief. Mehmed would know now that Radu still had use. The Italians would not risk another attack on the galleys, not after this. The Golden Horn was effectively neutralized.

Dawn broke, illuminating the remains of the battle. Though several galleys smoked, there were no significant losses on the Ottoman side. Radu saw more masts than should have been in the water though.

And then he realized they were not masts. The wooden poles reaching up to the sky to greet the dawn were stakes. And on each of them, slowly revealed as the light touched them, an Italian sailor was impaled. In the middle, on the highest stake, Radu recognized Coco himself.

On the hill above them, surrounded by Janissaries, a white-turbaned figure in a purple cloak sat on a horse.

Radu could not understand the scene in front of him. The Ottomans had won! They had decisively defeated the sneak attack. There was no reason for this, none, except to torment the city. It felt needless.

It felt . . . cruel.

Troubled, Radu watched the bodies as though his vigil could bring them peace. Or bring him peace. This seemed less like war and more like murder. And it was all because of him.

A commotion farther down the wall finally drew his attention away from the stakes. He leaned out just in time to see the first battered Ottoman prisoner dropped over the side. A length of rope secured around the prisoner's neck went taut, and the body swung limply.

Before Radu could shout, another prisoner had been hanged. And then another. And then another. He watched in horror as Ottoman prisoners were dropped like decorations, a tapestry of terror along the wall in response to the brutality across the horn.

Unable to stand it, he ran toward the hanging men. Someone had to end this. These soldiers would be held accountable for such cruelty to prisoners.

He stopped, though, when he saw the line of Ottoman prisoners waiting their turn. They were on their knees, some praying, some weeping, some too bloody and broken to do either. And standing behind them, staring out as tall and still as a pillar directly across from Mehmed, was Constantine.

Radu had been wrong. There were no good men in this city.

And there were no good men outside of it, either.

36

Mid-April

LADA EMERGED FROM HER tent to find her fire already
lit and a pot of water boiling. She had forced Oana to stay
behind to help run their base at Toma's estate, in part because
she trusted Oana to do it well, and in part because she did not
want anyone fussing over her wretched hair. Since then, Lada
had not woken to a fire.

"What are you doing?" Lada asked Daciana.

Daciana pointed to the pot. "Your options are weak pine
tea or weak pine tea. You really need better provisions."

"You know what I meant." Lada sat, taking a cup of blisteringly hot pine tea. It was weak, as promised. "I am not riding
through the country, charitably adopting all those who want to
join my merry band. I am taking men who can fight. Besides, it
is important that the land be tended to."

"Why do you care so much about the land?"

"Because it is mine. I have no desire to be prince of a country with no crops. People need to eat."

Daciana laughed. "You will be *prince*, then?"

Lada did not share her mirth. "There is no other title. I will be vaivode, prince of Wallachia. And I will make the land into the country my people deserve."

Daciana eased herself down, moving awkwardly with her swollen belly. "Very well, then. You take the men for soldiers and you leave the women to plant so that we do not all starve. And what will you do with the boyars?"

As though summoned, a letter from Toma Basarab was delivered at that moment by a smooth-faced boy.

Lada read the letter with a scowl. Nicolae sat next to her, trying to read over her shoulder. "What does he say?"

"He disagrees with my negotiating tactics." Her temper bubbled hotter than the tea. "And he says he is joining us to make certain I do not negotiate like that with any more boyars."

She threw the letter to the ground, standing and pacing. "Who is he to tell me what to do? You saw Silviu! You saw his land, what he was doing. Was I not right?"

Nicolae read over the letter with a resigned expression. "I am not saying you were not right. But . . . perhaps more thought and care should be taken with future boyars."

"Why?" Daciana said.

"We need them."

Lada snorted. "We need them? No one needs them. They are maggots, feeding on my land and doing nothing for it!"

Nicolae wore a long-suffering expression. "They are necessary for organization. They collect taxes. They run the farmlands. They muster troops from the men living in their provinces."

Lada leaned forward. "Tell me, Nicolae. Does it look like they are doing a good job?"

Nicolae smiled. "The roads are impassable with thieves. The fields are fallow or untended. The boyars are fat and wealthy while the people starve. The prince has no military support unless they decide to give it—which they never do. But the fact remains, that is how the country runs. Figure out how to use them better. Control them better. But you cannot get to the throne without them."

Lada sat in disgust. "Why not?"

"You are already using Toma Basarab. Trust that he knows what he is doing."

"I do not trust him at all."

Nicolae rubbed his scar. "Did you think he could just hand you the throne? You need allies. You need the boyars. You cannot skip past them, and to get them, you need him." Nicolae put an arm around Lada, drawing her close. "Make a deal with the devil until you are both over the bridge."

"Am I the devil, or are they?"

Nicolae laughed again, but he did not answer.

Bogdan sat on Lada's other side. His eyes lingered on Nicolae's arm around her shoulder. He offered her the inside of his bread. It was the softest part, her favorite. He took the crusts without expecting thanks. He simply did it, as he did everything for her. As he always had.

It sparked an idea.

"What if I take land—if I give the land to the people who deserve it, like Daciana's mother? I get their loyalty. The boyars claim things based on centuries of blood. The land is theirs by birthright. So I *take* it from those who oppose us. I *give* it to people whose vision for Wallachia matches my own. They have nothing to claim other than my favor, and they owe all allegiance to me." She met Bogdan's approving stare and offered him a smile. He ducked his head, a pleased flush spreading across his cheeks.

"You cannot kill *all* the boyars." Nicolae helped himself to some tea.

"Oh?"

Nicolae looked up sharply, narrowing his eyes. "They did not ask for their birthright. They have done nothing to you, and you have no guarantee that they ever will. I do not think you were wrong to kill that last pig, but slaughtering every noble in the country will have repercussions even you cannot handle." When Lada did not respond, he threw his hands up in exasperation, spilling his tea. "They are related to nobility in other countries. You will draw too much attention and too much ire. Someone will retaliate. Besides, they have families. They have influence. And they are *people.*"

Lada gazed into the flames, letting them fill her vision. "Of course. I will listen to Toma Basarab and accept allegiance from those who offer it. But no one keeps anything without meriting it. That goes for every Wallachian." She blinked, spots of light dancing in front of her eyes. "Including you, Daciana. So I ask again: why are you here?"

"You have no lady's maid."

Nicolae snorted. "You are mistaken. Our Lada is no lady. She is a dragon."

Bogdan growled low and angry in his throat. Lada laughed, patting Bogdan's knee. Then she tossed a handful of dirt and dry evergreen needles at Nicolae. "No one asked for your opinion."

"My opinions are gifts I distribute freely, asking neither permission nor payment."

"Take your gifts elsewhere," Bogdan grumbled.

Lada waved her hand. "Nicolae is right. I need no lady's maid, because I am not a lady. I am a soldier."

Daciana smiled, smug and self-satisfied. "Precisely. A soldier does not have time to wash her monthly courses from her clothes."

Lada's cheeks burned, and she looked at the ground rather than at Nicolae and Bogdan. Daciana's stomach loomed in the edge of her vision. And then she had a thought.

A terrible thought.

Lada stood, nearly falling into the fire. She grabbed Daciana's hand. "Come with me." The girl yelped, struggling to her feet. Lada dragged her away from the camp and into the trees.

"Tell me about being with child. How did it happen? How long did it take until you knew there was a—" Lada swept her hand toward Daciana's stomach, unable to tear her eyes away from it now. "How long until you knew that thing was in there?"

Daciana's dark eyes betrayed no emotion. "When was your last bleeding?"

Lada turned her back, stalking several feet away. "I am not asking about that, I only want to know—"

"I am neither stupid nor a gossip. When was your last bleeding?"

"Weeks. Maybe eight? Or nine." It had been before Hunyadi, when they were in the mountains of Transylvania. Her underclothes had frozen when she hung them to dry after washing.

"Do you bleed regularly?"

Lada shook her head. "No. Only a few times a year."

"That is fortunate. I am—" Daciana paused, taking a deep breath. "I was so steady you could track the moon by my blood. And when did a man last know you?"

Lada whipped around, snarling, "No man knows me."

Again, Daciana did not respond with any apparent emotion. "Your breasts would be tender and swelling already. You would be sick. Exhausted beyond anything you have ever known."

Lada shook her head in relief, then realized she was confirming Daciana's assumptions. Of course she was. She was a fool. Moving with Mehmed in the darkness, the feel of his skin, the feel of him inside her . . .

She closed her eyes, because she had worked so hard not to think of it. But as soon as she allowed the memories back in, she wanted to kill him. And she wanted to be with him again.

She did not know which impulse was stronger.

"My sister is like you." Daciana spoke as though they were discussing the weather. "She bleeds rarely. She is one of the only ones who has never been with child, despite many visits from our boyar, may his soul be damned forever." Daciana spat on the ground. "She was the lucky one. You will probably have similar fortunes."

Lada swallowed down some of her fear. It tasted like blood and bile. Daciana turned to go back to camp.

"You may stay with me," Lada said.

The girl smiled. "I know."

"You can sleep in my tent, if it makes you feel safer."

"That is very generous of you. I will be sharing Stefan's tent soon, though."

"You will?" She had never known Stefan to take up with a

woman. Though, of all her men, he would be most likely to do it without being noticed.

Daciana's smile grew into something sly and sharp. "He does not know it yet."

Lada laughed, and then the two women walked back together. It was a pity no one had given Daciana a knife when she was a little girl. Lada suspected she was as formidable as any of the men in camp.

37

May 5–16

UNWILLING TO SPEND MORE time repairing the wall—a huge section of which had fallen the day before with losses on both sides but no real change—Radu visited Orhan's tower, where all the Turks in the city were stationed. Here, at least, were Ottomans he did not have to kill.

Radu stopped to sit with the guard. He knew them all by sight, if not by name. They were outsiders here, committed to the city but never truly a part of it. Everyone viewed them with some measure of distrust.

"There is little food," the guard, Ismael, complained. "And no coin to buy it with. Orhan does as well by us as he can, but it is not easy."

Radu nodded. "The Venetians tried to flee yesterday. Giustiniani barely stopped them. Men are missing their shifts on the walls, staying in the city to try to find food for their families."

"Such is the nature of a siege. Death from without, rot from within." Ismael smiled ruefully. "We may yet make it out of this, though. Back to the way things were before. How I miss walking the streets and having mud thrown at me simply be-cause I am Turkish. Now we cannot leave our tower for fear people will think we are the sultan's men, inside the city."

Radu leaned back, the crate he sat on groaning in protest. Something inside caught his eye—an Ottoman flag. The crate held the rest of the flags they had not used for their messenger boat deception. Now, sitting here, useless and abandoned. Radu felt a surge of solidarity with the flags.

"Why did you stay?" Radu asked. If Mehmed won, Orhan's men were all dead. And even if Mehmed failed, they would still be pariahs in the city. Orhan would never be able to claim the Ottoman throne, not now that Mehmed had heirs. He was use-less politically.

Ismael rubbed his chin thoughtfully. "Orhan is a good man. He has grown up as a pawn, but he never let it turn him cruel or bitter. I have not heard the same of the sultan." He shrugged. "Either way, my fate was always at this city. Die inside the walls or against them. We chose to stay with a man we respect."

A few weeks ago, Radu would have wanted to strike Ismael for accusing Mehmed of cruelty. Now every time Radu closed his eyes, he saw a forest of stakes bearing their monstrous fruit.

The two men looked up as a procession of horses trudged through the mud in front of them. In the middle was Con-stantine. His shoulders drooped and his head hung heavy. The day before it had been his presence at the walls that kept the defenders fighting long enough to repel the attack. But Radu could see he was cracking under the pressure.

Mud flew through the air, landing on the flank of Con-stantine's horse. The soldiers at his side were immediately alert, looking for the assailant. Constantine sighed and shook his head.

"Heretic!" someone shouted from an alley. "Our children starve because you betrayed God!"

Constantine glanced to the side and saw Radu. He smiled ruefully. "Our children starve because the only silver left in the city belongs to God himself."

Once the emperor's procession had passed, Radu bid Ismael farewell. As he walked back to Cyprian's house, he saw evidence of suffering everywhere. It was one thing to see men die on the walls, and another entirely to see their children sitting on stoops listless and dull-eyed with hunger. There was food in Galata, and they still traded during the day with Constantinople. But if no one had money, all the food in the world was still out of reach.

Constantine's words trailed along in Radu's wake, nagging at him. *The only silver left in the city belongs to God himself.* Radu could do nothing to force an end to the siege. But perhaps he could alleviate some suffering in the meantime. Suffering he had helped cause by destroying food. Perhaps he could still do some good for his own soul.

Cyprian and Nazira were both in the sitting room when Radu burst through the door, reenergized.

"What are you so pleased about?" Cyprian asked.

"There is silver in the churches, yes?"

Cyprian nodded. "The collection plates are all made of it."

"And they are used to collect money for the poor. I think we should collect those plates to create money for the poor. Surely God would look kindly on such an endeavor." Radu could not imagine either god—the Christian one or the true God—would frown upon charity, no matter to whom it was given. It was one of the pillars of Islam, after all. He had not felt this genuinely happy about anything since he had come to the city.

Cyprian shook his head. "My uncle cannot take anything from the churches, not with his reputation. They barely let him worship there as it is. If he began demanding holy silver, the city would riot."

Radu smiled wickedly, holding out a hand to help Nazira up. "Your uncle will not demand anything, nor will he take it. I know my way around a foundry."

Cyprian bit his lips, his gray eyes dancing in delight. "I know where they mint the royal coins. It has not been in operation much lately."

"I know someone who is very adept at picking locks."

Nazira laughed, grabbing a black shawl and draping it over her head. "And I know someone who will be cleaning the churches, should anyone happen upon our merry band of thieves."

It was foolish, but it felt so good to be doing something other than fighting at the walls or hating himself. Radu practically skipped through the streets. Nazira was on one side, Cyprian on the other, and the night was as sweet as any he had known. They found a dim, unused church not far from Cyprian's house.

Nazira held her bucket of supplies in plain view, tapping a foot impatiently as though she wanted to get on with her work. The bucket conveniently blocked any view of Radu's lock picking. The door clicked open and they tiptoed inside. Radu

loved churches best when they were dark. The lavish, sumptuous decorations were muted, the silence holier than any liturgy
could be.

Cyprian made his way confidently to the altar, where he
pulled out a plate and held it up in triumph. Nazira tucked it
into the bottom of her bucket and covered it with rags.

Within three hours they had hit several churches. Nazira's
bucket was nearly full. Radu was too tired to skip, but he and
Cyprian kept laughing at the other's fumbling in the dark. In
one church, Cyprian tripped and fell backward over a bench, his
legs straight up in the air. Radu held himself, bent over, trying
not to laugh so loudly that they got caught. Rather than getting
up immediately, Cyprian had remained on his back, kicking his
legs, until tears streamed down Radu's face.

When the tenth church was stripped, they agreed to one
more. They weaved through the streets with secret laughter as
muffled as the city by fog. Radu did not know how it felt to be
drunk, but he suspected it felt something like this.

"I need it!" a woman screamed. They stopped, startled. Two
women pulled at a basket. Each had a child or two at their legs,
tugging on their skirts and crying. "My children are starving!"
one of the women shouted.

"We are all starving!" a man said, shoving between the two
women. One of them fell into the muddy street, taking a child
down with her. The other scrambled for the basket, but the
man got to it first.

"Give it to me," she begged, picking up her small child and
holding him in front of her as proof of her desperation.

"I have my own hungry children."

Cyprian and Radu stepped forward, unsure what to do but knowing something needed to be done. "You should be at the walls," Cyprian said to the man.

The man's face shifted into something ugly and brutal. "So you can take this food for your own? I will go back to the wall when I know my family is eating." He shoved past them, nearly knocking Nazira down. He did not so much as look back at the women he had stolen the food from. The one still standing stomped away, one child in her arms and the other hurrying after her.

Radu reached out to help the fallen woman up. She took his hand and stood, brushing off her skirt and using a clean section to wipe her child's face.

"You should go to Galata," Radu said, as gently as he could. "They have more food there, and your children will be safer."

"God will protect us," she said, and Radu did not know if it sounded like a prayer or a condemnation.

"But God is not feeding you."

She looked at him, aghast, then bundled her child into her skirts and hurried away, as though Radu's blasphemy were contagious.

She might as well have carried off all their easy happiness, too. But at least they knew this night was worthwhile. Necessary. "One more," Cyprian said, sounding tired. He pointed the way. "The monastery where they house the Hodegetria."

"What is that?" Nazira asked, linking one arm through Radu's and the other through Cyprian's. It did not feel quite right, with her in the middle. Less balanced. Radu had preferred when he was between them. But he carried the now-heavy bucket.

"The Hodegetria is the holiest icon in the city," Cyprian said. "A painting of the Virgin Mary holding the child Jesus at her side. Said to be brought back from the Holy Land by the apostle Luke. They parade it around the walls sometimes as protection, though the monks have been withholding it as punishment for my uncle's dealings with the Catholics."

"Do they really think a painting will save them?" Nazira asked, no sting in her criticism, merely curiosity. Radu cringed at her choice of words—*them* instead of *us*—but Cyprian took no notice. At least Radu was not the only one too comfortable around Cyprian.

"They say it has saved the city before," Cyprian said.

"Do you believe it?" Nazira asked.

Cyprian looked up at the stars peeking through the low cover of cloud and smoke that never really cleared. "I believe that the Virgin Mary would rather see us take care of our own than take care of a painting of her. Which is why I am going to go distract the guard so you two can sneak in and take what silver you find." He bowed jauntily, trying to recapture some of their fun, then walked around the corner of the monastery.

Radu leaned up against a small outer door, working the lock as quickly as he could. They entered through a pitch-dark back hallway. Feeling their way along the wall, they came to another door. It was locked.

"That is promising," Nazira whispered.

Radu picked this last lock. The air inside stung his nose with the remains of censer smoke. Radu dared to light a candle in the windowless room. As the light flared to life, the image of the Virgin Mary appeared in front of them. The icon, nearly as tall as Radu, was mounted on a pallet with poles extending for carrying.

"Too bad we cannot melt it down," Nazira said thoughtfully, looking at the heavy gold frame. Radu searched for silver. There were a few small pieces, and he pocketed them. Nazira stayed where she was, staring at the icon.

"I think that is Constantinople's problem," she said. "They look to a painting to save them, instead of to each other. They argue and debate over the state of their souls for the afterlife, while letting the needy in this life go hungry. No wonder this city is dying."

Radu put a hand on her shoulder. "I have what we came for."

Nazira did not move. Her eyes shone heavy with tears in the candlelight. "I hate them. I hate everyone in this city. I walk among them, I talk to them, and it is like conversing with ghosts. I want to wear mourning clothes every day." She was crying now. Reaching into one of the jars in the bucket, she pulled out a glopping handful of grease.

Radu grasped her hand before she could fling the grease at the icon. "No," he said softly.

"We should burn it. We should punish them."

"They are being punished enough."

"Your sister would burn it to demoralize them."

"My sister would do much more than that." He smiled, imagining what Lada would do if she were here in his place. Nothing in the city would be safe. "But Cyprian is outside. He would know."

Sniffling, Nazira nodded. She rubbed her hands along the pallet handles, trying to wipe off the grease. "I am sorry. I miss

Fatima so much it feels like ice has entered my soul. And it is hard remembering not to care about these people. I was so sure when we came that it would not be a problem. I wanted— I wanted them to suffer. I wanted to watch them fall."

Radu had never heard her talk like that. "To protect Islam?"

"For revenge," she whispered. "For Fatima. Her family was killed by crusaders when she was very young. They did horrible things. Things she cannot talk about even now. I wanted Constantinople to be ours to prevent more crusades, yes. But also to punish them." She dabbed at her eyes with a corner of her shawl. "I know it is not rational. None of the people here were responsible for what happened to Fatima. But their mindless hatred of us, their demonizing of Islam, is what let those men do what they did. It was wicked of me to come here with so much hatred in my heart. Hatred makes monsters of us all."

Radu pulled her close, hugging her tightly. "You could never be a monster," he said, as the Virgin Mary pointed solemnly at her son. Her face betrayed no emotion, no hint of judgment or mercy.

"I still think we are doing the right thing." Nazira fixed her shawl. "And I am trying to set my heart in line with God."

Radu nodded, taking her hand. Together, they left the monastery.

Cyprian met them outside. "The foundry is not far. No one will be there."

When they got to the foundry, the forge's fires were cold. It would take a while for them to be hot enough to melt down the metal. Nazira excused herself to go home and sleep.

Radu saw now that she wore her sadness like a cloak. She smiled so brightly, it was too easy to miss the sorrow swirling around her. Radu wished he could take it from her. But he knew that leaving this city and being reunited with Fatima would be what began her healing.

As they started the furnace, Cyprian found the molds for coins. "My father told me I would never make any money for the family. I wish he could see me now."

"My father did not even think about me enough to wonder whether I was worth anything."

"He sounds like more of a bastard than I am."

Radu laughed, and was rewarded with one of Cyprian's precious genuine smiles. They took turns stoking the fire. Cyprian leaned close, looking over Radu's shoulder to watch the flames. He had washed, and did not smell like the walls anymore. He smelled like clothing dried in the sun, with a hint of the breeze blowing off the sea. Radu found himself breathing in so deeply he was dizzy.

"You are very good at this," Cyprian said, his breath tickling Radu's ear.

Radu would have blushed at the praise—after his broken childhood, he devoured praise like a starving man took bread—but it was so warm he was already flushed. Soon the room was stifling. Cyprian peeled off his outer layers, finally taking off even his undershirt.

It really is uncomfortably hot, Radu thought, looking everywhere but at the other man.

When the fire was bright enough, they fed the silver pieces to it one by one, collecting the molten metal. The coins they cast were rough, obviously inferior to genuine money. But no one would examine them too closely right now.

Cyprian sprawled out on the floor, arms behind his head. Radu did not look.

Until he did.

Cyprian was lean and tall, with broad shoulders. Radu's eyes lingered on the space where his torso dipped from his ribs toward the line of his trousers.

No. He was tired, and it was—something. It was all *something*. He did not know what, could not form a coherent thought. Looking at Cyprian made him remember seeing Mehmed that night in Mehmed's bedroom, before Mehmed had known he was there. Radu felt an odd surge of guilt, like he had somehow betrayed Mehmed tonight. When he thought of how miserable he had been in Edirne, he wanted to laugh. He would give anything for that small distance from Mehmed, as opposed to the tangle of emotions and questions the walls separating them had introduced.

Except he did not think he wanted to give up this night, even with everything getting here had cost him.

Still, he kept his eyes on the table after that. If Cyprian caught him looking, how would he react? How would Radu want him to react? Radu focused intently on the coins. "How will you explain them to your uncle?"

"A dowry from a withered old crone who wants to marry me."

"You would be more believable if you said it was buried treasure."

"I happen to be very appealing to women of advanced age. My eyes, you see. They cannot get enough of my eyes."

Radu finally tugged his own shirt off, because the room kept getting hotter. He tried very hard not to look at Cyprian. He sometimes succeeded. All the while, he stayed on the other side of the table, glad it was between him and Cyprian. And glad his trousers were thick enough to hide the feelings his body would not accept should not be there.

Bodies were traitorous things.

38

Mid-April

"WE NEED DORIN," TOMA said. He sat tall and regal on his horse. "And he is a Basarab."

Lada pointed toward where they had come from. "He attacked us!" They had been met on the edge of Dorin Basarab's forest by three dozen poorly armed and terrified farmers. Ten well-trained soldiers with weapons had stood at the farmers' backs, leaving them no option but to fight. Before Lada had been able to open her mouth, one of the farmers had shot an arrow at her. Bogdan immediately cut the man down, then went after the next. It was a few minutes of bloody, screaming work to dispatch them. It was a waste of her time, and a waste of the farmers' lives.

Toma did not mind. He sniffed lightly, eyeing the manor ahead of them appraisingly. "Dorin will agree to back us. And we will not have another *incident*." He looked sharply at Lada. "I will placate him by offering him Silviu's lands when you are on the throne."

"No. I gave them to someone already."

Toma laughed. "To a peasant woman? Yes, I heard. That was amusing. Please leave land distribution to me. In fact, perhaps it is best if you stay out here with your men. I will handle everything."

He rode away, his men following. Lada watched his back with all the tension of a nocked arrow.

Nicolae put a hand on her arm.

"What?" she snapped.

He jerked his head behind them. She turned to see a line of peasants. A line of very angry peasants. They made no move toward her—probably owing to the mounted soldiers behind her—but she had no doubt they would kill her if they could.

"Who is in charge?" she asked, pacing her horse in front of them.

"My brother," one man grunted.

"Where is he?"

"Dead in the field back there."

Lada stopped her horse, glaring down her long, hooked nose at the man. "And you think that is my fault?"

"Your swords have blood on them."

Lada drew her sword. It gleamed, well polished. "My sword is clean. My sword was not behind your brothers and cousins, forcing them into a fight they were not prepared for. My sword was not hanging over your necks, forcing you to serve a man who cared nothing for your lives. My sword was not held by the guards of your boyar to ensure none of your sons and friends could run when they should have."

Nicolae cleared his throat. "Maybe not the best tactic to encourage them to fight with us," he said under his breath.

Lada turned her horse, disgusted and angry. "We are going to Tirgoviste," she said. "Join us."

The man looked to the side, rubbing his stubbled cheek. "Not right, a lady having a sword."

Lada knew that killing him would set a bad precedent. She knew that, yet her sword inched closer to him anyway.

"Why should we?" asked an old man with white and wispy hair like the clouds overhead. Loose skin beneath his chin wobbled as he spoke. "We were fine before you came. We want no trouble from Tirgoviste."

Lada turned toward him, sparing the other man. "And Tirgoviste has never troubled itself about you. It does not care. It does not care about your lives, or your families, or your welfare. What has the prince ever given you?"

The old man shrugged his sharp shoulders. "Nothing."

"If you are happy with nothing, by all means, flee and find another boyar to serve. Dorin Basarab will be with me. And when I am on the throne, I will remember every man who helped get me there, no matter his station."

"You want to be prince?" the first man asked. He was not angry anymore. He was confused. Lada preferred angry.

"I *will* be prince."

"What family are you from? Do they have no sons left?" he asked.

She opened her mouth to declare her lineage. Then she stopped. She did not deserve the throne because of her family. Because of her father. Because her brother would not take it. She did what she did not for herself or her family name but for Wallachia. She would *earn* the throne. "I am Lada Dracul, and

I will be prince." She lowered her voice, leaning toward the man and speaking like the sound of swords being drawn. "Do you doubt that?"

He shuffled back a step, finally seeing the truth in her face. She was not a lady. She was a dragon, and this whole country would know it before the end.

"If you fail?" the old man asked.

"Then you are no worse off than you are now. Your boyar will come crawling back. They always manage. But if I succeed—and I will succeed—I will remember *you*. Do you understand?"

The men nodded, some more grudgingly than others. The old man grinned toothlessly. "I think you are mad. But I will not say no to this offer." He bowed to her.

Lada looked over their heads toward the horizon. The effect was rather ruined by one of Toma's men riding up. "My lord says you can make camp behind the manor. You may join them for dinner, if you wish to."

Lada did not wish to. She gritted her teeth and nodded anyway.

39

May 16–24

As May passed its zenith and began slipping toward June, no end to the siege was in sight. The weariness with which Radu wandered through the days was broken only by scarlet bursts of horror. Everything else about that time was dirty—the dust, the clouds, his soul.

After the night in the forge, he had again done his best to avoid Cyprian. Nazira had few useful contacts left; Helen's disgrace at being associated with poor impaled Coco left her a pariah, and Nazira was swept along in that wake. Most of her time was spent trying to find food and delivering it to those in need. Radu never asked what the latter accomplished. He understood the need to extend kindness even as the very act devoured the soul with guilt. He understood the desire for penance, as well.

When Radu made it home to sleep, he and Nazira lay in the bed, not touching, not talking. Side by side, and alone together. The only thing Radu was certain of anymore in the sea of endless smoke was that Nazira would make it out alive. Everything else was negotiable.

On May nineteenth, the bells of the city jangled out their now-familiar call to the wall. *Panic!* they said. *Death!* they said. *Destruction!* they said. They were no longer instruments of worship, only proclaimers of doom.

Radu trudged past the Hagia Sophia. A sharp tug on his shirt startled him. He turned to find Amal. "I do not have anything for him," Radu said.

Amal shook his head. "He has a message for you."

Radu's weary heart stepped up its pace. Mehmed! His Mehmed. "Yes?"

"He says to stay away from the walls today. Find somewhere else to be."

Radu did not know whether to laugh in delight or cry in relief. Mehmed remembered him—and cared whether or not he was safe. "Why?"

Amal shrugged. "That is the message."

"Tell him thank you. Tell him—" *Tell him I miss him. Tell him I wish things could go back to how they were. Tell him I am terrified they never can. Tell him even if they could, I do not know if I will ever be satisfied with it again.* "Tell him my thoughts and prayers are with him."

Amal nodded, then held out his hand as though begging. Radu dug free a single coin and placed it in the boy's palm.

Radu turned to go back home, happy he could at least report to Nazira that Mehmed thought of them and had sent a warning. And then he remembered: Cyprian was already at the wall.

The wall Mehmed thought was dangerous enough it merited risking sending a message.

Radu could go home. He could wait and see what happened. He could stand at the window, watching for Cyprian. And if Cyprian did not return . . .

Radu ran for the wall. He would think of some reason, some excuse to pull Cyprian away. He did not question why it was worth the risk. He simply knew he had to.

When he got there, though, he stopped in shock. There were *towers* on the other side of the wall. Made of wood, they were covered in sheets of metal and leather hides to protect them from fire and arrows. Huge wheels stuck out from their bases. And they were making their way toward the city.

Where Mehmed had been keeping the towers was a mystery. No one around Radu knew where they had come from or when they had appeared. But their purpose was already being served. As the towers moved forward, the shielded men within them threw dirt and rocks and bushes into the fosse. Slowly but surely they were filling up the protective ditch.

Radu hurried past a line of archers, desperate to find Cyprian. Mehmed had not wanted him here, and he saw why now. The walls would fall today.

The archers shot burning arrows, but they bounced harmlessly off the towers' shielded exteriors. Small cannons were fired to little effect. The towers carried on without pause. Giustiniani pushed his way to the center of the wall, a few men down from where Radu crouched behind barrels. A constant barrage of arrows flew at the wall, preventing any concerted counterattack.

"What new hell is this?" Giustiniani said, peering between barrels. He noticed Radu and crawled over to him, gesturing toward the towers. "Did you know he had these?"

Radu shook his head, leaning back against the barrels, unable to face the towers.

All his previous anger at Mehmed had fallen away, like an

arrow bouncing off the armor Mehmed's message had supplied. But Mehmed protecting him and Mehmed trusting him were two different things. The towers had to have been in the works since the beginning. And Mehmed had never breathed a word about them to Radu.

Which meant one of two things: either Mehmed did *not* trust him, or Mehmed had deliberately withheld information because he had been looking for a way to get Radu into the city from the very beginning, and he had suspected Radu would be caught and tortured.

Even with the armor of Mehmed's warning, either option broke Radu's battered heart.

By nightfall the ditches were filled enough for the towers to cross them. Their progress was as slow and inevitable as the passage of the sun. As near as anyone could tell, men in the bottom pushed, inching them forward. The rain of arrows from the towers had not stopped. No counterattack could be launched, no run on the towers was possible. They crept forward at an agonizing pace, slowly bringing the city's doom. And still Radu had not found Cyprian. At this point he could not leave—because he did not have his friend, and because it would look as though he was running away.

Someone rode across the space between the walls on a horse pulling a heavily laden cart.

"Giustiniani!"

It was Cyprian. Radu perked up. The city was going to fall, but Cyprian was here! Radu could get him out, and they could get to Nazira and flee. Radu crouched, running along the wall to the ladder, then climbed down.

Cyprian was standing in the cart, arrows falling around him as he pushed a barrel off the end. Radu grabbed a discarded shield and ran forward, climbing on next to Cyprian and covering him while he worked. "We need to go!" Radu shouted.

"Almost finished!" An arrow thunked against the shield over their heads. Cyprian paused, giving Radu that smile that changed his whole face. "Well, that is another life I owe you. One of these days you will have to determine how I can repay you."

"What is this?" Radu asked as a few other men who had come to help lifted barrels down.

"Gunpowder."

"The cannons are too small to do enough damage to the towers."

Cyprian's grin shifted to something less warm but more appropriate to their surroundings. "Not for the cannons. Get these on the wall!" he shouted.

Radu jumped down, still shielding Cyprian as he directed the men. He kept looking toward the gate, wondering how he could get himself and Cyprian out. Meanwhile, Cyprian continued, oblivious to Radu's desperation. It was no small task leveraging the heavy barrels up the narrow ladders. They managed awkwardly, losing one man to an arrow. Radu followed Cyprian as they rolled the barrels along until they were positioned directly in front of the tower. Maybe if he helped Cyprian accomplish whatever he was doing, Radu could trick him into leaving.

Giustiniani gestured with concern. "This is nearly all the gunpowder we have left."

"It is doing us no good in the cannons," Cyprian said. "This is our best chance."

"But we do not have enough to take out *all* the towers. There are several more."

"The sultan does not know that, does he?"

Understanding dawned on Radu as Cyprian worked long fuses into the tops of the barrels. "You are going to blow up the towers." Radu laughed, his throat hoarse from exhaustion and smoke. It was exactly what Lada would have done. He should have thought of it himself.

No. He was not actually on this side. Radu tapped his head against the stones beside him, trying to knock some sense into himself. He should do something to prevent it. But he was trapped. He could not do anything for Mehmed, and he could not do anything to risk Cyprian's life.

Cyprian patted his vest, swearing. "I do not have a flint."

Radu held out his own. When Cyprian's fingers met his, there was a spark unrelated to the flint. Radu swallowed the mess of emotions blocking his throat and his breath.

Cyprian grinned at him, then struck the flint and lit the fuse. "If it bursts open when it hits the ground, we are blowing ourselves up."

Radu shrugged, sitting back. Perhaps that would be a kindness at this point. "At least I will have good company in hell."

Cyprian laughed. Giustiniani glared at them both. "On three," Cyprian said. The two other barrels were a few feet away. "One . . . two . . . three!"

Radu and Cyprian pushed the barrel up and over the wall while other soldiers did the same with theirs. They braced for an explosion, but none came. They peered over, holding their breath and watching as the barrels tumbled and rolled away from the wall and toward the tower. Giustiniani's veered too far to the right, lodging in debris. The third barrel lost momentum halfway there. But Cyprian's kept going, rolling right to the base of the tower.

"Get down!" Cyprian shouted, pulling Radu flat. Radu covered his ears, but the explosion was still deafening. He felt the concussive force of the blast passing right through him. The world hung in stillness for one soundless moment. Then debris pinged against the barrels, against his back, falling everywhere.

The tower was on its side, ripped open. Men ran forward to help the fallen Ottomans, not accounting for the other barrels. Radu and Cyprian ducked again, two more blasts coming in quick succession.

The scent of gunpowder almost covered the stench of burning flesh.

Giustiniani stood, pointing to a group of soldiers standing at the ready behind a sally port. "Burn everything! Kill anyone still moving!"

The port was flung open and men ran out. It was quick work, killing any Ottomans still alive and stunned from the last explosion. They poured pitch onto what was left of the tower's wooden frame and wheels. When lit, it burned so brightly that Radu could feel the flames warm his face.

Cyprian turned away from the killing, pulling his knees up and resting his head on them. His shoulders were shaking.

"Are you hurt?" Radu's hand hovered above the other man's arm. He did not dare touch him. Not on purpose, not in tenderness. He had defied Mehmed's order to stay safe because he could not abandon Cyprian. And in doing so, he had helped defeat this newest, best chance at the end of the siege. How many ways could a man turn traitor in one lifetime?

Cyprian looked up. Radu could not tell if he was laughing or crying. "I really thought that would blow us up. I thought there was a very good chance I was taking down our own walls and letting him in."

"But you tried it anyway?"

Cyprian wiped under his eyes, which left his face smeared with soot. "He is attacking us from every possible angle. Below the walls, outside them, above them. From the land, from the sea. He does not need everything to work. Just one thing. And eventually, something will." Cyprian leaned his head back, looking up at the smoke above them. "But not tonight," he whispered.

"But not tonight," Radu echoed. He did not know if he said it in relief or in mourning.

Cyprian's gamble paid off. When one tower fell, Mehmed pulled them all back. The bombardment continued unabated, but by now that felt almost normal.

Two days after the towers retreated, Cyprian received a summons to the palace. Radu was pulling on his boots to go back to the wall. Amal had not been at his place outside the Hagia Sophia. Radu had nothing but confessions and confusions to send to Mehmed anyway.

"My uncle has asked you to come, too," Cyprian said.

Radu frowned, surprised. "Why?"

"He does not say."

The small part of Radu's soul that had not been beaten down under the bombardment feared that he had been discovered. Perhaps he was walking to his death. He caught Nazira's eye from across the room. "Nazira, it seems quieter at the walls today. You should go over to Galata and see if there is any food you can buy there. Cyprian is losing weight."

"I am not!" Cyprian forced his stomach forward and patted it.

"He looks terrible." Radu smiled as though in jest but levied a meaningful look at Nazira. "Bring him some food from those beautiful fat Italians."

"*You* look terrible." Nazira narrowed her eyes and shook her head at Radu. "I am not going to Galata for anyone or anything. I will be right here when you come back from the palace."

Radu walked up to her and placed a kiss on her forehead. "Please," he whispered against her skin.

"Not without you." Then she pulled back and smiled, reaching up to rub at the stubble on his face. "Both of you eat at the palace. Save me the trouble of making you a meal. And while you are at it, see if the emperor can spare a razor, too."

With one last pleading look, Radu joined Cyprian. They walked in silence through the muddy streets. Though there were more religious processions than ever, they were fortunate enough not to run into any. Sometimes in his dreams Radu was stuck in the middle of one. Around the sound of the priest's liturgy, the women wailed and the children cried, while the smoke of the censer clogged his eyes and nose until he could neither see nor breathe. When the smoke finally cleared, everyone around him was dead. But the liturgy continued.

"Are you well?" Cyprian asked. "You keep shuddering."

Radu nodded. "Cold for May."

"Do not tell anyone else that. They will find some prophecy or other that states that a cold May signals the end of the world."

Radu tried to laugh but could not. If only Nazira had agreed to leave, he would feel at peace with facing his end. It was inevitable, at this point. He was always going to die here. He did not want her to.

At least he trusted that Cyprian was not the one who had figured it out. Cyprian wore his honesty painted across his face. If Radu was going to his death, Cyprian did not know it. It was poor comfort, but enough to give Radu the strength to keep moving, keep walking in this precious space before Cyprian found out the truth and never again looked at him with those beautiful gray eyes.

They passed several women and children dragging sacks full of rocks and rubble to repair the walls. When a stone cannonball shattered the wall of a house next to them, Radu and Cyprian ducked instinctively, before they had even processed what caused the noise.

The women and children had no such experience. One of the children lay in the street, broken and unmoving. A woman knelt over the child. She picked up the body and tucked it against the wall. "I will be back," she said, her hands bloody. Then she retrieved her bag and the bag of the child, and continued on to the wall.

"How can we go on?" Cyprian whispered. "Is this hell?"

Radu took Cyprian's hand, turning him away from the body of the child. The palace was before them. Radu knew it did not matter what he hoped or feared would happen. Death was unfeeling and random, as likely to strike down an innocent child as a guilty man.

They were met by two soldiers who escorted them past Constantine's study. They moved deeper into the palace, and then through a courtyard into another building. It was colder than the palace, the rocks leeching warmth from the day. The air smelled of mildew and despair.

"Why are we going to the dungeons?" Cyprian asked.

Radu allowed himself one moment of true sorrow for Nazira. He had failed. At everything, at all of it, but at this one most important thing he had promised himself and God. *I am sorry*, he thought as a prayer. *I am sorry. Save her.*

"Prisoners," one of the soldiers said, as though that explained everything.

When they emerged through a door at the bottom of a winding set of stairs, Constantine turned to face them. His face was hard. Next to him was Giustiniani. Radu took a deep breath, praying for strength. He met their gazes unflinchingly. He might still be able to barter for Nazira's life.

"There you are. Come on." Giustiniani gestured impatiently. Radu stepped forward, finally able to see past them.

Kneeling on the floor chained, bloodied, and dazed, was a man Radu had last seen being berated by his mother while delivering gunpowder. Tohin's son, Timur. How was he here?

"He has been speaking Arabic," Giustiniani said, "and we cannot understand him. Can you translate?"

"I should be able to. Where did he come from?" Radu asked, trying to control his voice.

"We caught him digging a tunnel under the walls. The rest were killed with Greek fire. Burned alive."

"I am the lucky one," Timur mumbled around a bloody, swollen tongue and broken teeth. He looked up at Radu and smiled. Radu did not know if the smile was one of recognition or madness.

Radu was not here to be tortured and killed. He was here to aid in the torture of a man he knew. A man with a family. Two children, he had spoken of. Or was it three? Radu could not remember. It seemed very important now to remember. *I am sorry,* he prayed again, this time with even more anguish. But Nazira was still safe. He held on to that light as a way to keep out of the darkness threatening to claim him.

Radu cleared his throat. "I know this man. His name is Timur. I met him briefly before fleeing the court."

Giustiniani grunted. "We need the locations of all the other tunnels. My men have been working on him for a while, but he has not given us any information." He pointed at a map of the walls. "Do whatever you can think of to get him to talk."

Blood dripped slowly down Timur's face, pooling on the stained stones beneath him.

Radu crouched in front of him. He only knew Arabic from the Koran, and he would not bring those sacred verses here. He did not want to use Turkish for fear Constantine and Cyprian would understand. "Do you speak Hungarian?" he asked in that language. He knew Cyprian did not speak it, and he was fairly certain none of the other men did. He looked at them, but they did not seem to understand.

Timur dragged his head up. His eyes widened for the briefest moment in recognition, then he hung his head again. "Yes," he answered in the same language. "A little. Can you save me." It was not spoken like a question. A question implied hope. Timur knew there was none.

"I can guarantee you a quick death. And—" Radu's voice caught. He took a deep breath, then pressed on. "And I will send word to Mehmed of your bravery. Your family will be taken care of forever. I swear it."

Timur shuddered, the last of the tension in his shoulders leaving. "What do they want?"

"The location of all the other tunnels. Will there be any men in them now?"

"Not now. Tonight."

"If we give them the information, they will act on it immediately. No more of your men have to die. The tunnels did not work. You tried your best. I am sorry it ended this way."

A sigh escaped the other man's lips. It smelled like blood, but it sounded like relief. "I did my part. God knows. You will tell the sultan that."

"I will." Radu gestured for the map. Timur pointed to several locations, tracing lines. The blood on his fingers worked as ink.

"He is telling the truth," Giustiniani said. "I suspected these two. This one we found this morning. But the others we did not know about." He rolled up the blood-marked map and handed it to a waiting guard who ran out of the cell.

With his back to the other men, Radu mouthed a benediction in Arabic that only he and Timur could see. Timur's face relaxed, and he closed his eyes. Radu pulled out a knife and drove it into the base of Timur's neck. He slumped to the floor, dead. There was very little blood. Whatever had been done to him before Radu arrived had already drained him of most of his blood.

Cyprian exclaimed in surprise. Radu pulled out a handkerchief and wiped his knife clean. His hands looked steadier than he felt. "I promised him a quick death in exchange for the information. He upheld his end of the bargain."

"But we might have needed him for something else," Giustiniani said, frowning.

Radu feigned his own look of surprise. "I am sorry. You told me to do whatever it took to get him to give us what he knew. That was what it took." He avoided Cyprian's eyes and bowed to Constantine. "Unless you have further use for me, I am due at the walls."

Constantine scratched at his beard. This close, Radu could see that the skin beneath his beard was red and irritated. "May we all meet such mercy at the hands of our enemies," he said, his voice so quiet he might have been speaking to himself.

The sound of boots racing down the stairs drew their attention to the door. A soldier burst into the cell, out of breath. "The boats," he said. "The boats we sent out. They have returned."

"And?" Constantine stepped toward the soldier.

The soldier shook his head, his face devoid of hope. "No one is coming."

Constantine dropped to his knees, hanging his head in the same pose Timur had been in when Radu arrived. There were no chains on Constantine, but he had only the same option of release as Timur. Radu watched as though from a great distance, and time seemed to slow, the space between heartbeats stretching out to eternity.

If Lada were here, Radu asked himself yet again, *what would she do?*

The door was right there. Giustiniani and Cyprian had turned away out of respect for Constantine's grief. Radu could jam the knife into the emperor's neck the same way he had into Timur's. He could end Constantine right now. The emperor held Constantinople together through sheer force of will. With his death, the walls meant nothing. The city would surrender immediately.

Lada would do it. She would have already done it instead of standing around, wondering. Radu was certain she had never in her life asked herself what he would do in her situation. He closed his eyes, despair washing over him. Mehmed had sent the wrong sibling into the city. Because he could end it all, right here, right now, and maybe even get out alive. Even knowing Constantine, even respecting him, Radu could do it. He had killed Lazar, after all. He had stuck his knife into his best friend to save Mehmed.

If he did the same now, it would end the siege. It would be almost a kindness to a man suffering under a burden too large for anyone to bear. The city would surrender and fall without looting or further damage.

The broken body of the child in the street loomed before him. Accusing. Pleading. If he killed Constantine, no one else had to die.

But as Radu ran through what he could do, what he should

do, he kept pausing on another image—the gray eyes that would never look at him the same if he did it. Radu was looking at Constantine, but all he could feel was Cyprian's presence.

Maybe if Cyprian were not here, maybe if Cyprian were not *Cyprian*, Radu could have done the right thing. Instead, he watched, impotent and useless.

The emperor wept, the innocent died around them, and Radu was incapable of offering anyone mercy. It was with this guilt looped like a noose around his neck that Radu followed the other men out of the dungeon and into the palace.

A visibly trembling servant shuffled up. "There is someone here for you, my lord."

Constantine waved them all to accompany him. It was doubtless the captain of the boat, ready to make a full report of his findings. Radu did not want to go. But there might be important information he could pass to Amal to atone for not killing Constantine when he had the chance.

The door opened to reveal no weary sailors. Instead, Halil Pasha stood in the center of the room.

40

Late April

Toma Basarab looked through letter after letter, smiling or humming thoughtfully depending on the contents. "Sit down before you pace a hole into that rug. It is worth more than anything you own." He paused for effect. "But then again, you do not own anything, do you?"

Lada glared at him, but she stopped prowling. "Well?"

Toma leaned back in his chair. They had taken residence in another Basarab family boyar's home. The study might as well have always belonged to Toma. His letters covered the desk, his wine next to his hand. Only Lada's sword was out of place.

They were close to Tirgoviste. So close Lada could not stand being cooped up in this house with these people, knowing how near her throne was.

Toma held up a letter. "The prince knows what we are up to."

"*And?*"

Toma smiled, the expression transforming him from a well-mannered boyar into something Lada understood far better: a predator. "And it does not matter. We have all the support we need. More than half the boyars are on my side." He paused, his smile shifting generously. "Our side. Most that are not will do nothing until they see where the advantage falls. He will not be able to draw a significant force in time to save himself. His sons and all the men he could ask for help are fighting at the walls of Constantinople at the sultan's request."

Lada closed her eyes, taking a deep breath. "I can go to Tirgoviste."

"Yes, my dear, you can," Toma answered, as though she had been asking permission. "I will follow."

"But not too closely." She opened her eyes and raised a knowing eyebrow.

He laughed. "No, not too closely. But you take all my hopes and prayers with you."

Lada picked up her sword where it leaned against a chair. "Keep your prayers. I do not need them."

————◆————

They had made it only a couple of hours before the scouts ahead of them shouted a warning. Lada spurred her horse to a gallop, quickly closing the distance between herself and her scouts.

It was too late. The two men, who had been with her since Edirne, were bleeding their lives out into the dirt. A band of a dozen dirty men surrounded them, pawing through their clothes.

They looked up at Lada. Their faces twisted with cruel pleasure, dead eyes greeting her. She drew her sword and killed two before the rest could react. By the time they realized she was no easy prey, Bogdan and a score of her men had caught up.

Several of the robbers scattered for the trees. "Kill them all," Lada said. She paused, thinking. One of the robbers had curled into a ball on the ground, arms over his head. "Leave this one."

She dismounted. Kicking him in the side, she pushed him over so he was forced to look up at her. His face was covered with the angry red spots of youth. He was probably only a couple of years younger than her.

"Are there any other thieves?" she asked, jerking her head down the road.

"No. No. Just us in this part."

"And in other parts?"

He nodded desperately. "Yes, miss. All over."

She leaned close, resting her sword against his throat. "Would you like a job?"

He could not nod. He could not even swallow. He whispered a tortured "Yes."

"Go down this road ahead of us. Find every thief, every robber, everyone preying on my people, and give them a message. These roads belong to Lada Dracul now. I declare them safe. And anyone who defies that will die."

She eased her sword away. The boy scrambled to his feet, bowing. "Yes. Yes, miss. I will."

She thought for a moment. Words were one thing. Evidence was another. She bent down and cut the ears off the nearest bodies. The first she mangled. The second she found the right place to slice. Nicolae blanched. The sound and sensation was unpleasant, but Lada rolled her eyes at him. "Take these." She held the ears out to the boy.

He looked as though he would lose his stomach, but he took the ears in trembling hands.

"Tokens of my sincerity. If you run, if you fail to deliver my message, I will know. And I will find you."

The boy squeaked an assurance that he would not fail, then, stumbling once, ran down the road away from them.

Bogdan returned a few minutes later, wiping his sword clean. "We got them all."

"Good." Lada stared at the quickly receding silhouette of the fleeing boy. It was a good message. But it was not quite enough. She had spent years in a land where every road was safe. The Ottomans were free to travel and trade, and their country flourished. She had not forgotten her lessons on the subject.

She had learned something from her tutors there, after all.

"These roads need clearer directions. Hang the bodies from the trees. Write 'thieves' on them." Several of the recent recruits looked worried. Most of them could not read or write. "Nicolae will write it," she said.

"This all seems excessive." Nicolae paused, halfway through dragging one of their scouts' bodies to the side of the road, where another soldier had started on a shallow grave.

Lada shrugged. "They are already dead. They may as well serve a purpose in death, as they did nothing with their lives."

<hr />

After a full day on the road and with Tirgoviste within reach on the morrow, they set up camp. Daciana had not yet moved into Stefan's tent, but Lada had no doubts it would happen soon.

Stefan watched Daciana move around camp with a sort of

confused fear tightening his eyes. He was so twitchy and nervous that Lada worried about sending him ahead to scout. Daciana paid him only the barest attentions, occasionally pausing in her work to comment to him, or to straighten his vest, or to remark on the color or length of his stubble, casually brushing her hand against it.

Lada did not understand the strange dance Daciana was performing. It seemed deeply inefficient. But seeing the way Stefan watched the girl, Lada became twitchy herself.

The place between her legs nagged at her at the strangest times, reminding her of how it had felt and could feel again in the future. She cursed Mehmed for introducing her to those sensations. Before, she had not known they existed. Now, she longed for them.

Daciana leaned close to Stefan, whispering something in his ear and then laughing.

Bogdan joined Lada at her fire. He was thick and menacing where Mehmed was lithe. Bogdan was a hammer to Mehmed's graceful sword. But hammers had good qualities, too. Lada looked at him, narrowing her eyes. "You would do anything for me." It was not a question.

He looked at her as though she had taken the time to inform him the sky was blue. "Yes."

"Come with me." She stood and walked into her tent. Bogdan followed.

It was much more efficient than Daciana's methods. And if she did not feel the same with Bogdan as with Mehmed, if the spark and the fire and the need were not overwhelming, Bogdan was as he had always been: loyal and serviceable.

Their second day on the road they met with no further thieves. They found evidence of campsites, hastily abandoned. Lada felt a stirring of something like what she imagined maternal pride to be. Her little robber boy was obeying her.

Bogdan rode closer to her than before, and occasionally in the midst of his inelegant protectiveness she caught a hint of newfound tenderness. It made her deeply uncomfortable. She knew Bogdan felt more for her than she did for him. She had always accepted it as natural, good even. He belonged to her, but she did not belong to him. Perhaps she had crossed a line she should not have.

Her discomfort was soon replaced with an inconvenient relief when she felt a gush of warm blood between her legs. She nearly prayed, she was so grateful. But she doubted that God cared one way or the other about the continued emptiness of her womb.

Lada pulled her horse to a stop and dismounted. In her bag she had extra strips of cloth. She peeled off her chain mail and draped it across her saddle.

"What is it?" Bogdan asked, halfway through dismounting.

"No!" She gestured impatiently for him to stay. "I will be back."

"You should not go alone," Nicolae said.

Lada glared at all of them. She could feel the blood still flowing. If she did not catch it soon, her trousers would be stained. Daciana, who rode on Stefan's horse with him, looked at how Lada walked with stiff legs. "Let her go. Lada is more frightening than anything in the forest."

Lada turned her back and marched toward the trees. "God's wounds, you are all ridiculous. Rest. Eat. I will be back."

She moved quickly through the trees, putting as much distance as possible between the massive party of men and her immediately pressing, deeply private needs.

She found a clear stream and squatted next to it. The water was freezing, but at least there was some warmth in the air. While she cleaned herself, she cursed the fact that she had to deal with this at such an important time.

But the blood was a welcome sight. Perhaps Bogdan had been a lucky thing, dislodging whatever had blocked her since being with Mehmed. She took it as confirmation that Daciana's thoughts were correct. Her body was not made for carrying babies. She hummed to herself as she rinsed out her underclothes and set them on a rock to dry next to her trousers. She took care to place the extra strips of cloth in her new underclothes to absorb the blood. Then, because she was happy and the day was warmer than any had been for a long time, she pulled off her tunic and rinsed it as well.

That was when she heard the sound of furtive footsteps. She froze, ready to curse Bogdan or Nicolae or whoever had disobeyed her. And then she realized the footsteps were coming from the opposite direction where her men were. For a moment the memory of other trees in another place, of another man sneaking up on her, paralyzed Lada. Her breath would not come. The memory of Ivan's weight on her, his hands . . .

She snatched her tunic out of the water, looking around desperately for somewhere to hide. The trees were too thin to climb, the stream was open and exposed. And she was alone, because of her stupid woman's body. She looked down at her arms clutching the dripping tunic against her chest. Her woman's body. Ivan had seen it as a weakness, as something he had power over.

The footsteps were getting closer.

Ivan was *dead.* Her body was a weapon. She could kill whoever approached, but ... Unbidden, Huma drifted across her mind's eye. The way she draped herself across furniture. The way she moved. Lada tried to recall everything about it, because Huma had been a weapon just as much as Lada was.

Lada picked up a knife where it lay next to her boots, holding it hidden behind her back. And then she let her tunic fall as three men appeared at the opposite end of the stream. Their tense grips on their weapons relaxed as their jaws dropped in shock.

"Oh!" Lada squealed, a poor imitation of what she thought a girl would sound like in this circumstance. She drew one arm across her unwieldy breasts.

One of the men averted his eyes, blushing. The other two had no such decency. "What are you doing here?" one of them asked, a puzzled smile on his face.

"I ..." Lada leaned down, picking up her tunic and hiding the knife beneath it. "I live there"—she gestured vaguely to her right—"and I was washing."

"You should not be here." The blushing soldier looked behind himself at something she could not see. "There are a lot more men coming."

"Oh! Oh no." Lada gathered up her trousers and her boots, feigning embarrassed clumsiness. She was grateful she had not put her trousers back on. Bundled as they were, it was not obvious that she did not have skirts.

"Go home," the man said, his voice tense but gentle.

The leering soldier grinned even bigger. "We will visit you after we take care of some trouble."

Lada did not know how to smile demurely, but she gave it her best shot. Then she hurried in the direction she had told them she lived. As soon as she thought it was safe, she yanked on her boots, shoving the rest of her things in her bag. She cut back toward the road, running as fast as she could. Her men would not be ready. They had gotten too used to being unchallenged. She had no idea how many soldiers were in the trees, but if they had the element of surprise, she did not like her forces' odds.

She burst onto the road much farther ahead of the troops than where she had left. Sprinting toward them, she waved her trousers in the air. She could not shout for fear the enemy was close enough to hear.

Nicolae noticed, waving tentatively back.

She pointed frantically toward the trees. Nicolae did not move for several agonizing seconds. Then he acted with all the practiced efficiency of a true soldier. Before Lada reached her men, they had all slid from the road and onto the opposite side, leaving an open expanse between themselves and the trees that hid the enemy. Lada joined them there, out of breath. She drew her sword from where it hung from her saddle.

"Lada," Nicolae hissed.

"Men. From Tirgoviste, I think. They are looking for us. I do not know how many, but they will be here soon. Spread word down the line. Crossbows first. We will surprise them."

"Lada," he said again. "Your . . ." He gestured wordlessly toward her chest. Bogdan moved so he was blocking Lada from view of anyone else. She looked down at where her breasts, still uncovered, moved up and down with her breathing.

Glaring, she yanked her tunic out of her bag and pulled it on. "Well, you can thank my"—she gestured wordlessly toward her chest as she tugged on her trousers—"for saving us."

Nicolae did not have time to inquire further about how, exactly, Lada's breasts had saved her men. The first enemy soldiers had begun coming out of the trees, moving with exaggerated stillness. Still believing the element of surprise was theirs, they looked up and down the road, then gestured for the others to join them.

It was not as big a force as her own, but if they had been able to use the cover of the trees and catch her men unaware, Lada did not want to think how it might have devastated her numbers. She lifted a fist, then lowered it. Crossbow bolts sang through the trees onto the road, cutting down half the men. The other half scrambled to load their own crossbows and form a rank, but by then it was too late. Lada's men roared out of the trees, an unbreakable wave of swords and strength.

When it was over and only a handful of their enemies remained, Lada joined them on the road. The men sat in a miserable circle, stripped of their weapons. Some bled. Bleeding was not always a weakness, though. Lada laughed to herself.

One of the soldiers on the road was the man who had had the decency to blush and look away. Lada pointed to him. "That one lives. Kill the rest." She ignored the messy work going on around the blushing man. "Did the prince send you?"

He cringed at the sound of sword separating soul from body. "Yes. We were supposed to kill you."

"And even though you were coming for me, you did not wonder if the girl in the woods was the one you hunted?"

He did not meet her eyes. "We assumed you would be somewhere safe. In a carriage, with guards. You are not what I expected. The prince said it would be easy."

"I am not so easy to get rid of." She offered him a hand. "You can go back and tell him that. Or you can stay and join my men."

He trembled from head to toe. "I will stay?" He finally glanced up to meet her eyes, and she knew he looked for confirmation of whether or not he had made the right choice. She had not lied to him—she would have let him go. But doubtless he thought that would have resulted in his death.

She nodded. "Very well."

"That was lucky," Nicolae said, leading Lada's horse out of the trees alongside his own horse. "You were right. Sometimes you do need to be alone."

Lada could not quite smile. It could have ended much differently. She pulled the reassuring weight of the chain mail around herself. Better to be a soldier than a woman.

Better to be a prince than anything.

41

May 24–25

"THIS MAN IS A snake and a liar," Halil said, sneering at
Radu. "I wondered where he had slithered off to."

Radu took a steadying breath, reminding himself of all the
times he had played a part to manipulate his old foe. He could
do it here. He had to. "I should think, given your peaceful views
of the city, you would envy those of us who had the courage to
leave the tyrant sultan and serve the cause of the emperor."

Halil snorted. "If you have courage, I am a donkey."

"That has always been my personal opinion of you, but I
never expected you to agree with me."

Halil's face turned a violent shade of red. "Get him out of
here."

Constantine held out his hands in placation. "I do not know
your history, but Radu has been instrumental to us. His advice
and information are testament enough of his loyalty." Constantine raised a single eyebrow. "And he has no towers named after
him in fortresses on my land."

Halil's scowl deepened. "You know I had no choice."

"There is always a choice. We appreciate your information and friendship, but you remain safely outside the walls. Radu is here."

"My position is not safe! No one's is. The camp is on the edge of riot. Daily we meet, and I urge negotiating peace, while others demand we give no quarter. I could not do that if I had not stayed with the sultan!"

Constantine rubbed his face wearily. "Tell me why you are here."

Halil threw a single piece of parchment on the table next to him. "Mehmed offers you terms of surrender. I will await your response." Leveling a murderous glare at Radu, Halil stomped out of the room.

Constantine read the letter, scratching absently at his beard. Droplets of blood broke through the skin. "He will let me go into the Peloponnese and be a governor there."

"We have wanted you to leave the city," Giustiniani said gently. "We need you safe, and then we can gather allies."

Constantine sighed. "If I leave the city, I am never getting back in. I cannot do it. But ..." He paused, tracing a finger over the bottom half of the letter. "If we open the gates, they will march through peacefully, leaving all citizens and property unmolested." He looked up at Radu. "Do you think he will honor that?"

"He will." Radu felt the first true spark of hope in ages. He had been right not to kill Constantine! Another way to end this siege had been given to him. "It is Muslim law. If you surrender, they have to respect that. There will be no prisoners, no slaves, no looting."

Giustiniani scoffed. "I doubt that very much."

"You have seen the order of his camp, the control he has over his men. He wants the city itself, not anything in it. He does not want to destroy it—he wants to own it. I will stake my life on his truthfulness in this matter. He will honor these terms. All your people will be spared."

"And the Christian capital of the world will be handed over to their god."

Radu chose his next words carefully. "If they take the city by force, they have three days for looting and doing anything else they wish. But if you surrender, the Ottomans treat their vassal states well. We would all have to run or risk death, but your people would not suffer under the sultan's rule."

Constantine's smile was as brittle as spring ice on a river. "The same cannot be said for my rule. How my people have suffered. How my city has darkened." He looked at Cyprian, fondness in his expression. "What is your counsel, nephew?"

Today Cyprian's eyes were not gray like the sea or the clouds. They were gray like the ancient, weary rocks of the city. Radu knew that the nameless child dead in the streets had come into the room with them. "We have lost so much. Perhaps this is a way to avoid losing everything. Our people would not be slaughtered or sold into slavery. You would live." He put a hand on his uncle's shoulder, his voice breaking. "I want you to live."

Constantine looked to Giustiniani, the other reason the city had survived for as long as it had. "You?"

Giustiniani shook his head. "If Halil is right, all we need to do is hold on for a little longer and Mehmed will be forced to leave. He may even lose the throne." After a pause, Giustiniani looked at the floor. "But I cannot promise we can hold on for even a day more. We have fewer than half of the forces we started with. The men are hungry and weary and frightened. The Venetians want to leave. My men do, too. I will not let them, but it may come to a point where I can no longer prevent them. With one victory, they could topple us—or with one victory, we could have enough momentum to sustain ourselves. We are balanced on the edge of a knife. I do not know whom the knife will cut. The choice is yours."

Constantine sat, his broad shoulders sloping as he picked up a quill and stroked the length of it. "I cannot do it," he said. Radu leaned heavily against the wall, all hope extinguished. "I will send Halil with an offer of peace. We will increase our tribute, and give the sultan the land under the Rumeli Hisari. We will give him Orhan, too, and abandon all attempts at de-stabilizing his throne."

Constantine was willing to sacrifice Orhan, a man he had used to manipulate the Ottomans for decades, even though Orhan had chosen to stay and fight. He would sacrifice Orhan, but not his pride. Not his throne. Radu shook his head, trying to keep the anger out of his voice. "Mehmed will not accept."

"I know. But I cannot abandon my city. I am sorry, my friends. I will fight until my last breath before I will see Otto-man flags in this palace and hear their call to prayer from the Hagia Sophia. It is in God's hands now."

But which god? Radu thought. With so many men on both sides sending up so many prayers, how could any god sift through the noise?

That night, the air was sweet with the promise of summer around the corner. The wind had blown strong from the horn, clearing the smoke from the city for once. Radu and Cyprian sat on the Blachernae Palace wall, facing the Hagia Sophia. Though they had not discussed it, neither man had gone to his scheduled position at the wall after leaving Constantine. They had ended up out here, silent, side by side.

It was almost quiet enough to pretend the world was not ending around them.

"The moon begins waning tonight," Cyprian said.

Radu remembered the prophecy that the city could not be taken on a waxing moon. "Do you believe in that one?"

"I believe in very little these days."

Radu looked toward the Hagia Sophia, where the full moon would rise over the city. A full circle of gold, like their coins, the moon was a protector of the city along with the Virgin Mary. Would the waning finally shift the tide of war?

Next to him, Cyprian sat up straight, a sharp intake of breath like a hiss puncturing the quiet of the night. In place of the full moon rising over the Hagia Sophia, there was only a sliver of a crescent moon.

The crescent moon of Islam.

"How is this possible?" Cyprian whispered.

Radu shook his head in disbelief. The moon was full tonight—*had* to be full tonight. But slowly lifting itself above the city's holiest building, the moon remained a crescent. The dark part was not as dark as normal, but rather a deep red. Stained like blood.

For hours Radu and Cyprian watched as the crescent moon hung over the city, promising an end to everything. Wails and cries from the streets drifted on the sweet breeze. For once the church bells did not ring warning. What could bells do against the moon? Finally, agonizingly slowly, the moon returned to the fullness it should have had all along.

"I might believe in prophecies now," Cyprian said in awe and wonder. "But I do not think I like this one."

Radu wondered what it must have been like to see the moon in the Ottoman camps. Surely Mehmed would have capitalized on it, claiming it as a prophecy of victory, even as the citizens of Constantinople saw it as a portent of doom.

It was just the moon. The moon did not take sides. But the blood-washed expanse of the Byzantine full moon seemed to promise otherwise.

They spent the night on the palace wall, not moving. Sometime in the small hours of the morning, clouds rolled in, obscuring the moon. "Where were you when we could have used you?" Cyprian muttered.

Dawn dragged itself free from sludge of night, bringing with it a smattering of rain and the promise of more to come. After Radu prayed in his heart, they began to walk toward a gate that would lead them to the wall over the Lycus River.

"Oh, hell." Cyprian cringed. "Oh, damn, I am going to be damned for swearing about this." They were near the monastery they had broken into that housed the Hodegetria. A massive crowd had gathered outside. Priests were already swinging censers, chanting and singing the liturgy. More people came in the street behind Radu and Cyprian, blocking them in.

"See if you can push through," Cyprian said. "They are

going to take the Hodegetria around the walls. If we get stuck in the middle, we will be trapped for hours."

A team of men exited the monastery, the pallet lifted onto their shoulders. One of them nearly lost his grip, struggling to keep hold. Radu remembered Nazira wiping her hands clean of grease—on the poles of the icon.

"God's wounds," he whispered, fighting an urge to laugh born of nerves and exhaustion.

Another man's hands slipped. He adjusted quickly, lifting the icon higher. A crossbearer in front began walking, followed by the priests. Men, women, and children surrounded them, all barefoot. A man near the front cried out in a voice loud enough to be heard over the low rumbling of thunder.

"Do thou save thy city, as thou knowest and willest! We put thee forward as our arms, our rampart, our shield, our general!"

Radu leaned close to Cyprian. "Someone should tell Giustiniani he has been replaced by a centuries-old painting."

Cyprian snorted, covering his laugh behind a hand.

The man continued. "Do thou fight for our people!"

"Do you think she will take our place at the wall?" Cyprian whispered.

Radu laughed. A man nearby gave them a furious glare, crossing himself.

"We are going to hell for blasphemy," Cyprian said.

"We are already in hell," Radu said, shrugging. "And with so much company." They tried to edge away from the crowd, but the street was narrow and clogged with people. The two men were carried forward in the surge of religious zeal, pushed along a seemingly random path.

"There!" Radu said, pointing to a narrow alley. If they could duck into it, they could wait until the crowd had passed and then backtrack.

Someone cried out in horror from the front. The Hodegetria was slipping. Though the men carrying it scrambled to counter its momentum, they could not get a good grip on the poles. The icon, the holiest artifact in the city, slid off into a thick patch of mud.

Everyone was silent for a few disbelieving heartbeats. Then the men sprang into action, trying to lift it. Though it was only a painting and there were several men, they could not seem to pull it up. The earth had decided to reclaim the Virgin Mary and would not relinquish her.

Several children started crying, their mothers doing nothing to shush them. A murmur like a tiny earthquake rolled through the crowd. Whispers of doom, damnation, the Virgin abandoning them. Of God judging them and deeming them unclean.

Radu was half tempted to tell them God had nothing to do with this—it had been a young woman with grease on her hands and sorrow in her heart. But it would do no good.

Finally, after far too long, the men managed to leverage the icon out of the mud and back onto their shoulders. A ragged cheer went up, but it would not have felt out of place at a funeral for all the happiness it held.

Then the world was lit for a single second in blinding white. Radu had time only to wonder if he truly was being struck down for blasphemy before a clap of thunder louder than any bombardment followed an instant later, shaking the ground. Screams and cries went up. A rushing sound moved toward them. Radu saw the rain before it hit. It was a solid wall of water, so thick and fast that it slammed into the crowd with the force of a river.

Something stung Radu's face. He touched his cheek to make certain he was not bleeding. Then another piece of hail struck him, and another. The hail fell with more fury than the arrows of the Ottomans. Another brilliant bolt of lightning struck nearby, the thunder accompanying it so powerful Radu could hear nothing for nearly a minute afterward.

All around him people were falling to their knees, unable to see or walk in the middle of the tempest. Radu knew God had nothing to do with the icon slipping. This, however, was difficult to attribute to anything else. The water fell so furiously that it began streaming down the street, rising to Radu's ankles and then to his knees. The narrow streets were funneling it, channeling it into a sudden river.

"We have to get out of this!" Cyprian shouted. Radu could barely hear him, though Cyprian's mouth was right next to his ear. He pointed at the alley they had been aiming for. Because of the slope, the water did not travel far up it. The two men pushed through the street, mud sucking at their boots, the hungry water pulling eagerly. A child in front of them went down, disappearing beneath the brown water.

Radu dove to his knees, pushing his hands down blindly. He caught a foot and pulled the child into the air. A woman rushed toward them. Radu handed her the child. Cyprian shouted, pointing to an old man who had gone down. They hurried to him, helping him up and dragging him through the water to the alley.

"There!" Cyprian waved toward a woman in the middle of the street holding an infant to her breast and unable to move. He started forward, but another blinding flash of lightning and an overpowering burst of thunder cracked through the alley.

Some of the cracking noises were not the thunder. The stones from the roof above them that had been struck fell in a jumble, taking Cyprian down beneath them.

42

April 28

WALLACHIA WAS FATALLY FLAWED when it came to keeping princes alive. The boyars were tasked with protecting the prince. They controlled all the manpower, all the troops, all the blades that stood between life and death. In theory, the purpose was to keep the prince loyal to the country and the people whom he depended on for survival.

It may have worked, were the boyars ever loyal to a prince. But the roads were open and clear in front of Lada like a field after harvest. She was grateful now that the boyars were never loyal to a prince. The few men the prince had been able to rally were dead on the road behind them.

"So, what is the plan?" Nicolae asked.

Lada shrugged.

"That—that is not a plan. You have no plan? Really? None?"

"We go in. We take the throne. That is all the plan we need."

"No, I definitely need more plan than that."

Bogdan grunted. "She told you the plan. Shut up."

Lada kept her eyes on the city growing ever larger in front of them. Homes were closer together as farmland gave way to life clinging to the edge of the city and the opportunity it provided. Which, judging by the condition of the homes, was not much.

Lada did not smile at the people who huddled in the dark doorways, watching her procession. But she could feel their stares, feel their whispers. Nicolae shifted defensively. She shook her head at him. She would not cower.

"Look," Petru said, pointing up at the sky.

Among the first stars beginning to pierce the night, there was one falling. It burned, light trailing behind it as it slowly moved through the gathering darkness.

"It is an omen," Daciana said from her seat in front of Stefan on his horse, her voice quiet with wonder.

Lada closed her eyes, remembering another night when stars fell from the heavens. She had almost been happy then, with the two men she loved. Now she had neither of them. But she had known that night what she knew now: nothing but Wallachia would ever be enough.

The stars saw her. They knew.

She lifted a hand in the air toward the burning sign as she rode forward, letting everyone see her pointing to the omen of her coming. Everyone would witness it.

They were her people. This was her country. This was her throne. She needed no intrigues, no elaborate plans. Wallachia was her mother. After everything she had been through, all she had done in pursuit of the throne, she was left with one thing only: herself.

She was enough.

The gates to the city were closed when they came to them.

Two men illuminated by torches stood at the top, a faint metallic clinking puzzling Lada until she realized they were trembling in their chain mail.

"Open the gates," she said.

The men looked at each other, unsure what to do. They looked over her shoulder, where her men lined up behind her. A murmur of noise like pebbles signaling an avalanche accompanied her.

"I come like that star, burning in the night." She raised her voice so everyone could hear. "Anyone on my side before I take the throne will be a salaried soldier. I reward merit, and there will be much opportunity for advancement of fortunes."

"How?" one of the men asked.

"Because anyone who opposes me will be dead. Those are my terms. They will not be offered again."

The gate opened.

Several men fell into line with her own as they rode into the city. "You," she said, pointing at one of them. "Deliver my terms to every guard you meet."

He sprinted eagerly ahead of Lada's troops. They continued at an unhurried pace. The streets were narrow, like spokes in a wheel going toward the castle. She looked back only once, to see her party stretching back to the gate and beyond, everyone squeezing in to follow. Their numbers had swelled to more than double the soldiers. Men, women, even children. The children danced and laughed in the torchlight like it was a parade. The men and women were warier, but an intensity shone in their eyes that had not been there before. She had done that.

She faced forward again. She had not romanticized Tirgoviste when she lived here, but after all these years and her time in the Ottoman Empire, it was not only smaller than she remembered, but also dingier, bleaker. Even the manors were pale and haphazard imitations of stateliness. Paint had chipped away to reveal the brown and gray stone skeletons of houses like flesh rotting from bone.

No one exited the boyar manors to join the procession. Their windows were curtained and shuttered against the night. Against Lada. They passed a fountain that she remembered running with clear water. She had dunked her head there once, trying to wash away the fear that living in the castle had bred within her. Now, fetid water lay still and stinking in it. But she was not afraid anymore, and had nothing to wash away.

The gates to the castle wall were open. Guards stood to either side, eyes on the ground, heads lowered as she passed. Nicolae and Bogdan looked around rapidly, shifting behind her, but she had no fear of assassins' arrows. Just as Hunyadi had ridden into the city wearing his confidence and rightness around him, so would she. No one could shoot her. No one could stop her.

She nodded toward the door to the castle. The guard who had run ahead opened it for her. She rode her horse straight through, its hooves clattering against the stone floor. No pretty tiles here, no rugs, nothing between the teeth of the castle and the people it devoured.

She liked it that way. Her horse plodded forward, tentative in the narrow halls with their burning torches. Behind her, she heard Bogdan and Nicolae trying to calm their horses. She did not stop or wait for them to reassure the nervous beasts. The throne room was ahead of her. The last time she had been here, she had watched her father pretend he had any power left as he addressed Hunyadi.

It felt right that as she entered high on the back of her horse, the Danesti prince sat stiff and sweating on the throne. A phantom memory of the scent of her father's beard oil teased her nose. She wished for one heartbeat that the man on the throne were her father. That he could see what she had become, in spite of him. Because of him.

The Danesti was saying something, but she had not bothered to start listening. Her eyes were caught on the curved length of the Ottoman sword still hanging above the throne. It was framed by two torches, flickering hypnotically. She guided her horse closer, entranced.

"I said, explain yourself!"

Startled, she looked down at the sputtering prince. His face was red, a sheen of sweat making his skin glow. She did not remember him from her time here as a girl. He had not mattered to her then, and he did not matter to her now.

She glanced around the room. There were several guards, but none moved toward her. She heard voices in the hall, someone swearing about a horse. She was alone.

It did not matter.

She addressed the sword. "I have delivered my terms already."

"I have heard no terms!" the prince huffed.

"They are not for you. They are for the Wallachians in this room. Land and wealth for those on my side. Death for those opposed."

"You have no right to offer them such things!"

She nudged her horse forward so that the Danesti had to scramble to the side of the throne to avoid the horse's long, velvety nose. Lada stood in the stirrups, reaching for the sword on the wall. She tugged it free, pulling it out of its sheath. It was dimmed by age but sharp enough. The sword of their enemies. The sword of their vassalage. The sword of their weakness.

Her sword now. She lifted it in the air, turning it to play with the torchlight. "I have the only right there is." She put the sword through the usurper's chest before he could answer her. He had nothing to say she cared about. She turned her horse, pulling the sword free.

"It is going to be a nightmare to clean that throne," Nicolae said as he walked into the room, followed by Bogdan and the rest of her men.

Lada smiled. "I *am* the throne. Put his body on a stake in the square as proof that I keep my promises. Loyalty rewarded. Cowardice cut down."

The gate guard ran forward eagerly, dragging the body from the throne. It left a trail of blood, black in the dim light. The only legacy this prince would ever have, his weakness written across stones as testament to Lada's superiority.

Bogdan took a knee, his deep voice booming through the room. "All hail Lada the dragon, prince of Wallachia!"

Lada's horse shifted, putting her directly in line with one of the narrow, high windows. Through it, perfectly framed, the falling star finally burned out. She lifted her face, closing her eyes, as her mother blessed her. A warmth settled deep inside, and she clutched the locket she always wore.

She was home.

43

May 25–26

"Do you think he will recover?" Radu asked, pacing anxiously. He had half carried, half dragged Cyprian back to the house. Though Cyprian did not appear to have suffered any significant visible damage, a cut on his head bled freely, and he had not yet woken up.

"Time will tell." Nazira finished cleaning up the blood. She gave Radu a concerned look that managed to pull her full lips nearly flat. "Sit down. You cannot worry him back to health."

Radu collapsed into a chair and put his head in his hands. "I know we greased the poles of the icon. But the way it refused to be picked up again—and then the storm. I have never been in a storm of such sudden fury. They brought out the Hodegetria to guide them, and instead they were swept away, carried off in the middle of a tempest."

"This city is getting to you, Radu. Even you see signs in everything now."

Radu nodded, rubbing his eyes and leaning back. "I know. I feel sorry for them. To see your own destruction reflected in everything around you—the moon, the weather, the shaking of the earth itself—I am amazed that anyone remains in this city. Why could they not leave?"

Nazira smiled sadly. "I persuaded Helen to. I know there was no reason for me to continue my friendship with her, but she was so sad and lost. I gave her the last of our money. Yesterday she slipped into Galata, where she has distant relations who can help her get to Athens."

"That was a good thing."

The door opened and Valentin appeared with a bowl of water and some clean rags. Nazira took them; then Radu held up a hand to keep Valentin from leaving. "Do you have any family in the city?"

Valentin shook his head. "My parents died two years ago. My sister, too."

"Aunts? Uncles?"

"No, sir."

"What about outside the city? Do you have anywhere to go?"

Valentin stood straighter, puffing up his chest. "No, sir, and if I did, I would not go anyway. My place is serving Cyprian, and I will stay where he is until the end."

"What if I needed to send a letter to my sister in Hungary? One that I could send only with someone I trust absolutely?"

Valentin smiled, with an expression too knowing and weary for a boy as young as he. "Then I would say I suspect you of tricking me, and anyway, I have heard your stories of your sister and would rather take my chances here."

Radu laughed, shocked at how much the boy had picked up

on. "Very well. But promise me one thing: If the city is falling around you, you do everything you can to get out. Do you understand? And if I am not here, you help Nazira and Cyprian get out."

Valentin stood even straighter, giving a dignified nod. "I will protect them with my life."

"Good boy."

Valentin left, closing the door softly behind him.

Cyprian moaned. Radu rushed to the bedside. "Cyprian? Can you hear me?"

Cyprian tried to lift a hand to his head, his eyes squeezed shut. "Radu?"

"Yes! You are safe, at home."

"I think—" he croaked, his voice cracking.

"I will get him something to drink!" Nazira hurried from the room.

Cyprian swallowed, still not opening his eyes. "I think the city fell down on my head."

Radu laughed in relief. "It did. But you Byzantines are remarkably hardheaded."

Squinting, Cyprian looked at Radu. "Radu! You are here!"

"Yes. I am right here."

Cyprian lifted a hand, searching in the air. Radu took it in his own.

"I went back for you." Cyprian's eyes drifted shut again.

"No," Radu said, gently. "I was not hurt. I brought you home. Remember?"

Cyprian shook his head, then cringed, crying out in pain. He squinted again. "No, I went back to Edirne for you."

What if the blow had permanently damaged Cyprian's mind? "We are not in Edirne. We are in Constantinople."

"I know that," Cyprian snapped, rolling his eyes. "You are very confused."

Radu tried not to smile. "You are right. I am the confused one."

"We never spoke, but your face ... The look you shared with him about the book. I never stopped thinking of you."

"What book?" Radu wanted to keep Cyprian awake and talking, even if it was nonsense.

Cyprian waved his free hand. "The book we gave the sultan. You understood how funny it was. The dragon book. I wished so much I could laugh with you. Even then I knew you would have a wonderful laugh. He did not want me to go back, you know."

Radu searched his memory, trying to figure out what Cyprian was talking about. Books and dragons? And then it rushed back. Last year. The delegation from Constantinople after Mehmed's coronation. It was the first time Radu had seen Cyprian. Back when Cyprian was a nameless ambassador delivering a book on Saint George and the dragon as a gift. Radu remembered that moment perfectly, too. That startling jolt when he had met Cyprian's clear gray eyes and seen the hidden laughter there.

"Who did not want you to go back to Edirne?" Radu asked, suddenly very interested in the conversation.

"My uncle. Too dangerous. I insisted, though. I wanted to speak to you."

Radu's heart was racing. "To ask me to come here and give information on Mehmed?"

"No." Cyprian's voice went far away and quiet. "I just wanted to speak to you. I wanted to hear you laugh." He smiled, lifting their clasped hands toward Radu's cheek. Radu leaned his head down, letting Cyprian's fingers brush against his skin. Though his fingers were cold, the touch felt like fire.

"I regret nothing," Cyprian murmured, and then his face relaxed into sleep.

The door clicked shut and Radu startled, looking up guiltily.

"Oh, husband." Nazira sighed, already in the room, for how long Radu did not know. "You almost make me believe in fate, for how unfortunate yours is."

She set down a bowl of broth and a mug of watered-down wine. Adjusting Cyprian's blankets, she knelt across the bed from Radu and looked up at him. "First a man with no heart to give you, and now a man who can never know your truths."

Radu stood, his pulse still racing, his cheeks flushed. "I— He was— I am not—"

Nazira looked tenderly at Cyprian, brushing some hair from his forehead. "I suspected, but I hoped I was wrong. It seemed too cruel, too absurd an irony."

"You know I am loyal to Mehmed!"

Nazira's face darkened faster than the tempest in the streets. "You owe him nothing more than your loyalty. Certainly not your love. Normally I would rejoice that your heart had stirred in another direction. But this . . ." She lowered her head onto the bed, hiding her face from him. "Oh, Radu. What will we do?"

A bell in the distance tolled *doom, doom, doom.*

———

Radu could not sit at Cyprian's bedside. He wandered the streets until nightfall. The storm had disappeared as suddenly as it came, the clouds taking residence on the earth instead. The air was still and dead, the city shrouded as if for burial.

As night fell, the fog thickened, masking all lights and making the city as dark as a cave. Radu had started toward home when muted cries of "Fire, fire!" broke through the fog. He turned, running in their direction, wondering if this was it, if the wall had finally fallen. Instead, he saw the roof of the Hagia Sophia flickering with light.

Horrified, he ran several steps toward the church before stopping. It was not fire. The light danced and moved along the roof, but it was the wrong hue for fire, more white and blue than yellow. And there was no smoke. Radu watched, transfixed, as the light gathered around the main spire and then shot upward into the sky.

He stared, blinking in the darkness, the afterimage playing across his vision. He had never seen anything like this, never heard of anything like it. But no—had not God appeared to Moses as fire? A cloud during the day—like the impenetrable fog—and a pillar of fire at night.

Radu could not breathe, could not comprehend what he had seen. Because the only way he could explain it was that he had seen the spirit of God himself. And God had left Constantinople behind.

But the fire had gone into the sky, not to the camps of the Ottomans. Perhaps all their prayers had canceled each other out. It was only men against men now.

God was right to abandon them. If anyone had decided on

mercy and reason over stubbornness, all these lives could have been spared. If Mehmed had allowed the city to continue its natural, slow death rather than needing to claim it. If Constantine had bowed to the impossible odds and opted to save his people over his pride.

Radu was so angry with both of them. Different possibilities spun through his mind. Killing Constantine, as he had considered. It would lead to surrender.

Using Mehmed's trust and sending a message into the Ottoman camps that Hunyadi was on his way with an army from the pope. That would tip things out of Mehmed's favor, forcing him to accept a new peace treaty.

Either was a bigger betrayal than Radu had it in him to commit, and for that he was as culpable as emperor or sultan. He could not make the hard decision, could not solve this where they refused to.

Radu wandered, lost in the fog. It clung to him, questioning, nagging. Radu was sorrier than he had ever believed possible. Somewhere in the past months he had grown to love this odd, superstitious, worn-down city. Somewhere in the past months he had grown to love the man who brought them here.

But an end was coming. If Mehmed did not take the city, it would be his end. Halil would see to that. More Muslims would die in Christian crusades, like Fatima's family had. And the city would still fall eventually. But if Radu helped the city fall now, he could save Mehmed. Radu could be at his side to see the future Mehmed would create.

Lada had despised Radu for the fact that he would always choose Mehmed. Nazira had told him that he did not owe Mehmed his love.

But he did owe Mehmed his life. And Mehmed was the only man who could fill the destiny laid out by the Prophet, peace be upon him.

He had imagined Constantinople, had wanted it for Mehmed. It had been simple and straightforward. But now he knew the true cost of things, the murky horrors of the distance between wanting something and getting it.

He had wanted Mehmed in ways he could never have him, and that, too, had slowly been destroying him.

What, then, did he have left?

Radu closed his eyes, remembering the light. God might have left the city, but Radu would never leave his God. And Constantinople as it was would always be a threat to Islam, bringing crusades, destabilizing the Ottoman Empire.

Some lives are worth more than others, Lada had told him. He had wondered when the scales would tip out of their favor, had thought her a monster for valuing their lives above all others. But he had valued Mehmed above all. He valued Nazira more than any innocents in this city. And the value he had to admit he held for Cyprian would break his own heart.

It was wrong, this weighing and measuring lives as though they were coins that could be spent or saved. He longed to be free of it all, to live among men seeing everyone as his brother, to view no one as his enemy.

But his choice was made. He walked toward the Hagia Sophia to find Amal. He would do everything in his power to give Constantinople to Mehmed, to the true and only God, and let his own heart break or stop as it would after.

44

Early May

"THE CASTLE IN EDIRNE was nicer," Petru said, looking dubiously at the whitewashed walls and plain stone floors of the dining hall.

"There were pigpens in Edirne nicer than this castle," Lada said. "You are welcome to go back and live in one of them."

"I like this castle! Really!" Petru said, scrambling to repair the damage he feared he had done.

Lada sighed and shook her head. "No one hates this castle more than I do. But this is the capital, so we live here now." She sat back, looking around the table. Nicolae, Petru, Stefan, Daciana, and Bogdan were with her. Lada had sent for Oana. If her old nurse was in charge of the kitchen, Lada knew she would be safe from any attempts to poison her food.

"Has anyone checked the treasury yet? Do we even have a treasury?" Lada realized how little of the actual running of a castle she had witnessed as a child. Mehmed had a legion of men employed to keep charge of his empire's finances. Lada did not even know where her resources were physically located—or whether she had any.

"I can hunt for treasure in the castle," Nicolae said.

"Me too!" Petru sat up, excited. Sometimes Lada forgot how young he was.

How young she was, too. She felt it more now, in the three days since she had taken the throne. She had focused for so long on getting here, that she was not quite sure what to do now that her only goal was behind her.

"I doubt there is much to find," Daciana said. "Would the previous prince have kept his family wealth here? Our boyar"— she turned her head to the side and spit—"and his family kept their wealth on their own land. The Danesti was not always prince. His wealth would be held by his family."

"You need taxes," Stefan said. Lada noticed that his right hand and Daciana's left hand were not on the table. Were they holding hands beneath it?

"You do need taxes," a man's voice said. "And for that, you need boyars. And for that, you need me."

She looked up to see Toma beaming at her, his arms open wide as though expecting her to run to him. At his side was Oana, who shifted away from him with a look on her face like she smelled something foul. Bogdan stood and embraced his mother. She patted his arm, then looked Lada up and down. Nodding, she tightened the apron around her waist and walked toward the kitchen muttering about getting things in shape.

Lada was surprised at how relieved she was to have Oana here again. It felt right.

Toma, on the other hand . . .

He sat down in the chair Bogdan had vacated, the one to Lada's immediate right. "Why are you meeting in here?" He looked derisively around the room. "You should be holding court in the throne room, or your chambers. I looked for you there first."

Lada had been staying in the tiny barracks with her men. That felt more like home than this castle. "I have not taken chambers yet."

"You must. And stop sitting with your men like a commoner. They should be standing at the ready near the doors, not treated like advisors. Appearances matter, Lada."

"Speaking of appearances," Nicolae interrupted—Lada suspected to spite Toma's pronouncement that her men were merely guards—"why are you here?"

Toma smiled, showing all his stained teeth. "Before I deliver the good news to Matthias, we need to discuss finances. Castles do not run themselves, I am afraid. And we will have to extend quite a few favors to secure the loyalty of the remaining Danesti boyars after what you did to their prince."

Lada sighed, making herself listen as Toma instructed her. The last time she had been forced to sit through tedious instruction in Tirgoviste, at least she had been able to demand to learn outside. Now she did not have even that luxury.

—————

The castle reminded Lada of a tomb, heavy stones waiting to claim her as they had her father before her. She did not want to live there—already, she craved escape, thinking longingly of the mountain peak in Arges. But she was the prince, and the prince lived in the castle.

She took her father's old rooms, throwing out everything

that had belonged to the dead Danesti. Some of it might have been left over from her father. She did not care either way. Daciana took over after Lada had cleared the rooms, securing enough furnishings for them to feel livable.

"Are you sure you do not want curtains?" she asked, hands on her hips, her belly jutting out.

Lada stared thoughtfully at the empty space above the narrow window. "My brother and I once used a curtain rod to push an assassin off a balcony. Maybe we *should* add them."

"Well, I thought they might be pretty. But, certainly, they can double as weapons. You are very practical."

Lada shook her head. "I hate this castle and every room in it. I do not care what it looks like."

Daciana nodded, not asking any questions. Lada liked that about her. She asked questions when she needed to and otherwise let memories lie where they would. Lada suspected it was because Daciana was equally reticent to talk about her own past. She seemed quite content in the present. She had appointed herself Lada's personal maid, but, contrary to convention, she did not sleep in Lada's rooms. Judging by the new expression of bemused happiness on Stefan's formerly blank face, Lada knew where Daciana had settled.

Daciana had decided what she wanted and had secured it. In spite of carrying another man's child, in spite of her circumstances, in spite of everything. Lada felt a pang of jealousy. To be able to want a man and claim him, heedless of anything else? She could have claimed Mehmed. She *had* claimed him. But it did not satisfy her. Why could Daciana find happiness when Lada could not?

No. That was wrong. Lada had decided what she wanted, and she had secured it. The throne was hers.

Mehmed's face and the feeling of his hands on her body still haunted her, though. She wished she could carve out his memory with a knife. Trace the lines of him that would not leave her, then cut them free. She would bleed, but she would not die. Still, he lingered in places no knife could ever reach.

Daciana gasped, bringing Lada back to the present. She was bent over, hands on her belly.

"Are you ill?" Lada asked.

"I think the baby is coming."

Lada was struck with a terror deeper than any battlefield could have presented. The need to flee was overwhelming. "I will go get the nurse. Oana, I mean."

Daciana nodded, breathing deeply against some internal pain Lada did not want to imagine.

The nurse was easy to find. After laughing at Lada's obvious horror, Oana escorted Daciana to another room. Lada waited outside with Stefan, who paced with nerves as though the child were his. Lada wondered idly what they would do with the newborn bastard. That was none of her business, though.

The hope on Stefan's face grew increasingly pained. It was obvious he loved Daciana. Lada wondered what that must feel like, to know someone loved you enough to take everything you were. To wait. To hope.

She wondered what it would feel like to be the person who loved that much, too.

She found Bogdan and invited him to her bedroom, but it did nothing to take the ache away from the edges of her memory of Mehmed. After, Bogdan wanted to linger. Lada dressed hurriedly and left her rooms. She did not have space in her heart for that. Not after last time. Not after loving Mehmed so much, and being so deeply betrayed by him.

No. Bogdan was safe. Bogdan was steady. And she did not and would never love Bogdan as she had Mehmed, which was both a relief and an agony.

When Oana told her that Daciana had safely delivered a little girl, Lada was unmoved. "They want to see you," the nurse said.

Lada did not want to see them. But Stefan was one of her oldest and most trusted men. So she entered the room, ready for the scent of blood and sweat and fear. Instead, she found a cozy, warm space. Daciana was curled in a nest of blankets, the babe at her breast. Stefan sat next to them, gazing in wonder at the tiny, mewling creature. Daciana looked up, beaming.

"Thank you," she said.

Lada frowned. "For what?"

"For giving me a world where I can raise my daughter how I wish. For giving us this Wallachia."

Lada felt something tender and sweet unfurling in her chest. It was a vulnerable feeling. A dangerous one. She cleared her throat. "Well. I guess I will have to find another maid."

Daciana laughed. "There is a boyar woman who has already hired me on as a wet nurse. It is amazing what they will pay for. But as soon as I am able, I will be back to fill your room with deadly curtains. You will help me, right, my little Lada?"

The endearment was very confusing. Stefan smiled up at her, nodding toward the baby. "We wanted to give her a name of strength."

Lada's face flushed. She had to clear her throat again. She leaned closer, trying to see the little bundle. "Is she pretty?"

Daciana held out the baby. Her face was red, squished and bruised from its violent entrance into the world. Dark hair sprouted from the top of her head, and one tiny fist was balled tightly and raised in the air. She was not pretty. But she screamed, and the sound was piercing and strong. "Do you want to hold her?"

"No!" Lada put her arms behind her back just in case Daciana and Stefan tried to force the baby on her. But Daciana seemed content to hold the baby herself. Lada tentatively smiled. "When she is old enough, I will give her a knife."

Daciana and Stefan both laughed, and though Lada had been serious, she laughed, too. But watching the tiny life, she promised herself she would do exactly that for this little girl and every other Wallachian under her rule.

She would make them strong.

45

May 28–29

THE LITURGY WAS PUNCTUATED by the ceaseless bombardment strikes. Radu wished they could have coordinated with Mehmed somehow, so that the distant sound and vibration of rock meeting stone could have matched up perfectly. As it was, the beats fell too soon or too late, a jarring mess guaranteeing no one could truly lose themselves to the worship service.

But that was never a possibility, anyway. Not tonight.

For the first time since Constantine had attempted to unite the churches, the Hagia Sophia was lit up. All their angry clinging to dogma and notions of religious purity had been abandoned, and they appealed to every icon, every relic, every link to God they had. If the Hagia Sophia could save them, they were finally ready to try it.

Outside the walls, the Ottoman camps were quiet. The bombardment had increased, everything they had left being flung at the city in anticipation of one final burst. Arrows came over the walls with scrawled warnings from sympathetic Christian soldiers:

The end is coming.

But they did not need the information written on arrows. It was already written in the massive stone cannonballs hitting the walls, in the day of rest and prayer Mehmed had given his men. One last assault, one last chance to defend or attack, to stand or fall, to live or die.

And so the people of the city came to church. The Hagia Sophia was packed, claustrophobic; people stood shoulder to shoulder. Radu breathed the same air as everyone around him. They exhaled terror and resignation, and he inhaled it until he could not catch his breath. He much preferred the Hagia Sophia dark, with the sound of birds fluttering near the roof. That had felt closer to worship than this.

Constantine stood at the front, looking upward as though he were already an icon himself. Nearby, Giustiniani stood, pale and sweating. He should have been sitting, but appearances were everything. He had been injured in the bombardment yesterday. The panic that spread through the city at the idea of losing him had been more dangerous than any cannon. And so Giustiniani stood when he should have been resting, prayed when he should have been sleeping, all so the people could see their emperor and their military commander and have some semblance of hope.

When the service ended, no one moved. Radu was desperate to get outside, to be away from all this. A hand tugged on his vest and he whirled around, ready to strike.

He looked down into the eyes of the little heir, Manuel. "Where is my cousin?" Manuel asked. Something in the way his lip trembled but his chin stayed firm stabbed Radu to the core. Manuel was expecting to hear that Cyprian was dead, and he was preparing himself not to cry over the news. Radu dropped into a crouch so he was face to face with the boy.

"Cyprian is resting at home. He was hit on the head with some rocks, but he will get better."

Manuel let out a breath of relief, grinning to reveal his first few lost teeth. "He promised to take me fishing when the siege is over."

"Well then, there you have it. He will heal quickly, because he would never break a promise like that."

Manuel nodded, quick to accept comfort. He slipped his tiny hand into Radu's hand, anchoring Radu with the weight of his innocence. John and their nurse soon joined them, the older boy solemn and ashen-faced. He nodded to Radu and Radu formally dipped his head.

"You will protect us," he said. Radu wanted to sink into the ground. John nodded again, and Radu realized the boy was reassuring himself. "The men and the walls will protect us."

Everyone turned, watching as Constantine, stately and regal, marched out of the church. As the door closed behind him, there was a whoosh of collectively held breaths released, along with wails and cries of despair. People scattered in every direction. Radu overheard snatches of plans to hide, places that might be safe, cisterns underground that no Turk would think to look in. At least they knew the limits of their faith.

Radu grabbed the nurse's arm as she tried to herd the boys away. "Stay here," he said.

She scowled in offense. "I am to take the boys back to the palace."

"If the walls are breached, the palace will be the first place the soldiers go looking for loot."

She lifted her nose defiantly in the air as though Radu's dour prediction were foul to smell. "Those filthy Turks cannot come past the columns. The angel of the Lord will descend from heaven and drive them away with a flaming sword."

Radu held back an exasperated huff, though it cost him dearly. Instead he smiled encouragingly. "Yes, of course. Which is why you should stay here. The Hagia Sophia is farther in the city than the angel will let the Turks get, so you will be safest here."

She frowned, weighing his words.

"And it will do the boys good to pray more."

No Byzantine nurse could resist the lure of forcing her charges to pray. She took both boys' hands and marched back into the center of the Hagia Sophia. Radu wished he could do more. But he knew Mehmed would want the Hagia Sophia intact, and would send soldiers to protect it if and when they breached the walls. It was safer than anywhere else in the city.

He walked out the doors, breathing the evening air with relief. Another little hand tugged on his shirt. He glanced down to see Amal. Taking a coin—his last—he placed it in the boy's palm. "Tell him to look to the gates at the palace wall. I will—"

"Where is my nephew?"

Radu whirled around. Constantine stared wearily back at him. Radu stammered in surprise and guilt. "He—he—he is resting. I think he will recover, but he is not fit to fight." He glanced to the side. Amal was gone.

Constantine nodded, something like relief in his eyes. "Take his place at my side, then."

Radu was swept along with Constantine's party. Stuck in the middle next to Giustiniani, he was unable to slip free. This was not where he wanted to be tonight. He had planned to position himself at the Circus Gate—a small gate opening into Blachernae Palace. He *needed* to be there. But there was nothing he could do to get away without looking suspicious. Constantine led them through the city, past the inner wall, and to the masses of soldiers clustered in front of the Lycus River section of the wall. It was here and at the Blachernae Palace section that their final stand would be made. The palace was visible in the distance. Nazira was there, as planned, and he was stuck here.

Constantine climbed onto a pile of rubble, looking out in the twilight over the heads of his men. "Do not fear the evil Turks!" His booming voice was punctuated by a distant impact. "Our superior armor will protect us. Our superior fighting will protect us. Our God will protect us! Their evil sultan started the war by breaking a treaty. He built a fortress on the Bosporus, on *our* land, all while pretending at peace. He looked on us with envy, lusting after the city of Constantine the Great, your homeland, the true homeland of all Christians and the protection of all Greeks! He has seen the glory of our God and wants it for himself. Will we let him take our city?"

The men shouted no angrily.

"Will we let the call to prayer corrupt the air good Christians have breathed for more than a thousand years?"

Another roar, even louder.

"Will we let them rape our women, murder our children

and elders, and profane the sacred temples of God by turning them into stables for their horses?"

This time the roar of anger was accompanied by the slamming of spear butts into the ground and the pounding of fists on shields. Radu could not point out that it had been a *Christian* crusade two hundred years before that had been guilty of all the above.

Constantine continued on. "Today is your day of triumph. If you shed even one drop of blood, you will prepare for yourself a martyr's crown and immortal glory!" He raised a fist in the air. "With God's help we will gain the victory! We will slaughter the infidels! We will bear the standard of Christ and earn our eternal rewards!"

The sound of the cheering and screaming was almost enough to drown out the bombardment. Constantine held his arms in the air, then lowered them and turned. His face was haggard and drawn, losing light as quickly as the day turned to night around them. "We lock the gates back into the city," he said quietly to Giustiniani. "We stand or fall where we are. No one gets out. If the wall falls, we all die together."

Giustiniani nodded grimly.

Radu watched the two men with a disconnected sense of farewell. In his time here, he had seen them be truly great, holding together a city against impossible odds. And he had seen them commit atrocities while doing it. He respected them, and he hated them, and he knew the world would be lesser for their deaths.

If they died.

He both hoped for and dreaded that outcome, impossible

to reconcile, just like everything else in this accursed city. He took a place on the wall next to Giustiniani. Although it was night, the Ottomans had lit so many fires the light bounced off the low clouds, creating an ominous orange haze everywhere. The defenders could not repair the walls, because there was no cover of darkness.

From his vantage point Radu could see the mustering area for the Ottoman troops. Somewhere nearby, Mehmed waited to find out whether his grand design would succeed or fail, whether he would fill the prophecies of generations. Maybe if Radu were out there with Mehmed, this would have all been exciting. It made him ill to think of it, to imagine who he could have been. How easily he could have wanted the end of this city and everyone in it.

It also filled him with longing, knowing it could have been simple. But he released that thought to the night, too, along with everything else. He would die on the wall tonight, between his brothers and his enemies, because he could no longer distinguish between the two. They had finally come to the end. Whichever side won, neither would triumph.

A stone cannonball slammed into the wall beneath Radu and Giustiniani. They fell to their knees, the impact jarring Radu from his toes to his teeth. He shook his head, trying to clear the strange ringing noise in his ears.

No. Not ringing. Screaming. He looked up past the defensive barrels to see a shouting horde rushing toward them. There was no order or sense to the approach. They ran like a swarm of locusts, over each other, pushing and shoving, each trying to get there first.

Those that did were cut down. But it did not matter. The ones behind them climbed over the bodies. When they, too, were killed by arrows, their bodies added to the pile. Radu shot into the melee, watching in disgusted horror as the irregular forces of Mehmed's army used the corpses—and sometimes the living injured—as steps. They clawed over each other, death itself a tool to crest the wall.

There were so many men that Radu could not help but hit someone with every arrow he fired. It was as effective as shooting at waves of the sea. The men never stopped coming. Giustiniani directed his own forces, anticipating whenever a group of irregulars would breach the wall. "There!" he shouted, pointing toward a stretch not far from Radu. Radu ran toward it, watching as the first few soldiers clawed and tumbled their way on top.

There were not enough men behind Radu. He had gotten there too fast. He hacked and slashed and blocked, but there was no hope. A man screaming in Wallachian barreled into him, tripping him. Radu fell flat on his back, looking up into the face of death. No matter where he went, his childhood followed. And now it would kill him.

Then the man was gone. Except for his torso, which fell across Radu's feet. Radu blinked away the dust and smoke. All the irregulars who had breached the wall had been cut down by one of their own cannonballs. Radu kicked the man's body away, laying his head back onto the wall and laughing.

Urbana and her cannons had saved his life after all.

He pushed himself up, rushing to Giustiniani. He was certain that he had been fated to die just then. But he was still here.

Which meant he could still accomplish something. This time, if an opportunity presented itself, he would not falter.

Much farther along the wall, Constantine threw a man over the side. He pointed and a spray of Greek fire lit up the night, burning the bodies of the living and the dead against the wall. The Greek fire moved up and down, consuming everything that wasn't stone. Men ran screaming, the attack's momentum gone.

"They are retreating!" Giustiniani roared. The men around Radu cheered, some crying and some praying. Between Constantine and Giustiniani, the city still stood a chance. Giustiniani clapped Radu on the shoulder. "You made it! I am glad." They ducked as a cannonball whistled overhead, falling somewhere in the space between the two walls. "Do you think we have them on the run?"

"They were intended to wear us down. Next he will send Janissaries." Mehmed would have saved his best men for last. And Radu knew without question that the next wave really would be the last. If numbers could not overwhelm the wall, only the Janissaries stood a chance. And if they could not win ... Mehmed was finished. He had nothing left to throw at them.

"We can hold. We will hold." Giustiniani favored his wounded leg as he limped toward a ladder. "Get something to drink and eat. You men, pick up the wounded. Take them to rest against the inner wall. We will shift positions to compensate, then—"

Everyone stopped as the music started. Radu watched as faces of weary happiness shifted into exhausted terror. They would have no break tonight. The metre music of the Janissaries crashed against the wall with as much force and intimidation as any bombardment. The white flaps of their caps glowed like skulls in the firelight as they rushed, screaming, toward the wall.

This was it. This last wave would overcome the wall and flood the city, or it would recede, taking Mehmed's chances with it.

Mehmed himself rode back and forth, just out of crossbow range. Radu could see him, would have known him anywhere. But his heart did not sing, did not yearn for him. So little land separated them, but that distance was soaked in blood and lit by flames.

Giustiniani shouted for Radu. "Cut the ropes! Throw down the hooks!"

Radu ran back and forth, hacking at ropes, dislodging hooks. Every man under Giustiniani followed his commands without hesitation or question. Radu could not see or hear Constantine, but he was certain that section of the wall was the same. Two men to hold back an empire.

Radu stopped, sitting with his back against a barrel and watching. All the men around him were Italians, Giustiniani's men. They were as good as the Janissaries, and they had the high ground. What could he do? Even if he stopped helping, stopped throwing down hooks and ropes, he would do nothing to turn the tide.

A man jumped over the wall next to Radu. Radu looked up at him in surprise, seeing Lazar's face under the Janissary cap.

No. Lazar was dead. Radu had killed him to save Mehmed. Radu pushed himself up, stabbing the Janissary and letting his body fall. But there were more. Janissaries leapt over this section of the wall, led by a giant of a man. He towered over everyone, the white of his cap gleaming above the mass of bodies. He held a broadsword. Unusual for an Ottoman, but fitting for his size. The man swung the sword from side to side, cutting down everyone who came at him with eerily silent efficiency. Protected by his fury, more and more Janissaries climbed onto the wall.

"With me!" Giustiniani slashed his way through to the giant. Radu followed in his wake, protecting his back. Not even Giustiniani could take the giant in hand-to-hand combat, though. As he got close, the man swung his sword. At the last moment, Giustiniani dropped to his knees. He swung his own sword with all the strength he had in him. The giant stopped, looking down in surprise. Then he slid to the ground, both his legs cut off at the knees.

The Janissaries around them stopped in shock. Giustiniani stood, raising his sword in triumph. And this time, when he knew what Lada would do, Radu did not hesitate. He swept his sword across the backs of Giustiniani's legs. Straight through the muscles and tendons. One swift cut to turn the tide.

Giustiniani fell. Radu caught him. "Giustiniani!" he shouted. "He is wounded! Help!"

The Italian's men rushed to them with all the energy they had left. The Janissaries remaining on the wall were quickly overwhelmed.

"What should we do?" one of the Italian soldiers asked, tears streaming down his face as he looked at the man he had followed in defense of a foreign city.

"We have to get him to the boats!" Radu stood, grasping Giustiniani under the arms.

"No," Giustiniani moaned, shaking his head. He was white

with shock and blood loss, eyes wild. "We cannot open the gate."

"We have to! To save him!" Radu nodded to the crying soldier, who carefully took Giustiniani's ruined legs. They maneuvered him down from the wall with the help of the rest of the Italians, passing him from one man to the other. Giustiniani groaned and cried out in pain, all the while telling them to stop.

They rushed across the open stretch, dodging arrows and cannonballs. All the Italians had followed, more than a hundred men this section of the wall could not afford to lose.

"The key!" Radu shouted. "Who has the key?"

"Giustiniani does!"

Radu heard shouting over everything else. On top of the wall, Constantine stood, gesturing. He was frantic, waving his hands and shaking his head. If that gate opened and men went through, it would be a mortal wound to the city. Too many would choose to flee if given the option. Men ran toward them to stop them, swords drawn.

"If they keep us here, Giustiniani will die!" Radu shouted.

The Italians, ever loyal to Giustiniani, drew their swords against the soldiers they had fought shoulder to shoulder with all these long weeks. Everyone stopped, waiting to see what would happen.

Radu reached into Giustiniani's blood-splattered vest and pulled out a heavy iron key. Giustiniani grabbed his hand. "Please," he said. His face was pale and bathed in sweat, but his eyes were lucid. "Do not do this."

Radu looked up at the wall. Constantine stood silhouetted

against the glowing night sky. His shoulders drooped. Then he took off his cloak, throwing it off the wall. His helmet, with a metal circlet on it, followed. He turned and joined the fight at the wall as one of the men he had lived with. As one of the men he would die with.

"It is the only thing I can do," Radu whispered. He tugged his hand free, then opened the gate. As soon as he was through, he ran toward Blachernae Palace. If any of Giustiniani's men noticed he did not stay with them, they were too busy saving themselves to stop him.

There were not many men left at the palace. Just a handful to guard the Circus Gate. And, in a stroke of luck or providence, they were all Italians. "Giustiniani has been wounded!" Radu shouted. "His only chance is to get to the boats! They need your help!"

The men stood still for a few seconds, then ran. The gate was his alone. Radu walked to it, his feet dragging. The bar across the door carried the weight of a thousand betrayals. He managed to lift it, and left the door open. He had chosen this one because it was the most poorly guarded, but it was not big enough to let a whole army in. He needed something more. If anyone could still claim victory in the midst of this, it was Constantine. Radu needed to break the defenders' spirits. If he did, the city would fall. He climbed back along the wall to the palace itself, where Nazira was waiting with a cloth-wrapped bundle.

She threw her arms around him, pressing her face into his shoulder. "I feared you were dead."

"Not yet." He pulled out the Ottoman flags they had stolen from Orhan's tower. They ran through the echoing palace, climbing and climbing until they reached the top. From there they heard the sounds of dying, the clash of metal, the screams of fury.

They tore down the emperor's flag, and in its place they hung the flag of the Ottoman Empire. Splitting up, they found every place they could hang a flag where the combatants would see it, finally meeting back on the wall above the gate that Radu had left open. He waved the last flag he had, before draping it over the wall above the way in.

He looked, then, at where Constantine stood between his city and destruction. Though it was too dark and Radu knew it was not possible, he felt as though they locked eyes one last time. A cry went up among the men; the desperate push at the gate to the city intensified. They thought the Ottomans were inside, and would abandon all to go save their families, or die alongside them.

Radu turned away. He had done his part. The pendulum had swung in Mehmed's favor and would never return to the defenders'. He had managed to kill Constantine after all. But too late to be merciful to any of them.

"What now?" Nazira whispered.

"Cyprian," Radu said.

They clasped hands and ran from the palace into the dark city, racing against the coming flood.

46

Mid-May

The body of Lada's brother Mircea rotted in a shallow grave a short ride from Tirgoviste. He had been heading for Snagov, the monastery island where their father had once taken them. He had not ridden fast or far enough to find sanctuary. Where he lay, the earth was nearly indistinguishable from that around it. Lada had only found his body because one of the soldiers who had run him down was now hers.

Ah, the loyalty of men.

She dismounted and kicked idly at the finally thawed ground. The morning mist had settled in the depression, softening everything. It was a beautiful morning, damp, with the slow promise of heat on the way. Petru and Bogdan stayed on their horses, scanning the field and distant trees for threats. Lada was prince now, which made her an even bigger target. But this was something she had felt she needed to do.

She could not share her victory with the brother she loved, so she would resolve the fate of the one she had hated.

Now that she was here, she did not know what she had

expected to accomplish. Rebury him? Bring his remains back to the castle? Say a prayer over his body, one that might as well be blasphemy for all the sincerity it held? She finally had to admit that she had seized on this adventure mainly as a way of escaping the city. Toma had been pestering her, wanting to talk about various Danesti boyars and their loyalties—how to gain them, why she needed them, what marriages might cement them. The other boyar lines were not thrilled with her ascension, but they would not object as long as they profited. The Danesti lines took it personally, though. Toma never passed up an opportunity to circle back to the subject of marriage with a Danesti, dangling the possibility in front of Lada with all the subtlety of a noose.

Finally she had told him she would meet with every Danesti boyar at the same time, and left him to plan it for her. She was certain his letter-writing skills far surpassed her own; he would know what to say to get the boyars to come. Her idea had been to tell them to come or forfeit their land and their lives. Toma had laughed like she had made a wonderful joke.

At least Mircea was dead, and she did not have to listen to him. That made him preferable to Toma. "How did he die?" she asked.

"He died well," the soldier said, voice tight as he stared straight ahead.

Lada snorted. "You are a liar. My brother was a bully and a coward. He would not have died well. He would have died fighting, or begging for his life. Which was it?"

The soldier shifted uncomfortably. "He died fighting."

"If he died fighting, why did you not say that to begin with?"

The soldier swallowed, saying nothing further.

"Dig him up."

The man finally met her eyes, horror shifting his dull expression into something childlike. "But—"

"Dig him up."

The man looked from the grave to Lada, then back again. "But we have no shovels, no tools."

Lada reached into her saddlebag and pulled out a hard loaf of bread. She broke off pieces and passed them to Bogdan and Petru. They dismounted and dragged an old stump over for Lada to sit on. She made herself comfortable. The soldier still stared dumbly. Lada pulled out a knife, setting it on the stump. "You have your hands. For now."

The man began digging.

The sun was directly overhead by the time he finished. His fingernails bled and he cradled his hands to his chest as he backed away from the body he had unearthed. Lada held her cloak over her nose. It would have been better had she taken the throne in the winter. It was warm enough now for her to smell him.

But that was not the troubling part. Her brother—Mircea the cruel, Mircea the hated, Mircea the dead—did not stare up at her with the accusing eyes of the dead. He did not stare up at all.

She was looking at the back of his head.

"Turn him over," she said.

Gagging, the soldier reached into the grave and maneuvered the corpse so it was faceup. Mircea's skin was waxy and thin where it had not been eaten away to the bone. His fingers, too, looked like the soldier's—nails broken and caked with dirt. Mircea's mouth was open in a scream, black with rot. Lada leaned closer. No—it was black with dirt, all the way down as far as she could see.

"You buried him alive," she said.

The soldier shook his head frantically. "I had nothing to do with it. It was Hunyadi's men and the Danesti prince."

"But you were there."

The man shook his head, then nodded, foolish tears of desperation leaking from his eyes. "But I did not kill him!"

Lada sighed, kicking the corpse of her brother back over so he could not see her. It was a terrible way to die. She imagined him twisting and turning, the weight of dirt suffocating him as he grew more and more disoriented. In the end, he had been clawing deeper into the earth, instead of toward the sun and freedom.

She wondered how her father had died. No one in Tirgoviste knew where he had been killed. Or, if they did, they were smart enough to say nothing. And she wondered about her own loyalty—and disloyalty—to Hunyadi, the man who had helped the Danesti boyars kill both her brother and father. The boyars whose support she was still courting. Guilt and regret warred with resigned exhaustion. She did not know how to feel about this. Why could she have no easy relationships? Why was there no man in her life she could feel only one way about?

"I did not kill him, I did not kill him," the soldier whispered, chant-like, as he rocked back and forth.

Lada *did* know how to feel about the soldier. She latched onto it with a startling ferocity. It offered her a lifeline, something solid and secure to react against. "I do not care if you killed him. He is dead. That problem is past us."

The soldier slumped in relief. "Thank you, my lady."

Lada sheathed her knife. "I am not your lady. I am your prince. And while the death of Mircea is not our problem, your lying to me is."

The soldier looked up, fear curling his lips to reveal his teeth, sticking out just like those in Mircea's agonized skull.

"Bogdan, a rope."

Bogdan took a rope out of his saddlebag. Lada tied it tightly around the soldier's wrists. She tossed the free end to Petru. He nodded grimly, then tied it to his saddle.

"What are you going to do to me?" the soldier asked through clattering teeth.

"We are taking you back to Tirgoviste as an example of what happens to those who do not honor the truth."

"What if he cannot keep up with the horses?" Petru asked.

Lada looked at the open grave of her brother, where his corpse once again faced the dirt that had claimed him. "That is what the rope is for."

She spurred her horse forward, going too fast for any man to run long enough to keep from being dragged to his death.

She did not look back.

47

May 29

DAWN CAME AT LAST. Birds circled overhead, dark silhouettes against the sky, drawn by the carnage beneath. Soon they would descend.

Nazira and Radu ran as quickly as they could. The streets had filled with groups of citizens, clustered together and panicking. "Is it true?" a man shouted as they sprinted past. "Are they in the city?"

"Run!" Nazira screamed.

The man dropped to his knees and began praying instead. Behind them, they heard the sounds of conflict drawing closer. There were no Byzantine soldiers in the city—no one left to fight—but the Ottomans surging over the wall did not know that. They would come ready to fight in the streets, and when they realized there was no one left to bar their way ...

"We have to get Cyprian out," Radu said, gasping for air. "Valentin, too."

"How?"

The way to Galata would be closed. The Ottomans would

anticipate that. The bells on the seawall began clanging a warning. If the Ottoman soldiers in the galleys knew the city had been taken, they would be eager to join the pillaging. The seawalls were barely manned now, and with word spreading through the city that the walls had fallen, everyone would abandon their posts, leaving the sailors free to climb over. No one wanted to miss out on the looting. Nothing was off-limits—gold, jewelry, people. Anything that could be moved and sold would be.

But if the seawalls were not manned, and all the sailors rushed into the city—

"The horn," Radu said. "We make for the horn. There are still the Italian ships. We may even be able to steal one of the Ottoman galleys."

"Are you certain we will meet no resistance?" Nazira asked.

Radu could not be certain of anything. "It is our best chance."

"What about Mehmed? You could ride out to meet him."

They collapsed against Cyprian's door. His home was deep enough in the city that no sounds of fighting had reached it yet. "I will not leave you and Cyprian here, not for anything," Radu said. "I can come back when the three days of looting are over and everything has settled."

Nazira squeezed his hand; then they ran into the house. "Valentin!" Nazira shouted.

The boy rushed down the stairs, nearly falling. "We heard the bells. Cyprian is getting dressed to fight. I told him not to, but—"

Nazira handed Valentin his cloak. "The city is falling. We are running."

Radu looked up to see Cyprian standing at the top of the stairs. His injury had left him unable to get out of bed for more than a few minutes at a time without becoming dizzy. He was as pale and bleak as the dawn. "My uncle?"

Radu shook his head. "It is over. If we do not run now, we will not get out alive."

Cyprian closed his eyes, taking a deep breath. Then he nodded, resolve hardening all his features. "Where do we go?"

"The horn." Radu turned to leave, then paused. "Wait!" He sprinted up the stairs, throwing open the chest in the room he had shared with Nazira. At the bottom, carefully folded, were the clothes they had worn on their journey to Constantinople. Radu yanked his robes on over what he already wore, then hastily wrapped a turban around his hair. Better to look like friend than foe to the invading army.

Cyprian nodded. "Like the flags," he said. For a terrible moment Radu thought Cyprian knew what they had done at the palace. But then he remembered the flags on the boats to help them sneak past the Ottoman fleet.

"Yes. Speak in Turkish," Radu cautioned. "Valentin, you say nothing."

The four of them paused on the threshold of the house. They had been happy here, after a manner. As much happiness as could be found in the slow, agonizing death of a city falling around them. Then they ran. Cyprian was in the lead, taking them on a winding route around the edges of the city, skirting populated areas in favor of abandoned ones. They were nearly to a gate on the seawall when they came across the first group of Ottoman soldiers.

A clump of citizens had been caught in the alley, and the soldiers ran at them, screaming and brandishing swords. Half of the group had been cut down before the soldiers realized there was no resistance and stopped. Radu thought nothing could be more horrifying than watching unarmed people hewn down.

Until the soldiers began claiming them. One young woman, her clothes already torn, was being tugged between two men. "I had her first!" one shouted.

"She is mine! Find your own!"

"There will be plenty," their commander said, going through the bags of the dead. He did not even look at the girl as the soldiers pulled off what remained of her clothes, arguing over who could keep her and how much she would be worth. The girl stared at Radu, her eyes already blank and dead, though she still lived.

If Radu were truly good, if he were not a coward, if he valued all life the same, he would risk drawing the soldier's attention and kill her right now. But he had to save Nazira, and he had to save Cyprian. "Come on," Radu whispered. They slipped back the way they had come.

At a gate to the thin shore of the horn, two remaining Greek soldiers huddled, debating whether or not to open it. Cyprian stalked up without pausing. "They are already in the city," he said.

"We will drive them out!" A small soldier, barely past his youth, stood in Cyprian's way. "The angel will come! We must hold them off until then."

"Does he have the key?" Cyprian asked the lanky soldier next to the boy. He nodded. Cyprian punched the boy in the face, then pulled the key from his vest. "The city has fallen. Do what you see best."

Crying, the young soldier stumbled away. The lanky soldier slipped out the gate as soon as Cyprian unlocked it. They followed him onto a narrow stretch of rocky beach lining the seawall. No boats were docked here. The Venetian boats had not fled yet, but from the movement onboard, they would soon. And, just as Radu had predicted, several Ottoman galleys were drifting not far from shore, completely abandoned. Someone had dumped logs into the water, where they floated by the hundreds, bobbing gently on the waves.

No.

Not logs.

Radu watched as a man who had managed to swim as far as the Venetian ships attempted to climb up the side. A sailor on the deck reached down with a long pole, pushing him off into the water.

"Why? Why not help him?" Nazira whispered, her hands covering her mouth.

Cyprian leaned back against the wall, the hollows beneath his eyes nearly as gray as his irises. "They fear being swamped. There are too many people trying to get on the boats."

Valentin shook his head in disbelief. "All these people. They could have saved them."

Many of the bodies in the water had wounds no pole could cause, though. The Ottomans must have gotten here at the same time as those people who had figured out the horn was a means of escape. The delay to get Cyprian and Valentin had likely saved all their lives.

"What do we do?" Nazira asked, turning to Radu.

"Can you swim?"

"A little."

He looked at Cyprian, who nodded. Valentin nodded, too, eyeing the corpse-strewn water with resigned weariness that had no place on such a young face.

"The smallest galley. We can row it out until we catch the wind. Once we have that in our sails, we can slip down and away."

"And then?" Cyprian asked.

"And then we keep going."

The bells of the Hagia Sophia, deeper and older than any others in the city, began clanging. Radu bade the church a silent farewell. Valentin slipped his hand into Radu's.

And Radu remembered two young boys. Still in the church, where he had left them. *You will protect us,* John had said.

Radu looked at Nazira, and Valentin, and Cyprian, and he knew then that the scales would never be back in his favor. But he could do this one thing. He could die trying to save two boys who meant nothing to him. Who meant everything to him.

"I am staying," Radu said.

"What? No!" Nazira grabbed his free hand, tugging him toward the water. "We need to leave now."

"I have to go back."

Her full lips trembling, Nazira nodded. "Fine. We go back."

Radu kissed her hand, then held it out to Cyprian. "No woman is safe in the city. Not today, not for the next three days. I cannot let anything happen to you. I promised Fatima. You have to go home."

Nazira stamped her foot, tears streaming down her face. "We have to go home together."

"You cannot go back in." Cyprian stepped past Nazira. He ignored her hand and grabbed Radu's, the intensity of his gaze overwhelming. "You will die."

"I know where John and Manuel are. I can save them."

Cyprian looked as though he had been struck. He closed his eyes, then stepped even closer, pressing his forehead to Radu's. "Their fate is in God's hands now."

"It was never in God's hands."

"No, it was in my uncle's, damn him and his pride. *He* has killed them, not you. Not us. If you stay, Mehmed will find you, and he will kill you."

Radu's final punishment was announced by a new bell pealing nearby, harsh and unyielding. He would not be allowed any mercy for the things he had done. He could not escape, and he could not keep anything he hoped to. Radu shifted his face, resting his cheek against Cyprian's for the space of one eternally breaking heartbeat. "He will not kill me," Radu whispered. Then he pulled back, forcing himself to look Cyprian in the eyes. Those eyes that had caught his attention even when Mehmed was his whole world. Those eyes that had somehow become the foundation of a hope that maybe, someday, Radu could have love.

"He will not kill me," Radu repeated, waiting for Cyprian to understand. The foundation in Cyprian's eyes crumbled like the walls around them.

Cyprian stumbled back, shaking his head. "All this time," he whispered.

"Will you still keep her safe?" Radu asked.

Cyprian stared at the rocks beneath them, as mute and stunned as he had been when lightning nearly killed him. "You could have escaped," he finally whispered. "You did not have to tell me. I would have— We could have—we could have been happy. We could have?" he asked.

Radu knew what Cyprian was asking, and if he had not already lost all hope it would have ended him. "I do not deserve happiness." The bells of the Hagia Sophia rang out more insistently. "John and Manuel are running out of time. Will you still keep Nazira safe?"

A single tear ran down Cyprian's face. He did not look at Radu. But he nodded. "I will," he said.

This one good thing, then, Radu had managed to do. He had not broken all his promises. Nazira threw herself forward, hugging him fiercely. "You come back to us," she hissed in his ear.

"Be safe," he answered. Then, his heart breaking all the more for knowing that he could trust Cyprian even now, Radu fled back into the city.

———•———

The street was slick beneath Radu's boots. He slipped, going down on his hands and knees. When he rose again, his hands were bloody. He had not felt them get cut, had not thought he had fallen hard. Then he realized that the blood was not a result of his fall, but rather the cause of it. The streets ran with it.

And so he, too, ran. He ran past soldiers throwing everything portable out of houses. He ran past women and children being dragged screaming from hiding places. He ran, and he ran, and he ran. He tried his best not to look, but he knew that what he saw that day would be seared in his memory.

Today, he saw the true cost of two men's immovable wills. He saw what happened when men were forced to fight each other for months on end. It was not merely sickness of the body that plagued sieges, but sickness of the soul that turned men into monsters.

Radu was nearly at the Hagia Sophia when he saw a boy thrown to the ground. A soldier flipped the boy onto his back, reaching down to undo his trousers. Radu slit the soldier's throat from behind.

He reached down and hauled the boy up, only to see the tearstained face of Amal. "Why are you back here?" Radu asked, shocked and despairing.

Amal shook his head, unable to answer. Radu dragged him along. That, with his turban, bloody clothes, and sword, were enough to make him blend in with all the other soldiers dragging people and things through the streets.

In the square outside the Hagia Sophia, soldiers not interested in immediately partaking of spoils secured their prizes. Beautiful children, girls and boys, were highly prized as slaves, as were young women. Anyone who looked wealthy was also carefully bound for future ransom. All around them were the bodies of those deemed too old or too sick to be of any worth.

Radu dragged Amal through the center of the fall of Byzantium, through the center of prophecy. Everything was profaned and ruined. There was nothing holy in this victory. God had truly left the city.

God was not here, but Radu was. And he still had a mission. His suspicion that Mehmed would send men ahead to protect the Hagia Sophia had proved correct. Several Janissaries stood in front of the church's barred door. But a growing mob of irregulars and other soldiers shouted and screamed for their right to three days' pillaging of everything. The guards and the bar would not last long. If Radu was not in the first wave of men inside, he did not want to think what would happen to two small, beautiful boys. There was the side door he had broken in through, but there were too many soldiers around to do anything unseen.

He shoved directly through the mob to the Janissary guards. One lowered his sword at him, but Radu brushed it impatiently aside. "Do you know what is in this building?" he asked.

The Janissary hesitated. "We are to leave it unspoiled. Mehmed does not want anything burned."

"All the wealthiest people in the city are hiding behind those doors. All the gold, the silver, the riches we were promised are behind those doors. We are not here to burn." He raised his voice to a shout. "We are here to grow rich on the fat of these unholy infidels!"

The mob behind him roared, pushing forward. The Janissaries, smart enough to know when they were going to lose, ran. Radu himself hacked through the bar, then pushed the doors open. The looters were greeted with screams and shrieks of despair. The mob fanned out, running to be the first to grab someone or something worthwhile. Radu scanned the faces, looking for the two he had come for. Amal stayed on his heels.

In the corner near the stairs leading up to the gallery, Radu saw the two boys. They stood in front of their nurse with straight backs. Radu ran, shoving several others out of the way to get there first.

"Please." The nurse pushed the two boys forward. "Spare me. These are the heirs! Constantine's heirs. I give them to you." The boys lifted their chins bravely.

A man nudged Radu. "They yours?" he asked, breathing heavily over Radu's shoulder.

"The boys are. You can do whatever you want with that woman." He reached out a hand to either boy, crouching down so he was eye level with them. Recognition dawned on their faces. Manuel burst into tears. John threw himself forward, looping his arms tightly around Radu's neck.

"Come on," Radu whispered. "We do not have much time. I know you are both very, very brave, but pretend you are scared and do not wish to go with me."

John released him and took Manuel's hand. Amal tentatively reached out and took John's other hand. Radu walked behind them, pushing them toward the stairs. "Why are we going up?" John whispered as they climbed past the gallery.

"There is no way out of the city now," Radu said. "I am going to hide you."

Fortunately no one had made it past the main floor. With so many people in the Hagia Sophia, the soldiers were busy grabbing as many of them as they could. Radu ushered the boys down the hall, then up the familiar ladders until they passed through a trapdoor and onto the roof.

Once they were on the roof, Radu jammed his sword into the trapdoor's hinges. It would not hold against any serious attempt to break through, but he doubted that men looking for the spoils of war would think to check the roof of a cathedral.

He led the boys away from the edge, where they could be seen from the street—and where they could see what was happening. John and Manuel, at least, had been spared those memories so far. Radu would keep it that way. They found a sheltered area and sat together. One heir huddled against each of Radu's sides, with Amal curled by his legs.

"Thank you for saving us," John said, trembling.

Radu looked up to heaven and closed his eyes, because he could not accept those thanks. He had not saved them. He had no way to get them out, no way to leave the city unnoticed. All he had done was delay the inevitable.

But unlike him, they were innocent. And so he would keep them safe for as long as he was breathing.

And he prayed that, somewhere out there, Cyprian would do the same for Nazira.

48

Late May

IN THE WEEKS AFTER her ascension, Lada spent as much time as possible outside. They were waiting for the end of May, when all the Danesti boyars had been invited to a feast. Anticipating it was a burden. Toma had taken over most of the planning, for which she was both grateful and annoyed. She knew she needed the boyars' permanent support if she was to keep her throne, but she did not know how to get it. If only she had Radu.

Radu.

She had received word that the siege against Constantinople was in progress. Where was he? Was he safe? Of all the things she held against Mehmed, jeopardizing Radu's safety was the greatest. If Radu was hurt, she would never forgive Mehmed. Radu was not an acceptable sacrifice, not for any city.

Though Lada herself had sacrificed her relationship with him to come here. Wallachia was different, though. Wallachia was hers. It was bigger and more important than any city. Besides, she had not put Radu directly in harm's way. Other than leaving him with a man he loved who would never love him back. Who would willingly send Radu into danger, never seeing that Radu would give up anything and everything for what Mehmed could never return.

If Radu had been harmed, she would avenge him. She would kill Mehmed. Thinking about that made her feel slightly better. She spent nearly as much time dreaming of killing Mehmed as she did of doing . . . other things to him.

But she needed Radu. She still did not know what to do with the boyars. There were some already in Tirgoviste. The ones who had supported her had come to pay their respects, but she suspected all the payments were forgeries, imitations of actual respect.

She often rode in the poorer parts of the city. Always she had men with her—the ones she knew, the ones she trusted. Bogdan and Nicolae. Petru. Stefan, if he could be found, and others of her old Janissaries when needed. She told herself it was because the Wallachian men who had joined her were not as well trained, but the truth was she still felt more at home among Janissaries than Wallachians. That preference filled her with gnawing guilt, but she reassured herself that it was because all her Janissaries had been Wallachian first. Just like her.

On this trip into the city, they stopped at a well to get a drink. Lada had noticed that none of the wells in the city had cups or ladles. Many of them did not even have buckets for drawing up water. Her bag clinked metallically at her side.

"Why is there no cup here?" Lada asked, projecting her voice.

A tiny girl, whose curiosity won out over others' wariness,

sidled closer. "No cups, Prince." She smiled shyly around the title, obviously delighted to address a girl that way. "People always take them."

Lada frowned. "You cannot even keep a cup here for the good of the people?"

The little girl shook her head. Lada knew all this. She had counted on it. Turning to the men with her, she continued talking, loud enough for the people lingering on the edges to hear. "Interview everyone. Discover any thieves. People cannot prosper if they cannot so much as get a drink without fearing theft."

"And when we find them?" Bogdan asked.

Lada jerked her head toward the castle. "Then they can go in the courtyard and join the soldier who represents dishonesty and the imposter prince who represents theft." There had been a steady parade of citizens come to gawk at the impaled bodies. Lada knew word of the prince's fate and the soldier's punishment had spread through all Tirgoviste. It had been the right thing to do.

She pushed the soldier's face from her mind. It mingled now with Mircea's rotting, dirt-covered face, staring at her in accusation.

She was doing the right thing.

"That seems a bit harsh," Nicolae said, his voice soft. He moved closer so no one could hear him. "These people are poor. They have nothing."

Lada raised an eyebrow. "They have me now. And they should know that things are changing." She reached into her bag, pulling out one of ten silver cups. The treasury at the castle was as sparse and depressing as everything else in this city. But she had no need for fine things. Out here they served a purpose.

They had attracted quite a crowd, people come to look at their new prince and whisper of her ascension and promises. Lada held the cup in the air. "This is from my treasury. My wealth is your wealth. I give you a cup for your well." The people gasped, murmurs of curiosity—and derision—rippling through them. Lada smiled. "This cup belongs to everyone. It is everyone's responsibility. I will not tolerate theft in my land, nor anyone who supports theft."

The grumbling grew louder. Lada held up a hand to silence it. "Theft cannot flourish in a country that cuts it out with swift and sharp vengeance. Thieves prosper among you because you allow it, which makes you complicit. I am tired of seeing Wallachia weak. We are better than that. Together, we are stronger than anything. We are stronger than any*one*."

There was more nodding than grumbling now. Lada smiled bigger. "This cup stays at this well." She handed it down to the little girl, who took it reverently. "It is everyone's responsibility to ensure it remains safe to serve your community." Lada's smile turned sharp and cold as steel. "I will come back to check on it. I expect it to be here the next time I want a drink."

There was no denying the threat in her words or her eyes. She saw it settle on the people. Some met it with fear. Some stood straighter, nodding, her own fierceness catching in their eyes.

As they rode away, Nicolae leaned close once more. "That was . . . dramatic."

Lada turned to him, exasperated. "Say what you mean, Nicolae."

"You know that cup will be stolen."

"No, it will not."

"What will you do if it is?"

"Make an example."

Nicolae scowled, his scar puckering where it separated his eyebrows. "You cannot fix a whole country in a few days, Lada. It will take time."

"Have you seen how long the average reign of a prince is? We have no time. I have to change things now."

"If you are so certain we have no time, why bother? Someone else will come and undo everything you have done."

Lada shook her head, tightening her grasp on the reins. She thought of Mehmed, all his careful planning. He had taken power and immediately made sure his empire was streamlined, efficient, and safe. He knew everything had to be settled at home before he could look outward.

Lada did not want to look outward. But she had to have safety and security here before she could hope to defend Wallachia—and her throne. If she could make the country stable for the common people, they would be hers. She did not understand the subtlety and machinations of the boyars. She *did* understand swift, assured justice. Her people would, too.

"Everything has to change now so that I *do* have time. We cannot go on as we always have. And the only way I know to shift our course is through severely fulfilled promises." She closed her eyes, remembering all her lessons at the hands of her early Ottoman tutors. The head gardener. The prisons. The corpses hung for everyone to see their crimes and learn from their punishments. If that was how her country would move toward prosperity, then so be it.

Mercy and patience were not options, not for her. The blood

of a few would water the land for the bounty of many. *Some lives are worth more than others,* she thought. *How many lives until the balance tips out of our favor?* Radu whispered back.

———•———

They found the castle's stores of wine. Nicolae presented them to her, with none of his usual good humor. "Should we sell it?" he asked. "Or keep them for when the boyars come?"

Lada stared at the barrels in front of her. It had taken them so long to get here, and now that they were, nothing felt the way it should. She was tired of being in control all the time, tired of worrying, tired of waiting. Tired of making hard decisions and wondering if they were the right ones.

"No," she said. She smiled at her friend. "We should get very, very drunk."

For the first time since they had arrived, Nicolae's smile was the same that had greeted her all those long years ago in a Janissary practice ring in Amasya. With Stefan, Petru, Bogdan, and a handful of Lada's other first Janissaries, they dragged the barrels up to one of the towers. It was the same tower from which Lada, with Radu at her side, had watched Hunyadi ride into the city. That day had heralded the end of her life as she knew it. This one, she hoped, would herald the beginning of her life as she demanded it to be.

Lada cleared her throat, holding a cup full of sour liquid. "I wanted to thank you. You rode with me. You stayed with me. And we won."

Nicolae cheered, raising his cup high, sloshing wine on Petru's arm. Petru laughed and licked it off, then hit Nicolae roughly so that even more wine spilled. Stefan almost smiled at her, which made Lada embarrassed at his effusiveness.

Bogdan gave her a heavy, meaningful stare. She raised her cup to cut it off, drinking deeply. She did not know if he knew how she really felt about him, but it was obvious what he felt was more. Longer. Deeper. Truer. That made her feel powerful, and she would not give it up.

The more they drank, the louder they got. Everyone traded stories, most about Lada and some outrageous thing she had done.

"Do you remember when we were outside Sighisoara, the goat I found?" Nicolae asked.

"Yes! That thing was so mean, and its milk was sour. But at least we had milk."

Nicolae tipped his head back, scar puckered and pulled tight as his cheeks shifted into a delighted smile. "I did not steal it like I told you I did. Well, not exactly like I told you. Though I suppose I did end up stealing it."

Lada knew he wanted her to demand he tell the real story. Normally she would have avoided asking just to tease him, but she was too warm and happy to pretend. "What really happened?"

"Do you remember the old farmer we ran into earlier that day? The one with the—"

"The long fingernails!" Lada finished, finally remembering. It took a lot to stand out in her memory of that time. But that particular man had had fingernails nearly as long again as his fingers. Each nail was twisted, yellowed, and cracked. He had offered to sell them food, but she could not stop looking at his nails and imagining what something they had touched would taste like. They had ridden on and camped nearby.

"Yes! I ran into him again as I was hunting. He had a goat with him that he had no need of."

"So he gave it to you?" Petru asked.

Nicolae shook his head, his smile growing even bigger. "He had no need of a goat, but he did have need . . . of a wife."

"No," Lada said, finally seeing where the story was going.

"Yes!" Nicolae doubled over with laughter. "I sold you to him! For a single goat! I told him I would take the goat back to camp and get you ready to be his bride!"

Lada shuddered, imagining being touched by those hands. "If I had known, I would have stabbed you."

"That is why I never told you. I think of him sometimes, staring forlornly out of his shack, still holding out hope that someday his bride will come."

"I cannot believe you sold me for a single goat."

Bogdan huffed indignantly. "Lada is worth all the goats in the world."

She knew he meant it sweetly, but she really would rather not be valued in terms of goats. "Next story," she said, throwing her empty cup at Nicolae. He ducked just in time, and it shattered against the stone tower.

Nicolae refilled Bogdan's cup. "What was she like as a child?"

"Smaller," Bogdan replied.

Lada laughed until her stomach hurt. "Tell them about the time Radu—" She stopped, cutting herself off. Because saying his name, bringing him into this space, made her realize that she would trade any of these men—her men, her friends—for Radu to be here with her.

Nicolae filled in the space her silence created, recounting the abuse she had hurled at the Janissaries in the woods to distract them from Hunyadi's forces. But soon they ran out of stories from the past year. When they had finally circled so far back in their history that the stories started taking place in the Ottoman Empire, everyone got quiet.

They had left it behind, but they still brought it with them everywhere. What they had learned. What they had done. What they had lost. Lada knew that was why she kept these men closest. Not because they were better trained, but because they had been hardened in the same fire she had. Only they understood the strange space of hating what a country made them, while being grateful for it at the same time.

Lada looked at the Radu-sized hole next to her. Then she looked up at the stars beginning to shine above them. "We are never going back to the Ottomans," she said.

"They will come for us," Bogdan said. "They always do."

Mehmed would not come. She had made it very clear what she would do if he did. But now, with the softening and dulling of the wine, she doubted her rash declaration. If he came to her, maybe she would not kill him. No one made her feel the way he did. He haunted her dreams. If he came to her, she would make him make her feel those things Bogdan could not manage.

And *then* she would kill him, if she still wanted to.

"Let them come," she said. "I will drink their blood and dance on their corpses."

Petru raised his cup. "I will drink to that!"

Nicolae was staring at the horizon, frowning. "Either I am far, far drunker than I thought I was, or something is wrong with the moon."

Lada was about to tell him to stop criticizing the poor moon, when she realized he was right. The moon had been almost full the night before. But tonight it rose as a slender crescent, barely there. The rest of the moon was washed darkest red.

"You see that, right?" Nicolae asked.

"It looks like blood," Petru whispered.

They sat on the tower and watched the moon in silence. Lada wondered what it meant, that the night she chose to herald the beginning of her new life was bathed in the light of a moon stained with blood.

49

May 29–June 12

THAT EVENING, WITH THE boys sleeping curled up
around each other like puppies, Radu went to the edge of
the roof and watched. He could tell from the activity in various neighborhoods that something was changing. Someone was
coming.

Mehmed.

But Radu did not *know* the way he used to, when Mehmed
had felt like a current running through his body pulling him
swiftly in the right direction. He knew now because he saw the
effects of the man rippling outward. Soldiers coming through,
clearing the streets, dragging bodies to the side.

Finally, Radu could see him. Mehmed rode straight and
proud through the city, his horse sidestepping occasionally
around a remaining body. Perhaps Mehmed was not riding so
straight-backed out of pride, but rather out of stiff revulsion.
His triumphant entry into the city of his dreams was paved
with bodies and decorated with death.

Mehmed picked his way slowly toward the Hagia Sophia,

and Radu wondered what to do. Go down and appeal to Mehmed's mercy? Wait and try to sneak the boys out of the city once things had calmed down? Find Cyprian and Nazira and live a fantasy life where they could all forget and forgive everything they had seen and done?

Sick and exhausted, Radu decided to sleep instead. He walked past the trapdoor—only to find his sword placed to the side. Horror clawing through his chest, he raced to where he had left the boys. Manuel and John were still there, sleeping.

Amal was gone.

Radu had not spoken with Amal, had not given him any instructions. But Radu had not been the one to send Amal into the city in the first place. Radu finally felt the tugging sensation of his connection to Mehmed return, and he walked slowly back to the edge of the roof.

Mehmed had entered the square. The soldiers there lifted their swords, cheering and yelling, praising God and Mehmed. Then a boy darted between them, running directly to Mehmed's horse. Mehmed's guards drew close, but Mehmed waved them off.

Amal pointed, and Mehmed looked up at Radu. Mehmed smiled, a look of relief and joy lighting his face. Once, Radu would have given anything to have Mehmed look at him that way. Now, Radu *had* given everything, only to find he was still empty. He sat on the edge of the roof, dangling his legs over the side. Doubtless Amal would have told Mehmed about the heirs, too. Radu could not hide them from Mehmed. He had saved them for nothing. They would meet the same fate as Mehmed's infant half brother, sacrificed for the security of the future.

Radu should do what he should have done to Constantine. He should get up and swiftly kill them as they slept.

Instead, he hung his head and wept.

———————

Small fires burning throughout the city gave it a cheery glow as, sometime later, the trapdoor opened. Radu did not turn around when Mehmed sat next to him, shoulder to shoulder.

"I am glad you are here," Mehmed said.

Radu smiled bitterly. "That makes one of us."

"The flags in the palace—that was brilliant."

Radu imagined himself before his time in Constantinople, how that person would have exulted in this moment. How he would have been filled to the brim with joy and pride to be recognized by Mehmed, to be truly seen. To be the more valuable Dracul.

He could not answer.

Mehmed put a hand on Radu's shoulder. It felt cold. "You turned the tide. You saw exactly what was needed, and you did it. As you always have, my dearest, my truest friend."

Several men climbed onto the roof behind them, bringing lanterns that cast sharp shadows.

"Where are the heirs?" Mehmed asked, standing and offering Radu a hand.

Radu did not take it. "What will you do with them?"

"Get them off this roof, to start with. It is no place for children."

Radu looked up at Mehmed, raising an eyebrow. "And down there is?"

Uncertainty turned Mehmed's expression angry. "Where are they, Radu?"

Radu stood on his own, then crossed the roof to where the boys still slept. Mehmed gestured, and one of the men handed him a bag. He reached in and, to Radu's immediate relief, pulled out a loaf of bread and a leather canteen. Mehmed knelt in front of the boys, who were now sitting up, blinking against the lantern light.

"Hello." Mehmed's voice was gentle as he held out the food. He spoke Greek. "You must be very hungry and thirsty after being up here all day. That was clever and good of you to stay out of the way. You are very smart boys."

Manuel looked up, finding Radu, his eyebrows drawn tight in concern. John, too, searched Radu's face. Radu put everything he had left into giving the boys a smile of reassurance. He had no idea whether or not the smile was the most damning lie he had ever told.

John reached out and took the bread, then handed it to Manuel. "Thank you," he said.

Mehmed sat across from the boys, passing the canteen after taking a small drink himself. "John, is it? And Manuel?"

The boys nodded, still wary.

"I am so glad I have found you. I sent my friend Radu to keep you safe." Mehmed smiled up at Radu. Radu looked off into the night, unable to play along. "You see, our city is hurting. I need your help. I want to rebuild Constantinople, to make it into the city it was always meant to be. To honor its past and bring it into its glorious future. Will you help me do that?"

John and Manuel looked at each other; then John nodded.

Manuel followed his example, his head bobbing with enthusiasm. Mehmed clapped his hands. "Oh, thank you! I am so glad to have you on my side." He stood, holding out a hand to help them stand. Each boy took his hand in turn, smiling up at their new savior.

Radu knew precisely how they felt. He knew how much they must worship Mehmed now, for coming in the darkness and saving them from it. Radu had *been* them, many years before. He wished he could accept Mehmed's hand with the same warm relief again.

Mehmed gave the boys into the care of his guards, promising he would see them again when they had gotten some rest, safe and sound in a real bed. Radu went back to the edge of the roof. Already dawn was approaching. The hours here moved all wrong—some crawling by and lasting days, others slipping like water through his fingers.

Mehmed joined him again.

"Will they really be safe?" Radu asked.

"Why would you ask me that?" Mehmed replied, his tone troubled.

"That was not an answer."

"Of course they will be safe. I will make them part of my household. They will be given the finest tutors and raised to be part of my empire. This is my city now, and they are part of my city. I never wanted to destroy Constantinople, or anything in it."

"We cannot always get what we want."

Side by side but further from Mehmed than he had ever been, Radu watched as the sun rose on the broken city. He shifted to look at Mehmed. Rather than pride, a slow expression of despair crept across Mehmed's beloved features. What he had sought for so long as the jewel of his empire was finally laid out before him in all its crumbling, dying glory. Even without the looting, the city was devastated, and had been for generations.

Perhaps, looking out over it, Mehmed saw what the beginning of his legacy would eventually lead to. Whatever Mehmed did, whatever he built, the greatest city in the world was irrefutable evidence that all things died.

"I thought this would feel different," Mehmed said, melancholy shaping his words like a song. He leaned against Radu, finally giving him the contact he had craved for so long.

"So did I," Radu whispered.

After a single day of looting, rather than the traditional three, Mehmed declared an end. He kicked all the soldiers out of the city, banishing them to the camp to go over their spoils and leave what remained of the city unmolested. The camp itself swelled to accommodate the nearly forty thousand citizens taken captive to be ransomed or sold as slaves.

Most of the churches had been protected by the guards Mehmed sent in, and all the fires that had been set were already extinguished. Mehmed himself had killed a soldier found tearing up the marble tiles of the Hagia Sophia. Then he had brought in his own holy men, and the jewel of the Orthodox religion was gently and respectfully converted into a mosque.

Orhan had died fighting in his tower, as had all the men

who attempted to hold out. One other tower had fought so long and so determinedly, though, that Mehmed visited and granted the soldiers there safe passage out of the city.

Two communities within Constantinople survived without harm. One was a fortified city within the city that had negotiated its own terms of surrender; the other, the tiny Jewish sector. Mehmed met with the leaders there and asked them to write to their relatives in Spain and invite all the Jewish refugees to relocate and settle their own quarter of the city. He even offered to help them build new synagogues.

Once the soldiers were back at the camp, word was sent throughout the city that anyone who had not been captured had full amnesty. Whether driven out by hope or starvation or simply exhaustion, slowly the survivors appeared.

Mehmed vowed to build something better, and Radu knew that he would.

He simply could not shake the cost of what it had taken to get there.

In the days that followed, Radu wandered the streets in a daze, listening to Turkish in the place of Greek and finding he missed the latter. Over and over he returned to Cyprian's house, but he could never bring himself to go inside. It would not be the same. He would never see Cyprian again, and Cyprian certainly would never want to see him again. Not now, not after what he had done.

In a city filled with the dead, where tens of thousands now suffered horrible fates outside its walls, Radu knew it was horrendous to mourn the loss of his relationship with Cyprian. And yet he could not stop.

Kumal found him sitting outside the Hagia Sophia. His old friend ran up to him, embracing him and crying for joy. Then he looked around. "Where is my sister?"

Radu felt dead inside as he answered. "I do not know."

Kumal sat heavily next to Radu. "Is she . . . ?"

"I sent her from the city on a boat with a trusted friend. But whether they got out, and where they went if they did, I do not know." He had inquired after the boat and received no concrete word of its fate. His only hope was that once news traveled that Constantinople was open to Christian refugees and Ottoman citizens alike, Nazira would return.

"God will protect her." Kumal took Radu's hand and squeezed it. "We have fulfilled the words of the Prophet, peace be upon him. Her work in helping us will not be forgotten, nor go unrewarded by God."

"How can you say that? How can you be so sure of the rightness of this? Did you not see what it cost? Were you not at the same battles I was?"

Kumal's kind smile was sad. "I have faith because I must. At times like this, it is only through God that we can find comfort and meaning."

Radu shook his head. "I despair that my time here has cost me even that. I do not know how to live in a world where everyone is right and everyone is wrong. Constantine was a good man, and he was also a fool who threw away the lives of his people. I have loved Mehmed with everything I am since I was a child, and I have longed to enter this city triumphant with him. But now that we are here, I cannot look at him without hearing the cries of the dying, without seeing the blood on my hands.

Nazira and I—we ate and dreamed and walked and bled with these people. And now they are gone, and my people are here, but I do not know who I am anymore."

Kumal said nothing, but he held Radu close as Radu cried.

"Give yourself some time," Kumal whispered. "All will come right in the end. All these experiences will lead you to new ways to serve God on earth."

Radu did not see how that was possible. He loved Kumal for trying to comfort and guide him, but he was no longer a lost little boy in a strange new city. Now he was a lost man in a broken old city, and no amount of prayers and kindness could undo what had been done.

———◆———

Two weeks after the city fell, Mehmed asked Radu to meet him in the palace. He had set up a temporary residence there, already beginning construction on what would be his grand palace. A home to rival all others, a refuge from the world.

Radu passed a woman in the hallway.

"Radu?"

He blinked, focusing on her. "Urbana? I thought you were dead!"

Half her face was shiny with new scars, but she smiled. "No. And I got the forges at Constantinople, after all. I won!"

Radu tried to meet her happiness, but it was too large a task for him. "I am glad for you."

"You are welcome to help me any time you want." She patted his arm, already distracted and doubtless planning her next cannon. Radu watched her walk away, glad she had survived.

Then he saw two other familiar faces. Aron and Andrei Danesti. "Radu," Andrei said. "I know you now."

Radu did not bother bowing or showing respect. He was too tired for pretense. "Yes."

"It is good to see you," Aron said. "Will you take a meal with us later?"

"Do you mean that, or do you want something from me?"

Aron's face and voice were soft. "Only the company of someone who speaks Wallachian and understands some of what we have been through these last months. And I want to apologize for our youth together. We were cruel. There is no excuse for that. It does my heart good, though, to see the man you have grown into. I would like to get to know you."

Radu thought he would like to know himself, too. He felt like a stranger in his own skin. Sighing, he nodded. "Send word when you want me to come."

Andrei nodded silently, and Aron clasped Radu's hand. Then there was no one between Radu and the room that held Mehmed.

"Ah, Radu!" Mehmed stood when Radu entered, embracing him. Radu noted that they were alone. No stool bearer, no guards.

"What can I do for you, my sultan?"

Mehmed drew back, frowning. "Your sultan? Is that all I am to you?"

Radu passed a hand over his eyes. "I do not know. Forgive me, Mehmed. I am tired, and I have been pretending for so long, I can no longer remember what I am supposed to be and whom I am supposed to be it for."

Mehmed took Radu's hand and led him to sit in his own chair. "Well, that is part of what we are doing today. I know who you are, and you need a new title to reflect it. How do you feel about Radu Pasha?" Mehmed grinned. He was making it official that Radu was someone important in the empire.

Before he could think better of it, Radu answered, "I thought I was known as Radu the Handsome."

In the shadow that passed over Mehmed's face and the way he immediately looked away, it was confirmed. Mehmed had known about the rumors. He had known, and he had said nothing to Radu.

"Is that why you sent me away? To kill the whispers about us?"

"No! I never sent you away. You were always close to me. Every day I looked at the city and trained my thoughts on you, wishing you well and worrying for you. I am so sorry that your time in the city was terrible. Soon it will be as a dream."

"It was not all terrible," Radu said. Something in the way Mehmed's expression shifted to deliberate casualness made his next question anything but innocent.

"The ambassador, you mean? He quite liked you. I could see it at Edirne."

Radu realized with a sickening lurch of his stomach that Mehmed was dancing around a question, trying to determine whether or not Radu cared for Cyprian in the same way. Which meant that Mehmed knew Radu had the feelings for men that he was supposed to have for women.

Which meant Mehmed could not possibly be unaware of the feelings Radu had nurtured for him all these years.

Shame welled up in him, but a new feeling came, too. Radu felt . . . used. If Mehmed had known all this time, but had never acknowledged it, not even to gently tell Radu it was impossible . . . Nazira had said Mehmed would never fail to pursue an advantage. And having a friend so deeply in love with him that the friend would do anything in his service was certainly useful to any leader.

But even now, as angry and hurt as he was, Radu could not look on Mehmed's face without love. He was still Mehmed, Radu's Mehmed, his oldest friend. And in spite of everything, Radu would not give him up. Radu had made his choice. He had chosen to save Mehmed at the expense of an entire city.

Mehmed smiled, and it was the sun. Nazira was right. Mehmed was both more and less than a man. He was the greatest leader of generations, he was brilliant, he was a man other men would follow to their deaths.

And because of that, just like Constantine, he was a man who would leave death in his wake as he built greatness around himself.

"I have a surprise for you," Mehmed said, his eyes dancing.

Radu had one last dark spike of hope that finally, finally he could have what he wanted. They were reunited. The city was Mehmed's, and Radu had given it to him. They both knew how Radu felt. Maybe if Radu could have Mehmed, he could forget everything it took to get there. The same way Mehmed could forget what it took to get Constantinople, now that he had it.

Radu leaned forward. Mehmed turned, clapping his hands together. A guard opened the door. "Bring him in!" Mehmed said, his tone and expression gleeful.

Halil Vizier entered the room, the hems of his robes betraying the trembling of his knees. He bowed deeply. "How can I serve you, my sultan?"

"Not merely sultan anymore. Caesar of Rome. Emperor. The Hand of God on Earth."

Halil bowed deeper. "All this and more is your right."

Mehmed winked at Radu, then began pacing in circles around Halil, prowling like a cat. "You asked how you can serve me. I have an idea. I would like a member of your family for my harem."

Halil straightened, swallowing so hard Radu heard it. Even now Radu could see the wheels turning in the man's head. He nodded eagerly. "I have two daughters, both lovely, and—"

"No," Mehmed said, holding up a hand. "Not *that* harem. The other one."

Halil turned pale. "I do not understand."

"Yes, you do. My other harem. The one you were so fond of telling people I had. The one that would ask for sons instead of daughters. I heard all about that harem. Didn't you, too, Radu?"

Radu had so long nurtured a hatred of the detestable man now visibly shaking in the middle of the room. He had devoted so much time to defeating him, had played a game in which Halil was the spider and Radu the valiant friend protecting Mehmed from the spider's web. But now, seeing Halil finally fall, Radu felt neither pleasure nor triumph.

"Halil Vizier," Mehmed said, not waiting for an answer from Radu, "you have worked against me from the beginning. I sentence you to death for your crimes. I will grant you this one kindness: you may choose whether your family dies before you, or whether they watch you die before dying themselves."

Halil hung his head, then lifted it, his eyes staring straight ahead. "Please kill them first so they have less time to be afraid."

Mehmed nodded in approval. "A noble choice." He gestured and the guards moved forward, taking Halil away. Mehmed watched until the door closed, and then he spun around, robes and cape flaring. "One more enemy defeated! Your reputation is restored, Radu Pasha!" He beamed with pride, waiting for Radu to thank him.

"No," Radu said.

"What do you mean?" Mehmed's eyebrows drew together. He looked at Radu as though looking upon a stranger. And perhaps he was. Radu was not the same person Mehmed had sent into the city.

"Do not kill his family. They should not be held accountable for his guilt." Radu knew Halil's second son, Salih. Had used him. Had taken advantage of Salih's attraction to him to get what he needed. He looked at the floor in deepest shame. He was no better than Mehmed in this matter.

"But if I kill Halil, his family will be against me."

"Send them away. Banish them. Strip them of their titles and forbid anyone in power to marry into that family. But if you do this for me, spare them."

"If that is what pleases you," Mehmed said, waving his hand with a puzzled expression. He spared their lives as easily as he had condemned them.

Radu bowed to hide his expression of sorrow. Sorrow for Halil's family. Sorrow for Constantine and Constantinople.

Sorrow for the person he had left behind when he crossed the wall for the first time. Sorrow for leaving Lada to pursue her own fate, while he stayed with someone who saw it as a gift to protect Radu's "reputation" against the truth of his actual affections.

Mehmed put his hand on Radu's head, like a benediction. Then with one finger under Radu's chin, Mehmed lifted Radu's face to look searchingly in his eyes.

"Do you still believe in me?" he asked, suddenly the boy at the fountain again. His brown eyes were warm and alive, the cold distance of the sultan gone.

"I do," Radu answered. "I always will." It was the truth. He knew Mehmed would build something truly amazing. He knew that Constantinople needed to fall for Mehmed to hold on to his empire. He knew that Mehmed was the greatest sultan his people had ever known. But, like his love for Mehmed, it was no longer simple.

Radu had seen what it took to be great, and he never again wanted to be part of something bigger than himself.

50

May 29

"Let me handle any talk of the prince," Toma Basarab said. He eyed Lada critically.

Lada had dressed for battle. Over her black tunic and trousers, she wore chain mail. It rippled down her body, the weight familiar and comforting. At her waist, she buckled the sword she had ripped free from the wall. On her wrists, she slid knives into her cuffs. *The daughter of Wallachia wants her knife back.*

She shuddered. She was not her father. She would not become him.

Her only concession to finery was a bloodred hat in the style of the courts. In the center of it, she pinned a glittering star, with a single feather sticking up from it. Her comet. Her omen. Her symbol.

Her country.

"Do you have a dress?" Toma asked.

She did not answer him, so he continued. "They will demand reparations, and of course we will make them. Every Danesti boyar will be at this meal. It may be overwhelming for you. I will handle everything."

"I do not need you to do that."

He smiled and set his dry, warm hand on hers. Lada pulled her hand away. "I have also had word from Matthias. He is very pleased with your success. The king of Hungary has taken ill, and Matthias has stepped in to make all decisions."

Lada felt a small stab of guilt. She had promised Ulrich that the boy would have a quick and painless death. Another promise broken.

"I am drafting our letter to the sultan right now. We feel it is best to continue in the vassalage—appraising Matthias of any developments or troop movements."

"Continue in our vassalage? I have no intentions of paying anything to Mehmed, or anyone else."

"Oh, that will not work. We already owe money to the throne of Hungary and several Transylvanian governors. They will expect to collect soon."

"Do *you* have debts to them?" Lada raised an eyebrow. "You keep saying 'we,' but I have no debts to those countries."

"I believe you burned a church and slaughtered sheep? If you want good relations with our neighbors, we must make amends. Just like tonight is for making amends to the Danesti families." Toma opened the door. "Come, they should be eating now. We cannot keep them waiting."

Toma insisted a show of wealth was as necessary as a show of strength, and so the food they served was finer than any Lada had swallowed since Edirne. Finer than any her starving people ate. She resented every mouthful she imagined going into the boyars' privileged bellies. The smells of roasted meat and sour wine assailed her as she walked into the room. Somehow Toma had managed to enter before her.

The massive table, lined with Danesti boyars, stretched from one end of the room to the other.

Lada had expected cold glares and hard looks as she threw her shoulders back and strode through the room behind Toma. Instead, she was met with a few curious, even amused glances. Most of the boyars did not stop eating or speaking to their neighbor.

She had dressed for battle and was met with indifference. Would she have to fight the battle to be seen her whole life?

The walk to the head of the table took an eternity. She wished she had not insisted she be alone for this. She wanted someone trusted by her side. Nicolae, with his incessant questions? Bogdan, with his dogged loyalty? Petru, or Stefan, or even Daciana?

She realized with a pang whom it was she missed. She wanted Radu on her right. And she wanted Mehmed on her left. They had made her feel strong, and smart, and seen. They had made her feel like a dragon. Without their belief in her, who was she?

She stood at the head of the table and waited. And waited. Nothing changed. No one ceased conversation, or bowed.

"Welcome," she said. Her voice was lost among the general buzz of activity. She cleared her throat and shouted it, the meaning of the word probably lost with her angry tone.

Finally, taking their time, the boyars' chatter quieted and then stopped. All eyes turned toward her. Eyebrows lifted. Corners of mouths turned up or down. Nowhere did she see the anticipated anger. Most of the boyars looked . . . bored.

She looked desperately to a side door, where Nicolae stood smartly at attention. He mouthed *Thank you for coming.*

"Thank you for coming," Lada blurted, then immediately

regretted it. She cleared her throat again, standing straighter. "We have much to discuss."

"I want compensation for the death of my cousin," a boyar near her said, his tone flat.

"I— We will get to that, but—"

"Yes, of course," Toma said. He sat next to the head of the table, on her right. "I think we can work out payments, and extra land as redress."

Lada froze, grasping for words. Why had he answered for her? Already they had put her on the defensive. This was not how it was supposed to go. How could they come in here, demanding compensation for the deaths of their relatives, while her own father and brother rotted because of their betrayal?

Toma smiled encouragingly, as though nudging her. "That is how you will answer for the deaths, right?"

Lada closed her eyes, then opened them, smoothing her expression to match Toma's tone. "I will answer the same way they will answer for my brother lying facedown in a grave outside the city. Or my father, who has no grave."

Toma cleared his throat, giving her a minute shake of his head and a small, disappointed frown. "This is all very bleak talk for the dinner table. We should speak of something else. How will you disperse your men?"

"You mean to clear the roads?" She had not had a chance to finalize her plans for making the roads safe for travel and commerce. Why was Toma pushing her to talk about those ideas now? "I had thought we would divide it by area, and—"

Toma held up a hand to cut her off. "No. You misunderstand. As prince, you are not allowed to have a standing military force. It is part of our treaties with Hungary and the Turks both. Matthias Corvinas specifically mentioned it in his most recent letter." He smiled patronizingly. "I know this is all very new, and you were so young when you left us. Of course you did not know, but your men far outnumber a traditional guard. You may keep . . ." He paused as though thinking, stroking his beard. "Oh, twenty? That should more than meet your needs. The rest we will divide among our estates. Since I already have a relationship with them, I volunteer to house the bulk of your forces."

Lada had more than three hundred men now. Good men. Men who had given up everything to follow her. "They are *my* men," she snapped. "I have made no promises to Hungary or to the Ottomans, but I have made promises to my men."

A dark-haired, rat-faced boyar near the middle of the table spoke up. "Promises you were never entitled to make. *Princes*," he said with a sneer that made it clear what he thought of a woman holding the title, "cannot defend themselves. It is not done. A prince is the servant of the people. It is the duty of the boyars to hold soldiers to be called upon in times of need. If we decide the need is urgent, we will organize our men."

Toma nodded, reaching out to pat Lada's hand. "You have been gone too long. A prince is a vassal, a figurehead. Any attempt to build an army or even so much as a tower to defend yourself is seen as an act of aggression. You have nothing to fear now, though. The boyars are your support."

"So your strength is my strength," Lada said, eyes half closing as she let the sea of faces in front of her blur. "That is comforting."

Some of the men and women laughed. Many went back

to their conversations. None of this had gone as she thought it would. She had expected opposition, challenges, arguments. Instead, they all seemed perfectly willing to accept her as their prince.

And then she realized why. They were happy to have her because they were happy with weakness. The more pliable the prince, the more power they had. And who could be more pliable than a simple girl, playing at the throne? No wonder Toma had supported her. He could not have designed a better avenue to power for himself than a female prince. If Lada died, the Danesti line would put their own back on the throne. And until then, they would do whatever they saw fit.

If she had Radu, if she had a way to manipulate them, then maybe she could manage all this. But they worked with weapons she had no training in. Despair washed over her.

Toma leaned forward conspiratorially. "You did very well. I will stay on as your advisor. No one expects you to understand everything."

All the change she saw sweeping the country in the shadow of her wings had been an illusion. These people ran everything, and nothing had changed for them.

"Which one will she marry?" a woman a few seats down asked.

The man sitting next to her snorted into his cup of wine. "Aron or Andrei, whichever one, what a pity for them. First they lose their father, and then they have to marry the ugliest murderess in existence."

"Still, it will be good to get the Draculesti line under control."

Lada stood. Her chair scraped back loudly. "Lada," someone said from the door nearest her. She turned to see Bogdan. Something was wrong. She could see it in his pale face and downturned mouth. She hurried to him.

"What is it?"

"Come with me."

No one called after her. She followed Bogdan down the hall and into the kitchen, where a large wooden table had been cleared of food. It was now laden with a body.

Petru's body.

Lada stumbled forward. His eyes were closed, his face still. His shirt had been pulled up to reveal a ragged hole of a wound that was no longer bleeding, because his heart no longer pumped. Bogdan turned him gently on his side. The origin of the wound was his back. Someone had stabbed him from behind.

"How did this happen?" Lada touched Petru's cheek; it was still warm. He had been with her since Amasya. She had watched him grow up, into himself, into a man. One of her men. One of her best.

"We found him behind the stables," Stefan said.

"Were there any witnesses?"

Bogdan's voice was grim. "Two Danesti family guards who were arguing with him earlier said they saw and heard nothing. They suggested perhaps he fell on his own sword. Backward."

Lada clenched her jaw. She stared at the body on the table until her vision blurred. Petru was *hers*. He represented her. And he had been stabbed in the back by men who represented the Danesti boyars. "Kill the guards. All of them, not just those two. Then bring my first men—those who have been with us since before we were free—into the dining hall."

Lada turned around. She walked back toward the room holding the Danesti boyars. Dining with boyars. Dealing with Hungary. Pleading with the Ottomans for aid. Had she become her father this quickly?

She slammed through the door, the noise drawing the attention of everyone who had not noticed her absence. "Someone's guards killed one of my men. I want to know who allowed it."

"Why?" Toma asked.

"Because an attack on my men is an attack on me, and I punish treason with death."

Toma grimaced a smile at the table, then leaned close. "I am certain it was a misunderstanding. Besides, you cannot ask for a noble life in exchange for a soldier's."

"I can do anything I want," Lada said.

Toma's expression became sharp. "Sit down," he commanded. "You are embarrassing me. We will talk about this later."

Lada did not sit. "How many princes have you served under?"

Toma narrowed his eyes even more. "I would have to count."

She leaned forward against the table, gesturing toward everyone. "I wish to know how many princes you have all served under."

"Four," the rat-faced boyar said with a shrug of his shoulders.

Many nodded. "Eight," another said. "Nine!" someone else countered.

A wizened old man near the back shouted out, "I have you all beat. Twenty-one princes have I seen in my lifetime!"

Everyone laughed. Lada laughed loudest and sharpest. She

kept laughing long after everyone else stopped, her laugh ringing alone through the room. She laughed until everyone stared
at her, confused and pitying.

She stopped abruptly, the room echoing with the silence left
in the wake of her laughter. "Princes come and go, but you all
remain."

Toma nodded. "We are the constants. Wallachia depends
on us."

"Yes, I have seen Wallachia. I have seen what your constant
care has created." Lada thought of the fields empty of crops.
The roads empty of commerce. The hollow eyes and the hollow stomachs. The boys missing from the fields, their corpses
against the walls of Constantinople now. The lands eaten away
by Transylvania and Hungary.

So many things missing, so many things lost. And always,
ever, the boyars remained exactly as they were.

She, too, had been lost. Sold to another land, for what? For
her father to be betrayed and murdered by the men and women
in front of her now, eating her food. Patting her hand. Calculating how long this prince would best serve their needs until they
found another.

The Danesti boyars were a poison that would be her even-
tual end. In the meantime, they would try to marry her into
their families, and would siphon the life from *her* Wallachia.
She had promised the people a better country. A stronger country. And now, finally, she understood how to create it. There
were no compromises, no gentle pathways. She could not keep
power the way anyone else had before her, because she was like
no one else before her.

"Your mistake is in assuming that because I have been far away, I do not understand how things work." She reached over and plucked the knife from beside Toma's plate. "I *have* been far away. And because of that, I understand perfectly how things work. I have learned at the feet of our enemies. I have seen that sometimes the only way forward is to destroy everything that came before. I have learned that if what you are doing is not working, you try something else."

She stabbed the knife into the top of the table, embedding it in the wood. Then she looked up to see her men entering the room and lining the walls of the hallway. "Who killed my father and brother? And who is responsible for the death of my soldier Petru? I demand justice."

No one spoke.

"Very well. Lock the doors," she said, her voice cold.

A murmur arose among the boyars. They shifted in their seats, watching as each exit was closed and locked. Finally, they had the sense to look uncomfortable. Finally, they truly saw her.

Lada drew her sword, looking down the curve of it. She had thought it like a smile, before. Now she saw what it was: a scythe. Without a word she shifted and plunged it into the chest of Toma. The man who had used *we* to talk about their plans, when he meant himself and a foreign king. The man who had thought that through words and advice, he could take Lada's soldiers, Lada's power, Lada's *country* without ever fighting her. She watched his face as he died, committing it to memory.

A woman screamed. Several chairs clattered as people hastily stood. Lada pulled her sword from Toma's chest, then gestured to the table.

"Kill them all," she said.

Her men did not move, until Bogdan drew his sword and stepped forward, swiftly killing two boyars. Then the work of harvesting began in earnest.

Lada picked up a cloth napkin and used it to wipe the blood off the length of her sword. The screams were distracting, but she was used to distractions. *Hold hands with the devil until you are both over the bridge.*

Or kill the devil and burn the bridge so no one can get to you.

It took a few moments for her to notice the screaming had finally stopped. She looked up. Bodies littered the room. Men and women slumped over the table or lay in their blood on the floor where they had tried to escape. Her men had not even broken a sweat.

It was good that Radu was not here after all. She did not want him to see this. Maybe it would not have been necessary if he had been here. Maybe, together, they could have found another way.

But he had chosen Mehmed, and she had chosen this. She could not stop now. Lada sheathed her sword. "Take the bodies to the courtyard. Everyone needs to know a new Wallachia has been born tonight. After they have been displayed, we will give Petru the memorial he deserves."

"What about their families?" Bogdan asked.

"Kill any Danesti heirs. They have nothing to inherit now. I will give their titles and land to those who actually serve me."

"Lada." Nicolae grasped her elbow. His sword was still sheathed. "Do not do this."

"It is already done."

"But their children—"

"We cut out the corruption so we can grow. I am making Wallachia strong." She turned to face him, her eyes as hard as her blade. "Do you disagree with me? They killed my family. They would have killed me, too, when it suited them. And they wanted us to continue under the Ottomans. They would sell our children to the Turkish armies, just like you. Just like *Petru*. You know I am right."

Nicolae looked down, scar twisting. "I— Yes, I know. I wish we could have done it another way, but I think you are right. The Danesti boyars would never have supported a new Wallachia under you. But their children are innocent. You can afford to show mercy."

She remembered the choice Huma made to assassinate Mehmed's infant half brother to avoid future civil war. Kill a child, save an empire. It was terrible. Sometimes terrible things were necessary. But unlike Mehmed, who had his vicious mother, no one would make these choices for Lada. No one would save her from this. She had to be strong. "Mercy is the one thing I cannot afford. Not yet. When Wallachia is stable, when we have rebuilt, then yes. What we do now, we do so that someday mercy will be able to survive here."

"But the children." Nicolae's voice was as empty as a boyar's promise.

"You said you would follow me to the ends of the earth."

"God's wounds, Lada," he whispered, shaking his head. "Someday you will go further than I can follow." He let go of her arm, then grabbed Toma's body and dragged it from the room.

She had done what was necessary. She watched as each body was removed. She would mark their passing, and acknowledge their unwilling sacrifice. Because with each body they drew closer to her goal. She clutched her locket so tightly that her fingers ached.

She was a dragon. She was a prince. She was the only hope Wallachia had of ever prospering.

And she would do whatever it took to get there.

51

To Lada Dracul, Vaivode of Wallachia, Beloved Sister,

Constantinople has fallen. Mehmed is sultan, emperor, caesar of Rome, the new Alexander. He has united East and West in his new capital. As his vassal, I ask your presence to celebrate his victory and to negotiate new terms for Wallachia's taxes and Janissary contributions.

He wishes to see you, as do I. I think of you often, and wonder whether I chose right after all. Please come. Mehmed will offer you good terms, and I dearly wish to spend time with you. I have much to talk about with you.

Your visit is eagerly anticipated.

> With all my love, and the official
> order of the sultan, emperor, and
> caesar of Rome,
>
> Radu Pasha

52

To Radu, my brother,

I do not acknowledge your new title, nor Mehmed's. Tell the lying cow-
ard I send no congratulations. He sent none to me when I took my throne
in spite of him.

You did not choose right.

Tell Mehmed Wallachia is mine.

With all defiance,

Lada Dracul, Prince of Wallachia

DRAMATIS PERSONAE

Draculesti Family, Wallachian Nobility

Vlad Dracul: Deceased vaivode of Wallachia, father of Lada and Radu, father of Mircea, husband of Vasilissa

Vasilissa: Mother of Lada and Radu, princess of Moldavia

Mircea: Deceased oldest son of Vlad Dracul and his first, deceased wife

Lada: Daughter and second legitimate child of Vlad Dracul

Radu: Son and third legitimate child of Vlad Dracul

Vlad: Illegitimate son of Vlad Dracul with a mistress

Wallachian Court and Countryside Figures

Nurse: Oana, Mother of Bogdan, childhood caretaker of Lada and Radu

Bogdan: Son of the nurse, childhood best friend of Lada

Andrei: Boyar from rival Danesti family, son of the replacement prince

Aron: Brother of Andrei

Danesti family: Rival family for the Wallachian throne

Daciana: Peasant girl living under a Danesti boyar's rule

Toma Basarab: Boyar from Basarab family

Ottoman Court Figures

Murad: Deceased Ottoman sultan, father of Mehmed

Halima: One of Murad's wives, mother of murdered infant heir Ahmet

Mara Brankovic: One of Murad's wives, returned to Serbia

Huma: Deceased mother of Mehmed and concubine of Murad

Mehmed: The Ottoman sultan

Halil Vizier: Formerly Halil Pasha, an important advisor in the Ottoman courts whose loyalties are to Constantinople

Salih: The second son of Halil Vizier, formerly a friend of Radu

Kumal: Devout bey in Mehmed's inner circles, brother of Nazira, brother-in-law and friend to Radu

Nazira: Radu's wife in name only, Kumal's sister

Fatima: Nazira's maid in name only

Amal: A young servant who has aided Radu and Mehmed in the past

Suleiman: The admiral of the Ottoman navy

Timur: An Ottoman citizen working for Mehmed

Tohin: An Ottoman citizen expert in gunpowder, mother of Timur

Urbana of Transylvania: An expert in cannons and artillery

Lada Dracul's Inner Military Circle

Matei: An experienced former Janissary, one of Lada's oldest men

Nicolae: Lada's closest friend

Petru: Lada's youngest soldier from the Janissary troop

Stefan: Lada's best spy

The Hungarian Court

John Hunyadi: Hungary's most brilliant military commander, responsible for Vlad Dracul's and Mircea's deaths

Matthias: John Hunyadi's son, high up in court politics

Elizabeth: The mother of the young king, Ladislas Posthumous

Ladislas Posthumous: The ill young king

Ulrich: The king's regent, advisor, and protector

Constantinople Court Figures

Constantine: The emperor of Constantinople

John: The heir of Constantinople, nephew of Constantine

Manuel: John's brother, nephew of Constantine

Coco: An important naval captain

Cyprian: An ambassador for the court, bastard nephew of Constantine

Giustiniani: An Italian, Constantine's most important military advisor

Helen: A citizen of Constantinople, Coco's mistress and Nazira's friend

GLOSSARY

bey: A governor of an Ottoman province

boyars: Wallachian nobility

censer: A metal ball with slits or small holes into which one puts burning incense, then swings through the air on a chain; used during religious processions and worship

concubine: A woman who belongs to the sultan and is not a legal wife but could produce legal heirs

dracul: *Dragon*, also *devil*, as the terms were interchangeable

fosse: A ditch dug around the exterior of Constantinople's walls to prevent easy attack

Galata: A city-state across the Golden Horn from Constantinople, ostensibly neutral

galley: A warship of varying size, with sails and oars for maneuvering in battle

Golden Horn: The body of water surrounding one side of Constantinople, blocked off by a chain and nearly impossible to launch an attack from

Greek fire: A method of spraying compressed, liquid fire known only to the Greeks and highly effective in battles

Hagia Sophia: A cathedral built at the height of the Byzantine era, the jewel of the Christian world

harem: A group of women consisting of wives, concubines, and servants that belongs to the sultan

Hodegetria: A holy relic, said to have been painted by an apostle and used for religious protection in Constantinople

infidels: A term used for anyone who does not practice the religion of the speaker

irregulars: Soldiers in the Ottoman Empire who are not part of officially organized troops, often mercenaries or men looking for spoils

Janissary: A member of an elite force of military professionals, taken as boys from other countries, converted to Islam, educated, and trained to be loyal to the sultan

liturgy: Religious worship performed in Latin or Greek, depending on whether the church is Catholic or Orthodox

metre: Loud music performed by Janissary troops as they attack, extremely effective at demoralizing and disorienting enemy troops

Order of the Dragon: Order of Crusaders anointed by the pope

pasha: A noble in the Ottoman Empire, appointed by the sultan

pashazada: A son of a pasha

postern: A small gate designed to let troops in and out of Constantinople through the inner walls

regent: An advisor appointed to help rule on behalf of a king too young to be fully trusted

Rumeli Hisari: A fortress built on one side of the Bosporus Strait as companion to the Anadolu Hisari

spahi: A military commander in charge of local Ottoman soldiers called up during war

Transylvania: A small country bordering Wallachia and Hungary; includes the cities of Brasov and Sibiu

trebuchet: A medieval engine of war with a sling for hurling large stones

vaivode: Warlord prince of Wallachia

vassal state: A country allowed to retain rulership but subject to the Ottoman Empire, with taxes of both money and slaves for the army

vizier: A high-ranking official, usually advisor to the sultan

Wallachia: A vassal state of the Ottoman Empire, bordered by Transylvania, Hungary, and Moldavia

AUTHOR'S NOTE

Please see the author's note in *And I Darken* for more information on resources for further study on the fascinating lives of Vlad Tepes, Mehmed II, and Radu cel Frumos.

As a note in this book, I would like to personally apologize to the nation of Hungary and its incredible history. The Hunyadi family legacy is worthy of its own trilogy, but in the interest of not writing three-thousand-page-long books, I had to dramatically simplify and compress things to suit my narrative needs. In the end, these books are works of fiction. I try to incorporate as much history as respectfully as I can, and encourage anyone intrigued to further study this time period and region.

The characters in the series each interact with religion, and more specifically Islam, in various ways. I have nothing but respect for the rich history and beautiful legacy of that gospel of peace. Individual characters' opinions on the complexities of faith, both Islamic and Christian, do not reflect my own.

Spelling varies between languages and over time, as do place names. Any errors or inconsistencies are my own. Though the main characters speak a variety of languages, I made an editorial decision to present all common terms in English.

ACKNOWLEDGMENTS

First, in correction to an error of omission for *And I Darken:* Thank you to Mihai Eminescu, the brilliant Romanian poet who wrote "Trecut-au anii" (translated into English as "Years Have Trailed Past"), a beautiful and deeply affecting poem that ends with the line that inspired the titles for these books: "Behind me time gathers . . . and I darken!"

Thank you to Michelle Wolfson, my tireless agent. I couldn't do this without you, plain and simple. Here is to many more years of me sending you "I wrote a strange thing, please figure out how to sell it" emails.

Thank you to Wendy Loggia, my brilliant editor, whose guiding hand is on every page of these books. I'm so deeply fortunate to have you shaping my words and my career.

Special thanks to Cassie McGinty, who somehow escaped being thanked in book one, but who was a phenomenal publicist and champion of the series. And thank you to the devastatingly lovely Aisha Cloud, who called dibs on Lada and Radu's publicity, much to my everlasting delight.

Thank you to Beverly Horowitz, Audrey Ingerson, the First In Line team, the copy editors, the cover designers, the marketing department, and everyone at Delacorte Press and Random House Children's Books. You are the absolute best team and absolute best house I could have asked for. I'm constantly amazed by your dedication, innovation, and intelligence.

Thank you to Penguin Random House worldwide, in particular Ruth Knowles and Harriet Venn, for getting our vicious Lada into the UK and Australia with such style. I'm so jealous she gets to hang out with you.

Thank you to my first and last critique partners (that sounds more ominous than it is), Stephanie Perkins for the save-me-please emergency reads and Natalie Whipple for the save-me-please emergency moral support. We all know I wouldn't be here without you.

Thank you as always to my incredible husband, Noah, without whom these books would have never existed, and without whom my life would suck. I'll never get over how lucky I am to have you. And to our three beautiful children, thank *me* for marrying your father and passing along such excellent genes. (But also thank you all for being the delightful center of my life.)

Finally, I always feared people wouldn't connect with my brutal, vicious Lada and my tender, clever Radu. I should never have doubted you. To everyone who embraced the Dracul siblings and these books: thank you, thank you, thank you. A girl could take over the world with you on her side.

CLAIM THE THRONE.
DEMAND THE CROWN.
RULE THE WORLD.

New York Times bestselling author of AND I DARKEN
KIERSTEN WHITE
BRIGHT WE BURN

RULE THE WORLD

Turn the page for a preview of the epic conclusion to
the bestselling AND I DARKEN series.

1

1454, Wallachia

Lada Dracul had cut through blood and bones to get the castle.

That did not mean she wanted to spend time in it. It was such a relief still, to escape the capital. She understood the need for a seat of power, but she hated that it was Tirgoviste. She could not sleep in those stone rooms, empty and yet still crowded with the ghosts of all the princes who had come before her.

With too far to go before reaching Nicolae, Lada planned to camp for the night. Solitude was increasingly precious—and yet another resource she was sorely lacking. But a tiny village tucked away from the frosted road beckoned her. During one of the last summers before she and Radu were traded to the Ottomans, they had traveled this same path with their father. It had been one of the happiest seasons of her life. Though it was winter now, nostalgia and melancholy slowed her until she decided to stay.

Outside the village, she spent a few frigid minutes changing into clothes more standard than her usual selection of black trousers and tunics. They were noteworthy enough that she risked being recognized. She put on skirts and a blouse—but with mail underneath. Always that. To the untrained eye, there was nothing to mark her as prince.

She found lodging in a stone cottage. Because there was not enough planting land for boyars to bother with here, the peasants could own small patches of it. Not enough to prosper, but enough to survive. An older woman seated Lada by the fire with bread and stew as soon as coins had exchanged hands. The woman had a daughter, a small thing wearing much-patched and too-large clothes.

They also had a cat, who, in spite of Lada's utter indifference to the creature, insisted on rubbing against her leg and purring. The little girl sat almost as close. "Her name is Prince," the girl said, reaching down to scratch the cat's ears.

Lada raised an eyebrow. "That is an odd name for a female cat."

The girl grinned, showing all the childhood gaps among her teeth. "But princes can be girls now, too."

"Ah yes." Lada tried not to smile. "Tell me, what do you think of our new prince?"

"I have never seen her. But I want to! I think she must be the prettiest girl alive."

Lada snorted at the same time as the girl's mother. The woman sat down in a chair across from Lada. "I have heard she is nothing to look at. A blessing. Perhaps it can keep her out of a marriage."

"Oh?" Lada stirred her stew. "You do not think she should get married?"

The woman leaned forward intently. "You came here by

yourself. A woman? Traveling alone? A year ago such a thing would have been impossible. This last harvest we were able to take our crops to Tirgoviste without paying robbers' fees every league along the road. We made two times again as much money as we ever have. And my sister no longer has to teach her boys to pretend to be stupid to avoid being taken for the sultan's accursed Janissary troops."

Lada nodded as though hesitant to agree. "But the prince killed all those boyars. I hear she is depraved."

The woman huffed, waving a hand. "What did the boyars ever do for us? She had her reasons. I heard—" She leaned forward so quickly and with such animation half her stew spilled, unnoticed. "I heard she is giving land to anyone. Can you imagine? No family name, no boyar line. She gives it to those who deserve it. So I hope she never marries. I hope she lives to be a hundred years old, breathing fire and drinking the blood of our enemies."

The little girl grabbed the cat, settling it on her lap. "Did you hear the story of the golden goblet?" she asked, eyes bright and shining.

Lada smiled. "Tell me."

And so Lada heard new stories about herself, from her own people. They were exaggerated and stretched, but they were based on things she had actually done. The ways she had improved *her* country for *her* people.

Lada slept well that night.

———◆———

"Did you know," Lada said, scanning the parchment in her hand, "that to settle a dispute between two women who were fighting over an infant, I cut the infant in half and gave them both a piece?"

"That was very pragmatic of you." Nicolae had ridden out to the road to meet her. Now they were side by side, their horses meandering through the ice-glazed trees. This winter was preferable to last, though, oddly, she found herself missing the camaraderie of camping as a fugitive alongside her men. Now they were scattered. Scattered doing important work for Wallachia, but any chance she had to reunite with them, she took. She had been looking forward to this time with Nicolae.

He guided them toward the estate that had formerly belonged to her advisor, Toma Basarab. Before Lada's rule, Toma had been alive and well, and these roads had been nearly impassable without an armed guard for protection. Now, Toma was dead and the roads were safe. Both of those—death of boyars and safety for everyone else—were patterns of Lada's rule so far.

The frigid air stung her nostrils in a way she found bracing and pleasant. The sun shone clear, but it was no match for the blanket of ice that Wallachia slept under. Perhaps that also contributed to the safety of the roads. No one wanted to be out in this.

Lada preferred it to the castle with a fierceness that was as sharp and pointed as the icicles she passed beneath.

She waved the parchment with the story of her unusual methods of solving family disputes. "The most offensive part," she said, "is that the story is deeply unoriginal. The Transylvanians got that one from the Bible. The least they could do is make up *new* stories about me, rather than stealing from Solomon." She should print the stories the woman and her daughter had told last night. Spread *those* rumors instead.

Nicolae gestured to the bundle of reports he had given her. "Did you see the new woodcut? Very skilled artist. It is the next page."

She was sorting through as best she could while riding, dropping each page to the road as she finished. None had been anything but slander. Nothing important. Nothing true. Her thick gloves were not suited to manipulating thin sheets, but she shuffled until she found the illustration. "I am dining on human flesh amid a forest of impaled bodies."

"You are! Meals in Tirgoviste have changed since you sent me out here."

Lada adjusted her red satin hat, a jeweled star in the middle representing the falling star that had accompanied her ascension to the throne. "He got my hair all wrong."

Nicolae reached out and tugged one of her long, curling locks. "It is difficult to capture such majesty with simple tools."

"I have missed you, Nicolae." Her tone was acidic, but her sentiment sincere. She needed him where he was, but she missed him at her side.

He gestured to the star in the center of her hat, beaming. "Of course you have. I dare say I am one of the brightest—nay, the very brightest—point of your existence. How have you scrambled in the dark these long six months without me?"

"Peacefully, now that you mention it. Such blessed quiet."

"Well, Bogdan's strength never has been conversation." Nicolae's smile twisted, puckering his long scar. "But you do not keep him around for talking."

Lada gritted her teeth. "I *can* kill you. Very quickly. Or very, very slowly."

"As long as the Saxons make a woodcut of my demise, I will accept it with grace." He stroked his chin. "Please ask them to get my face right. A face such as this should never be poorly represented."

Nicolae was not wrong about Bogdan, though. Bogdan, her childhood companion and now most stalwart soldier and supporter, did not speak much. But lately even that had been too much. A break from him had been one of her motivations in making this trip alone. She was meeting him in Arges, but she had deliberately given him a task that took him from her before then.

Bogdan was like sleep. Necessary, sometimes enjoyable. She needed him. And when he was unobtainable, she missed him. But she liked that she could take him for granted most of the time. His opinion on that issue did not matter to her.

Mehmed would never have tolerated such treatment. She scowled, pushing him from her mind. Mehmed deserved no place among her thoughts. He was a usurper there, just as he was everywhere.

They passed a frozen pond, patterns of frost telling a story she could not read. The trees opened up ahead to rolling farmland softened with snow. "Why did Stefan not stay after delivering these letters? He knew I was due here soon."

"He wanted to get back to Daciana and the children. And he was probably worried if he saw you before that, you would send him away again and he would not get a chance to stop in Tirgoviste."

Lada grunted. That was true. She wanted him in Bulgaria, or maybe Serbia. Both were active vassal states of the Ottoman Empire, and likely staging areas for any attacks. She did not *expect* an attack. But she would be prepared, and for that, she needed Stefan. He had spent the last couple of months scouting in Transylvania and Hungary to get a feel for their political climates, whether there were any active threats toward Lada's rule. She wanted to speak with him in person. Daciana should not take priority over that. Nothing should.

Daciana ran the day-to-day business at the castle, all the details and mundanity that Lada could not begin to care about. Lada was grateful for her work. It had been a stroke of luck, finding her during their campaigning last year. But there was nothing at the castle that required Stefan's attention. Daciana was safe and busy. He should know better than to waste all their time.

Lada scanned the neatly ordered reports impatiently. Stefan had written his own observations and coupled them with the woodcut printings. In Hungary, Matthias was king. He did not go by Hunyadi, as his father did, but had styled himself Matthias Corvinus. Lada was not surprised. Matthias's relationship with his soldier father had been fraught. Of course he would not honor the man who had cut the path to the crown for him. And Lada had helped, in the end. She had betrayed Hunyadi's legacy and committed murder for Matthias.

And then she had had to do everything by herself, anyway, because the aid of men was never what they promised. It always came with hooks, invisible barbs to tug her back when she got close to her goals.

Matthias was not having an easy time of being king, at least. According to Stefan's report, he spent all his time and money flattering nobles and trying to buy back his crown from Poland. The Polish king had taken it for *safekeeping* years before when the previous king had been killed in battle. It was an important symbol, and Matthias was desperate for the legitimacy it would give his questionable claim to the throne.

Lada skimmed that information. Matthias was a fool if he thought a piece of metal would give him what he wanted, and she did not particularly care about any of his machinations as long as they were directed toward other countries. It also served the benefit of keeping him distracted. As far as Stefan could tell, he had no designs on Lada despite her refusal to defer to his authority.

The woodcut printings demonstrated Transylvania's continued opposition to her rule, but aside from the artistic flair, they had no organized opposition. There did not seem to be any attempt to destabilize her militarily. Stefan mentioned the downside to losing them as allies—they had long served as a buffer between Wallachia and Hungary—but there was nothing to be done. She had, after all, spent much of the previous year burning their cities. But if they had not wanted her to do that, they should have allied with her sooner.

All things considered, it was as good of news as she could have hoped for. But she had questions for Stefan. And concerns, now. She did not care for his split loyalties. Daciana was hers. Stefan was hers. She did not like them being each other's before that.

She tucked the papers into her saddlebag. "And how have you managed?"

"I sleep well at night, and my appetite remains consistent. Some days I feel a touch of melancholy, but I combat it through long walks and deep barrels of wine." He grinned at Lada's exasperated look. "Oh, were you not asking about me, personally? I was born to be a lord. This much authority suits me nicely. My crops flourished, the fields are ready for the thaw, and the people on my land are happy. Revenues should be robust this year. Good news for the royal treasury, which is—"

"Still empty. And the men?" Along with the farmland, they had set aside a portion of Toma Basarab's estate for training Lada's soldiers. Princes had never been allowed to have a standing army. They were expected to depend entirely on the boyars and their individual forces. It was a disorganized, messy system. And a system that saw prince after prince dead before their time.

But Lada was like no prince before.

Nicolae tugged down his hat. In the cold, his nose had gone bright red, and his scar almost purple. "Everything is going well. You were right to send us out here. It is easier to control the men and instill discipline when there are no city temptations. And everything I learned from the Janissaries is being put to use. This will be the greatest group of fighting men Wallachia has ever had."

Lada was not surprised, but she was pleased. She knew her methods were better than what had always been done. Power was not split among meddling, selfish boyars. It flowed in a direct line of command to her. She rewarded merit, and she punished disloyalty and crime. Both with very public efficiency. And she knew from her stay the night before that word was spreading. Her people were motivated.

They passed two frozen bodies hanging from a tree. One had a sign that said DESERTER. The other, THIEF. Nicolae grimaced and looked away. Lada reached up and straightened one of the signs.

She had been focusing on making the roads safe and preparing for the spring planting. She had also been pruning the boyars. But Nicolae's work was just as important for the future of Wallachia, and she would invest whatever she had to. It was a different type of seed to nurture.

Nicolae stretched, holding his long arms above his head and yawning. "How are things in the capital? Any problems with the boyars? I heard rumors that Lucian Basarab was angry." Nicolae's casual tone was as artfully constructed as a Transylvanian woodcut. Lada knew he had not forgotten nor forgiven her choices at the bloody banquet.

Though she had mostly killed Danesti boyars, the family most directly responsible for the death of her father and older brother, Toma Basarab had also been eliminated. It did not go over well with the Basarab family, including his wealthy and influential brother, Lucian. She was not sorry. The fewer boyars alive to betray her, the better. They had outlived far too many princes. This had made them comfortable and lazy, assured of their own importance. If boyars now lived in constant fear for their lives? She did not think that was a problem. They needed to know they were the same as all Lada's citizens: They served Wallachia, or they died.

But Nicolae always wanted more delicacy. More mercy. It was part of the reason she had sent him out here, even though he was one of her best. She had no use for his counsel on moderation and placation. Neither of those were skills she had any interest in cultivating. If boyars served a purpose, they could remain. But they so very rarely did.

And mercy was a luxury Lada's rule was not yet stable enough to afford. Perhaps someday. Until then, she knew what she was doing was both necessary and *working*.

She breathed in the sharp, cold air, the scent of woodsmoke beckoning them toward warmth and food. They rode across the fields, through the Wallachia she had carved free from the failure of the past. "I addressed Lucian Basarab's concerns. It is all taken care of. I am a very good prince."

Nicolae laughed. "When you are not busy cutting babies in half."

"Oh, that takes almost no time. They are such small things, after all."

A few days later, satisfied that Nicolae had her troops well under control, Lada rode along the same banks she had traveled twice before. Once, as a girl with her father discovering her country. And then with her men in an attempt to take that country back.

This time she rode alone. She paused at a bend in the river where a hidden cave contained a secret passage down from the ruins of the mountain fortress.

But they were ruins no longer. There was no solitude to be found here today. Lada listened to the chisels, the shouts of men, the clinking of metal chains. Here, at last, a promise fulfilled: she had come back to rebuild her fortress.

She rode slowly along the narrow switchbacks leading up

the steep mountainside. This morning after she left the village she had dressed in her full uniform, complete with her red satin hat marking her as the prince. Where she passed, her soldiers bowed. And the men and women working cowered, ducking out of the way.

Near the top, as the new walls of her fortress loomed gray and glorious from the peak, Bogdan came out to meet her. She let him help her down from her horse, his hands lingering at her waist.

"How is it?" She devoured the walls with her eyes. Her silver locket, given to her by Radu and filled with the flower and tree clipping she had kept with her all their long years away, felt heavy around her neck as though relieved to be home, too.

"Nearly finished."

A man in chains staggered past, pushing a cart filled with stones. His clothes were ragged and stained, only a hint of their former finery showing through. She much preferred Lucian Basarab this way. Behind him, his wife and their two children pushed more carts. The children were dead-eyed, trudging numbly along. Lucian Basarab looked up, but did not seem to see her. He collapsed on the side of the path.

One of her soldiers hurried forward, a club in his hand. Lada did not know whether Lucian Basarab was dead. It did not matter. There were more to take his place. Just like the rest of her Wallachia, the fortress was being remade at remarkable speed thanks to the unwilling efforts of those who opposed her.

At last she had found something that boyars were good for.

"Show me my fortress," Lada said, striding past her foes and into her triumph.

Please enjoy this special excerpt of Kiersten White's chilling
new novel which speaks to the fears we all bury deep inside.

NEW YORK TIMES BESTSELLING AUTHOR
KIERSTEN WHITE

THE
DARK
DESCENT
OF
ELIZABETH
FRANKENSTEIN

SHE'S NEVER BEEN
MORE ALIVE.

ONE

TO BE WEAK
IS MISERABLE

LIGHTNING CLAWED ACROSS THE sky, tracing veins through the clouds and marking the pulse of the universe itself.

I sighed happily as rain slashed the carriage windows and thunder rumbled so loudly we could not even hear the wheels bump when the dirt lane met the cobblestones of the edge of Ingolstadt.

Justine trembled beside me like a newborn rabbit, burying her face in my shoulder. Another bolt lit our carriage with bright white clarity before rendering us temporarily deaf with a clap of thunder so loud the windows threatened to loosen.

"How can you laugh?" Justine asked. I had not realized I was laughing until that moment.

I stroked her dark hair where strands dangled free from her hat. Justine hated loud noises of any type: Slamming doors. Storms. Shouting. Especially shouting. But I had made certain she had endured none of that in the past two years. It was so odd that our separate origins—similar in cruelty, though differing in duration—had had such opposite outcomes. Justine was the most open and loving and genuinely good person I had ever known.

And I was—

Well. Not like her.

"Did I ever tell you Victor and I used to climb out onto the roof of the house to watch lightning storms?"

She shook her head, not lifting it.

"The way the lighting would play off the mountains, throwing them into sharp relief, as though we were watching the creation of the world itself. Or over the lake, so it looked like it was in both the sky and the water. We would be soaked by the end; it is a wonder neither of us caught our death." I laughed again, remembering. My skin—fair like my hair—would turn the most violent shades of red from the cold. Victor, with his dark curls plastered to his sallow forehead accentuating the shadows he always bore beneath his eyes, would look like death. What a pair we were!

"One night," I continued, sensing Justine was calming, "lightning struck a tree on the grounds not ten body lengths from where we sat."

"That must have been terrifying!"

"It was glorious." I smiled, placing my hand flat against the cold glass, feeling the temperature beneath my lacy white gloves. "To me, it was the great and terrible power of nature. It was like seeing God."

Justine clucked disapprovingly, peeling herself from my side to give me a stern look. "Do not blaspheme."

I stuck my tongue out at her until she relented into a smile.

"What did Victor think of it?"

"Oh, he was horribly depressed for months afterward. I believe his exact phrasing was that he *languished in valleys of incomprehensible despair.*"

Justine's smile grew, though with a puzzled edge. Her face was clearer than any of Victor's texts. His books always required further knowledge and intense study, while Justine was an illuminated manuscript—beautiful and treasured and instantly understandable.

I reluctantly pulled the curtains closed on the carriage window, sealing us away from the storm for her comfort. She had not left the house at the lake since our last disastrous trip into Geneva had ended with her insane, bereft mother attacking us. This journey into Bavaria was taxing for her. "While I saw the destruction of the tree as nature's beauty, Victor saw power—power to light up the night and banish darkness, power to end a centuries-old life in a single strike—that he could not control or access. And nothing bothered Victor more than something he could not control."

"I wish I had known him better before he left for university."

I patted her hand—her brown leather gloves a gift Henry had given me—before squeezing her fingers. Those gloves were far softer and warmer than my own. But Victor preferred me in white. And I loved giving nice things to Justine. She had joined the household two years earlier, when she was seventeen and I was fifteen, and had been there only a couple of months before Victor left us. She did not really know him.

No one did, except me. I liked it that way, but I wanted them to love each other as I loved them both.

"Soon you will know Victor. We shall all of us—Victor and you and me—" I paused, my tongue traitorously trying to add Henry. That was not going to happen. "We will be reunited most joyfully, and then my heart will be complete." My tone was cheery to mask the fear that underlay this entire endeavor.

I could not let Justine be worried. Her willingness to come as my chaperone was the only reason I had managed this trip. Judge Frankenstein had initially rejected my pleadings to check on Victor. I think he was relieved to have Victor gone, did not care when we had no word. Judge Frankenstein always said Victor would come home when he was ready, and I should not worry about it.

I did. Very much. Particularly after I found a list of expenses with my name at the top. He was auditing me—and soon, I had no doubt, he would determine that I was not worth holding on to. I had done too well, fixing Victor. He was out in the world, and I was obsolete to his father.

I would not let myself be cast out. Not after my years of hard work. Not after all I had done.

Fortunately, Judge Frankenstein had been called away on a mysterious journey of his own. I did not ask permission again so much as . . . leave. Justine did not know that. Her presence gave me the freedom I needed here to move about without inviting suspicion or censure. William and Ernest, Victor's younger brothers and her charges, would be fine in the care of the maid until we could return.

Another burst of thunder, this one rumbling through our chests so we felt it in our very hearts.

"Tell me the story of the first time you met Victor," she squeaked, clutching my hand so hard that the bones ached.

The woman who was not my mother pinched me and tugged my hair with brutally efficient meanness.

I wore a dress that was far too big. The sleeves hung down to my wrists, which was not the style for children. But it covered the bruises that in turn covered my skin. The week previous I had been caught stealing an extra portion of food. Though I had often been bloodied by her angry fists, this time my caregiver had beaten me until everything went black. I spent the next three nights hiding in the woods at the lake, eating berries. I thought she would kill me when she found me; she had often threatened to do just that. Instead, she had discovered another use for me.

"Do not ruin this," she hissed. "Better for you to have died at your birth along with your mother than to be left here with me. Selfish in life, selfish in death. That's what you come from."

I lifted my chin high, let her finish brushing my hair so that it shone as bright as gold.

"Make them love you," she demanded as a gentle knock sounded at the door to the hovel I shared with my caregiver and her own four children. "If they do not take you, I will drown you in the rain barrel like the cat's last litter of runty kittens."

A woman stood outside, surrounded by a blinding halo of sunlight.

"Here she is," my caretaker said. "Elizabeth. The little angel herself. Born to nobility. Fate stole her mother, pride imprisoned her father, and Austria took her fortune. But nothing could touch her beauty and goodness."

I could not turn around lest I stomp on her foot or punch her for her false love.

"Would you like to meet my son?" the new woman asked. Her voice trembled as though she was the one who was scared.

I nodded solemnly. She took my hand and led me away. I did not look back.

"My son, Victor, is only a year or two older than you are. He is a special child. Bright and inquisitive. But he does not make friends easily. Other children are . . ." She paused, as though searching a candy dish for just the right piece to pop into her mouth. "They are intimidated by him. He is solitary and lonely. But I think a friend like you would be just the gentling influence he needs. Could you do that, Elizabeth? Could you be Victor's special friend?"

Our walk had brought us to their holiday villa. I stopped dead. I was amazed by the sight. Her momentum tugged me forward and I stumbled, stunned.

I had had a life, before. Before the hovel with mean and biting children. Before the woman who cared for me with fists and bruises. Before a life haunted by hunger and fear and cold, crammed into the dirty darkness with strange bodies.

I stepped one toe gingerly over the threshold of the villa the Frankensteins had taken for their time at Lake Como. I followed her through those beautiful rooms of green and gold, windows and light, pain left behind as I stepped through this dreamworld.

I had lived here before. And I lived here every night when I closed my eyes.

Though I had lost my home and my father more than two years before, and no child could remember with perfect clarity, I knew it. This had been my life. These rooms, blessed with beauty and space—so much space!—had graced my infancy. It was not this villa, specifically, so much as the general sense of it. There is a safety in cleanliness, a comfort in beauty.

Madame Frankenstein had brought me out of the darkness and back into the light.

I rubbed at my tender and bruised arms, as thin as sticks. Determination filled my child's body. I would be whatever her son needed if doing so gave me back this life. The day was bright; the lady's hand was softer than anything I had felt in years, and the rooms ahead of us seemed filled with hope for a new future.

Madame Frankenstein led me through the hallways and out to the garden.

Victor stood alone. His hands were clasped behind his back, and though he was not much more than a year older than me, he seemed almost like an adult. I felt the same shy wariness I would feel approaching a strange man.

"Victor," his mother said, and again I sensed fear and nervousness in her voice. "Victor, I have brought a friend."

He turned. How clean he was! It filled me with shame to be wearing a much-patched, too-big dress. Though my hair was washed—my caregiver said it was the best thing I had to recommend me—I knew my feet inside my slippers were dirty. I felt, as he looked at me, he must surely know, too.

He tried on a smile like I tried on castoff clothing, shifting it around until it mostly fit his face. "Hello," he said.

"Hello," I said.

We both stood, motionless, as his mother watched.

I had to make him like me. But what did I have to offer a boy who had everything? "Do you want to find a bird's nest with me?" I asked, the words tumbling out in a rush. I was better at finding them than any of the other children. Victor did not look like a boy who had ever climbed a tree to spy on nests. It was the only thing I could think of. "It is spring, so their chicks are all nearly ready to hatch."

Victor frowned, his dark eyebrows drawing close together. And then he nodded, holding out his hand. I stepped forward and took it. His mother sighed with relief.

"Have fun! Do stay close to the villa, though," she entreated us.

I led Victor out of the garden and into the spring-green forest that surrounded the estate. The lake was not far. I could smell it, cold and dark, on the breeze. I took a wandering path, keeping my eyes trained on the branches above us. It felt vital to find the promised nest. As though it were a test, and if I passed, then I could stay in Victor's world.

And if I failed . . .

But there, like hope bundled into twigs and mud: a nest! I pointed to it, beaming.

Victor frowned. "It is high."

"I can get it!"

He considered me. "You are a girl. You should not climb trees."

I had been climbing trees since I could walk, but his pronouncement filled me with the same shame my dirty feet did. I was doing everything wrong.

"Maybe," I said, twisting my dress in my hands, "maybe I can climb this one, and it will be the last tree I climb? For you?"

He considered my proposal, and then he smiled. "Yes, all right."

"I will count the eggs and tell you how many there are!" I was already scrambling up the trunk, wishing my feet were bare but too aware of myself to take off my shoes.

"No, bring the nest down."

I paused, halfway to my goal. "But if we move the nest, the mother may not be able to find it."

"You said you would show me a nest. Did you lie?" He looked so angry at the idea that I had deceived him. Especially that first day, I would have done anything to make him smile.

"No!" I said, my breath catching in my chest. I reached the branch and scooted along it. Inside the nest were four tiny, perfect eggs of pale blue.

As carefully as I could, I worked the nest free from the branch. I would show Victor and then put it right back. It was difficult, climbing down while keeping the nest protected and intact, but I managed. I presented it to Victor triumphantly, beaming at him.

He peered inside. "When will they hatch?"

"Soon."

He held out his hands and took the nest. Then he found a large, flat rock and set the nest on top of it.

"Robins, I think." I stroked the smooth blue of the shells. I imagined they were pieces of the sky, and that if I could reach high enough, the sky would be smooth and warm like these eggs.

"Maybe," I said, giggling, "the sky laid these eggs. And when they hatch, a miniature sun will burst free and fly up into the air."

Victor looked at me. "That is absurd. You are very odd."

I closed my mouth, trying to smile at him to let him know his words had not hurt my feelings. He smiled back, tentative, and said, "There are four eggs and only one sun. Maybe the others will be clouds." I felt a warm burst of affection for him. He picked up the first egg, holding it to the light of the sun. "Look. You can see the bird."

He was right. The shell was translucent, and the silhouette of a curled-up chick was visible. I let out a laugh of delight. "It is like seeing the future," I said.

"Almost."

If either of us could have seen the future, we would have known that the next day his mother would pay my cruel caregiver and take me away forever, presenting me to Victor as his special gift.

Justine sighed happily. "I love that story."

She loved it because I told it just for her. It was not entirely the truth. But so little of what I told anyone ever was. I had ceased feeling guilty long ago. Words and stories were tools to elicit the desired reactions in others, and I was an expert craftswoman.

That particular story was almost correct. I embellished some, particularly about remembering the villa, because that was critical to lie about. And I always left off the ending. She would not understand, and I did not like to think about it.

"*I can feel its heart,*" Victor whispered in my memory.

I peeked out the edge of the curtain as the city of Ingolstadt swallowed us, its dark stone homes closing around us like teeth. It had taken my Victor and devoured him. I had sent Henry to lure him home, and now I had lost them both.

I was here to get Victor back. I would not leave until I had.

I had not lied to Justine about my motivation. Henry's betrayal stung like a wound, fresh and raw. But I could survive that. What I could not survive was losing my Victor. I *needed* Victor. And that little girl who had done what was necessary to secure his heart would still do whatever it took to keep it.

I bared my teeth back at the city, daring it to try to stop me.